To Harry.

I hope you enjoy and recognise some of the events!

[signature]

For Ray who brightened my days with his humour, wit and humility.

Forward

Within every family there are those members of an older generation who have a plethora of stories, anecdotes and experiences to share if only they were asked. Unfortunately with the advent of mass media and the frenetic pace at we which we 'live' our lives, there seems little time or inclination to do so; and even less time to listen. Within all of us there is a story to be told.

1933 like most years, was a year of memorable events. All over the world governments were changing as the great depression began to lift and political focus shifted to other issues and problems. There were natural disasters, technological advances and people were born or died.

January 1933

The building of the Golden Gate Bridge begins in San Francisco. Political violence causes almost 100 deaths in Spain. The US Congress votes favourably for independence in the Philippines, against the view of the President, Hoover. In Germany, Adolf Hitler is appointed Chancellor. The Lone Ranger is broadcast for the first time on American radio.

February 1933

German Chancellor Adolf Hitler gives his

'Proclamation to the German People' in Berlin. A second international conference on disarmament ends without results. Officers on a US ship record a 34-meter high wave in the Pacific Ocean. The first singing telegram is introduced in New York. There is an attempt to assassinate F D Roosevelt, the President elect but the assassin misses and hits Anton Cermak; the Mayor of Chicago. Germany's parliament building is set on fire under suspicious circumstances. A decree following the Reichstag fire is passed, taking away many German civil liberties.

March 1933

'King Kong' the film starring Faye Wray premiers at the Roxy Theatre in New York City. A powerful earthquake hits Japan, killing approximately 3,000 people. In America Franklin D. Roosevelt replaces Herbert Hoover as President. He declares a Bank Holiday, closing all United States banks and freezing all financial transactions. The Nazis gain 43.9% of the votes in the German election. The Mayor of Chicago dies of the wound he received on February 15. Legislation brought into being by Congress, which begins the first 100 days of the New Deal. 117 people are killed during an earthquake in California. FDR addresses the nation for the first time as President of the United States, in the first of what becomes known as his 'fireside chats'. An Austrofascist dictatorship is started by the Austrian Chancellor, Engelbert Dollfuss when he keeps members of the National Council from convening. Dachau, the first Nazi concentration camp is completed. Adolf Hitler is made the Dictator of Germany. Japan leaves the League of Nations.

April 1933

The Nazis boycott all Jewish-owned businesses in Germany. England batsman Wally Hammond scores a record 336 runs in a cricket test match against New Zealand. An anti-monarchist rebellion occurs in Siam (Thailand). The first flight over Mount Everest takes place, led by the Douglas Hamilton. 73 of the 76 crewmen are killed when the American airship AkIan crashes off the coast of New Jersey. It is decided by a court in The Hague that Greenland belongs to Denmark. FDR' announces an order which makes it illegal for U.S. citizens to own substantial amounts of monetary gold or bullion. Sale of some beer is legalized in the United States under the Cullen-Harrison Act of March 22, eight months before the full repeal of Prohibition. The first law of the new Nazi regime directed against Jews (as well as political opponents) is passed in Germany. A Children's and Young Person's Act is passed in the United Kingdom. The United States officially goes off the gold standard.

The Nazis outlaw the kosher ritual Shechita. Jewish physicians in Germany are excluded from official insurance schemes, forcing many to give up their practices. The Gestapo secret police is established in Nazi Germany by Herman Goering

May 1933

The first alleged modern sighting of the Loch Ness Monster occurs. Hitler prohibits trade unions in Germany. In the South of Ireland, the Oath of Allegiance to the English Crown is abolished. The *New York Times* reports on the detection by of radio waves from the centre of the Milky Way Galaxy by Karl Jansky. Mohandas Ghandi begins a 3-week hunger strike because of the mistreatment of the lower castes. The Nazis stage massive fires in which they burn books in Germany. Paraguay declares war on Bolivia. Vidkun Quisling and J Hjort form the National-Socialist Party of Norway. The Nazis introduce a law to legalize eugenic sterilization. The World's Fair opens in Chicago.

On May 31st 1933 – Raymond John Dagnall is born in an ordinary hospital, to ordinary parents in the extraordinary city of Liverpool, England.

Part One

Chapter One – Nazi bugs and Zeppelins

"Help, we're being attacked!" He screamed as he stared into the sky horrified; frozen to the spot and not quite believing his eyes. He'd seen this before, but that had been in his nightmares and soon forgotten within the embrace of his mother who'd gone and comforted him when she heard his screams. He wasn't sure she could make this alien thing go away, but the thought of his mother moved him to action. He ran as quickly as his small legs would carry him, peering over his shoulder in a mix of fear and dread as the shape emerged from the clouds looking like a glittering torpedo and cutting a path across the sky as effortlessly as any bird. A ray of sunlight reflected off the metallic outer shell, reinforcing the alien nature of the craft.

He reached the door he'd been looking for and banged on it repeatedly. "Ma....MA; you need to come and see this!" He kept banging as he yelled. "Ma, please hurry up; it's Ming the Merciless; he's trying to take over the world!" He wasn't sure what his mother could do to stop the invasion given that even Flash Gordon found Ming a handful, but he had every faith she'd have a few ideas as she seemed to know most things.

After what seemed like forever the door finally opened and hi s mother emerged into the sunlight. She was a formidable looking woman of medium height with scraped back hair and horn rimmed glasses.

"What on earth are you going on about Raymond; who is trying to take over the world?"

"Look!" He pointed into the sky as the huge cylindrical craft slid overhead, almost soundless except for the quiet drone of its engines. As he looked around he saw crowds of people gathered in the street watching in awe, but not doing anything to try and bring the craft down. "Ruddy hell Ma, why isn't anybody trying to stop it, it's bound to start firing the death ray any minute?!" He said as he hid behind his mother's skirt and gawped up into the sky. He was quite small for a five year old and only reached up to her thigh, but he had an abundance of energy, a very active imagination and a mischievous glint in his eye. His attention was momentarily distracted as he received a clip around the ear.

"Raymond Dagnall, you watch your language young man or I will wash out your mouth with soap and water again!" Olive Dagnall ruled her small kingdom of 29 Colinton Street with a firm grip and alien invasion or not, she was not prepared to allow her son to use such profanity.

"I'm sorry" he said as he continued to gaze on in astonishment as the craft started a slow turn towards the Mersey. "But what are we going to do; I don't fancy being taken into space and being treated like a slave?" He pictured himself chained to a wall in a dark and dingy cave just like his hero, Flash; only being allowed out to clean the toilet or mop up the blood after Ming had seen to another of his enemies.

In that moment Olive decided she needed a strong word with her husband about taking their son to the local cinema to watch 'Flash Gordon's Journey to Mars'. He'd had nightmares ever since and seemed obsessed with the planet Mongo and Flash Gordon's arch nemesis Ming the Merciless. As the craft finally came around so the entire vessel was in profile, they noticed the large red tailfin, and on it was painted the symbol that people around the world had come to know and loathe over recent years.

"Raymond, look at the swastika on the tail; it's not a spaceship at all, it's a Nazi Zeppelin. There isn't anybody attacking us or trying to take over the world." As the words left her mouth, a whispered "yet" came unbidden to her lips as she took in the sight of emblem. "It wouldn't surprise me if Mr. Hitler didn't have some spies in that gondola under the balloon taking photographs of the docks."

This knowledge inspired her son to even greater profanity "Flippin heck!" he said, dodging the swipe from his mother as he ran off down the street, grabbing a stick as he went. Now he knew Ming wasn't on board, his fear vanished as he felt quite confident in taking on Nazis spies and overpowering them; more confident than deterring Ming from conquering the earth anyway.

He was joined by several other boys who were as eager to bring down the airship with their imaginary tracer bullets. They made repeated massed volleys of "Dadadadadada!" and "Peow" and "trumph" to no avail. However, Ray was convinced he'd scored a direct hit with a particularly forceful "Ptush".

"I hit it!" he said as the ship dipped slightly to the left. He was in the process of jumping up and down in triumph, when he was grabbed by the collar and unceremoniously dragged back towards his house.

"What did I tell you about using bad language Raymond?!" Olive growled as she pulled him over the threshold. "Get over to the sink and scrub your mouth with soap".

"But Ma it was the Nazis, they made me say it" He wailed as he made his way reluctantly towards the sink in the kitchen. He knew it was pointless in arguing, but didn't particularly look forward to the taste of the carbolic soap. "It was hearing you say it was a Nazi that brought the words out because I know how much you hate them."

"I do not hate people Raymond; and that is a poor excuse for using bad language!" He received another clip round the ear as he rubbed some soap onto his fingers. His mother was very strict and fervently religious. "And you will be asking God for forgiveness for your trashy mouth before I'll allow you any tea!"

After he'd given his mouth a rudimentary swilling he went into the front room to tell Nana what he'd seen. Nana was Olive's mother who lived with them in the bay window. For as long as Ray could remember, she'd been bed ridden, but didn't seem to mind very much. Given that she had given birth to twenty three children, his mother being the youngest; he thought she probably needed the rest.

"Nana, did you hear all the commotion outside? It was a Nazi aspirin."

"They are a bit of a pain those Nazis. If my Peter were still alive he'd sought them out." Peter had been her husband who was a six in hand coach driver and who'd driven the state coach for the Lord Mayor, but had unfortunately been killed when one of the horses kicked him in the head as he put it into harness.

"I thought we were being attacked Nana, because it didn't half remind me of Ming the Merciless' spaceship. I thought he was going to blow up the house and the school!"

The house was an end terrace in an area of terraces and had two rooms upstairs, two rooms downstairs and a kitchen. There was no bathroom and the toilet was in the yard at the back. The house faced Hey Green Elementary school where Ray had recently started to attend.

"That's nice dear."

He looked at his grandparent as if she was an alien from the planet Mongo. "It wasn't nice Nana, it was ruddy scary!" As soon as he said it, he knew he was in trouble even though his mother wasn't in the room. She had an uncanny knack of honing in on the slightest misdemeanour and dispensing punishment rapidly.

"Raymond that's it; get up to your room! You will not be getting any tea and you stay up there until you learn not to use bad language!" He suspected he might grow old and become bed ridden like Nana if he wasn't allowed out until he learned something. He knew his mother didn't tolerate any naughty words, but he couldn't help using the odd profanity; everybody else did outside of their house. He also suspected he'd end up having to confess his 'trashy mouth' to the entire congregation at the coming Sunday service that was to take place 'over the water' on New Brighton beach, which it did most Sundays during the summer months.

His mother had a habit of making him stand up and preach a sermon to the gathered crowds, which he didn't mind too much as he was normally rewarded with sweets and even the odd coin on occasion; but having to confess to using bad language filled him with a kind of dread. If they were as judgemental as his mother, there'd be no rewards this week.

However, those thoughts could wait as he reflected on the wonder he'd seen and his heroic act of defending his home. He'd overheard adults talking for months now about the menace of 'Hitler and his Nazi thugs' and he'd heard his father refer to 'Hitler's tyranny whipping up the Nazis' on several occasions when he'd been discussing world affairs with his mother and Nana. As he lay on his bed he pictured these 'Nazis thugs' as being some form of super bug, a bit like nits only very much bigger with Hitler controlling them with a huge whip called 'Tyranny' and ordering them to attack people and eat their brains; a bit like Ming the Merciless. He also imagined himself, armed to the teeth and firing repeatedly at the enemy to save the country from the tyranny of Hitler's rule. This image took the form of a man who looked a lot like Ming, surrounded by giant nit creatures, waving around a big whip yelling;

"No one can defeat me and my Nazi bugs and my whip called Tyranny" he then went about chopping the heads off defenceless civilians and fought on and on regardless of the amount of times Ray, who looked a lot like Flash Gordon, shot him.

Chapter 2 – Sermon on the Beach

He awoke early as was the norm on a Sunday; went downstairs and out into the yard to go to the loo. As he stood in the chill of the yard, which had yet to receive any sun, he wished he lived in a house where the toilet was inside. He'd heard they existed and that if you bought a new house, you would definitely get one. He also didn't like using cut up newspaper to wipe his bum as it often left print on his hands, and his behind. He determined that once he'd defeated Hitler and his Nazi bugs the king would be so grateful he would reward him with whatever he wanted.

As he parked his backside on the freezing cold wooden seat, he decided that top of the list would be a brand new house with a toilet in every room, and they would only use toilet paper that was soft and definitely had no print. As he made his way back into the house after he was done, he thought how nice it would be to have everyone fall over themselves to give him what he wanted. Any idea of such a scenario lasted as long as it took him to open the back door.

"Wash your hands and face Raymond and then eat your breakfast quickly" his mother said as she pointed towards a large slice of bread and can of condensed milk. These ingredients would allow Ray to make his favourite meal; a connyonny butty, which involved pouring the milk over the bread until it was sopping wet. "As soon as you've finished go and get dressed and remember to put your best pants on. And please hurry up we have a long way to go".

Ray dutifully did as he was told and shortly afterwards him, his mother and his father set off for the Pier Head. He always got excited about his journey to Sunday service when they took place on the beach as it meant a trip on the tram and then on the ferry. They didn't have far to walk in order to catch the 'Bone Shaker' as there was a depot for the trams at the bottom of Smithdown Road near Penny Lane.

Upon paying the tuppence to journey into town, he eagerly claimed the window seat and watched the world go by. The journey was somewhat uncomfortable as the backs of the chairs were made of wooden slats and the tram had little in the way of suspension. There were no doors either, which was fine during the summer as it allowed a cooling breeze to wash over the passengers, but in winter could leave you feeling raw and frozen. He loved seeing the buildings go by and spot the odd car as he rarely ventured further than the local shop or church and there were no cars in any of the streets near him.

"Why haven't we got a car Dad?"

His father pondered the question before answering, which was pretty normal for him. John Dagnall was a man of medium height and weight who was reflective about most things. He was normally quite quiet and placid, but Ray loved him dearly and believed him to be the wisest person alive.

"How many people do you know who have a car Ray?"

Ray thought for a second. "None I suppose."

"And why do you think that is?"

Ray really didn't have a clue. "Is it because they like to ride on the tram?"

His father smiled "That may be part of the reason; the other part is that cars are really expensive, which means that not many people can afford them."

As Ray went back to watching the world go by he made a mental note to add a car onto his shopping list when he defeated the Nazi bugs.

As they pulled up at the pier head he refused to leave the tram. "Please Ma, can we just wait until everyone's got off"

"For goodness sake Raymond; we have to catch the ferry!"

"Please Ma, it will only take a second and there are always huge queues anyway."

His mother relented, which enabled him to approach the conductor as the last passenger disembarked. "Can I flip the seats for you mister?" he asked as he put on his most angelic face.

"Go on then lad."

Ray then proceeded to run down the centre aisle with his arms outstretched and flicked the back of the seats so they crashed over, resulting in them facing the other way, and enabling the passengers to look forward on the outbound journey.

The Dagnall family then joined the crowds waiting to board the ferry. Ray never ceased to be amazed at how many people seemed to live in Liverpool. The queue was always huge and it didn't seem to matter how early you got up, by the time you arrived at the landing stage, there were always hundreds of people in front of you already waiting. Whole families would be patiently standing around, laden down with picnic hampers, bottles of lemonade and a wide assortment of beach toys and blankets. There were also couples with swimming costumes in bags over their shoulders and many, many children running around adult feet, screeching with delight as they chased each other around and around and receiving annoyed retorts from parents and strangers alike.

You could always tell the moment the ferry came near to docking as a ripple of invisible energy went through the crowd. It was almost a palpable sensation as the children's excitement grew and parent's tension increased. Then fathers would start to heave baggage over shoulders and mothers ordered children back to their positions around her feet with instructions to keep hold of her skirt and not to let go. This reminded Ray of a mother duck with her ducklings, which always made him giggle.

"What are you laughing at Raymond? Make sure you keep hold of my hand and don't dawdle; we have to get on this ferry if we are to be in time for the service".

The passengers were literally crammed into every conceivable space with barely enough room to breathe, let alone move. The sailors shoved people on until there was no more space on board before embarking on the thirty minute journey across the Mersey. Ray loved the thrill and the growing excitement and although he couldn't swim, he loved the idea of being on water. To survive the crush, he pretended he was a statue, standing perfectly still looking out over the river with his eyes wide so he wouldn't blink.

"Raymond, what are you doing? Stop being silly you look like an idiot."

"I'm not an idiot Ma, I'm a statue!"

His mother sighed heavily all too used to Ray's eccentricities so he remained in the same position for the rest of the journey.

As they docked at New Brighton the crowd seemed to take a leaf out of Ray's book and freeze in anticipation as the sailors tied the boat to the jetty before the gates were opened to allow people to disembark. As this happened there was a stampede as people jostled to leave the boat and many started to run down the landing stage in order to avoid the crush. Whilst being slightly scared by this, Ray also found it quite exhilarating and he shrieked with glee as his mother barged her way through less determined opponents.

"Excuse me please." She said as she shoved an elderly gentleman out of the way.

"Excuse me indeed." He replied grumpily.

Ray supposed they were so polite to each other because it was a Sunday.

As the crowds dispersed in different directions, some going towards the beach and many heading towards the outdoor swimming pool, he thought how lucky he was to live so close to such a popular destination during the summer. Even though it was still fairly early, the beach was packed with virtually no space to set up deckchairs and windbreaks. Not that he would be spending much time relaxing as he had to attend the Sunday service and preach to the congregation.

As they passed the pier and Ray caught his first glimpse of the roped off area that acted as their place for congregation, he began to feel rather apprehensive even though he'd done it before. It was not so much the idea of standing up and talking about what God meant to him in front of hundreds of people, it was more to do with what he would do if he got an itch or he had to sneeze or burp. He knew his mother would be furious and if she was, then so too would God.

However, he delivered his lines just as he'd rehearsed with his mother, and proclaimed that God influenced his life in many positive ways. He saw her smile on several occasions and his father looked on affectionately nodding encouragement when Ray stalled for just a second as he talked about how merciful God was and how he forgave our sins. The reason Ray stalled was that a question emerged for just the briefest of moments that centred on the fact that if God was merciful and forgave our sins as long as we said sorry; then why did his mother give him a good hiding for using the odd naughty word when he always apologised? However, the thought was fleeting and Ray dismissed it as just another example of the mysteries of life before continuing with his preaching.

Being the centre of attention did have its benefits though. After he'd finished he was patted affectionately on the head by a multitude of adults with many an "Ah, how cute was he" or "you must be so proud of him Olive" to his mother. The minister even handed over a bag of sweets, which was decent payment for three minutes of work and more than made up for the fact that he wouldn't get the chance to go to the pool or sit on the beach.

Olive was so pleased she even bought him an ice cream and they went for a stroll along the prom, looking out over the sea of humanity who had come to bask in the sunlight before the real sea. As he walked along the promenade he was struck with how happy and relaxed people seemed to be and how the simplicity of making sand castles and digging holes in the sand could lead to such a sense of achievement for both adults and children alike. Little did he know that in the coming months the holes that would be dug would be to defend and protect and the castles would still be made of sand, but placed within canvas bags to resist bomb blasts and shrapnel. 1939 was just around the corner and Mr. Hitler and his Nazi bugs had plans for world domination that could not be put on hold.

Chapter 3 – Riding the Dog, Uncle Walt and Other Routines

In the months that followed Ray's sermon on the beach, life continued as normal with daily routines unchanged. His father still worked down at the docks doing what, he wasn't quite sure and his mother had her part time job in the jam factory. Ray loved jam and looked forward to when his mother was able to bring home a pot she'd purchased cheaply due to a jar being not right or a seal that had cracked on the lid. He'd dollop a pile onto a piece of bread and savour it in front of the fire, loving the sweet sticky taste and licking his fingers for minutes after he'd finished.

"Will you be getting some jam today Ma?" he said as his mother got ready for work.

"Maybe, it depends if they have any jars that are damaged." She responded as she took her wedding ring off. It always puzzled him why she did this so decided to ask.

"Why do you take your ring off and leave it on the sideboard every time you go to work Ma?" He suspected it was because she didn't want to lose it or was afraid of catching her hand in some sort of machinery.

"It's because they don't like you to be married, so I pretend that I'm not." She then put her coat on and left leaving Ray utterly baffled as to what she meant. Who were 'they' and why didn't they like her being married? The other thing that amazed him was that his mother had all but admitted to lying, something she would have battered him for doing and probably sent him to bed without any tea. It annoyed him sometimes the way grownups had one set of rules for their children and another for themselves. He decided to ask his Nana so went to sit on her bed."Nana, why don't they like me Ma to be married? And who are 'they' anyway, and why is it alright for grownups to tell lies but not children?"

His nana loved to talk so he thought she'd appreciate having so many questions to ponder, but she didn't seem particularly impressed.

"Raymond stop bothering me, I'm trying to listen to the radio!" She then threw a newspaper at him to ensure he left the room.

He hated having a question, which no one would answer, so he spent the rest of the day sulking around the house feeling sorry for himself, and thinking about how boring his life had become since he'd done his sermon on the beach. If he'd asked a question then, everybody would have fallen over themselves to answer it. As he moped around he concluded he didn't like being ignored and treated as if he was too young to have his questions answered properly. When his father returned from work he therefore pounced even before his father had time to remove his jacket.

"I've already asked me Ma and Nana and they didn't answer me, so you have to give me a proper answer, Okay?"

His father looked rather bemused but agreed. "Whatever you say Ray, what would you like to know?"

He had to admit his father had a canny way of calming a situation down. If he'd spoken to his mother as he just had, she'd have flown off the handle and probably given him a clip around the ear, but by remaining calm his father always managed to sort things out without things getting out of hand.

"Well, me Ma takes her wedding ring off before going to work each day and she said it was because 'they' don't like her being married so she pretends not to be, so I want to know who 'they' are; why they don't like her being married and why is it ok for grownups to tell lies but not kids?" He was quite out of breath by the time he'd finished so he sat quietly while his father constructed his answer in his mind.

"Well firstly 'they' are the people who own the factory. Secondly, they don't like women being married because they might have a baby, which means they'll be off work and thirdly, pretending to not be married was the only way your mother could get the job so I suppose there are certain occasions when it's better to pretend than be totally honest; for grownups that is; children should always tell the truth."

Ray was fairly satisfied with the answers he received but still felt that grownups should follow the same rules that kids had to. They seemed to break the rules at every turn and didn't even bat an eyelid; such as every Saturday when they'd ritually go to Uncle Walt's in the afternoon.

Walt was one of Olive's many brothers and only lived around the corner in a house that backed on to the railway. When they visited he was actually never there as he was a train driver, but his wife and normally several other members of the family were in attendance. When they arrived Ray would always try and sneak away to the back yard as quickly as possible where Sabre, Walter's dog was kennelled. The dog was a huge wolfhound with long fangs and a shaggy grey/black coat that truly ponged when he got wet. He was a lot taller than Ray and was so docile he allowed him to climb onto his back and ride him as if he was a horse and Ray was Hop Along Cassidy. Many an hour was spent riding around the yard on the beast's back shooting imaginary bad guys.

If he was really lucky he'd be given a list of shopping and allowed to take Sabre with him as he went to the local corner shop at the end of the street. He was the envy of every other kid as he jumped on the dog's back and nonchalantly rode him to the store, saying 'Howdy' to everyone he passed. When he got back, he'd return to the yard and listen intently for the whistle of an approaching train. At 4:15 pm precisely, Ray would hear the tootle of the whistle and then run in doors.

"He's coming, He's coming" Ray would shout.

"Stop shouting Raymond and go and bring Sabre in quickly". Ray would then run out and jump on Sabre's back and ride him into the kitchen before the train passed. The weekly ritual would then include somebody, usually Olive saying

"I wonder what we'll get this week; I hope it's fruit; maybe some lovely oranges" and then the whole family would stand at the window and watch as uncle Walt passed in his train and hurled some sort of contraband that had come into his possession from god alone knew where, into his back yard. He would then wave before receding into the distance and the family emerged to see what treasures had literally fallen into their laps that week.

One Saturday afternoon in November it was raining outside so Ray was allowed to bring Sabre into the back room to play whilst the adults sat and talked in the front room. Whilst it was fun to roll around with the dog, he soon became bored and looked around the room for something to distract him. On the sideboard he saw Walter's bowler hat, glasses and a packet of cigarettes.

"How would you like me to do a little performance for you boy? You would? Okay then." He donned the hat and glasses and placed a fag in his mouth and began to, quite accurately in his mind, mimic Walt's walk and voice as he paced around the room saying "Why have I got so many ruddy relations?!"

Sabre seemed most impressed and wagged his tail enthusiastically. He even jumped up, placing his paws on Ray's shoulders and licking his face all over.

"Did you like that boy?"

The dog yapped excitedly and wagged his tail even more.

"I think it's only fair that you have a go as well." He then put the glasses on the dog's head, jammed the bowler hat over his ears and placed a cigarette in his mouth. He was just about to strike a match to light it when his mother walked into the room.

"Raymond we are leavi....." She stood frozen for what seemed like ages, which made Ray think she was in training for a trip on the ferry; and actually doing really well in her attempt at becoming a statue. However, she suddenly exploded into frantic gestures that were directed at both Ray and the dog and screamed; "John, get in here! Look what your idiot son has done to Walter's bowler hat". She quickly grabbed

Ray by the arm and dragged him out threatening all kinds of retribution. As he was led through the door, Ray saw Sabre drop the fag and jump up on his dad's shoulders and give him an affectionate lick, still wearing the glasses and bowler hat. He also noticed that his father was trying his utmost not to laugh and failing miserably, which made up for the fact he was sent to bed without any tea.

Chapter 4 – Jigger Shelters, Gas Masks and Railings

As winter turned to spring in 1939 it was clear to Ray and just about everyone else that war with Hitler and his Nazi bugs was imminent. Every evening the family would gather around the radio and listen as one crisis after the other was reported by announcers with clipped accents who seemed unbelievably calm given they were reporting on the savagery of the war in Spain, the German invasion of Czechoslovakia and the promise of the British Prime Minister, Mr. Chamberlain that Britain would defend Poland if Germany should invade them.

When walking across the street to school or going to church with his parents on a Sunday, it was not difficult to pick up on the cloud that was hanging over everybody. It was as if the adults were permanently distracted and only half paid attention when asked questions by their children. Of course Ray used this to his advantage whenever he could.

"Do you think there'll be war John; please answer me honestly?" His mother asked one evening as they sat around listening to the news on the radio.

"I think it's inevitable with the way that tyrant Hitler is behaving."

"Oh John, what will we do, you'll be called up." His mother wailed.

Ray didn't really appreciate the importance of his parent's conversation, but felt now would be a good time to slip into the conversation his own news in the hope it might escape their attention.

"What will happen if the Germans invade Poland Dad? I got the slipper in school for making silly noises while we were meant to be listening to a story." He'd hoped asking about an event in the news before slipping in the fact he'd been naughty in school might have allowed him to escape further punishment. However, as nobody seemed relaxed anymore he received a sturdier whack than normal.

"How many more times are you going to get into trouble for making stupid noises Raymond?!"

He was pretty sure he didn't know the answer to that particular question, but thought he'd better offer something "Four?" He received another whack for his efforts and was sent to bed.

As he lay sulking he reflected on the unfairness of life and blamed Hitler and his Nazi bugs for making the adults in his life tense and liable to snap at the slightest sign of his natural exuberance.

Even though the threat of war seemed nearer every time they switched the radio on, the day to day routines did not change. He still got up, went to the loo in the yard, got washed in the sink in the kitchen and had a bath once a week in a tin enamelled bath that was brought from the shed to the back room every Saturday evening. He still went to school each day, Walt's on a Saturday and to church service on a Sunday. However, there were exceptional events that marked an evolution for the Dagnall family. One such development happened in March as Ray was finishing his breakfast.

"Raymond, I want you to go straight to your Aunty Sydnah's from school. I'll drop some clothes off for you, and you are going to be staying there for the next few days."

Sydnah was Olive's best friend and Ray had known her all his life. He liked her but she could be very strict.

"Why do I have to stay with Sydnah? She's not even my proper aunty."

Olive gave him a look that would melt ice and that sent a clear message that he should not say another word. "Sydnah is a very good friend of mine and has kindly agreed to take you in and look after you whilst we have electricity fitted. You do want electricity don't you?"

Ray nodded his head eagerly and apologised for his petulance. "Wow, are we really getting electricity?! In that case I don't mind staying with Aunt Sydnah one little bit."

It would be a lot less of a burden if it gave him bragging rights over most of his friends. He only knew of one or two people in his street that had electricity, most people still used gas lights, and so he headed off to school feeling pretty special indeed. Unfortunately, this feeling only lasted as long as it took him to cross the road and enter the playground. He bounded onto the yard expecting to be the centre of attention when people found out he was getting electricity.

"We're all getting it Ray, the corpy are putting it into all of their houses."

Therefore, whilst it was still exciting to be able to flick a switch in order to turn a light on and off; once the novelty had worn off, and after he'd received several clips around the ear for standing by the switch and flicking it up and down repeatedly, he decided it wasn't such a big deal after all and quickly became used to the new routine.

The weeks passed by until it was summer once again with the shadow of war hanging over them like an invisible membrane that sucked the fun and vitality out of normal routines and left people concerned and lacking in hope. The Dagnalls endeavoured to continue as normal, but everywhere they turned there were indications of the changes being wrought on people. Even as they headed to Sunday service on the beach at New Brighton, Ray noticed there seemed to be a lot less laughter, and whilst he still looked forward to the trip, the atmosphere was not as exciting as it had been the year before. This may have also been down to the fact that now he was six years of age he'd been replaced by a new sermoniser who was only four. When he first heard he was to be replaced he was fuming.

"Four years of age!" he growled at his mother indignantly. "Four years of age! What does he know about how God forgives our sins; he can't have any sins to forgive!"

Ray expected his mother to reprimand him in some way as she often did, but instead of some retort accompanied by a sanction, she looked at him and guffawed with laughter.

"Oh Raymond, you are just what the doctor ordered" she said as she leant down and embraced him. "And you're absolutely right, what does a silly four year old know about God's mercy compared to my little man."

Ray was rather taken aback by this. Firstly he didn't really understand what his mother meant by "the doctor ordered". To his mind a doctor only ever ordered you to take some foul tasting medicine that made you feel worse before it made you feel better. If his mother was saying he was like some foul tasting medicine, he wasn't particularly impressed. However, her laughter and embrace indicated this was not what she meant.

Secondly, whilst he loved his mother dearly, she did spend most of her time chastising him for some wrong doing or other and this more affectionate side was quite rare. This epiphany put into perspective his earlier rant about the four year old and as he hugged his mother back he said;

"I'd rather sit next to you during the service anyway ma so I don't really care if he gets the sweets off the minister". His mother hugged him again and Ray was sure he saw a tear in her eye as she did so.

The possibility of war was brought home to him further at the beginning of July as he helped his mum and dad put up large black curtains on all the windows of their house. "Why are we doing this dad?" Ray huffed as he heaved a curtain above his head so his dad could hang it above the window.

"We're practicing to make sure that if we go to war, the enemy bombers can't see any lights from the air and so won't be able to bomb us."

"Wow, if we do end up in a war will you have to fight in it?"

Ray's dad paused, concentrating on the curtains before he answered. "I hope it doesn't come to war, but if it does I will probably join the navy. Seeing that I work at the docks already it would be the obvious thing for me to do."

Most of Ray's uncles were in the navy in one form or another so he thought it was obvious too. "Will I have to fight?" he said, quite excited by the prospect, picturing once again his battle against Hitler and his bugs in which he was armed to the teeth with machine gun and grenade. His father laughed.

"No young man, you will have to look after your mother". Ray raised himself to his full height, rather proud of the fact that if his father went away to war he would be the man of the house. Having said that, he quickly became deflated because the idea of telling his mother what do was a rather daunting prospect.

"I hope you don't have to go away dad."

"So do I Raymond, so do I." But by the way he said it; Ray reckoned his father wasn't convinced.

When he broke up for the summer holidays he thought things would be better as he had six whole weeks off. However, there was a gloom that rested over everything; even the weather seemed to sense the imminent clash of nations as it was dull most days and rained every other meaning Ray was cooped up indoors most of the time. Then at the end of August he was told by his mother he had to attend school the next day. He was furious as he believed he had several days until he had to return and the weather had finally decided to cheer up.

"Why do I have to go to school ma? We don't go back till next week."

His mother sat him down at the kitchen table and then sat down herself. "Listen Raymond, we have been told that all children who live on the side of the railway towards town are to be evacuated to Wales so that if there is a war, they will be safe."

He wasn't sure what evacuated meant, but it didn't seem to be relevant as the Dagnalls lived a few yards on the other side of the railway. "Why aren't I getting evacuated then?" He said a little petulantly feeling rather put out that he wouldn't be going to Wales; the furthest he'd been was New Brighton.

"If there is war, then the Germans will probably target the docks and we live far enough away for us to be deemed safe from the bombs."

He was still rather confused and he still fancied a trip to Wales. "But why can't I go, and why do I need to go into school?"

His mother's patience was starting to wear thin. "Look Raymond, those children who are being evacuated are going to have to leave their parents and travel to Wales on their own. Do you want to have to leave me?" She paused as she brought her impatience under control. "You have to go to school tomorrow because your teachers want to give you instructions on what will happen in the event of war and also, you're going to be given a gas mask."

"A gas mask?" Ray said "What's a gas mask?"

"If the Germans decide to drop poison gas, the mask will protect you. You have to learn how to put it on properly. That's why you have to go to school".

He felt much better after hearing he was being given a present and so the next morning he headed off out the front door feeling pretty cheery. However, a new sense of gloom hung over the playground as he saw many of his classmates standing with parents and accompanied by suitcases, hats and coats, which had cardboard tags pinned to them. Many were crying as they hugged mothers close and he could hear the sobs as he made his way to join them, confused as to why his mother hadn't accompanied him and wondering what the heck was going on. Before he had a chance to ask anyone what was happening, his teacher approached him from across the yard and escorted him into a classroom where there were a handful of other children.

"Right, you lot are not being sent to Wales so I am going to hand out a gas mask to each of you and show you how to put it on. These are not toys and should only be used if we are attacked with gas."

She proceeded to hand around cardboard boxes, which had string handles. Inside were the masks, which to Ray, looked like the face of one of the aliens that Flash Gordon might fight. He was shown how to take it out of the box and how to put it on. He then had great fun trying out different voices to see which one scared the girls the most.

"You will do as you're told or I'll destroy you!" he

pronounced in a rather effective voice, which made the girl who sat next to him squeal with horrified delight.

"Dagnall, what did I say about the mask not being a toy? You are only to wear it if we are attacked with gas!" She then gave him a clip round the ear, which caused him to bash his nose on the tubular piece that sat on the front of the mask.

"Ouch miss that hurt!"

"Not as much as it will hurt if you come to use that thing only to realise you've broken it by messing!"

He decided she probably had a point and took the mask off and replaced it in the box. To his surprise, he was then told he could go home so he was through the door and down the corridor before the teacher told him what was to happen the following week. As he made his way across the playground he realised the children who had been there earlier had gone, and now there were only a small number of mothers who were being consoled as they sobbed quietly into their handkerchiefs.

As he left the school site he couldn't resist the urge to wear the mask one more time, and thought it would be fun to see how many people he could scare. He donned the mask and pretended he was an alien monster making guttural noises whilst sloping down the street with shoulders hunched and arms swinging.

"I will rule the world!" he said in his best Ming the

Merciless voice. Several people gave him strange looks and one old lady tutted loudly as she passed by. He was rather put out by this so turned to give her his loudest roar, but as he did so, he tripped and fell head first into the railings that surrounded the school. Luckily, his head impacted at a point where one of the bars was slightly bent so his head passed cleanly between two of the metal rods. However, when he came to remove it, he realised his head was stuck solid.

As he knelt there wailing and shouting for help, he realised he didn't like the gas mask after all and indeed grew to hate it over the forty five minutes he was stuck there before the fire brigade came and cut him loose. By the time he was free there was quite a crowd watching; so it was with a sense of huge embarrassment that he made the rest of the way home.

That evening whilst listening to the news it was announced that Germany had invaded Poland. Ray knew that Mr. Chamberlain had said that if Germany did this, Britain would declare war on them, but as he listened to the radio it was unclear whether this had happened. His parents seemed as unclear as him and so he spent a restless night dreaming of being stuck in the railings as Nazi bugs queued up to kick him up the bum and laugh and make jokes about him.

The next day was Saturday and although they kept to their normal routine of visiting Walt's, the tension was palpable. Even Sabre seemed to sense it and was listless in the yard, not letting Ray ride him. After returning home and bathing, they once again gathered around the radio and heard that Mr. Chamberlain would address the nation the next day; Sunday September 3rd at just after 11:00 am.

Ray gathered with his parents and grandmother in the front room of their house. They had even postponed Sunday service so people could listen. When Mr. Chamberlain came on air everyone was totally still. His mother held his hand in her right and his father's in her left. There was a couple of seconds of static before Chamberlain said.

I am speaking to you from the Cabinet Room at 10 Downing Street. This morning the British Ambassador in Berlin handed the German Government a final Note stating that, unless we heard from them by 11 o'clock that they were prepared at once to withdraw their troops from Poland, a state of war would exist between us. I have to tell you now that no such undertaking has been received, and that consequently this country is at war with Germany. You can imagine what a bitter blow it is to me that all my long struggle to win peace has failed. Yet I cannot believe that there is anything more or anything different that I could have done and that would have been more successful. Up to the very last it would have been quite possible to have arranged a peaceful and honourable settlement between Germany and Poland, but Hitler would not have it.

He had evidently made up his mind to attack Poland whatever happened, and although He now says he put forward reasonable proposals which were rejected by the Poles, that is not a true statement. The proposals were never shown to the Poles, nor to us, and, although they were announced in a German broadcast on Thursday night, Hitler did not wait to hear comments on them, but ordered his troops to cross the Polish frontier. His action shows convincingly that there is no chance of expecting that this man will ever give up his practice of using force to gain his will. He can only be stopped by force.

We and France are today, in fulfilment of our obligations, going to the aid of Poland, who is so bravely resisting this wicked and unprovoked attack on her people. We have a clear conscience. We have done all that any country could do to establish peace. The situation in which no word given by Germany's ruler could be trusted and no people or country could feel themselves safe has become intolerable. And now that we have resolved to finish it, I know that you will all play your part with calmness and courage. At such a moment as this the assurances of support that we have received from the Empire are a source of profound encouragement to us. The Government have made plans under which it will be possible to carry on the work of the nation in the days of stress and strain that may be ahead. But these plans need your help. You may be taking your part in the fighting services or as a volunteer in one of the branches of Civil Defence. If so you will report for duty in accordance with the instructions you have received. You may be engaged in work essential to the prosecution of war for the maintenance of the life of the people - in factories, in transport, in public utility concerns, or in the supply of other necessaries of life. If so, it is of vital importance that you should carry on with your jobs.

Now may God bless you all. May He defend the right. It is the evil things that we shall be fighting against - brute force, bad faith, injustice, oppression and persecution - and against them I am certain that the right will prevail. "

The announcer then came on and said that people should keep listening as there would be a series of announcements by the government. He then said that Mr. Chamberlain had completed what he wanted to say.

As Ray looked at his mother he saw a tear slowly roll down her cheek, and his father sat stoically determined as church bells sounded over the radio. He was lost for something to say and so just sat and listened as another voice came over the air. He was shocked by what he heard. All entertainment was to be stopped immediately. Cinemas and theatres were to be closed as it was thought to be too dangerous for lots of people to congregate in one place due to the potential threat from bombs. Churches though, would remain open for the foreseeable future, which he found to be a bit of a contradiction and slightly unfair. He'd much rather go to the cinema than to church!

As the announcer continued, the reality of what was happening dawned on him as he heard that all sirens, bells, whistles or horns were to be prohibited so they could be used to warn people of impending attacks. People were told what the warning would sound like and that when the raid was over there would be a continuous note that would last for two minutes. He saw a look of fear pass between his parents as the announcer said that if they heard the sound of wooden rattles it would indicate a gas attack and everybody should don their gas masks until they heard hand bells, which would indicate it was safe for them to be removed.

He felt sick at the magnitude of what he was hearing, but quickly bucked up when the next thing to be announced was that all schools were to be closed for at least the next seven days and possibly longer. Ray was so distracted by the prospect of having a continuous holiday that he almost missed the next section that advised that people should keep off the streets to avoid being exposed and that everybody, particularly children, should have their names and addresses written onto card or envelopes and sewed onto their clothes. He was slightly indignant by this statement as he was pretty sure he knew his name and address and didn't need a tag sewn into his clothes to remind him. He was also not too impressed with having to carry a gasmask around with him everywhere he went. He had quickly fallen out of love with the cumbersome device since getting his head stuck in the railings two days before.

The announcer then went on to talk about unemployed people and what they should do about claiming benefits, but Ray wasn't listening. It was only when the national anthem was played that he rose to his feet unbidden, and joined his parents in a silent salute to their king and nation.

When it ended Ray dashed from the room and threw open the front door before stepping out onto the street. He stood listening for many seconds before looking to the left and then to the right and then up into the sky. Where were they? The announcement said that they were now at war and Ray was convinced he would be able to hear the gunfire at the very least and probably see the German bombers in the sky. However, there was nothing except for a dog that paused to give him a perfunctory sniff then walked over to a lamppost, cocked its leg and urinated profusely before loping off down the street. He felt somehow let down by the anti-climax to the tension he'd experienced with his family as they listened to the radio. When they had stood for the national anthem, he'd been convinced their lives would change immediately, but nothing happened. He supposed he would have to wait until tomorrow for it to begin properly.

However, the next day nothing much had changed other than being off from school, having his name sewn in his clothes and not being allowed out, which was not a good thing for an energetic six year old. By the afternoon he was literally bouncing off the walls.

"For goodness sake Raymond, just go out and play but make sure you don't go wandering off. I want to be able to see you if I look out the front door."

As he left his house he concluded that a number of other parents had seen sense and freed their children from captivity. He therefore spent several hours playing war with the others, shooting imaginary Nazis and defending his homeland.

That evening they heard that a British passenger

liner, the Athenia had been sunk by German U boats and one hundred and twelve people had lost their lives.

"And so it begins." John said as he hugged his wife.

They had heard bulletins about the fighting in Poland and they'd seen images of war from the newsreels played in the cinema depicting the war in

Spain, but hearing of British lives lost brought home the very real fact that the country was now at war itself.

"I am so scared." His mother said as she sniffed into her hanky. This did a lot to scare Ray himself because his mother was the scariest person he knew, so for her to be scared by something meant they should all be worried.

"Don't worry Ma, I'll look after you." He said it as a way of trying to hide his own fear, but it seemed to do the trick.

"My big strong boy, I'm sure you will." She said as she hugged him close.

The first direct impact of the war that he experienced came several weeks later when a lorry pulled up in front of his house and a number of workmen got out and headed off down the 'jigger' or alleyway that ran down the back of the houses. When he finally persuaded his mother to let him out he immediately approached one of the workmen

"Hey mister what are you doing?"

"We're going to build you a shelter just in case that nasty Mr. Hitler decides to send his bombers over."

Ray was intrigued. "How are you going to build it?"

"Well we're going to put reinforced concrete slabs on top of the walls in your jigger, which will make a roof. Then if there's an air raid you can just run down here and you'll be safe.

There was some sense in what the man was saying, but he thought it was quite a way to run if the bombs were falling all around you. "But why can't you build a shelter out front? It'd be a lot easier to reach."

"You're a bright little tyke aren't you?!" the man replied. "We're actually doing exactly that in the other streets round here, but you've got the school across the way so we can't do that here."

As Ray headed to the shops with his mother that afternoon he witnessed for himself, the hive of activity as men swarmed in the streets nearby, hurriedly constructing shelters. He didn't know much about what destruction a bomb would cause, but he didn't really understand why you'd build a shelter out of the same material houses were built. If you weren't safe in a brick built house, then why would you be any safer in a brick built shelter in the middle of the street? However, he was sure the people who made the decision to build them, knew what they were doing and at least he knew they had a reinforced concrete roof over their jigger, which he assumed was a lot harder to hit than one in the street, because the jigger was so much narrower.

Chapter 5- Barrage Balloons and the German Butcher

The winter as 1939 became 1940 was a hard one. The snow fell early and remained for weeks on end, drifting up against the kerb and doorways and making it difficult for people to get out of their houses. For young boys though it was magical. The dreary street was transformed over night into a white wonderland that offered loads of new fun filled activities such as making snow angels, building snowmen and the obligatory snowball war between the gangs of kids who lived in the streets around the school. Initially, Ray would spend hours stalking anything that moved and then bombard whatever it was with snowballs. However, when the snow showed no signs of melting after several days, some of the older kids' organised teams and the 'war' became more organised. There were eight in Ray's team ranging from a girl who was a year younger, to lads who were nine and ten. They took up station on the corner of the street and actually built snowy ramparts, which offered some form of protection and also offered a ready means of ammunition once their stockpile was used up. From this base they would then roam around in groups of no less than two looking for targets to attack.

On one occasion Ray was guarding the ramparts of

their base with a boy from down the street called Derek. They'd heard screams of delight and anguish coming from round the corner so were ready for any eventuality and armed with a snowball in each hand. Suddenly, Derek pitched forward, falling over the edge of their barrier.

"What's wrong?!" was all Ray managed to say before he too was hit on the back of his shoulder. He spun round to discover they'd been duped by the screams and had in fact been snuck up on by their opponents. There was little either of them could do as a second wave of the enemy came round the corner in front of them. They were basically caught in a pincer movement and although they put up a gallant defence, were soon overrun and pelted relentlessly with snow.

"Alright we surrender! Please stop!" wailed Derek as he received three hits simultaneously in the head.

Their leader considered his plea for the blink of an eye before replying. "No way, this is too much fun!" and then continued with his relentless assault.

Ray was receiving the same level of abuse as Derek, but he was still refusing to submit and fired off as many missiles as he could manage. He'd just scored a direct hit on their leader's nose when he felt a hard thwack against the side of his head and blackness descended.

When he came round he was lying on the sofa in his back room with his mother pressing a towel to his head. When she removed it he saw there was a large red stain and realised he was bleeding.

"What happened?" he said groggily and winced as pain raced around his brain.

"You were hit by a snowball that had a stone stuck in it. That's it Raymond, you're not to play with the big boys anymore!"

He attempted to argue but the pain in his head was too strong and he knew by the look on his mother's face it would be pointless anyway. His new routine therefore became quite difficult. Instead of being able to play out with the other kids, he was given various snow related chores to complete each day. It fell to him to make sure the pavement in front of the house was kept clear and to clear away any snow from the back yard between the house and the loo. His difficulty arose as soon as he'd open the front door as the wind would blow the top of the drift down the hallway, before melting and wetting everything in its path.

"Raymond, for goodness sake, will you use the back door to go out! And try not to get wet"

Sometimes his mother's rationale amazed him. How was he supposed to clear masses of snow and remain dry? It got to a point where he actually wished he were back in class.

Hey Green Elementary had not reopened due to it being taken over by the RAF and becoming a base for a barrage balloon. To begin with Ray would pine away the couple of hours spent doing classes before escaping to watch as the men practiced inflating the massive piece of canvas before releasing it into the sky and then repeating the whole manoeuvre again. If he were honest, the novelty of the routine soon wore off, but he still gained pleasure from not having to be in class, particularly seeing that his mother had volunteered their house for the lessons to take place. Therefore, each morning he got up, went downstairs and into his back room where a teacher would be waiting with half a dozen other children.

"Dagnall, for the love of god why are you late? You live in this house for goodness sake; and will you put that sandwich away!" He regularly received a telling off for traipsing in still eating his connyonny butty. When the goo inevitably ended up dripping all over his work, the teacher's patience would run out.

"Go and stand in the hall until you've finished!" Unfortunately, standing in the hall would in turn attract the wrath of his mother.

"Why have you been sent out again Raymond?"

"It wasn't my fault Ma, it was the connyonny butty." He'd then receive the obligatory clip round the ear before his mother stomped off angrily. He felt this to be utterly unfair as the back room was where he normally ate and it wasn't his fault it had been changed into a classroom.

After some perfunctory learning that covered the basics of English and Mathematics, the teacher would leave with the other children leaving Ray to his own devices. His mother was too busy working in the jam factory, looking after her mother and trying to purchase enough food to live off to devote much time to Ray, which meant he was free to roam around. After the initial warnings about not going out, things had relaxed somewhat since there had been no attacks, so he wandered the streets, heading onto Picton Road and even venturing as far as Smithdown Road, a good half mile away. He was not alone of course as there were a number of other children with little to do. It was inevitable they'd get up to mischief, which happened rather too regularly for Olive's liking.

One particular mishap, which brought Ray a good deal of shame, involved a local butcher. The man had owned his corner shop for many years but he had the unfortunate surname Schmidt and had originated from Germany shortly after the First World War. He'd married an English girl and lived in the community ever since. However, in those months following the outbreak of war, the children of the local area made his life a misery.

It began when Ray came across some older boys while he was out wandering one day.

"I dare you to throw some mud at his window." The largest of the boys said to his companions.

Two of them looked at each other. "I will if you will."

"Alright, we throw after three and then leg it!"

The two boys counted down and left two large muddy stains running down the shop front window. When Mr. Schmidt came out of the shop to see what had happened, they ran off laughing calling him names such as "Boche" and "Hun" and "Nazi scum".

Ray and his mate Johnny stood giggling as Mr. Schmidt, who was a rather rotund man, waddled down the street trying to grab hold of one of the offenders and failing miserably.

"That was so funny!" Johnny said "Did you see the way he ran after them?!"

As they stood there laughing, the older boys returned. "Do you think you'd be brave enough to try something like that?" the leader said rather scornfully.

"Yeah of course we are, aren't we Johnny?" Ray responded, although he was not absolutely sure he was. Johnny agreed uncertainly, which encouraged the older boy further.

"Go on then take these stones." He said picking up a couple of stones and handing them to Ray and his friend "And go and show the Nazi swine that we won't put up with Hitler or any of his kind around here."

The way the boy put it made Ray believe they'd be striking a blow for justice and freedom in the war against Hitler's tyranny and his Nazi bugs, so he crept up to the shop window with Johnny. When they were a matter of inches away Johnny turned to him

"I will count to three and then we'll both throw at the same time."

Ray was slightly surprised as Johnny never showed much aptitude for counting and he was unsure if he could actually count to three. "Are you sure?" he said looking at Johnny a little dubiously. "Why don't we just throw the stones and run?" Johnny just ignored him and began counting.

"One" Johnny raised his hand; "Two" Ray quickly raised his hand also; "Three!" Ray threw his stone and it sailed through the window, shattering it into hundreds of pieces. He turned to run and realised that Johnny must have been so taken with counting to three successfully, he'd forgotten to throw his stone and just ran off leaving Ray a glimpse of his back as he disappeared around the corner. Before he could run further than five paces he was grabbed by the collar.

"Why would you do such a thing? Do you know how much it will cost to have that window repaired you young ruffian?!" Mr. Schmidt glared at him, his face becoming redder and redder as he shook him by the shoulders.

"What have I ever done to you young Raymond?" It was at that point that Mr. Schmidt began to cry and Ray suddenly felt very guilty.

"The big boys told me to do it". He wailed. "They

said you were a Nazi bug and deserved everything you had coming to you." He still hadn't quite grasped the concept of a Nazi thug and still imagined giant insects that originated from Germany. In his mind's eye this meant that Mr. Schmidt was only disguised as a human and the thought of an insect lurking under this man's skin terrified him.

"Please, I'm sorry, let me go, please don't eat me, I'm sorry!" he sobbed so loudly that Mr. Schmidt released him and he ran as quickly as he could to his house.

However, he'd only just managed to sneak passed his mother and head to his room so she wouldn't see him crying when there was a knock on the front door. He heard his mother answer the knock and then felt the blood drain from his face as he heard Mr. Schmidt's voice giving his mother an account of what he'd done. Several minutes later the door closed and he heard his mother's footsteps pounding up the stairs. His door swung open and his mother stormed into his room.

"How could you?! Have I brought you up to treat people that way? I'm disgusted with you!" It was these last words that hurt far more that the good hiding he received; or the early bedtime without any tea; or the grounding from being allowed out for two weeks; or even having to write an apology to Mr. Schmidt and deliver it personally. As Ray lay awake that night, quietly wiping away the tears and snot from his face with the sleeve of his pyjamas, he vowed he would never call anybody a Nazi bug ever again and he'd think twice before listening to older boys. He also vowed he would make his mother proud of him once more.

In the weeks that followed Mr. Schmidt had his windows broken several times until one day as Ray and his mother headed passed the shop, they realised it had been closed and Mr. Schmidt had moved away. This added to the difficulties faced by Ray's mother as by now most foods were rationed and it was becoming harder to find fresh fruit, vegetables and meat. Not having a local butcher meant a further journey to find meat and no relationship on which to build any perks.

Although life had subtly changed for all of them, they quickly adapted to new routines. Each evening they'd gather around the radio in his grandmother's room and listen to updates of what was happening on the world stage. This was not a new routine, but whereas it had once been a means of relaxing after a day's toil, now it was an anxious means of following what was happening with the war and learning what they might expect in the future.

However, after the initial expectation of bombers and invasion the war seemed to settle down into a series of battles at sea and invasions of far away countries; many of which Ray had never heard of. The conflict felt like a distant thing and even when he learned that three of his uncles had had their ships sunk from under them, he still didn't appreciate the immediacy of the growing conflict as his uncle's had all survived and seemed quite merry when they'd returned home on leave.

However, In May events started to increase rapidly.

They heard that the allies were to evacuate their forces from Norway and then they heard the Germans had invaded Belgium, France, Luxembourg and The Netherlands. On the same day they heard that Neville Chamberlain had resigned as Prime Minister and been replaced by Winston Churchill. Within a matter of weeks the Germans had overrun every obstacle in their way and the allies had retreated to a place called Dunkirk. When he looked at a map, which his teacher had brought to a lesson he was shocked to realise how close the war had come to Britain's shores.

"But that Dunkirk place is only on the other side of the sea."

"That 'sea' as you put it is called the English Channel." His teacher corrected him.

"Whatever it's called miss, it's very close to England."

"God help us all Raymond, but you're right, it's very close to our shores."

When he confronted his father with his new found knowledge that evening he was looking for some sort of confirmation that everything would be alright.

"If the Nazi's kick our army out of France what will stop them from being able to invade us dad?"

His father contemplated his answer as normal. "We've still got a strong navy and air force so they'll have to try and neutralise them before they launch anything, but if they manage to do that then nothing will stand in their way. Maybe then I'll be called on to fight."

Much of what his father had just said went straight over Ray's head, but he did know that since the day after war was first declared, his father had tried to join up. It wasn't that he wanted to go away to fight and leave his son and now pregnant wife alone to fend for themselves, it was that he felt it was his duty to help defend his country.

His parents hardly ever argued, but Ray heard heated exchanges on several occasions.

"What am I going to do if you go off to fight and the bombs start to fall?" He heard his mother state one evening towards the end of May. "How am I going to get Raymond and my mother to a shelter, we won't stand a chance." His father was always a quiet mannered man so Ray was surprised to hear him raise his voice.

"Look Olive, I've been turned down by the Navy and the Air force because they say my job at the docks is too important to the war effort; but all I'm doing is painting camouflage onto the ships. Can't you see how frustrating it is for me? Every evening we hear that the Nazis have pushed further into France. We're not winning Olive. The army needs every man it can get and I need to feel I'm doing something worthwhile."

As Ray listened from the stairs he was quite sure he'd never heard his father say so much in one go and was therefore not surprised when there was a lengthy silence when he finished as he was sure the exertion of such a long speech would've exhausted him. Eventually he heard his mother say in a far more soothing voice.

"John I understand, truly I do, but if the authorities have said you are doing an important job, then you must start to believe you are. Your work is potentially saving lives." Ray wasn't quite sure how painting a ship could save lives, but he didn't dwell on it as his father responded.

"Olive, I've made up my mind. I will go down to the recruitment office tomorrow and try to join the army. If they will not take me then I'll accept that I will have to fight this war from home, but please don't try and dissuade me from trying." In all things domestic, Ray could not remember a time that his mother didn't get her own way so he was flabbergasted when he heard her quietly capitulate.

"John, you do what you have to do. I will be here for you regardless of what happens." There was then silence as he heard his father's footsteps cross the room and it was with shock and disgust that he realised his parents were kissing!

The following day John did as he'd promised and went to try and join the army, but was once again disappointed when he was told that his job painting camouflage onto ships was too important to the war effort and so he had to resign himself to contributing in that way. He did however; decide to become a member of the Air Raid Precaution (ARP) organisation. A couple of days later he entered the kitchen kitted out in his uniform, which consisted of a set of overalls, wellington boots and an armlet; along with a black steel helmet, which had **W** for Warden in bold white writing across it and a small silver-coloured badge. Ray thought he looked equally as proud as if he'd been wearing the battle dress of an infantry man and concluded that his father had finally found something of use to do, even though in Ray's mind, camouflaging ships was useful.

After some initial training in first aid and the responsibilities of his role, John started to don his uniform every other evening and go out on patrol. He was basically tasked with ensuring the blackout was stringently adhered to, which meant yelling at anybody who allowed any light to shine from their house. For somebody as quiet as Ray's father this was quite a challenge, but he embraced the responsibility wholeheartedly and became quite adept at projecting his voice across vast distances. He also had to make sure that everybody in his designated area had access to a shelter and that the shelters were kept in good condition for when they were needed. In the weeks that followed the collapse of France and the evacuation of the allied forces from Dunkirk, everybody knew it was only a matter of time before the British mainland itself was attacked and so preparations and drills increased significantly.

Ray noticed this increase first hand by looking out of his bedroom window to see how often the RAF personnel would practice raising and lowering the barrage balloon. Whenever he heard an increase in yelling he would jump up from whatever he was doing and go and watch.

"Pull your bloody finger out Smith and get your arse to that rope!" was a fairly common curse pronounced by the sergeant. Another particular favourite of Ray's was when the sergeant would scream "For the love of Christ, how many bloody times do I need to bloody tell you to keep clear of the bloody guide ropes when the bloody balloon is on the way up; you bloody moron!"

There were plenty of other curses and oaths fired off

during their routine, but Ray reckoned they were so filthy his mother would probably wash his mouth out just for him hearing them.

He looked forward to these drills, particularly when one of the mobile anti aircraft batteries would pull up and the crew would practice the firing routine for when German planes were flying overhead. However, he still didn't seem to appreciate the imminent nature of why they practiced so much. This changed on a sunny evening towards the end of July. He was sitting on his front doorstep as the crew of the balloon ran to their stations ready to inflate and then raise the balloon. The trick was for the men holding the guide ropes to manoeuvre the balloon into position once it had been inflated so that it could then be winched into the air using the steel cable and huge winch mechanism that was fixed to the back of a lorry. On this occasion the men had successfully completed this task, when the familiar voice of the sergeant bellowed across the yard.

"Smith, move away from that bloody rope before it wraps itself around your leg!" As Smith looked down and made to take a step away, he stepped into the rope by accident as it snapped up. The rope tangled around his leg and the more he struggled, the more it tangled. Before anybody else could react he was whisked forty feet into the air along with the balloon.

"Oh my God, help me!" he screamed as he tried unsuccessfully to bend up and untangle his leg.

"Don't do that you idiot, you'll fall on your head if you come loose. You there, get the bloody thing down before he falls!" There was chaos as airmen ran to winch the balloon back down, but as the balloon started to descend the vibration caused Smith to weave about and as he did so, the rope quickly came loose and he plummeted to the ground. He landed head first and Ray could hear the crunch of his skull from where he was sat.

The last thing he saw was Smith twitching violently before his sight was obscured by the man's colleagues as they crowded around. Several minutes later an ambulance arrived and Ray saw them lift the body into the back, a blanket covering the face of the now dead Smith. Ray made the decision there and then he didn't want to join the RAF when he was older and something inside clicked making him realise at last, that war had well and truly arrived.

Chapter 6 – Signals and Raids

By the beginning of August he'd heard the warning sirens sound on a number of occasions and had always responded by running to the shelter in the alley behind his house. However, up until now, they'd always been either practices or false alarms. Then one evening in the second week of August, he was playing in the street in front of his house when he heard the sirens once again. Instead of hurrying towards the shelter, he dawdled a bit and noticed the RAF crew of the barrage balloon were also heading towards the back alley; something they hadn't done before. It was then that he heard the distant drone of what sounded like thousands and thousands of insects vibrating in the air, and he was once again reminded that his idea of the Nazi's being some form of giant bug might not be as farfetched as he'd been led to believe.

He was still unsure what the droning was, but he increased his pace as he started to hear the boom, boom of anti aircraft fire and then, far off, the sound of lots of explosions. Once in the alley shelter he was joined by his parents and they sat nervously for several hours listening to the pounding of guns and the concussion of the exploding bombs. It was fair to say he was definitely nervous, but he couldn't honestly say he was scared. He knew that when he'd been naughty, he was afraid of what his mother would do. He knew what fear felt like when the light was first switched off and he couldn't see a single thing until his eyes adjusted to the dark; he even got scared when he was alone on the street and big kids came round the corner. But the feeling he now experienced was something different.

"Dad, are you scared?"

His father looked at him for several seconds. "I'm certainly nervous, but by the sound of the explosions they seem to be targeting the city centre or even the Wirral so I think we'll be alright. You try and be strong and don't let your mother know you're scared."

Ray was somewhat indignant. "I'm not scared!"

"No of course you're not." Was all his father said, but Ray was convinced he didn't believe him so he pondered his emotions a little longer and came to the conclusion that what he was actually experiencing was a sense of anticipation. It was like waiting to go in and see the nit nurse; you were nervous, but you also had a morbid fascination and eagerness to see what she'd find. In short, Ray reckoned that deep down he was actually excited and this unnerved him further. He'd just come to this realisation when he became aware his grandmother was not with them.

"What have you done with Nana ma; is she still in bed?" He knew she couldn't walk properly, but he thought it was a bit much just leaving her whilst bombs were falling.

"Don't worry about her" his dad replied "we've brought your mattress down and put it on top of her, she'll be fine."

Ray wasn't so sure this would be the case if a bomb dropped on the house. By the sound of the explosions he didn't think there'd be much left of his Nana, let alone his mattress. Selfish as it may have been, he spent more time thinking of what he'd sleep on, than the fate of his relation in the event of a direct hit. However, it did take his mind off the noise and before he realised it the all clear had sounded and they made their way back into the house where they found Nana soundly asleep; snoring as loudly and sounding remarkably similar to the droning of the hundred or so bombers that had been overhead shortly beforehand.

As he lay in bed later that night on his mainly undamaged mattress (except for some rather large drool stains), he reflected again on why he hadn't been terrified. The noise, even though the bombing had been far off, had still been ear splittingly loud and the amber sky he'd seen as they emerged from the shelter had indicated the destruction the bombers had wrought should have made him petrified; but they hadn't. He supposed it may have been because he'd been surrounded by his family and they seemed quite calm;

on the outside at least. However, the more he thought about it the more he realised that deep down, it wasn't anticipation or excitement he'd felt; it was actually relief that at last things had started to happen. As this occurred to him his thoughts began to tumble through his brain. They'd spent months expecting the bombs to drop and fear and the tension caused by the unknown had been excruciating. He realised he'd been building up an horrific image in his mind of what a raid might feel like, and was more than a little relieved that the reality of this evenings attack was not half as bad. As he finally drifted off to sleep, it was with a sense of satisfaction that he'd coped so well with the first raid, but he also felt a bit guilty for being relieved that war had finally come.

The next day they found out the raid had fallen on Birkenhead and whilst information was still sketchy, it didn't appear that anybody had been killed. All that day Ray listened intently for the sound of sirens and the drone of aircraft, but to no avail. Just before tea he moved across the road to hang around the railings of his school, watching as the airmen raised the barrage balloon. As they finished their task the men broke off and headed in different directions. Some entered the school, whilst others sat around smoking or playing cards. One chap came over to stand near him.

"Hey mister, do you think we'll be attacked again tonight?" he asked as the soldier took a drag on his cigarette.

"I expect things will hot up quite considerably from here on in, but don't you worry, we'll sort them out." He said confidently.

"When do you think they'll come again mister?" will it be night time again? The airman considered this for several seconds before answering.

"I think you're right lad, they'd be a bit ruddy stupid if they tried bombing us in daylight as they'd be sitting ducks. However, shall I let you in on a little secret?" Ray leant in eagerly. He was about to be let in on top secret information.

"Now before I tell you, will you swear not to tell another living soul?" Ray knew that his mother would swill his mouth out with soap again if she heard him swear but this was too great an opportunity to turn down. "Go on, I want to hear you swear not to tell another living soul."

"Bloody; shit and crap!" he pronounced solemnly. "I won't tell another living soul."

The airman's eyebrows nearly disappeared into his hairline as he stared open mouthed at Ray. "That wasn't quite what I meant." He said as he tried to stop himself from laughing too much. "But I suppose it's as good an oath as any." He then indicated for Ray to look towards the railway line. "Can you see the signal pole on the railway over there?" he said pointing over at the far end of the street. Ray nodded eagerly. "Well, when the light turns to red it means that German planes have been sighted over the South Coast and when it turns green, it means they are over Birmingham and that's when you need to get in the shelter."

Ray was astounded by this information and sat on his front step until his mother called him in, not taking his eye off the lights. Obviously, he had several false alarms as the lights also changed when a train was coming, but just as he was responding to his mother's beckon, he saw the lights change to red and there was no sign of a train.

"Ma, come here!" he yelled into the house with such urgency his mother rushed to the front door. "Look Ma, please don't ask me how I know because I can't tell you as it's a military secret, but the Nazi bombers are heading this way again." Olive looked at her son with a mixture of bemusement and concern.

"What do you mean the bombers are coming again, how can you possibly know?"

"Ma, I told you it's a military secret!" Just then, the light turned to green. "Come on, we need to head to the shelter." His mother was just about to object and return indoors when the sirens started up their eerie wail and almost immediately they could hear the distant sounds of anti aircraft fire.

After his mother had thrown his mattress over Nana once more, they rushed towards the shelter.

"You need to tell me how you knew there was going to be a raid young man?"

He was quite flattered by being called 'young man' but he wasn't going to divulge national secrets because of a bit of flattery. "I'm sorry Ma but I can't"

His mother therefore had to settle herself on a bench and glower at her son while he pretended he couldn't see her and refused point blank to catch her eye. As he sat listening to the explosions he realised this raid also seemed to be in the distance and the atmosphere in the shelter was calm and almost jovial except for his mother who refused to be fobbed off with his refusal to spill the beans.

"If you don't tell me Raymond Dagnall, I will ground you until you are twenty!"

He knew the threat was an empty one as she'd already threatened good hidings, starvation and a myriad of other tortures. She'd even threatened to never allow him another connyonny butty, but he kept his promise and refused to divulge his source; opting for stubborn silence as his form of resistance.

"If you don't tell me how you knew about the raid" she said after a period of silence "I'm going to tell your friends you still wet the bed!"

"But I don't wet the bed!" he replied before realising she'd succeeded in getting him to speak. His mother looked triumphant as she probed the chink in his armour.

"That may be so Raymond, but your friends don't know that."

He was astounded his mother would stoop so low as to tell lies. "But that would be a lie and you said you don't tell lies. If you said that, I'd have to tell the vicar!"

The look of shock on his mother's face was something to behold. It was clear she never believed her son could be so crafty as to use bribery and blackmail as a strategy; these were techniques reserved for adults; but it was with new respect in her eyes that she asked him one final time.

"Raymond please; if I know how you learned of the attack I can make sure Nana is properly safe instead of just throwing your mattress on top of her. You want to keep Nana safe don't you?"

This was a cruel change in tactic. He was sure he could withstand the threats and the bullying, but when he was called on to think of others it was a lot harder.

"Ma, please stop asking, I swore I wouldn't tell anyone." As soon as he said it he knew he'd thrown away his advantage and sure enough, his mother pounced immediately on his slip up.

"You swore?!" She said as she closed in on him, towering over him and intimidating purely by her presence. "What oaths did you happen to say?"

He knew that one way or another he was done for. All of his mother's earlier threats had been half hearted and fairly empty; but now she had some solid evidence with which to punish him. He therefore decided partial honesty was his best chance of escaping really bad retribution.

"I just said a few words that I heard the sergeant use when he was ordering his men around, I'm not sure I can remember them exactly. The airman said they were fine."

With a look of victory, Olive nodded slowly. "So it was one of the airmen that told you. Well that's alright then." And with that, she went and made herself comfortable at the bottom end of the shelter.

Moments later the 'all clear' sounded and Ray realised he'd barely noticed the raid so intent had he been on defending his secret. As he headed back round to the front of his house he wondered if the whole battle of wills with his mother had been her ploy for taking his mind off the bombs and destruction.

The next day, they found out the bombs had once again been dropped on the Wirral; this time it was Wallasey that saw the brunt of the attack. Ray was thankful once again that Liverpool had not been targeted, but there was still a niggling sense of anticlimax. Over the following days the sirens didn't go off at all and even though he spent hours watching the railway signals, they never marked the beginning of a raid, leading him to suspect the airman had been pulling his leg.

Ray's father spent more and more time patrolling the streets making sure the blackout was adhered to and ensuring the streets were safe and shelters tidy. This meant he only caught brief glimpses of him first thing in the morning before his father left for the docks, and then another brief glimpse as he grabbed something to eat in the evening before heading out on patrol. He missed him a lot as it was his father who mostly told him stories before he went to sleep and it was his father who'd taken him to the cinema before they'd closed. However, he supposed he was still lucky as he got to see him and knew that he was safe. Most of his friend's fathers were away fighting.

A week after the bombings of the Wirral, he was

sitting as had become his custom, on the front step of his house looking down towards the railway line still in the hope that he possessed military intelligence.

It had been a sunny day and he'd spent the morning tediously learning his times tables up to 5 and then after he'd been dismissed, played cricket in the street with some of the children who were still living locally. They used a bin as the wicket and a tennis ball. Ray had played a couple of times before, but on this day, he realised he could bowl really well. He had no idea how he did it, but as the ball left his hand, he was able to make it swing through the air and when it landed, make it change direction quite dramatically. Time and time again he would take five or six paces up to the jacket they were using for the non strikers wicket and release the ball.

Because the pace was slow, the batter assumed he was going to be able to slog the ball for sixes and fours, which meant they would be able to hit one of the houses or knock the ball well onto the playground. This was rarely the case and he became more and more unpopular as he took wicket after wicket. At one point, several of the airmen asked if they could have a go and were duly impressed when this scrawny seven year old was able to bowl unhittable balls that invariably went on to hit the wicket.

As he sat reflecting on his glory and basking in the memory of being applauded by the adults of the RAF, there was the rumble of an engine as a lorry swung around the corner with a huge anti aircraft gun on the back. It pulled up directly in front of him and the crew swarmed out and mounted the gun, preparing it for action. Everything then seemed to happen at once. He noticed the lights on the railway had changed, the sirens started to whine, his mother came running out of the house and he started to hear the boom of anti aircraft fire and the now familiar drone of enemy planes.

However, this felt different to last week. This evening the drone of the engines seemed closer and he could feel the vibrations of the antiaircraft guns as they fired. As he made his way towards the shelter, he looked up into the sky and saw the source of the noise. He was instantly reminded once again of the image of Nazi bugs as the sky appeared to be in the process of being consumed by black winged beasts that seemed to coalesce to block out the last remaining rays of sunlight. As he began to run in earnest towards the shelter he realised he was, for the first time, truly scared.

In the moments after being deposited in the shelter he thought back on what he'd just witnessed. In the moment of frozen shock before he ran, he saw the gun, which was only a matter of yards in front of him, start to fire into the darkening sky. The rate at which the gunners fired, ejected the spent cartridge and reloaded again was truly impressive and made the many hours of practice worthwhile. In the seconds it took for his mother to drag him to safety, the gun had fired twice and fired a third time shortly later.

The noise was indescribable and forced Ray to sit with his hands over his ears as he felt the floor under him shake from the exploding shells. When he opened his eyes during a moments reprieve, he realised he was covered in dust from the quaking walls of the shelter.

"Ma, are we going to die?" he yelled as the explosions started once again. It was a genuine question born out of curiosity rather than fear, although he was undoubtedly scared.

"Come here son." Was all his mother was able to say as she hugged him close before there was another explosion nearby. "I'll protect you." As each concussion hit them she'd squeeze her son tight as if the strength of her arms was all he needed to keep him safe. For Ray, this became rather painful and pretty annoying.

"Ma, you're crushing me I can't breathe!" he yelled after a particularly close call. His mother released him slightly and giggled somewhat hysterically.

"I'm sorry Raymond; I was a little shaken by that last one."

Ray thought he'd best try and comfort his mother before she did the job the Nazi's were trying to do. "Don't worry Ma, I'll look after you."

His mother shed a tear at hearing those words, but thankfully released her grip somewhat. "I'm sure you will Raymond, I'm sure you will."

After roughly forty five minutes the noise finally subsided from its crescendo and settled into more distant explosions. However, the all clear didn't sound and so they remained in the shelter.

"When can we go back into the house Ma, I'm tired and I want to see what's happened to Nana?" He had to admit, he hadn't even considered his grandmother as the bombs were falling overhead and so it was out of a sense of guilt that he now wanted to find out.

"To be honest I'm not sure; I suppose we have to wait until the 'all clear' sounds.

However, just as she said this the calm was once again shattered as a second wave of bombers flew overhead and began dropping their loads somewhere nearby; although it didn't feel as close as it had earlier. Moments later, Ray's father entered the shelter.

"It looks as though they're targeting the docks with

a mixture of high explosive and incendiary devices." He said as he made his way over to sit by Olive. "I'm going to have to go back out in a while to see if there's any more damage locally."

Ray was fascinated to know what it was like out in the open so he went to sit on his father's knee. "What did it look like dad?"

His father thought for a moment before answering. "It's actually an amazing sight" he started to say before Olive interjected ferociously.

"John, how can you say such a thing? It is utterly horrific! Every one of those bombs brings destruction and death." Olive's face had gone a deep shade of purple and Ray was quite concerned she was about to explode just like a bomb. However, his father made conciliatory gestures as he put his arm around her shoulders and the colour started to dissipate ever so slightly.

"I know, I know, I'm not saying it's a good thing, it's just that with the search lights, the explosions of the ack-ack, the fires and the bomb explosions it is quite a sight. It looks like hell has descended onto earth and is consuming half of Liverpool." Having finished another long speech, his father lapsed into silence contemplating the way he'd just described the attack and evidently thought it an accurate description as he nodded several times before rising to his feet.

"I'm sorry darling but I have to go back out there." He was moving towards the entrance when Olive shot out of her seat and strode after him. Grabbing him by the shoulder, she turned him round, hugged and then kissed him; right there in front of everybody. Ray was shocked and disgusted with his parents for the second time in a matter of months. He would have to have words with one of them when they weren't together, but was unsure of exactly what it was he would say.

"You look after yourself out there and don't do anything stupid." Olive said as she straightened his helmet and brushed dust from his shoulders. She stood for several seconds after he left just staring into the darkness before she returned to her seat and resumed her knitting.

Chapter 7 – Nana and Shrapnel

In the weeks that followed the raids became more frequent and towards the end of August they were taking place each night. Some bombs fell fairly close; one even hit the church in Mossley Hill, which infuriated Ray's mother.

"How could they target a house of God?!" she ranted as they stood looking at the damage.

It didn't look too bad to Ray. There was a big hole in the roof, most of the windows had been blown out and some of the brickwork looked dodgy, but it still looked like a church. Some of the houses he'd seen nearby were just piles of rubble and in a far worse state, so he reckoned God was lucky it had escaped with such minor damage; he did have other houses after all.

Anyway he wasn't that interested in looking at a church; he was obsessed with a new hobby that had sprung up with the children of the area that involved scouring the landscape after a raid in the hope of finding bomb fragments, and then swapping the grisly mementos for all sorts of things; even sweets. A frenetic market had developed and Ray was determined to find something near the church. When he'd first started looking earlier that week, he was amazed at how far shrapnel could travel. He'd found pieces hundreds of yards from where the bomb had exploded and loved the sensation of discovering a new piece. It wasn't just bomb fragments that were valued; anti aircraft shells rained shrapnel down after they exploded in the air leaving pieces strewn everywhere after a raid.

The most prized pieces were any with writing on and any chunks that looked as though they were from the same bomb. Kids would spend hours trying to piece them together fragment by fragment, but to date he hadn't seen anything that remotely looked like a complete missile, except perhaps, the tailfin from an incendiary device, which had been awesome. As he looked around the graveyard he didn't expect to find anything as good as that because he'd heard it was high explosive that had been dropped the previous night and unless the bomb hadn't exploded, there were normally only fragments left.

He sauntered away from his mother so he could investigate the surrounding ground. He started by walking along the side of the church close to the wall, but there was nothing there so he widened his search until he was almost at the boundary wall when he spotted something reflecting in the sunlight. His heart quickened as he approached the dull, jagged object that was embedded in the wall. Once he was certain it was indeed shrapnel, he couldn't contain his excitement. Not only was it a piece of the bomb, it also appeared to have writing on it, which he presumed was German as he didn't understand what it said. This was amazing; he didn't know of anybody who'd found a piece like this. He'd heard stories, but those owners were legends and people who'd been put on a pedestal by those who recounted their adventures. He would be the envy of the entire city! There was one small problem though; the shrapnel was stuck firmly into the wall and although he tried with all his might, he couldn't budge it. However, he refused to be defeated and so he took out his penknife, which had been a present from his father for his seventh birthday and proceeded to dig around the metal frantically. He only had seconds as his mother looked as though she was coming to the end of her conversation with one of the parishioners, so he attacked the stone with as much force as his young muscles would allow. In his moment of triumph as the metal finally came loose, all of his excitement and happiness were lost as the shiny blade from his most prized possession snapped in two. He was distraught, but only had time to pick up the shrapnel and broken blade and shove them in his pocket before his mother came over.

"What's the matter Raymond? There's no need to get upset; God will punish the Nazi's for damaging his church."

Ray suddenly realised what had happened and was

even more appalled. He too had been damaging the house of God and so God had punished him by snapping his knife. As he traipsed after his mother as they headed home, he felt a fleeting wave of sympathy for the Germans, because if God could destroy his beloved knife just for chipping at the wall surrounding the church, he didn't like to think what he'd do for dropping a bomb on the church itself.

When they arrived home he was told he had to sit with Nana whilst his mother went to visit with Aunty Sydnah.

"Can't I come with you?" he pleaded rather too desperately.

"No you can't. I need someone to look after Nana, and with your father on patrol I need it to be you."

It wasn't that he particularly wanted to visit Sydnah as he found her rather intimidating, but he'd rather go with his mother than sit with Nana on his own. She babbled on and jumped from one topic to the next leaving him baffled as to what she meant. She also didn't smell very nice having an aroma that smelled musty and a little bit like wee. Regardless of his reservations he dutifully spent the afternoon half listening to her ramblings, giving grunts for answers and the occasional yes or no.

"And did you hear about your uncle Bert? No you

probably haven't. He lost a leg in the Great War you know. Anyway, when he came home he became a bouncer at the Wellington Pub."

Ray merely responded with "Oh" before she continued.

"He was only little, but he couldn't half fight. If anybody got out of hand he'd whip off his false leg and batter them with it!" She then giggled to herself hysterically as Ray nodded and smiled.

"His wife was a bit of a bitch though; because she didn't like him working in a pub, she made him sleep in the shed in the yard and wouldn't let him in the house."

Ray couldn't believe his ears. "Nana, you don't want to let me Ma hear you using language like that because she'd wash your mouth out with soap if she did."

Nana seemed oblivious and continued her babbling. "I was such a pretty girl when I was young. I couldn't walk down the street without one boy or other whistling or asking me out for a date."

He felt a little uncomfortable on hearing this and also couldn't quite believe what he was being told as the woman who lay in front of him was incredibly fat with lank grey hair and a rather large nose. However, he was prepared to give her the benefit of the doubt as twenty three children must mean she had something about her.

That afternoon though, he noticed something was different about Nana. She tired quickly and kept stopping halfway through one of her stories so she could catch her breath. Half way through one story the room went silent and when he looked up form doodling on some paper, he realised she'd fallen asleep. He made the decision to talk to his mother about it when she got home; in the meantime he felt his time would be better spent searching for more shrapnel and perhaps showing off his knew find to the other kids of the area. He may even be able to charge money to let people look at it and save enough to buy a replacement penknife before his parents found out he'd broken his other one.

As soon as he showed his find to one of his friends he knew he'd been right to think he'd be the envy of the other local kids. They gathered around him, eager for a glimpse of his shrapnel with writing on. He was offered a wide range of treasures to swap the metal including a yoyo, a toy metal car and even a catapult; but he declined every one. As he was about to head home though, one of the bigger boys came up to him. Ray had known him for a number of years and made sure he kept out of his way because he was a real bully. His name was Kenneth or "Kenny" as he liked to be known and he was big, even for a ten year old; with quite a podgy face, fat legs and a belly that hung over the waist of his knee length grey pants.

"What's that you've got Dagnall?" He said as he pushed the smaller children out of the way. "Let's have a look then."

Ray reluctantly brought the metal from out of his pocket and held it up in a firm grip so Kenny could take a look without touching. "It's just a piece of shrapnel Kenny."

As he went to put it back in his pocket Kenny grabbed his wrist. "Not so fast Daggers, what's that on the side there?"

Nobody had ever called him 'Daggers' before and as he brought his hand back out, he realised he quite liked it; it made him sound quite sinister and hard. "Watch out, here comes Daggers" or "Daggers will get you for that!"

As he lifted the metal, Kenny let go of his wrist and went to take it from him, but instead of handing it over like Kenny and everybody else expected, Ray, bolstered by the strength of the nickname said. "You don't need hands to look Kenny. It's got German writing down the side. I can just make out ACH."

There was an intake of breath form most of the kids who were standing around and Kenny looked as though he'd been slapped in the face with a wet kipper. His mouth hung slightly open and his eyes went wide as if he'd had a shock, which in many ways he had.

"What did you say?"

"I said it has German writing down the side and I can just make out an A, a C and an H." Ray pointed to the faded letters on one of the jagged edges of the metal. He knew he was probably about to get a beating, but something inside him spurred him on to stand up to the bigger boy. "Look Kenny, if I give this to you, you'll just walk off with it like you did with Johnny last week. I ruined my best penknife getting this out of a wall and I'm not about to just hand it over to you."

There was another intake of breath, but this time Ray noticed there were a number of kids nodding in agreement with what he was saying and several of them started to edge around the circle so they were stood behind him. Johnny had been distraught after Kenny had played the same trick on him and just walked off with a prized piece of shrapnel in his hand.

Kenny stood catching flies in his open mouth for several seconds before he clenched his fists and started moving slowly towards him. "You can either give it to me Daggers, or I take it from you; either way I'm having that piece of shrapnel."

As Kenny loomed over Ray he didn't know what to

do. It was too late to run and he didn't think he'd get very far as he was hemmed in by the other children. He was also uncertain of the support the others would give him. Nobody particularly liked Kenny, but they were afraid of him and it was unlikely they'd create a united front and openly defy him. He realised he had just two choices; he could hand over the shrapnel or he fight him. Ray was not a fighter; his father had taught him some basic boxing moves, but he'd never used them against anybody and he didn't think he had it in him to take on this much larger boy.

"Kenny if you hit me I'll tell me Ma and she'll be around to your house quicker than you can say Flash Gordon. If she tells your mum, she'll batter you." Ray had overheard Kenny's mother talking to Olive earlier in the summer about how she dealt with Kenny's naughtiness since his father had gone away to fight with the navy. From what he overheard, he didn't think Kenny would relish being hit with his father's belt.

He realised he might be onto something as Kenny paused in his movement and a look of hesitation came into his eyes. Before he lost the momentum from the exchange, Ray decided to push his advantage and try and extricate himself from the situation without Kenny or him losing face. "If you want the shrapnel, I'll trade you for it. I've turned everyone else down, but if you've got something worthwhile I'll let you have it."

He knew this was a long shot, but if Kenny decided the wrath of his mother was worth beating him up, there was little he could do to stop it. To his amazement, Kenny looked as though he might consider a swap.

"What would you take for it?"

"Well I wrecked my penknife getting it out of the wall so I'd swap yours for it." Ray knew Kenny had the exact same knife as he had, and as he said it, he knew that's what he needed more than the shrapnel.

"Ok deal." And with that Kenny pulled out his knife and gave it to Ray in exchange for the shrapnel. He breathed a huge sigh of relief as he turned to head home and was surprised that several of the other boys followed him, patting him on the back and proclaiming 'Daggers' to be their hero.

Chapter 8 – Missing fingers and the Dangerous Lamppost

As summer turned to autumn in 1940, the raids on Liverpool and the surrounding area increased in a sporadic pattern. The bombers would arrive each consecutive night for two or three nights in a row and then there'd be a break of several days or even weeks before they would return once again. This undoubtedly took its toll on people's peace of mind and left them in a constant state of tense anticipation and nervousness. However, they went about their daily routines with a determination not to give in to panic or despair.

Ray was particularly impressed with his mother. When a raid was on she would be awake most of the night making sure that he was behaving himself in the shelter, worrying about her husband who was out checking people were safe and fussing about anything in order to keep her own mind off the falling bombs. She'd then be up at the crack of dawn to see to Nana and then go out to do the shopping, while her back room was used as a classroom. Shopping for food was a challenge in its own right as she first of all had to try and find a shop with any stock, before queuing for hours in order to stand any chance of picking something up. She'd then come home and cook the titbits she'd found, clean the house and keep track of what he was up to. She did all of this with a calmness that made the whole experience seem like it was just a common routine.

"Don't you ever get tired Ma?" he said to her one day as she was putting washing through a mangle.

"I haven't got time to be tired son and besides, you get plenty of time to sleep when you're dead."

This frightened him because she said it as though she might die any day and the thought of a world without his mother was hard to imagine. "You're not going to die are you Ma?" he said with a trembling lip.

"Of course I'm not! I'm saying that we should all make the most of everyday that God grants us because who knows what will happen tomorrow."

He supposed this was true, especially seeing that a bomb might drop on them any minute, but he didn't want to dwell on it so he changed the subject.

"When are the Irish men arriving Ma?"

His mother had for some reason seen it as her Christian duty to volunteer to house four Irish navvies who'd been recruited by the local authority to dig bodies out of the rubble and act as rescuers for when people were trapped by bomb blasts.

"Any day now so you make sure you don't leave any of your things lying round; and woe betides you if you're rude to our guests."

He didn't have a clue what 'woe betides' meant, but he supposed it had something to do with not burping or breaking wind in front of them seeing that she said in conjunction with being rude.

The arrival of the Irishmen meant that Ray had to share a room with his parents whilst they took over his room and the back room downstairs. The increase in humanity in such a small dwelling brought a range of hardships that he found difficult to handle. Whenever he wanted the loo, he'd traipse outside only to find it occupied and then when he finally gained access, he'd discover all the paper had been used up, which meant traipsing all the way back into the house to find some more. He got to the point on several occasions when he thought he may as well go in the yard, but fear of what his mother would do stopped him. Mornings were the worst as there was always a mad rush as the Irishmen rummaged around collecting their things so that they might vacate the back room for Ray to have his lessons.

"Ma, why on earth did you take in the Irish? There's nowhere for me to do anything and I keep having to hold on before I can go to the loo; it's giving me stomach aches!"

"It is my Christian duty to support these men Raymond. We all have to make sacrifices in a time of war and you feeling a bit uncomfortable and giving up your room can be yours."

However, he suspected her generosity may also have had to do with the extra rations she received, plus the rent the Irishmen paid. Nevertheless, he took her advice to heart and started to become friendly with the men. He found out that they were all amateur boxers and spent many a happy hour being coached on how to stand, move and punch. He had to admit he wasn't convinced by the advice he was being given because they didn't seem to be very good at what they did. Each Thursday evening they'd go off to a local gym to take part in matches against other clubs, but when they returned, they looked as though they'd been mauled by a savage beast. Invariably there would be swollen eyes, bloodied noses and nasty cuts.

"Ryan, aren't you very good at boxing?" Ray asked their self appointed leader as he stared at the mass of cuts and bruises on his face. Ryan laughed.

"Why do you ask that laddie?"

"You always seem to get beaten up?"

"What yer talkin about me laddo, this is nothing. I nearly always win. If you want to see beaten up you should take a look at the chap I was fighting."

Ray was quite sure he didn't if Ryan's face was anything to go by, but he decided to glean as much as he could about the pugilistic arts and practiced each day, punching Ryan's hands and then skipping out of reach as he threw a counter punch.

Each evening the Irishmen would go on duty leaving Ray and his mother to sit and keep Nana company. If there was no raid, Olive would play her organ, which she did with some expertise, and Ray would sit and doodle on some paper or just listen to his mother play. The organ was Olive's prize possession, which she polished daily and made sure her son kept his distance from.

"If I see you within five feet of my organ I will tan your hide Raymond!"

It was a mantra he'd learned from the moment he could walk, and was so ingrained that when he entered the front room where the instrument was kept, he'd actually walk in a curved line in order to avoid crossing the invisible boundary that marked the five foot proximity.

He had to admit though; his mother was very good. She'd even been recruited to be the church organist at the City Mission since the previous incumbent had gone off to join the army. He loved listening to her play tunes she'd play in church, but especially the ones she'd learned by just listening to Reg Dixon on the radio. Reg was an amazing organist who used to broadcast from Blackpool Tower Ballroom, but Ray reckoned his mother was just as good, and so they'd spend several happy hours with his mother at the organ, Ray clapping along and his Nana babbling to herself contentedly.

If there was an air raid, sometimes Nana would have Ray's mattress plonked on top of her and he and his mother would go to the shelter. However, this was happening less and less as Nana was becoming very frail so they tended to all stay in the house and crowd under Ray's mattress. On one occasion, the morning after a raid, Ray overheard his mother speaking to his father in the kitchen.

"I don't think Nana will be with us much longer" she said in hushed tones intending that no one else should hear. "She doesn't seem to be lucid most of the time and she isn't eating much at all."

Ray was confused by what he'd heard and ruminated for the rest of the morning about what his mother might have meant. He just couldn't see where Nana could possibly go; she couldn't even get out of bed so he found it hard to believe she'd want to go and live somewhere else, and as for food, everything was rationed so he wasn't surprised she didn't eat much; he didn't get much either. In the end he gave up trying to find an answer and went to do something far more productive instead; search for shrapnel.

However, understanding dawned only a week later when he returned home from one of his forages.

"Raymond come and sit down next to me." His mother said in quite an unusual voice. "Try and not get too upset, but I have to tell you that Nana has gone to heaven."

At first, he was just as mystified as he'd been the week earlier. "But how did she get there, she can't walk?"

His mother gave him a rather incredulous look as if to say, 'Are you kidding me?!' However, when she realised he was serious, she clarified the situation further. "No Raymond, I mean she's died. She went to sleep earlier and just didn't wake up."

Even though he'd seen the soldier die on the playground opposite, seen dead birds in the road and even a dead cat in the kerbside, his concept of death was influenced by the westerns he'd watched in the cinema in which you could get shot one week and then appear in a different movie a couple of weeks later.

"When will we see her again Ma?"

His mother misinterpreted what he said and looked at her son as if he'd just asked a most profound question. As she hugged him tight she said. "Oh Raymond, it's difficult to say, but you can be sure we will meet again someday."

He wasn't allowed to go the funeral as his mother said she didn't want him to get upset, but if he was honest, he didn't feel that sad. He felt sorry of course that Nana had gone, but when he really thought about it, he was mainly relieved because she had become someone other than the person he'd known. He was also quite pleased they finally had a bit more space in the house, which resulted in him moving out of his parent's bedroom and back into his own. As for his mother, she dealt with her grief as she did all things; with quiet efficiency and little emotion. He was sure she must have cried, but he never saw it and routines returned to normal within days.

This didn't last long as only a couple of weeks later his mother went out one afternoon and didn't return for several days. Sydnah came to look after him, but when he asked where she was he was just told; "the babies coming". Now Ray was a rather naive seven year old and in his mind this baby must have been coming from an awfully long way away if his mother had to wait for it for as long as this. When she did finally return, she brought with her a mewling, puking, very smelly bundle of humanity in the shape of his new sister Enid who took over his place in his parent's bedroom.

"You need to be especially good from now on Raymond and you need to look after your new baby sister."

He had no idea how he was supposed to look after a baby when he couldn't look after himself, but he just nodded and poked the child in an imitation of affection.

In a moment of unselfish reflection, Ray contemplated how difficult it must be for his new sister being born in the middle of a war such as this. He found it difficult to cope with the noise and danger sometimes, so he reckoned his sister must be really struggling. They rarely spent a whole night in their beds as the sirens went off on an increasingly regular basis, meaning they spent night after night in the shelter, which interrupted sleep patterns and routines. Sometimes the raid would be in the far off distance and the noise would just be carried on the wind, but other times the bombs dropped extremely close.

On one such occasion, Ray had been sat on the front step when he noticed the lights had changed to green. He must have been distracted as he hadn't noticed them turn to red. "Ma, we need to go to the shelter quickly!"

Olive no longer questioned her son's military secret and came rushing out of the house, Enid in her arms and already crying. Even before they'd reached the corner of the house they could hear the drone of the planes louder than ever before, and as they ran passed one of the soldiers who was rushing to find his own cover they heard him say "It's going to be a ruddy heavy one tonight!"

Olive grabbed her son's hand and increased the pace towards the entrance as the bombs started to fall. As he ran, Ray was more excited than afraid as the first thing that went through his mind was the fact there would be lots of great shrapnel trophies to be had the next day. As he settled once again into his regular spot in the shelter, he vowed to get up extra early so he could go treasure hunting before his lessons.

As he sat there a short while later, he heard an unfamiliar sound in amongst the cacophony of other explosions, drones and booms. It sounded like the rat-tat-tat-tat of a snare drum that the boys' brigade played at Sunday service, but he thought that was highly unlikely during an air raid. He also felt the faint vibrations of numerous things impacting on the roof of the shelter. Almost immediately the RAF crew from the barrage balloon came diving through the entrance, landing in a heap on the floor in front of Ray.

"Bloody hell, there's shit landing everywhere!" the sergeant said to everybody and anybody who would listen. "We nearly got our arses shot off just getting in here!"

Olive rose out of her seat, Enid still wailing in her arms and strode over to the sergeant, her face stony and her eyes blazing. "Excuse me young man, I don't care what has just happened or how you speak to your men, but you will certainly not use that sort of language in front of me or in this shelter. If you insist on doing so I will have to ask you to leave!"

As Ray looked on he was pretty sure the sergeant was not used to being spoken to like this, and was convinced the man was going to give his mother a mouthful. There were several seconds of silence as the sergeant thought through how unlikely it would be for anybody to throw another human being out into a raid such as this, and the fact that he was a sergeant and she was just a housewife. However, one look at Olive's face and the steely determination in the set of her body convinced him that this woman most certainly would and probably could.

"Sorry Ma'am, it's just that it's a bit hairy outside, the bastards.... sorry, the Hun have just machine gunned us."

"Well that's no excuse for using foul language particularly in front of children. However, I will accept your apology just as long as it doesn't happen again."

With that she returned to her seat and the sergeant, looking rather relieved to have escaped her wrath, lit a cigarette and went over to stand by the entrance. He stood looking out at the devastation being wrought as he took deep drags from his fag. Ray was intrigued by what he'd just heard and so walked over and tapped the sergeant on the back.

"Excuse me, did they really just try and shoot you with their machine gun?"

"Too ruddy...sorry, too true they did! There were bullets flying everywhere. They even hit the shelter. Didn't you feel them?"

As Ray nodded, he felt shocked that the Nazis would resort to shooting at people as well as bombing them, but he supposed that one was no worse than the other. He also reckoned that if he could find a German bullet it would even surpass the shrapnel he found with the writing on. He decided he would have to get up even earlier in the morning.

"Do you think I'd be able to find some of those bullets tomorrow?" he asked the sergeant in the hope he would give him directions to where they landed.

"I suppose you could if you had something to dig them out of the walls with because they bury themselves pretty deep. You live in this end terrace don't you?" the sergeant asked as he stuck his hand out of the shelter to flick ash from his cigarette.

"Yes I do"

"Well there was a whole spread of bullets hit your gable end as I ran passed so you should definitely be able to...."

There was a high pitched whizzing sound from outside the shelter's entrance and the sergeant pulled his hand in quickly; except his hand was missing the two fingers that had been holding the cigarette and blood pumped steadily from the stumps where they had once been.

"I was enjoying that bloody fag!" he said before collapsing to the floor clutching his hand to his chest.

As his colleagues gathered around and administered first aid, Ray reflected on what he'd heard his mother often preach about how cigarettes were bad for your health, heedless of the cynical looks she received from her audience. Perhaps they would not be so cynical if they'd just witnessed what had happened to the sergeant? However, even Olive could not have predicted that smoking could also result in having your fingers sliced off by flying shrapnel.

When he shared his experiences with his father the next morning even he found it difficult to believe. However, Ray's story was not the only remarkable incident from the night before, and as they sipped their tea his father shared what had happened to him.

"I'd finished work painting camouflage onto a merchantman and then boarded the overhead railway in order to head home. However, I'd barely travelled a mile when the sirens went off and I had to get off and walk the rest of the way home"

"That's not very exciting dad, you've had to do that loads of times."

"Ah yes, but last night I had to sneak from one shelter to the other in order to avoid the bombs and I can tell you that was very exciting indeed!"

Ray could well imagine the adventure his father must have had dodging bombs and bullets as he made his way home.

"Anyway that's not the point of the story. When I finally arrived home the second wave of bombers was approaching so I just had time to put my warden overalls and helmet on before Archie was knocking on the door asking me to help out due to the severity of the attack. He told me there was an unexploded bomb lying in the middle of Tiverton Street."

"What was it dad?" His father had previously told him of the various types of bombs that were being dropped; from small incendiary, to huge sea mines that were meant to be dropped into the Mersey but often missed.

"Well Ray, it was very dark last night with the only light to see coming from burning buildings. When I arrived on site I found a mound of rubble and what looked like the tail of a rather large high explosive bomb."

"What did you do?" his son asked eagerly.

"The first thing I had to do was try and make sure that if the bomb exploded it would cause as little damage as possible so me, Archie and Fred stacked sandbags around the steel tip we could see protruding from the rubble. I can tell you, it was no easy feat as the Germans kept coming wave after wave. It was also really dark so I kept tripping over"

"Were you scared? I think I would've been."

"At first I didn't have time to be scared as there was a big job to be done, but when we came under fire from German machine guns, I have to say I was terrified."

"They shot at you as well?" Ray was horrified to think of his father being targeted when he was trying to help people.

"I don't think they were shooting at me specifically, I just think they were spraying bullets here, there and everywhere. At one point I was dragging a sandbag into place when I heard the rat-tat-tat-tat of the machine gun and I actually felt the disturbance in the air as bullets whipped passed my head."

Olive blanched at this "I don't think you should be telling him this John, you'll give him nightmares."

"He won't Ma, this is brill! What did you do next dad?"

"Well, by the time I'd moved the sandbag in place, there wasn't any sand left in it and when I looked more closely, I found a neat row of four bullet holes almost dissecting the bag in two."

"Wow!"

"After a few hours we reckoned we'd done as much as we could to make the site safe until the army could arrive in daylight to diffuse the bomb."

"So did you just leave it and come home?" Ray had been asleep when his father arrived home so was unaware of what time he'd arrived back.

"No, I suggested that somebody should stay with it to make sure none of the residents went back into their houses or anybody came close. I'll tell you what; the sweat was pouring off me even though it was a cold November night."

"Who stayed?"

"Well Fred said we were stupid if we thought he'd stay as he reckoned if the bomb exploded, whoever was anywhere near it would be a goner"

Ray reckoned Fred was right but he was also concerned "What if people moved back into their homes and it went off, it would've been a disaster."

"That's exactly what I said so I volunteered to stay behind."

John recalled how his colleagues had told him he was either stupid or a ruddy hero and that either way he deserved a medal. He remembered how he'd felt as he guarded the site on his own until daylight. "I stood about thirty feet from the bomb" He didn't tell them this was well within the "kill zone" should it go off "So I could see passed the mound of rubble to the other end of the street. It was pretty hard keeping the local residents away and not knowing from one minute to the next if the bomb would explode."

"Dad, you are so brave!"

"I'll let you in on a little secret; I spent most of the time thinking how nice it would be to win a medal and pictured myself being awarded the gong by the King himself with you, your mum and Enid looking on, glowing with pride."

"You didn't?" Olive said with amused incredulity "How very modest of you!"

"Well I had to do something to pass the time. Anyway, as the blackness gave way to the grey light of dawn, I kept making cautious glances towards the bomb to gauge if there'd been any changes and to determine if there was a chance of it going off before the bomb disposal boys arrived. As the shape became clearer, I started to make out the metallic outline and it didn't look right. As I edged closer, my heart was pounding and I'm sure it skipped a beat."

"You know what dad, you do deserve a medal and the king should give it to you himself; you were so brave."

"Thanks for saying that son, but I wasn't that brave; you see as I got right up close to it, I realised I'd risked my life guarding a blinking lamppost!"

"What?" Ray and his mother cried in unison.

"There had been a bomb, but it had exploded and brought down the lamppost and in the dark, the wreckage looked like a bomb."

"I don't think the king gives out medals for guarding lampposts dad!"

All three laughed for so long and so hard they had tears rolling down their cheeks.

Chapter 9 – Direct Hit

The next day, John was unable to get to work due to the devastation caused by the previous night's raid, so after breakfast he took his family to witness the damage as he felt it would be better if they saw it together rather than Olive and Ray seeing it by themselves. At first Ray was put out because he'd been determined to escape in search of shrapnel and bullets as early as possible, but now he was being dragged along by his parents. He was therefore rather sulky and petulant.

"Raymond, if you don't stop dragging your feet, so help me, I will tan your hide for you in front of everyone!"

This threat didn't do much for his mood, but he picked up his feet to keep up. However, as they walked around the streets and the magnitude of the havoc the raid had caused became apparent, he was thankful he was accompanied by his parents. Every direction he looked there were piles of rubble where there had once been houses, interspersed with the odd anomaly of a house or even two houses together that appeared completely unscathed other than a broken window.

As they turned the corner into Stevenson Street he was appalled to realise that a whole stick of bombs had landed down the middle of the road, blowing out the fronts of houses on either side and destroying the row of shelters that had been built there. As he watched rescuers pouring over the rubble in search of survivors and bodies, he was reminded of his thoughts when the shelters were first built. Perhaps he was mistaken after all, and the powers that be did not in fact know how to protect innocent people from the ravages of high explosive bombs.

After looking at such chaos he felt numbed to the devastation and whilst it was still disturbing, his youthful exuberance soon took over.

"Can I go and look for some shrapnel now?" he asked as he saw other kids crawling over the remains of a house. "I promise I won't go far and I'll be back before tea." He didn't really expect to be allowed, but his parents were obviously distracted by what they were seeing and so gave him perfunctory warnings to be careful and to be back well before tea. He quickly shot off and began his search for grim souvenirs before they could change their minds.

Since the raids had begun in earnest, he'd come up with a strategy for finding the best bits by avoiding where the other kids were looking. He therefore searched for quiet little nooks and crannies to scour, and on this occasion, looked for an area where the damage was not as pronounced, but which lay within the range of flying shrapnel. He found the perfect spot on the embankment of the railway not far from his house. The bombs had fallen at the other end of the street, but he could still see plenty of evidence that shrapnel had ripped into walls and a car that had been parked near where he stood. As soon as he started looking through the grass he detected several fragments of metal and within minutes he had a small bag full. The thrill of making a find never got tiring and even though these were pretty run of the mill pieces, he was still made up to discover them.

He was about to call it a day when he came across the dun colour of black metal. Even before he moved the grass from around it he knew he'd hit the jackpot, as lying before him was a complete tailfin from an incendiary bomb. These bombs weren't very big, the idea being that when they hit the floor, a detonator in the nose would ignite the chemicals inside, causing an intense fire that was difficult to extinguish. He'd seen a couple of the tailfins before as crowds had gathered around the lucky kid who'd found one, patting them on the back and offering the world to swap it. He felt goose bumps on his arms and a chill of excitement ran down his spine as he fell to the floor in order to clear the area around it. As he moved the grass out of the way he was surprised to notice how good the condition was. Normally, there would be signs of melting and burning, but this one seemed in perfect condition. He then realised the reason for this; the bomb was in its entirety. He jumped up and took a few steps away before coming back and dancing in glee. Nobody he knew had come across an entire bomb before. Even his father couldn't boast to finding a whole bomb, although he thought he had the day before. He was therefore ecstatic as he carefully picked the bomb up and carried it home as if it were an injured bird.

When he arrived home he'd hoped to find the family all there so he could show off his treasure, but his parents were still out and the Irishmen were nowhere to be seen. He therefore took the bomb upstairs and hid it under his bed for fear that some untrustworthy lout might sneak into his house and pinch it off him to make it their own. He then waited for someone to return so he could share his triumph, but when the Irishmen returned later that afternoon, they just sat around the kitchen table glumly sipping their cups of tea not saying anything at all.

"Did you have to do much digging after last night?" He asked as a means of trying to manoeuvre the conversation around to digging for shrapnel.

"We did too much digging my boy, too much digging indeed." Ryan replied before he sank once again into a morbid silence.

"Did you dig the people out of the shelters in Stevenson Street?"He asked, innocently thinking that although the shelters got bombed, the people surely survived. However, when they refused to answer he concluded that this was perhaps not the case.

"I'll tell you this boyo, there was over a square mile of Wavertree destroyed last night. Hundreds of families were made homeless and god alone knows how many people lost their lives."

Ray felt at this point they needed cheering up and was just about to go and fetch the bomb he'd found, when the sirens sounded once again. This was the third night in a row that the Luftwaffe had targeted Liverpool and although people were obviously stressed, the bombing had failed in its intention of destroying the moral of the populous

"Here we go again." His father said quite light-heartedly.

"They're going to run out of bombs soon if they keep dropping them on us aren't they dad?" he said as the family made their way to the shelter and the Irishmen went off for what appeared to be yet another busy shift.

As he walked with his dad holding his hand, Ray looked up into the sky and once again clearly saw the bombers overhead. They hadn't lost any of the resemblance to giant insects in Ray's mind and just like insects, they had become an annoyance, which he wished somebody would swat. Just as he was entering the alleyway he saw the bomb doors open on a plane almost immediately overhead. The next second there was a flash and Ray turned to his dad.

"Wow dad, did you see that; the ack ack hit that plane?!" Ray was convinced he had mental powers that had directed the anti aircraft fire onto the bomber, but just as he was about to say so, his father looked up and immediately grabbed him and threw him into the shelter; throwing himself on top of him in the process. Seconds later there was a huge explosion the likes of which Ray had never experienced before. The ground shook, the walls of the alley crumbled in places leaving him and the other people in the shelter covered in small pieces of debris, and the noise left him with ringing in his ears for several hours afterwards.

"Blimey that was a close one; I reckon it hit the school" John said as he brushed brick from his shoulders and made sure Ray and his wife where safe and settled.

"Do you think the plane crashed?" Ray asked his dad thinking back to the flash he'd seen before his father had thrown him into the shelter.

"No Ray, what you saw was the bombs actually

dropping from the bomb doors and light being reflected off them as they were caught in a searchlight beam."

"Wow, wait until I tell the lads I saw the bombs falling, I bet nobody's seen that." He was excited by the prospect and sat out the rest of the raid working through the story he would tell the next day.

When the all clear sounded several hours later the Dagnalls decided to enter their house through the backyard. They went through the gate, through the yard and into the kitchen. At first everything looked quite normal other than objects being strewn across the floor having fallen from shelves. It was only when they opened the kitchen door to lead into the rest of the house that they realised the rest of the house no longer existed. As they stood there in total shock each of them reacted in different ways. His mother brought her free hand to her mouth and bit down on her fingers to stop any wayward emotion escaping. Enid wailed as normal from his mother's other arm. Ray himself stood open mouthed as he stared out at his school in shocked fascination as to why he could see it, when he should be looking down his hall at the front door. John looked out onto the rubble that had been his home and started to laugh.

"John, why are you laughing at a time like this? We've lost everything!"

"Not quite everything, Olive my dear. If your mother had lived for a few weeks more, there is a very good chance we would have been in the house with her and the lot of us would have been blown to smithereens." Olive nodded slowly and hugged her baby to her whilst putting the other arm around Ray.

"And another thing," John said, winking at Ray "our Ray actually saw the bomb that destroyed our house leave the plane. Now how many people can say that?!"

Whilst Ray was impressed by his father's calmness and levity at such a time, he was convinced it wasn't the Nazis who'd destroyed his house; it was him. He should never have hidden the unexploded bomb under his bed. It must have detonated and quickly consumed the house. He was utterly mortified as he took his father to one side.

"Dad, I have something to tell you; it was me who destroyed the house, I'm so sorry!" He began to sob and his father took him in his arms.

"Don't be silly Ray you're just in shock. How could you have possibly destroyed the house? You saw the bombs fall from the plane."

"It's my fault!" He then proceeded to whisper between sobs how he'd found the incendiary and hidden it under his bed.

"You did what! Do you know how dangerous that was, you could have killed yourself?!" He hugged his son close. "Don't you EVER pick up anything that looks like an unexploded bomb again" He then hugged him again before whispering "Whatever you do, don't mention this to your mother she'd have a fit."

He was somewhat bewildered by his father's reaction. If he were honest, he didn't really understand why his actions had been so dangerous, but he was more confused as to why he shouldn't mention it to his mother.

"But dad, I burnt the house down, we should tell her."

"Raymond, it was a high explosive bomb that destroyed the house. Your bomb would have caused a fire, not demolish the entire front of the house, but if you tell your mother you brought an unexploded bomb home, the damage the bomb caused won't be anything compared to what she'll do to your backside; you'll not be able to sit down for a month and probably won't be allowed out until you're at least eighteen!"

Ray decided to take his father's advice and never mentioned the incendiary ever again in front of his family.

Chapter 10 – The End of an Era

His father's levity didn't seem as appropriate later that night when they reported to the police station on Picton Road to inform the authorities they were still alive and the fact they no longer had anywhere to live.

"Right you are Mr Dagnall" the duty sergeant said after Ray's dad informed him what had happened. "I'm afraid you'll have to spend the rest of the night in the cells as it's been a busy couple of days and every shelter, bed and breakfast and hotel is full."

Ray was part terrified and part thrilled to be spending the night in a prison cell. He imagined that "Daggers" had been tracked down by the law and finally captured, but he was sure that his trusty gang would break him free.

His trusty gang turned out to be Auntie Sydnah who arrived at the station early the next morning having discovered her best friend's house had been destroyed. She was overjoyed to find the family safe and well and offered to put them up for as long as was necessary.

"I'll not hear of you staying anywhere else, so please don't try and argue." She said as she took Enid from his mother and headed towards the door. Ray was pretty sure none of them had intended arguing as they were desperate for somewhere to stay. He hadn't enjoyed sleeping in the cells at all and vowed never to become a criminal.

"You just come home with me and I'll put the kettle on for a nice cup of tea; and don't worry about your things, I'll organise a lorry and we'll go and collect what we can tomorrow."

Quite how she organised everything so quickly Ray never knew, but the following morning they were allocated a van by the Corporation in order to root through the rubble and retrieve as many possessions as they could from the wreckage of their home. The caveat was they only had the van for one trip and so they had to be selective in what they took. Heartbreakingly for Olive, her organ was too large to fit on the van or in Sydnah's house and so as they pulled away, she wept at the site of the instrument standing forlornly in the gutter.

Sydnah had always been a generous woman. Her door was always open and people would drop in for a cup of tea and a chat. She was very tall, standing at well over six feet, weighed over twenty stone and she was old fashioned in the way she dressed; wearing high collared blouses and long skirts with the addition of small round spectacles. Perhaps her most marked feature was her very straight hair that was held off her forehead by a clip.

She'd spent her life devoted to two things: the City Mission, where she took on many responsibilities and looking after her mother Ninph. She'd never married and in many ways was naive about the ways of the world; especially about the way children behaved.

"Children should be seen and not heard" she'd say whenever Ray showed even the slightest signs of enthusiasm.

This made no sense to him because unless you were going to be a statue (which he didn't think he could sustain for a whole week, although the challenge was quite tempting), you were bound to make some sort of noise at some point. You couldn't go a whole week without coughing or sneezing or burping or trumping; it was impossible. He usually couldn't get through an hour without doing at least one of those things. Her attitude towards his behaviour made him slightly scared of her and probably accounted for why she intimidated him.

He therefore spent most days sitting incredibly still and bored; being reprimanded if he showed the slightest indication that he was a seven year old or being dragged along with his mother as she did the daily trawl of local shops trying to find enough food for them to eat. He found little time to go off on his own, which made him feel hemmed in and trapped. He chafed at the bit to escape and look for souvenirs from the raids, but Olive had become very protective towards him since the bombing of their house and refused to let him out of shouting distance.

"But Ma I'm bored!" he whined as he sat at the kitchen table with nothing but a rolling pin for company. "Can't I just go out for a little bit, I won't go far?"

"No Raymond, we don't know when the next raid will be and I don't want you out of my sight."

He didn't even have the escape of lessons as they'd been cancelled until a new location could be found and his Irish friends had found new lodgings and so he didn't even have their boxing stories to keep him company.

It was therefore with a good deal of relief when his father announced one evening that his parents had offered them a room in their house; Olive was not impressed.

"I hope you're kidding John? Why would we want to go and stay with them?"

The way she said 'them' made it sound as if his father's parents were infected with some deadly disease.

"What's wrong with them Ma?"

"There's nothing wrong with them Raymond" his father answered. "And they have a three bed roomed house, which means there will be more space for us.

Sydnah has been incredibly kind, but you can't deny Olive, it's too cramped with us all here."

"John I'm not sure I could stand living with your mother, she can be so uncouth."

Ray had no idea what uncouth meant, but the way his mother said it made his Grandma sound quite wild and exciting. He'd rarely seen his paternal grandparents and heard them spoken about even less.

The decision made, he was intrigued and a little nervous as they packed their few remaining possessions once again, and headed off on the short walk to their house.

Within minutes of arriving he began to understand why his mother was loathed to stay there. Grandma Dagnall was loud, flamboyant and liberal in the face of Olive's quiet, straight laced conservatism. She was also covered in tattoos and told stories of once performing as part of a circus.

"We had quite a time of it youngster." She said as she took a drag on her pipe. "We used to travel from town to town; and the parties we used to have when we got there; dear God they were wild!"

"What did you use to do in the circus Gran?"

"I had a couple of acts, but my favourite was knife throwing."

To a boy of nearly eight this made her the most

amazing person he'd ever met. "Wow, can you show me how to throw a knife?!"

"You're a bit young at the moment, but I will one day when you've grown a bit."

In the days that followed he'd sit on the floor by her feet for hours at a time as she drank beer from a bottle and smoked her pipe whilst regaling him with stories of elephants and lions and travelling the country. At the same time, his mother would sit on the opposite side of the room quietly seething and shaking her head.

His granddad was a bricklayer who drank most of his earnings in the pub on the way home and usually returned singing loudly and laughing a lot, which only added to Olive's disgust and quiet contempt. To Ray though, these were exciting people who made it easy to forget about the fact the bombs were still dropping and the fact that they literally only had the clothes they stood up in. The house was always filled with loud laughter and garrulous bickering, which often included words that he would have had his mouth washed out for saying.

"Norman, look at the bloody state of you, you drunken git!" his grandmother would often growl as she gave her husband a kick as he lay sprawled on the floor in a stupor.

"I love you even if you are a bleeding cow to me!" Norman would respond. He was one of those men who became very jolly when he'd had a drink, regardless of what his wife said or did.

"Get off your arse and go and sleep it off!"

His grandfather would then invariably stagger towards their bedroom and vanish for the rest of the evening, the only evidence of his presence being the resounding snores that reverberated around the house and which could be heard down the entire street.

Olive coped by spending most evenings visiting Sydnah and bemoaning her lot whilst gossiping about her in-laws. "Honestly Sydnah, they are unbearable. They drink, they smoke and they use foul language. Just the other day, his mother..." she would never use her Christian name and always referred to her as 'John's mother'. "They are just so common. I'm not sure how much longer I can stand it."

Sydnah had been sat listening sympathetically and suddenly made a decision. "Olive, you don't need to worry any longer I will speak to Mrs. Hetherington-Smythe today and sort you out with a house."

Olive was unaware that Sydnah knew Mrs. Hetherington-Smythe, who was a member of a very rich and influential family and lived in a huge house in Childwall. She therefore didn't particularly hold out much hope of her being able to deliver on her promise.

However, to her amazement, three days later there was a knock on the door of Ray's grandparents' house.

"Go and see who that is will you Ray?" his grandmother said between puffs on her pipe as she sat rocking back and forth whilst knitting. "I can't afford to drop a stitch at this point."

He went out into the hall and opened the door to a tall, elegant woman dressed in clothes he'd only seen in the really posh shops on the few occasions he'd gone into town with his mother.

"Ah, you must be Raymond Dagnall," she said in an accent that reflected her clothes; rich and finely tailored.

"Er yeah." Ray replied feeling very common indeed as he realised he hadn't sounded the "s" as his mother so often reminded. He resolved to try much harder from there on in. "I am awfully sorry I meant to say 'yes'. Can I ask how you know my name, ma'am?" He'd meant it to sound like "marm", but it came out like "mam" and made him sound more common than ever.

"Your Aunty Sydnah asked me to do her a little favour and I was only too glad to oblige." At this point, Ray's mother entered the hallway.

"Raymond who was it at the d... Mrs. Hetherington-Smythe! What an honour! Please do come in; Raymond why didn't you tell me Mrs. Hetherington-Smythe was here?!"

Ray had rarely seen his mother as flustered in his

life. She almost curtseyed as she led the woman into the front room and was mortified when Ray's Gran came into the hall, looking their guest up and down with distaste.

"Who's this then?" And upon finding out it was Mrs. Hetherington-Smythe, adding "Very posh I'm sure; well It's very nice to meet you; fancy a brew?"

Mrs. Hetherington-Smythe extended her hand with her fingers bent in what Ray assumed was the delicate etiquette reserved for the very rich and well to do. She was therefore rather taken aback when Grandma gripped her hand as if she was greeting a docker and shook it vigorously. "Charmed, I'm sure," Gran said as Mrs. Hetherington- Smythe winced and gently extricated her fingers from the vice-like grip.

"Might I have a word Olive dear?" And with that Mrs. Hetherington Smythe took Olive into the front room and closed the door.

"She's a stuck up cow!" Grandma whispered as she winked at Ray and headed back to her knitting.

This left him alone in the hall to try and listen to what was being said on the other side of the door. He stood with his ear pressed up to the wood, but could only hear the mumble of voices and then his mother's voice as she said with earnest, "You are too kind!"

"You'd be better using a glass if you want to hear what's being said."

Ray spun round to find his father standing there with a wry grin on his face. "Who's is the Rolls Royce parked outside the house?"

"Rolls Royce; there's a Rolls Royce in the street?!" Ray dodged around his father and headed towards the front door. He'd only ever seen a Rolls Royce on the cinema screen as they drove the King somewhere, and he never dreamed he would actually get to see one in the street outside the house where he lived. He burst through the front door and then stood open eyed and open mouthed at the marvel of modern engineering that stood in front of him; complete with uniformed chauffeur in peaked cap. His father joined him and they spent several silent moments appreciating the sleek lines and ostentatious figure head of the winged Spirit of Ecstasy on the front of the bonnet.

"She's a beauty isn't she Ray?"

"Too right she is; can you imagine what it must be like to ride in one? You must feel like royalty; just look at those seats."

Their reverie was interrupted by the elegant voice of Mrs. Hetherington-Smythe. "You are quite right Raymond; one does feel rather special when one is journeying in such a car. How would you like to see for yourself what it feels like?"

"You mean I can have a go in the car?!" He said open mouthed and giddy with excitement.

"Well yes, I have just been telling your mother that I am going to arrange for you to receive some new accommodation."

At that point Ray and his father didn't care too much about the accommodation, but both were extremely sure they'd love to go on a trip in the Rolls Royce. They nodded eagerly and the next thing they knew, the chauffeur was standing next to the door holding it open as Ray, followed by his mother holding Enid, his father and Mrs. Hetherington-Smythe sat back in the plush leather seats. As he sank into the seat, the feeling was indeed what he'd expected and as they drove down the street, people actually came out of their houses to stare as he waved regally back at them.

When they reached the town hall their plight was put into perspective when they were met by hundreds of people who were in the same position as themselves; namely having had their homes destroyed by the Nazi bombers. However, the feelings of being VIPs lasted a little longer as they bypassed the queues accompanied by Mrs. Hetherington-Smythe, and entered what was obviously her office.

"Now we have three properties for you to view. I assume you would prefer a garden and an indoor bathroom? The rent will be the same as you were paying on your old property."

Ray couldn't believe his ears; a garden *and* an

indoor bathroom. A bathroom, not just a toilet but a bathroom! By the look on his parents' faces, they were as flabbergasted as he was.

"Yes please Mrs. Hetherington-Smythe that would be absolutely wonderful." His mother said as she rang her hands, before needlessly smoothing down her skirt.

"Well come with me and I'll fetch the keys. We will look at a rather nice property on Clavelle Road. It's double fronted; you don't mind it being double fronted do you?" The Dagnalls just shook their heads in unison and followed Mrs. Hetherington-Smythe back to her Rolls Royce.

After another luxurious journey sat in the back of the car, they eventually pulled up in front of a house, which as soon as Ray saw it, knew would become their new home.

The first thing that struck him was the space. The road was wide and the pavement had a grass verge running along it. There were even trees and they'd passed several parks on the journey to this new address.

"Oh Mrs. Hetherington-Smythe we love it! We don't need to see the others, we love this one already." Olive said as her eyes took in the elegance of the house in front of them.

"But you haven't seen the inside yet. It's not quite finished being renovated so it will be several weeks before you can move in."

As they moved around to the side of the house and entered the front door the wonders that lay within were revealed to them. In front of them on the left hand side was a staircase leading upstairs, and on the right was a door that led into the main room of the house. Further down the hall was a second door leading to a slightly smaller room. A door on the left led into a huge kitchen that could easily double as a dining room.

As Ray pounded up the stairs he found two good sized bedrooms plus a third smaller one and then the thing he had dreamed of for as long as he could remember. As he opened the door to the bathroom, he was in awe even though it was not yet complete. He could see the bath, which had already been installed and next to it the sink that looked as though it had spaces for two taps; a hot and a cold one, but the highlight, the thing that would separate Ray from everybody else he knew, was the indoor toilet; white and glistening in its newness. He reverently stepped towards it and parked himself, ever so lightly on its closed lid and contemplated the countless hours of pleasure he'd now be able to have in the warmth of an indoor bathroom.

Having looked around the house both Olive and John confirmed to Mrs. Hetherington-Smythe they would not need to look at any other property, and so as they drove back towards the town hall to sign the lease on the property, Ray realised that a chapter of his life was coming to an end and couldn't help but feel incredibly guilty because no matter how hard he tried, he could not help but feel grateful that the Nazis had bombed his house enabling him to move into 57 Clavelle Road where he would have indoor plumbing.

Part Two

Chapter 11 – New Beginnings and a Wooden Leg

As he sat in the front compartment of the van as it trundled along Mather Avenue towards his new abode, Ray felt butterflies of excited anticipation rolling around his stomach. It had been several months since the Nazi bombs had destroyed his previous dwelling and a number of weeks more since he'd first laid eyes on the palace that was to become his new home.

However, the day had finally dawned and they were now on their way. He somehow felt different already as he looked out once again at the amount of greenery and open spaces. He had been used to streets of brick and concrete, crammed closely together; so this alien environment made him feel as if he was embarking on a brand new adventure in a new land; even though it was only three miles from where he used to live.

For starters he would actually have a room to himself rather than sharing with his sister, Enid who had moved in with him since they'd been bombed out. She was quite a placid baby given the noise of continual bombing, sirens and anti-aircraft fire, but she did still feel the need to cry just when he was in a deep sleep.

He quickly settled into his new home but continued to revel in the luxury of being able to arise from his bed and walk just a few steps to the bathroom in order to go to the loo. His mother even bought some proper toilet paper to mark the occasion. The downside of having a bath and sink in a fixed location was that he was expected to have more than one weekly bath and he seemed to continuously be reminded to wash his hands.

In the days that followed the move he was free to explore the local area in more detail. His mother was less protective as Allerton had seen less bombing than Wavertree and she also had her hands full with his new sister. This allowed him time to wander further afield than he'd ever done before. He discovered green fields and woods, a large cemetery and a park with a huge deserted mansion in it; he also discovered a pill box that was used by the home guard during their exercises.

As he was exploring the park with the pill box, he came across a boy who looked to be a similar age to him. He was quite a bit taller though and much stockier, with a mop of sandy coloured hair. The boy was throwing stones at the windows of the mansion trying to see if he could smash one. After his experience with the German butcher, Ray was rather anti throwing stones at windows.

"Why are you doing that?" he asked in a tone that showed he didn't approve.

"Why not?" The boy said as he picked up another stone and threw it at a ground floor window, missing narrowly. "It's not as if anyone lives there. Why don't you have a go?"

"The last time I threw stones at a window I got caught and me ma battered me. She also said it made me no better than the Nazi thugs." Ray winced at the memory of the good hiding he's received after smashing Mr. Schmidt's window.

The other boy was about to throw another stone, but upon making the connection between his mindless act of vandalism and what the Nazis were doing, he made the decision to find other activities to fill his time. He dropped the stone and turned to Ray. "I'm rubbish anyway. I must have thrown twenty stones already and missed every time. My name's Ian." He said as he extended his hand. "Ian Davies, what's yours?"

Ray eagerly extended his own hand and the boys shook vigorously. "Ray Dagnall, we've just moved into Clavelle Road as we were bombed out of our house in Wavertree."

"Wow, what was it like?" And so he proceeded to tell him all the exploits of living with the raids. To Ian, who it turned out also lived in Clavelle Road, this made Ray something of a hero, as whilst he'd seen the devastation, he hadn't been so close that he'd had shrapnel whizzing past his head or been targeted by Nazi machine gunners.

"And there was the time when I found an

unexploded bomb and had to make sure no one went near it; I stayed up all night and then discovered it was a blown up lamp post." He knew he was getting a little carried away with the truth, but Ian seemed to be lapping his stories up so he continued to embellish. "There was also the time a lad I know found a whole incendiary bomb and took it home to hide under his bed. I had to get it off him and drop it in a bucket of water, because that's what you do to stop them going off." He actually amazed himself at how creative his stories were becoming, but the look of admiration in Ian's eyes was clearly stimulus enough. As the two boys started to climb trees, a firm friendship began to blossom like the leaves on the trees in which they climbed.

It was a strange relationship because on paper, they had little in common in terms of background and upbringing. Ray's dad was basically a painter and decorator whilst Ian's dad was an underwriter for Lloyds. Ray had spent his life going outside to the loo, whilst Ian had always had the luxury of an indoor bathroom. Ray had a baby sister whilst Ian had an elder brother of seventeen and two gorgeous sisters who were older still. Ian showed no interest in girls whilst Ray fell in love with Ian's sisters as soon as he saw them.

It happened the first time he went round to Ian's

house; he'd walked into the large kitchen as Susan was getting ready to go to work.

"Sue, this is my new friend; Daggers." Ray had made sure that Daggers was the nickname he liked to be known by. "Daggers, this is one of my elder sisters, Sue."

She must have been about nineteen and was tall and slim with blonde hair and she had the most amazing blue eyes, which when turned upon him, made Ray's stomach go queasy and his tongue so tied in knots that all he could do was drool. She'd ruffled his hair and giggled as she left the room.

"Wow!" he managed to exclaim as she slammed the front door. To Ray that giggle had been the single most beautiful sound he'd ever heard, and he vowed never to wash his hair again where her hand had made contact. Unfortunately a vow that was broken that same evening when his mother made him have a bath.

Every day for an entire week he tried to catch a glimpse of his beloved. He would walk passed the front of Ian's house in the hope that she would appear and when she didn't, he'd walk back again pretending he'd forgotten something. Each time he failed to see her he would repeat the action until he looked like a yoyo as he went one way and then the other. He also looked for any excuse to gain entry into Ian's house and when that still failed to allow him access to her beauty, he tried to persuade Ian that they should play for whole days round at his house in the hope of him glimpsing her again.

"Oh go on, you're house is great and we can play in the garden."

"You've just got a crush on our Susan." Ian said as they headed up the path.

"Susan? Who's Susan?" It was a poor attempt at deflection, but Ian let it go with a laugh. However, seven days after first seeing the love of his life he met Ian's other elder sister and his affections shifted like a leaf on the wind. Mary had the same features as Susan; the blonde hair, height, figure and dazzling blue eyes; but what set her apart from her sister and immediately replaced her in Ray's affections, was her uniform. She was in the Wrens and upon seeing her sat at the kitchen table bickering and sharing banter with her brother, he became quite breathless and made a vow to make her notice him and bestow him with a smile. He actually achieved this quite quickly by clowning around with Ian and so he made yet another vow to make her fall in love with him, even though he didn't have a clue what he'd do if he succeeded.

Sadly, Ray's fairy tale relationship ended rather quickly as he discovered on his next visit that Mary had been posted away somewhere and Susan had a boyfriend who she intended to marry. This left Ray sat at the same kitchen table with Ian and his brother Peter, who went everywhere dressed as Sherlock Holmes complete with long coat, deer stalker hat, magnifying glass and pipe; even when he sat at the kitchen table.

After an hour of being interrogated by 'Sherlock' regarding his whereabouts over the last seven days and being scrutinised with a magnifying glass to see if he had any dog hairs on him, his final vow was to invite Ian round to his house in the future!

All good things come to an end and for Ray, his time for missing lessons ended all too quickly. The following week his mother informed him that he'd be starting at Springwood Elementary school, which was just round the corner and had barely closed since 1939. It was therefore with a good deal of reluctance that he dragged himself through the school's gates the following day. As he walked onto the playground he was immediately confronted by a group of three girls who appeared to be a couple of years older than him.

"Look what the cat dragged in" the taller of the girls said as she looked Ray up and down disdainfully.

He looked down at himself and sadly understood what the girl was talking about. He had lost most of his belongings in the bombing so was stood there in a threadbare shirt and faded grey short pants that had a patch sewn into the behind.

"Do you live on the streets boy?" the girl said as she

looked around for encouragement from her friends.

"Er no, we've just moved into Clavelle Road after we were bombed out of our other house."

"Oh, they are really lowering the tone of the area." To which she received appreciative giggles from her two friends.

Ray wasn't too sure what she meant, but he had an idea that it wasn't a compliment. He was about to say something horrible about the girl's teeth, which were rather wonky and protruded over her bottom lip, when a fourth girl walked over.

"Audrey leave the boy alone, can't you see he's obviously lost everything when his house was bombed?"

"Oh alright Joyce, if you fancy him you just have to say so." And with that they walked away bickering between themselves.

Ray headed into school and was taken to see the headmaster. He was left sat outside the office for what seemed an awfully long time, but was probably only a couple of minutes before a deep voice resonated through the oak door.

"Enter." Ray didn't realise that the "enter" was directed at him and so continued to sit nervously waiting.

"I said enter." Ray looked around him, wondering if the voice was talking to somebody else, but he still didn't move.

"New boy, I said enter!" and with that the door swung open and the headmaster limped out into the hallway. "Why are you still sat there boy? Why are you not standing before my desk?"

Ray looked up at the headmaster, afraid and tongue-tied. He tried to speak but could only mumble nonsense.

"Stop mumbling boy, get into my office."

Ray moved quickly past the man, tripping over his own feet and sprawling flat on his face in front of a large wooden desk. The headmaster limped back around the desk and sat down.

"For goodness sake, stand up and slowly tell me your name."

Ray got to his feet and tried to calm himself by taking several deep breaths. "R-R-Raymond John Dagnall."

"Raymond John Dagnall, *sir*! You will always call me sir or Mr. Little."

Ray wasn't quite sure why he should call him Mr. Little when he looked like a rather large man. It was only later, once his nerves had calmed down that he realised that Mr. Little was his name. Ray was not usually as intimidated as this by teachers, but he'd never come across a male teacher before as most had joined the armed forces. The reason Mr. Little sat before him rather than fighting the Nazis was the fact the he only had one leg, the other being wooden.

"Y-yes sir, Mr. Little sir." Ray stammered and then realised that his best way of surviving this encounter was to say as little as possible and so firmly closed his mouth and stood as straight as he possibly could, pretending he was a statue as he'd done so often before on the ferry.

"Right Dagnall, I want you to work hard and do everything your teacher tells you. I don't want to see you standing in this office again. If I do, it will mean you are in trouble and woe betide you boy if you get on my wrong side. Now come along with me and I will take you to your class." He then proceeded to rise quickly from his seat and limp out of his office and down the corridor with Ray having to run to keep up with him. Considering he had a wooden leg, Ray was impressed with the speed at which he moved. When he abruptly stopped outside room 6b, Ray collided with his wooden leg and almost fell to the floor. Swinging round, Mr. Little said, "What are you doing boy?!"

"Sorry sir, I must have been too close."

"Never mind just get in there." And with that Mr. Little flung open the door and Ray entered.

"This will be your new class and your class teacher, Miss McEvoy." As Mr. Little had a private word with Miss McEvoy, Ray looked around the class and immediately noticed Ian grinning at him from the back of the room.

"This is Raymond Dagnall everyone, say hello to him." Miss McEvoy said as Mr. Little strode from the room keeping his eye on Ray all the way.

The class responded with a monotone "Good morning Ray Dagnall." And then Ray was asked to greet them in return. He decided he'd play it for laughs and so with huge exaggeration and as animatedly as possible, he took a large breath and said, "Good morning class, good morning Miss McEvoy." His satire was lost on most of them, but Ian found it hilarious and let out a bellow of laughter.

"What are you guffawing about, Davies?! Go and stand in the corridor."

So began a pattern of events that became an almost daily routine. Ray would play the clown; Ian would respond with loud laughter or silly comment and end up getting into trouble for it. On the other hand, Ray became rather popular with his class mates and before long was at the centre of a small gang who were the scourge of their teacher.

Several weeks later, with Ray firmly established as the class clown, Miss McEvoy decide to treat her class to an afternoon's field trip to the local park. As was the routine, the children all had to pair up and walk hand in hand down the road. Ray and Ian drew peals of laughter as they pretended to be sweethearts; swinging their arms, skipping along and blowing kisses to one another until Miss McEvoy had had enough and made them hold her hands for the rest of the way. When they arrived at the park they were instructed that they had to go off and find examples of the different types of wildlife, local to the area. Ray, Ian and another member of their new gang Tony Blains decided they could accomplish this in a fraction of the time they'd been allotted.

"All we have to do is find some bugs and note down any animals we see. We don't even have to see them; we can just make it up." Tony or 'Blainsey' as he liked to be known was something of a maverick who some people actually called psychopathic. He was certainly fearless, incredibly reckless and found Ian and Ray hilarious, which was why they'd become close friends. "I reckon we have a game of hide and go seek instead, which will be a lot more fun."

Several hours later the boys had failed to collect any specimens and the time was nearly up for them to present the fruits of their labour. As they approached Miss McEvoy, they were still arguing about what the best excuse would be.

"I reckon we say that we came across a wasp's nest and accidently knocked it, which caused the wasp's to chase us and we dropped all of the stuff we'd gathered."

Ray was quite impressed with Ian's creativity, but thought his idea was still more exciting. "I still reckon we say we found a Nazi parachutist, captured him after a fierce fight and handed him over to the army."

Blainsey agreed "Dagger's idea is way better than yours Ian; I like the idea of beating up a Nazi."

It was agreed they would go with Ray's excuse and were just about to respond to Miss McEvoy request for them to produce their findings, when they heard the sirens sounding in the distance. For the past four nights Liverpool had been hit hard and so Miss McEvoy understandably panicked.

"Quickly children, take cover!" Pandemonium broke out, instigated primarily by Ray and his gang, who ran off all over the park screaming "Take cover! Take cover!" and ran in zigzag lines doing impersonations of planes as they dived into bushes and threw acorns at each other. It was at this point however, they realised the raid was real as three Hurricane fighter planes screamed over their heads and turned towards the Mersey.

"Wow that's strange, I can't hear any bombers."

Normally within minutes of the siren going off you would pick up the undeniable drone of massed planes, but on this occasion there didn't appear to be any. The next minute there was the unmistakable sound of machine gun fire and the boys looked up to see the three Hurricanes chasing down a lone Nazi bomber in the distance. The German seemed to be putting up a good defence as it weaved left and right and spat fire back towards the three attacking planes.

"Come on lads, you can do it; shoot the bugger down!" Blainsey shouted as he rang his fist at the enemy. The other lads joined in and within seconds were yelling and screaming into the sky. Their support appeared to work as suddenly they saw debris fly from the engine on the right wing of the bomber and flame and smoke started to spurt backwards into the oncoming Hurricanes. The boys cheered hysterically as the plane sank below the tree line and disappeared.

"That was awesome!" Ray exclaimed over the babble of voices as each of his mates described the dogfight from their perspective. "That must be the best fieldtrip ever!"

Things didn't seem as awesome, however, when Ray returned home later that evening only to discover that Miss McEvoy had reported them as missing and there were now police and volunteers out looking for them. He felt the wrath of his mother that made it difficult for him to sit down for several days and also received the obligatory grounding.

However, on the third evening of him not being allowed out, he came up with a ruse that allowed him to escape the house and spend a little time at least, hanging around with his mates. Shortly after he'd finished his tea he complained of having a stomach ache and so went to sit on the loo. The bathroom had become Ray's favourite room in the house and it was not uncommon for him to spend several hours sat reading a comic whilst he emptied his bowels. So now when he locked the door to the bathroom, he knew he should be safe for a couple of hours at least without being disturbed. He locked the door, climbed out of the window and down the drainpipe as quickly as a ferret.

The first time he escaped he'd barely reached the bottom of the road when the sirens went off and he had to quickly dart back to the house before his absence was discovered. He only just managed this in time before his mother shouted, "Raymond have you finished yet? We're heading to the shelter so hurry up!"

Though they could still hear the explosions and anti aircraft fire, their new home seemed somehow safer. It was that bit further from the docks and now they had a garden, they also had an Anderson shelter dug into the flower beds out back and although it was probably less safe than the shelter in the alley, it didn't feel that way. It was almost cosy compared to what the family had experienced before.

Chapter 12 – The Best Chip Butties and New Headquarters

May of 1941 proved to be a particularly destructive month for Liverpool and the surrounding area. The bombers returned night after night and struck randomly at targets in an attempt to annihilate as much of the populous and infrastructure as possible.

"There doesn't seem to be any strategy to what they're doing." John said as they sat in the shelter once more and listened to the sound of devastation raining down from above. "One day they'll target the dock, which is understandable given the amount of food and resources coming in; but then they'll target residential areas the next night."

"They're trying to destroy our morale John, but I'll tell you something, I feel more determined to withstand them now than I ever did before it started."

"You know you're right, the feeling down at the docks is really positive. It's as if everyone's come together to resist. Strange really; I suppose it's the sense that we're all in it together. It doesn't matter who you are or where you come from, the bombs have the same effect."

Ray had no idea what his parents were going on about. All he knew was that these raids were leaving him feeling pretty tired after spending all night in the garden, which left him grumpy and bad tempered. As he and Ian walked to school one morning he was stopped in his tracks by a deep voice.

"Well if it isn't little Daggers?"

As Ray turned towards the voice he came face to face with Kenny, the bully who he'd swapped shrapnel for a penknife. Kenny seemed to have evolved over the months since he'd last seen him and was now even taller and his voice had changed into a deep growl.

"What are you doing around here Kenny!?" He hadn't meant to sound so aggressive, but the tiredness made his question sound as if Kenny was an irritation; rather like the Nazi bugs.

"Who do you think you're talking to?!" Kenny said as he punched Ray hard in the stomach. "I was only trying to be nice."

As Ray crouched on the floor trying to get his breath back, Ian stepped forward. "Look Kenny or whatever your name is; he didn't mean anything, it's just that he's tired because of all the raids."

"We're all ruddy tired mate, but he didn't have to snap at me like that; I was only trying to be nice."

As Ray got back to his feet he thought he'd better apologise. "I'm sorry for snapping Kenny; I didn't mean it to sound the way it did. Why are you around here?"

"It's not just me who's moved into the area; there are loads of families moving out because we've been bombed out."

"Oh right; look Kenny I am sorry; maybe I'll see you around sometime." Ray grabbed Ian by the arm and quickly moved off, vowing that if he ever saw Kenny again, he'd hide until he was out of sight.

Kenny had been right though about the increase in people moving into the area. When he got to school that morning, there were four new kids in his class and when he arrived home that evening; it was to find that his father had asked if his mate from work could move in with his wife for a few days as they'd also been bombed out. Olive agreed and so the next day Joe and Dolly moved into the smaller of the downstairs rooms.

In many ways this felt more normal to Ray who had always known his home filled with additional bodies; Nana, the Irish navvies and now Joe and Dolly. The couple were nice enough and everyone quickly settled down into a new routine. The only bug bear for Ray was with more people, time in the bathroom was put at a premium and it put added pressure on him when he needed to use it as an escape route when grounded.

When after a week, Joe and Dolly had failed to find alternative accommodation, matters were made worse when he informed them that Dolly's mother and sister had also been bombed out and asked if they too could stay for 'a couple of days'. Through gritted teeth Olive agreed, but said they would all have to pay rent; her Christian duty only went so far. 57 Clavelle Road therefore had four extra occupants living in one room downstairs and Ray had even less time to spend in the bathroom.

He always believed however, that things a balanced themselves out, so whilst he had to sacrifice his escape route, he was rewarded with the cooking of Dolly's mother; particularly her homemade chips. As a thank you for letting them stay, Dolly and her mother had pooled their ration tokens and saved up to get some potatoes, which was a rarity in 1941. The mother had then peeled and chopped them into thick slices and managed to find some oil in which to fry them. The first time he tasted the crisp yet fluffy chip inside a piece of bread, he actually thought he'd died and gone to heaven. They melted in the mouth and he was instantly addicted. He begged for them on a daily basis but was denied by his mother who believed them to be an unnecessary indulgence.

"But ma they are so good, I've never tasted chips like them." Later, he would realise his mistake, but at the time he was desperate to taste the flavour of the fried potatoes once again. "Didn't you think they were the best things you'd ever tasted?"

His mother had a look that she reserved only for those people who really ticked her off and she now turned that steely gaze on her son, who paled as shivers ran down his spine.

"W-what have I done?! What have I said? I only said she makes the best chips." It was then it dawned on him what had irked his mother so. She prided herself on her ability to source ingredients in this time of austerity and create palatable dishes that nourished and allowed him to thrive. Yet here he was as good as saying that her best just wasn't good enough. "Look, I'm sorry; I'm not saying that her cooking is better than yours. You cook really well and you make the best connyonny butties ever."

Olive continued to stare at him in silence and so he felt the need to continue. "Forget about the chips; you're right, we should be more careful with our rations, I'm sorry!" He left the kitchen and went up to his room. As he went through the door he was almost certain he saw his mother smile smugly to herself and it was only later he realised she hadn't actually said a word. That one look was enough.

The 'couple of days' seemed to have been forgotten as May became June and June became July with Joe, Dolly and her mother and sister still living in the downstairs back room. Ray never mentioned the chips again to his mother, but he came to an understanding with Dolly's mother that when Olive was out and rations allowed, she would secretly make him some chips and have the kitchen spotless by the time his mother returned home.

In addition to the chips, he was also thankful for his baby sister Enid. It wasn't that he felt particularly affectionate towards her; he was now a boy of eight and she was just a baby, but she did take up an awful lot of his mother's time, which meant she was less inclined to focus on him thus leaving him free to get up to mischief with Ian and his other new found friends.

As the nights got lighter the raids slackened off somewhat as it was easier for the defenders to see and therefore hit the enemy bombers. This meant Ray and his gang had whole evenings in which to roam and cause mischief. One evening they were horsing around in the park when they ended up outside the deserted mansion where Ray had first met Ian.

"That would make a great base" Blainsey said, pointing at the rather forbidding structure that loomed before them.

As Ray had got to know Blainsey better he came to realise the prefix of 'psycho' was well earned. He was indeed reckless, but some of his escapades were downright dangerous. On one occasion he threw stones at the park warden just so he would chase them; on another, he picked a fight with a much older boy, only to run off laughing as the boy turned on his friends as they stood frozen to the spot.

"Come on let's see if we can get in." He went up to the house; climbed through some railings and moved from window to window and door to door to see if there was any weakness they could take advantage of.

Ray was a little dubious and very nervous. If they got caught they'd be in serious trouble and he reckoned he wouldn't see the light of day for at least a year, let alone the hiding he'd receive if his mother found out.

"Here you are." Blainsey said as he pulled a loose wooden board from a window. "We can get in here. This must be the cellar; this is going to be so good!" He then pulled a second board off and disappeared into the darkness within.

The other boys were far more reluctant to head into the unknown but nobody was prepared to appear to be the weakling, so one after the other they followed Blainsey into the house. Once inside a lot of the fear started to vanish as they were caught up in the excitement of the adventure. There wasn't much left in the house but the possibilities of what they could get up to were not lost on any of them. They moved from room to room, their enthusiasm growing as they realised there were still comfy chairs they could sit on and even running water. They were just emerging into the reception area, which had a huge staircase sweeping up to the first floor when Ray realised that Blainsey was missing.

"Hey, has anybody seen Blainsey since we've been in here?" The other boys looked around and shook their heads. Ray was just about to call his name when there was a huge crash and the floor shook. He jumped about a foot into the air and actually peed his pants a little as he looked down and saw a huge piece of masonry a matter of inches from where he stood.

"Ha! Ha! Ha! You should see your faces". Ray looked up to see Blainsey balancing between two beams looking down on them from a hole in the ceiling and holding his sides as he guffawed at his joke.

"You could have killed me, you ruddy idiot." Ray screamed as the realisation that he was inches away from being crushed swept over him and he began to shake. From shock or from rage he wasn't sure, but through all of the air raids and bombings he'd never felt as he did now. "Get down here you psycho so I can knock your ruddy lights out!" Now Ray was not a fighter so was utterly bemused as to why he'd offered to punch the hardest person he knew. As Blainsey disappeared from the hole in the ceiling, his common sense started to return. He realised he needed to beat a hasty retreat, but he also needed to try and save face with the others at the same time. He therefore shouted at the top of his voice.

"It's a good job I'm late for me tea Blainsey or I would have had to teach you a lesson." With that he ran as fast as he could, out of the cellar and into the park. In fact he didn't stop running until he reached his house; never looking behind him for fear he'd see psycho Blains chasing him.

After a sleepless night in which he had nightmares of the various ways in which psycho was going to hurt him, he arrived at school bleary eyed and feeling sick. He'd been tempted to try and persuade his mother he was too ill to attend but he knew he'd be just putting off the inevitable; and if his sleepless night was anything to go by, the beatings his imagination had served up were hopefully a lot worse than the reality of what Blainsey might do to him. That was his rationale anyway.

Typically, the first person he saw was Blainsey who strode across the yard looking grim and somewhat feral. The other kids on the yard sensed, as only kids' can, there was the potential for violence in the air and quickly gathered around in hope. "Er, hi Blainsey."

Blainsey replied by cracking his knuckles and loosening his shoulders. "You said you were going to punch my lights out." He then flicked his neck from side to side, which caused Ray to swallow hard.

"Er, did I?"

"Yeah, and you said you were going to teach me a lesson. Well come on then, what's this lesson you're going to teach me Daggers?"

In that moment Ray made the decision to fall back on his one true strength – humour. "Well, see this string?" he said as he pulled it out of his pocket. "I'm going to teach you how to tie a special knot." With that he proceeded to demonstrate a rather complicated routine his dad had taught him. At first he was unsure how Blainsey would react as he just stood there staring as Ray wove the string together, but then he let out a bellow of laughter and slapped him on the back sending him sprawling.

As Blainsey picked him up he flung his arm around his shoulder and proceeded to lead him into school leaving the rest of the kids to make their way disappointedly to their classes. "You're a ruddy idiot you are Daggers!"

"So are you Blainsey, so are you." Ray said as he heaved a huge sigh of relief and vowed never to threaten anybody ever again.

Chapter 13 – The Trouble with Cartoons

School didn't really interest Ray that much; he enjoyed meeting his friends and playing football at break, but most other things bored him. He spent much of his time in lessons doodling or drawing cartoons of his classmates or Miss McEvoy when he should have been writing a story or doing long division. However, all the practice actually made him into quite a proficient artist.

During one particularly mind numbing lesson about the British Empire, he had completely switched off from the drone of his teacher's voice, which sounded remarkably similar to the drone the Nazi bombers made and could be just as destructive. He therefore became absorbed in drawing a cartoon of one of his best mates, Mousey Johnson. In this particular picture Mousey was dressed as Flash Gordon and he'd just vanquished Ming the Merciless, who looked a lot like Adolf Hitler. It was clear that Mousey had won as he was seen kicking his nemesis up the bum. Ray was rather pleased with his creation and was in the process of adding the finishing touches when a shadow fell across the paper and he felt a presence at his shoulder.

"What do we have here Raymond?" Miss McEvoy leaned over to take the picture. He knew it was too late to hide it, but he instinctively tried to sweep the paper into his pocket.

"Er nothing miss, just some notes on what you were saying." He was far too slow and Miss McEvoy snapped it out of his hand before it was even half way off the desk.

"Raymond, this is really good. I'm not sure exactly how it fits in with what we are doing but it is really good none the less, really good indeed!"

In many ways he felt rather sorry for Miss McEvoy. Since joining the school he had not made her life particularly easy and yet she never seemed to give up on him. She seemed determined to find something he was good at and then nurture that talent or channel his eagerness into something positive rather than mischief. Up until now she'd failed abysmally, but by the look on her face he believed she may have found a new vehicle on which to focus her attention.

"Er Thanks"

"That's Eric Johnson isn't it?"

"Mousey, yeah that's right." Ray was rather pleased his characters were at least recognisable and his fear of being in trouble started to subside.

"Well I think we've discovered you have a real talent for Art Raymond. I want you to take this picture to show Mr. Little and tell him I sent you."

As he stood up and moved slowly towards the door he could see Miss McEvoy beaming with delight. Her face reminded him of how he imagined St Paul's face would have been after he'd had the epiphany on the road to Damascus; full of awe and wonder. Quite how she was going to use her new found intelligence to turn Ray into a productive student and useful human being, he was not so sure. However, he was pleased he'd finally made her happy as he'd never deliberately intended to make her cry and felt a little guilty at the frequency at which he seemed to achieve this.

As he headed towards Mr. Little's office he imagined he'd probably have to stand up in assembly and show off his brilliance at Art to the rest of the school. He pictured himself being awarded a prize, with his mother applauding thunderously from the back of the hall as tears of pride trickled down her cheeks. He also pictured examples of his work being displayed throughout the school; attracting hoards of admirers who would look on his skill as being a gift from God. It was therefore with a high degree of self assurance that he knocked on Mr. Little's door and then nonchalantly entered, almost before he was told he could do so. As he walked into the office he was met with a rather bad tempered headmaster who looked him up and down distastefully.

"You again Dagnall?!" Mr. Little had the annoying habit of stating the obvious. "What have you done this time boy?! He also had a habit of asking a question and not waiting for an answer before he'd made up his own mind what that answer would be and summarily passing judgement and meting out punishment. "I am sick and tired of your stupid sense of humour!" he ranted.

Ray felt this seemed like something of a contradiction as humour, by its very nature, is stupid.

"You are a clown and a fool and I will not stand for it any longer!"

Again, Ray was left feeling a little confused as he listened to contradiction after contradiction. In his mind, a clown and a fool were the same thing and he actually considered it a compliment as he loved playing the fool.

However, the way Mr. Little said it, he was pretty sure he wasn't intending to be nice. He'd also said he wasn't going to stand for it any longer, but he was already sat down? He was tempted to say something, but decided to ride out the tirade in silence, as when he'd attempted to contribute to these 'conversations' in the past, it had never ended well. He therefore looked for the tell tale signs that Mr. Little was nearing his conclusion.

The conversation would normally begin with Mr. Little calling him names, which Ray thought was a little childish for a man of his age and responsibility. He'd then usually work himself up into such frenzy that he'd go very red in the face and then pound the desk with his fist. On one hilarious occasion he'd done this and accidently knocked his cup of tea over; tipping scalding hot liquid into his lap. It was a good job it landed on his wooden leg as Ray was sure it would have really hurt, but he barely seemed to notice.

The final stage of his tantrum normally involved him rising from his desk and limping up and down wildly gesticulating in such a way that Ray was amazed he never took off. He was at that stage now, so he knew he may get a window of opportunity to answer the original question, as sometimes Mr. Little would pause his tirade and simply say "Well?!" On other occasions though, he'd move towards the drawer and pull out 'the slipper', which indicated an imminent beating and no opportunity to answer any allegations.

Ray was coiled like a spring ready to jump in with an answer. However, it appeared today was going to be one of those occasions when Mr. Little wasn't interested in anything he had to say as he headed towards the drawer. He was slightly disappointed as he saw the images of the award, his exhibition and the tears of pride trickling down his mother's face transform into the tartan of the familiar size ten slipper and the inevitable sting when it impacted with his behind. He was in the process of assuming the position when there was a polite tap on the door and Miss McEvoy entered.

"What is it?!" Mr. Little snapped before he realised it was a member of staff. "Oh, sorry Miss McEvoy, I thought it was a child. You're just in time to see me punish Dagnall once again. What is it he's done this time?" As he said this, he was giving the slipper some practice swipes through the air, limbering up and loosening his muscles; a sure indication that today's session was going to be particularly painful.

"But Mr. Little, Raymond hasn't done anything wrong. In fact I sent him to you so he could show you the wonderful picture he's drawn."

By the look on Mr. Little's face you would have thought somebody had just beaten him with a slipper, so pained was his expression. His right eye had begun to twitch and he began panting as if he was a dog who needed a drink. Ray assumed this reaction was caused by the realisation that on this occasion, it was Mr. Little who was acting the fool but unlike Ray, he obviously didn't enjoy playing this role one little bit.

"Surely he must have done something wrong. I mean it's Dagnall we're talking about here?!" Ray felt a little insulted by that remark, but once again decided to say nothing.

"No Mr. Little, if you just take a look at the picture you will see how talented Raymond is. I think we have finally discovered real potential here, and if we just channel it ...." Miss McEvoy didn't get the chance to finish her defence as it was clear that Mr. Little was too far gone to accept he was in the wrong. He snatched the picture from Ray's hands and threw it onto his desk without even looking at it.

"And was he meant to be drawing in your lesson?"

"Well no, we were looking at the history of the British Empire, but if you just take a look..." Miss McEvoy was once again interrupted as Mr. Little's face lit up as if he'd just received the best present imaginable.

"Ah well there you are then! Once again this boy is flouting the school rules and not doing what he should; thank you Miss McEvoy that will be all."

"But...." Ray looked at the shock and pain etched on his teacher's face and actually felt sorry for her as he saw tears in her eyes as she mouthed "I'm so sorry" before obediently leaving the office; but rebelling ever so slightly by slamming the door behind her.

"Right, where were we?" Oh yes, assume the position Dagnall." He then proceeded to beat him with relish.

Ray didn't feel resentful as he left the office rubbing his sore behind. In the big scheme of things there were plenty of times he'd caused all sorts of mischief and not been caught. He therefore treated today's injustice as the universe's way of balancing things out.

However, he vowed to keep any other talents he had

well and truly hidden if this was the result of bringing them out into the open.

Chapter 14 - The Gang

His life became a daily torture of boredom and polite rebuttals of Miss McEvoy's varied attempts to engage him in some sort of learning. She tried cajoling, threatening and even blackmailing and bribery in her ever more desperate strategy to stimulate him. To be fair, Ray sometimes found these tactics quite enjoyable, but never enough to sustain his interest beyond one or two days. He yearned for the hands of the clock to work their way around to the golden hour of 3:00 pm, which would mark his release. He was usually out of from his desk and through the door before Miss McEvoy had reached the first 'S' of 'Dismissed'. He'd then run as fast as his legs would carry him beyond the school premises and wait for his mates to catch him up.

His gang had grown somewhat over the months he'd been living in Clavelle Road. In addition to Ray, Blainsey and Ian, there was now Johnny and Jimmy Featherston whose father worked with Ray's dad down at the docks and who had been gassed whilst he fought in the trenches during the Great War. He was fine most of the time, but on occasion, he could literally drop down onto the floor without any warning and start twitching uncontrollably. The first time Ray witnessed this, he was left shocked and somewhat unnerved by the casual attitude displayed by his two friends as they stepped over their father's gyrating body and continued with whatever they were doing as if he wasn't there at all. However, after he'd experienced this on several different occasions, he too became rather flippant; and their father seemed none the worse when he eventually came back to his senses.

Another aspect to note regarding the twins was the habit their mother had of not allowing them to use the outside loo during winter months as she thought the cold would be bad for their digestive system. Often were the times Ray would accompany them home after school, only to have them disappear behind the sofa where two warm potties waited. Ray found it hilarious to watch their two faces resting on the back of the sofa as they squeezed in unison to empty their bowels.

If Blainsey was the natural leader of the gang, the most talented was undoubtedly Mousey Johnson. He was only a small boy, hence the nickname, but he was brilliant at everything he did. He was by far the best runner, the best footballer and the best thrower of a stone or ball. He could also do amazing things with a piece of wood. He'd sit for hours in one of the comfy chairs at their base, whittling away with his knife and a block of wood he found in the park. At the end of his endeavours there would appear as if by magic, a life like depiction of a bird or a dog or even a tank or ship or plane. Ray looked up to Mousey (or rather down), as he respected his talent enormously. He was also intelligent, quick witted and fearless. There was inevitable friction at times between Mousey and Blainsey for Blainsey resented Mousey's natural talent. However, Mousey would never back down even though Blainsey could batter him. Instead he would deflect Blainsey's aggression onto a rival gang or teacher and Blainsey would go off like a bull that had been shown red, to cause havoc and mayhem as he wreaked his retribution on them.

Lionel Henry was a member of the gang who'd been inadvertently recruited by Ian after a camping accident. Lionel lived just around the corner from Ray and Ian and one day had decided to set up a tent on the large grass verge that ran alongside the tram tracks on Mather Avenue; one of the main thoroughfares leading towards the city centre. He'd erected the main structure and had gone inside to secure the poles and sort out the ground sheet when Ray and Ian came along. Ian decided to lend a hand and hammer the tent pegs into the ground. However, he failed to let Lionel know he was going to do this and as he brought the mallet down onto the peg that was situated in front of the entrance, Lionel popped his head out to see what was going on and met the full force of the downward blow. The sound of the impact made Ray feel sick, as did the way that Lionel slumped to the ground unconscious.

However, when he came round he didn't seem any the worse for wear, other than a large egg shaped lump on his forehead. He also saw the funny side straight away, which made him a most suitable addition to their gang.

The last member of the gang was Obie Macintosh who was a large, affable child who didn't mind being the butt of jokes and could usually give as good as he received due to his quick wit and imagination.

On one occasion Blainsey thought it would be funny, as well as strategic, to set fire to a clump of bushes where Obie was hiding during one of their games of war. The gang had split up into two sides and it was the aim of one side to avoid capture by the other. The only difference between this and hide and seek was the fact that in hide and seek you didn't get tortured. In this game if you got found, it would result in you being 'interrogated' in order to ascertain the whereabouts of your comrades. Blainsey took great pleasure in punching you very hard to give you dead legs or arms and if you could withstand this form of punishment, he'd often resort to wedgies, which gave him much fun whilst the victim writhed in agony.

On this particular occasion Obie was the final member of the opposition still avoiding capture and Blainsey was losing patience with his opponent. "Obie, we know you're hiding in these bushes." He yelled so as to make sure Obie could hear him. "If you don't show yourself in five seconds, I'm going to set them on fire."

Nobody truly believed he'd go through with his threat as he counted down from five, but no sooner had he reached one he pulled a box of matches out of his pocket, struck two together and dropped them into the very dry vegetation. Ray was sure Blainsey didn't intend to kill Obie, but as soon as the flames licked at the dry scrub, an inferno leapt up suddenly forcing Blainsey to leap back.

"Obie, get out there quick you idiot; the whole bush is on fire!" He screamed into the flames, which grew higher and higher. No sound came from the bush except the crackle and spit of the flames as they crept swiftly across the field consuming everything in their path including the space where Ray knew Obie had been hiding.

Mousey attempted to breach the flames to see if he could save him, but was quickly beaten back. When they realised there was no hope, they were horrified and overcome by panic; they ran. Nobody made a conscious decision to run; it was as if their muscles were beyond their control. One minute they were stood screaming into the flames, the next they were hurtling through the trees towards the park's exit, tears streaming down their cheeks. Whether from the smoke or from the grief of killing their friend nobody would say.

"What the ruddy hell are we going to do?" Ray asked having regrouped with his remaining friends at the bottom of the road that led to Obie's house.

"Why do you have to be such a bleeding psycho Blainsey; you didn't need to set the whole place on fire!?" Mousey had actually fronted up to their leader and even though he was much smaller, stood with his fists clenched ready to fight.

"I didn't mean to kill the bugger; I just meant to flush him out!" It wasn't much of a defence and it showed on the faces of the rest of the gang. "Anyway why didn't you stop me?"

"Because we didn't think you'd be ruddy stupid enough to go through with it!" Mousey yelled incredulously.

"There's no point in arguing amongst ourselves, we need to decide what we're going to do." Ray felt sick to the core of his being, but knew they needed to decide on a course of action.

"We'll have to go and tell his parents." Ian announced with a look of anguish. There was silence as they reflected on the impact the news would have. Obie's parents were devoted to him and they were quite sure the news would destroy them.

"You're right Ian, but Blainsey has got to be the one who does the talking. After all, he's the one who bleeding killed him!" Mousey gave Blainsey a look of disdain and turned away.

"Alright I will, but you lot have got to come with me because I'm not going on my own."

It was therefore with a great deal of anguish and trepidation that the gang traipsed up the path to Obie's house leaving Blainsey to knock on the door. When Obie's mother opened it and smiled at the boys, they felt foully guilty and Lionel started to cry. It broke their hearts to think what the news of her son's death would do to her. As Blainsey opened his mouth to speak, Obie's mum interrupted.

"I'm sorry boys; Owen can't come out at the moment, he's about to have his tea."

The boys looked at one another in confusion. How could Obie be about to eat his tea when they knew he'd never be eating his tea, breakfast, lunch or any snacks in between ever again; because Obie was dead; burned to a crisp in the nearby park.

"He'll be out in about an hour after his food has gone down." The way she said it made her sound as though she never had a care in the world.

Ray was about to scream at her that her son was dead when he saw the curtain twitch and there, standing as bold as brass in the window, was Obie looking rather smug and definitely not burned to a crisp.

"I got bored hiding so came home." He mouthed through the window. "Did we win?"

Blainsey was so relieved he almost collapsed onto the floor, only being stopped by Ray who put a supportive arm around his shoulder. "Ok Mrs. Macintosh, we'll see Obie later."

With that she closed the door and left the boys to laugh and clap each other on the back as Blainsey just stood and pointed at Obie in the window. From the look on his face, Obie was a little confused and rather unnerved by what Blainsey was doing, but his mother came to drag him away for tea leaving the boys to celebrate their lucky escape.

Chapter 15 – Choir and Clogs

Ray was not left up to his own devices all of the time however; there were still routines to which he had to adhere. The following Sunday morning, he was informed they would be travelling once again to New Brighton for a church service on the beach. It had been many months since he'd travelled into the city; let alone cross the Mersey, so he was excited as they headed down to Mather Avenue where they could catch a tram to the Pier Head. The journey though, turned out very different than when he'd taken it the year before, and became quite a harrowing experience. He'd already witnessed firsthand the damage caused by the bombing so didn't believe he could be shocked by the aftermath of what was becoming known as the 'May Blitz'. However, the closer they travelled into the city centre; the magnitude of the devastation became far more apparent, and it felt overwhelming. There were piles of rubble where there had once been communities and in places buildings had literally been raised to the ground leaving only a vague imprint of where people had once lived and worked.

As he looked out of the window he heard a loud sniff and looked up in surprise to see his mother quietly crying into her handkerchief. This unnerved him somewhat as he'd rarely seen her cry; even when her own mother had died. He decided to save her embarrassment by focusing even harder on the view from the window and noticed that even though it was a Sunday, men and women were crawling like ants over the rubble working tirelessly to create some sort of order out of chaos. Trucks lined up to be filled with debris and men and women rummaged through the remains of buildings to find salvageable bricks ready to be used again when the city would be reborn.

Practically every building had been damaged in some way but as they got off the tram in the middle of Liverpool, Ray realised that shops were still doing business and would be open the next day as usual. The people too, were something to behold. Despite the horror that had descended from above, they seemed to be going about their lives as if nothing had happened. In fact if anything, he thought most people seemed more animated than ever. Everywhere he turned he saw people smiling or laughing, sharing banter between friends and strangers alike.

"Why does everyone look so happy when they've lost everything?" He asked his father as they watched an old man throw a shop room dummy onto a pile of rubbish.

"I'm not sure Ray; maybe it's just the way we scousers are."

It felt to Ray as if it was more than that. "Do you reckon it's got something to do with what me Ma said a few weeks ago about not giving in to Hitler?"

His father looked at him mildly confused.

"I mean if you look at everyone, they seem to have made the decision to try harder than ever to be jolly so they can show Hitler that our morale will never be destroyed."

John looked at his son with admiration. "You know what Ray; you don't half surprise me sometimes." He then looked around and added. "I think you're right, but look around as well." He gestured in a sweeping motion, which took in the alien landscape. "Just imagine; if you'd lived through this level of destruction, you'd be pretty happy just to be alive."

Ray looked at his dad with wonder as this wisdom made such sense. He began to smile because he too had survived the blitz; had good mates and a loving family. In fact he was very happy to be alive as well. As they walked along he looked up at his father "You know what dad; you don't half surprise me sometimes as well."

When they reached the Pier Head there was still the inevitable queue waiting to board the ferry, but there were noticeably less people and Ray didn't need to practise his statue skills as they headed towards the landing stage. Having seen what had happened to Liverpool, he supposed people were just too busy trying to rebuild their shattered lives to spare the time to enjoy the sunshine or take a stroll down the promenade. There were a number of couples who appeared to be relaxing, but it was clear from their uniforms that these were servicemen and women making the most of their leave before returning to wherever they were stationed.

When they finally arrived at the service area there were people already gathered, but again, less than normal. Even before they'd found a place to stand, the minister came over.

"Ah Olive, as you can see we are rather short of people to sing in the choir so I was wondering if you would be so kind as to oblige?"

Olive loved the idea of having responsibility within the church and had in fact, led the choir and played the organ up until Enid had been born; she therefore agreed with alacrity. However, she also volunteered Ray's services, which did not go down well with him at all.

"Ah eh Ma, I'm not singing in no choir; my voice is so bad I don't even sing in the bath!" His moaning had little effect on Olive who merely grabbed him by the arm and dragged him across the sand to where a handful of others were warming up ready to lead the congregation. "I'm not singing Ma!"

"Enough Raymond; you sing each week at our church service so this is no different, you will just be at the front!"

"But I don't sing. I just open me mouth and mime the words."

Olive gave him 'the look' before whispering through tight lips. "Raymond, you are going to sing in this choir and that is that! I don't want to hear any more about it. Is that understood?!" She then let go of his arm and went to talk to some of her cronies.

Ray contemplated giving her the slip and sneaking away to hide somewhere but he realised that if he did, he may as well run away permanently because when his mother found him, his life wouldn't be worth living. Had he been a couple of years older, a life at sea would have been a real option as he was sure there must be at least one ship who'd take on a lad who was prepared to work hard and who was too afraid to ever step foot in Liverpool again. The simple fact though, was that he wasn't old enough. He therefore capitulated with ill grace and stood sullenly in the front row, opening his mouth, but only making a sound when he felt his mother's elbow nudged him sharply in the ribs. With each nudge, the desire to join the navy as a stowaway grew.

At the end of the service the minister was so delighted with how things had gone, he begged Olive to rejoin the choir permanently. She was so thrilled to be asked, she agreed immediately and whether out of a true desire to spend more time with her son or as a punishment for giving cheek, she also volunteered his services, which the minister readily accepted. During the journey home those feelings of being happy to be alive he'd felt as they boarded the ferry to New Brighton, had diminished dramatically.

Luckily for Ray, or so he thought, Olive made the decision to join a new parish only a couple of weeks later. All Souls was only round the corner from where they lived, so she felt it would make it easier for her to worship and cope with a one year old. However, on the first Sunday they attended, she offered her services to the choir and insisted that Ray join her. He therefore spent week after excruciating week standing in his cassock deliberately singing out of tune in the hope that the choirmaster would ask him to leave; but he never did.

Ray deduced there could only be two possible answers as to why not; either their choirmaster was tone deaf, which was a strong possibility given the atrocious sound the choir normally produced; or his mother was bribing him in some way in order to torture her son by making him sing each week. This was also quite possible as he was sure his mother would go to any length to keep him involved in the Sunday service. Either way, he began to dread Sunday morning with a passion.

In the end it wasn't Ray's ingenuity that ended his

weekly torture, but the Canadian Red Cross. The war had now entered its third year and whilst people had become used to the scarcity of items of basic goods and accepted it as a way of life, it was still not easy on a day to day basis. Food was hard to come by and even items such as bread and milk needed to be savoured and cherished. There was certainly no waste in the Dagnall house particularly since they'd lost most of their belongings when they were bombed out. This left Ray wearing pants with patches on the patches and shoes with cardboard insoles to cover the holes in the bottom. Being nine years of age, he was also growing apace so what clothes he did have, were invariably too small.

There was therefore a good deal of excitement when John arrived home one day with a large parcel, which had come from the Canadian Red Cross.

"It's not Christmas is it?" Olive joked as the whole family, including Joe's lot, who were still with them after nearly a year, gathered around the kitchen table as she cut the string and neatly wound it up to be used again. As she opened the package it did indeed feel like Christmas all over again. There were tinned fruit, tinned potatoes, some soap and a variety of other treasures. At the bottom of the package there was a pair of red wooden clogs, which Ray thought were the best shoes he'd ever seen.

"Oh my word, they are brilliant!" he exclaimed as he lifted them out of the box. "Do you reckon they'll fit me?" He quickly pulled his tattered shoes from his feet and hurled them into a corner before trying on the clogs.

To be fair, he'd always had a weird sense of fashion; particularly when it came to footwear, so it came as no surprise that he pounced so quickly upon the garish item before anybody else could claim them. "Wow Ma, how cool do I look?!"He said as he admired himself in the mirror. He had on a green jumper that was two sizes too big, which he'd been told he'd 'grow into'; a newish pair of black short pants with no patches; knee length grey socks and now the bright red clogs. As he clomped up and down the hall, his mother smiled indulgently. If he was happy, who was she to disillusion him by telling him he looked awful.

"They look wonderful Raymond; just make sure you look after them."

"Too right I will Ma; you don't have to worry about that!"

The following Sunday, dressed in his best clothes; which naturally included his new pants and clogs, Ray made his way to church. His mother had drawn the line at the green jumper and persuaded him he'd be too warm if he wore that on top of his blue shirt. He therefore headed off feeling very dapper indeed.

All Souls was a large church on the corner of Mather Avenue, with a marble floor throughout. As he stepped foot inside the doors the clogs rang out as he clip clopped towards the choir stalls, occasionally skidding as he slipped on the shiny surface. The noise echoed around the vaulted ceiling bringing the choir to a halt as they warmed up. As the choirmaster turned round, his mouth dropped open as he took in Ray's new shoes.

"In the name of God Dagnall, what are you wearing?!"

Ray was delighted his clogs had been noticed and offered a little exhibition up and down as he put on his cassock. "They're my shoes I got off the Red Cross, aren't they brilliant?!" He was oblivious to the sniggers from the rest of the choir as he made his way into position and stood glimpsing down at his shoes when he thought no one else was watching. As the service started and the choir began to sing the entrance hymn he began to tap out the rhythm in an attempt at keeping pace with the song. This was nothing new as he was rarely able to keep pace with the organ and was always slightly out of time. However, on this occasion his new footwear made a loud 'clack' every time he brought his foot down resulting in mild chaos with the rest of the choir and congregation. The Vicar was glaring at the choirmaster and the choirmaster was glaring at Ray who was oblivious to it all, merrily clacking as he concentrated furiously on his out of time rhythm and his out of tune voice.

At the end of the song the choirmaster made his way over to where he sat. "Raymond, can you please refrain from tapping your feet; it is most off putting." He said in a terse whisper.

"But I can't help it; I have to tap to try and keep up."

"I don't care, just stop it!"

The choirmaster didn't seem to realise that the gesture was instinctive and so the second hymn was no better than the first and perhaps even worse as Ray tried harder to keep in time following the criticism, and therefore tapped harder and fell further behind in the rhythm.

By the time the offertory hymn came around the two people on either side of Ray had been instructed to stand on his feet; however, when it came to a competition between soft leather and wood, wood won out. By the first chorus the clacks were back and the two foot guards were feverishly trying to regain their dominance by stamping on Ray's feet, which annoyed him somewhat and resulted in the three of them scuffling throughout verses three and four.

"Will you get off me and leave me alone!" he cried as they grabbed him by the arms and tried to wrestle him to the floor.

"The choirmaster told us to stop you, it's not our fault!"

The Vicar was outraged and tutted loudly, shaking his head and shifting from foot to foot in his agitation, which caused the choirmaster to collapse in floods of tears as the three choristers, rolled around in the aisle quietly cursing each other and trying to sing at the same time.

At the end of the service the choirmaster dragged Ray to one side. "I *never* want to see you in my choir stall again Dagnall; is that understood?!"

"Absolutely choirmaster, does that mean you don't want me to sing in the choir as well?" He didn't realise he was being facetious, but the choirmaster rolled his eyes.

"Get out of my sight you insolent boy!"

It was therefore with a high degree of elation, that Ray clomped his way down the aisle and out into the sunlight; leaving vivid scratches in the marble and the vicar with his head in his hands as the choirmaster tried to console him.

Chapter 16 – Yanks and Eyeties

Ray really wanted to join the Boys Brigade but knew he'd have to wait at least two years until he was eleven. He therefore made do with sitting next to his mother each Sunday, imagining he was a member of the brigade, but instead of playing drums and bugles, they'd go on secret missions behind enemy lines to capture Hitler, defeat the Nazis and bring peace to the world. The violence of these day dreams was not particularly religious, but the aim was to bring world peace, so he was sure God wouldn't mind.

One Sunday, shortly after returning home from church, he was allowed to go off and play with his mates. His mother had taken Enid to Sydnah's and his dad had gone to a training session with a football team made up of his mates down at the docks, which he'd recently started coaching. Ray was really quite proud of this and would often throw into conversations that his dad was a part time football manager.

"I've got a few hours until my Dad comes back from coaching his football team so what shall we do?"

"Daggers we were impressed about your dad managing a football team the first eight times you told us, but it's starting to wear a bit thin now." Mousey said as he gave Ray a dig and the others laughed.

"Yeah, but that's where he is so I've got the whole afternoon free" he said rubbing his arm. "So let's do something different for a change."

As they sat ruminating on how they would spend their time, the Featherston twins started to argue. "I'm telling you they were Germans." Jimmy said as he punched his brother on the arm.

"And I'm telling you they were ruddy Italians." Johnny said as he returned the favour twice as hard on Jimmy's leg.

"What are you two arguing about?" Blainsey wasn't the most patient of people and wasn't in the mood for bickering. He therefore went over and knocked the two boys' heads together.

"Ouch! We saw a load of prisoners of war being escorted to the camp in Speke the other day and I reckon they were Germans and he's saying they were Eyeties, but I reckon I'm right; they were definitely Germans."

"They were Eyeties!" His brother responded.

"Pack it in the pair of you!" Blainsey warned. "Whatever they were, I reckon I know what we can do with our afternoon. Why don't we go down and see if we can't get close to the camp; you never know we might be able to speak to them."

This idea was met with general approval so they set off on the half hour walk to Speke in order to find the camp.

However, they covered the distance in a fraction of

the time by having races between each other and pretending they were Hurricanes and Spitfires versus German bombers and ME 109's. As they ran down the streets towards the camp they made a right racket and caused several residents to come out of their houses to see what was happening before cursing the boys and telling them to keep the ruddy noise down.

As they neared the end of Mather Avenue there was suddenly an even louder noise in the shape of a low rumble from the road behind them. As he turned, Ray saw three large trucks with white stars on the bonnet and sides that marked them as Americans. He knew that troops had been pouring into Britain since the Japanese had bombed somewhere called Pearl Harbour, but he'd yet to see any. As the boys stood and gawped, the lead truck pulled up as it came along side them and a soldier poked his head out of the window.

"Can you guys tell me how to get to the airfield?"

Now Ray had seen the many posters that had been adorned on buildings and walls all over the place teaching the lesson that "Careless talk costs lives" so reckoned they should keep the whereabouts of any military installation secret. "I'm sorry mister, but for all we know you could be German spies dropped by parachute with the sole purpose of wreaking havoc and attacking bases; you'll have to find your own way."

He thought he was doing the sensible thing, which

would gain the approval of his mates and a few pats on the back. Instead he received several digs to his arms and Blainsey pushed him to the back of the group.

"Don't listen to him Sarge, he's just messin' about. We're going in the same direction so if you give us a lift, we'll show you." Ray was outraged that the others were prepared to pass on information that could potentially lead to sabotage. The airfield was the base for a squadron of Hurricane fighters as well as being the launch pad for brand new planes as they came off the production line of the nearby Routes factory.

"Wait a minute, what if these are Germans dressed as Americans; I've heard they did something similar in Poland just before the war started." He pleaded as his mates looked at him as if he were mad. "What if they're about to attack the base as part of a full blown invasion" He looked frantically up into the sky to see if he could see any enemy planes or parachutes.

"Daggers, have you gone ruddy daft or what?" Ian said as he grabbed him by the collar and dragged him towards the truck. "I think we'd know if they were about to launch the invasion and I reckon there would be more than three trucks!" He then unceremoniously kicked Ray up the bum and forced him into the back of the truck whilst Blainsey gave directions from the cabin.

As he was helped up into the back by one of the

American soldiers, he realised he may have got a bit carried away with his accusations as it wasn't packed with enemy troops armed to the teeth; there were just three men and a number of crates and they didn't even have any weapons. As he settled down on a bench, he listened as his friends fired questions at the yanks.

"So where are you from mister?" "Have you met Hop Along Cassidy?" "Do you know Flash Gordon?" "What's it like over there, do you have trees and grass; and does it snow in winter?"

The Americans must have felt as if they were under attack as they looked at each other in shock. "Whoa, hold up a minute guys", the eldest of the three said. "What's with the interrogation? We're just three normal fellas from New York. Here have some candy." He then rummaged in his pocket and brought out a huge bar of American chocolate for the boys to share.

"Wow, thanks mister, but we don't call it candy, we call it chocolate."

Whatever they called it, the chocolate did the trick for the Americans as the boys sat quietly whilst they devoured the sweet taste of something they'd not had in several years. After the truck dropped them off near the airfield, they sat on the grass verge savouring the taste and taking the mickey out of Ray for being far too sensible. Ray believed he deserved their wisecracks as, with hindsight, he must have sounded like a right

Wally.

When they got to the site, they were surprised to discover that whilst there were obviously fences, barbed wire and guards, the prisoners were actually free to wander around. Ray had pictured a prisoner of war camp being something like what he'd experienced when he'd had to sleep in the cell at the police station. In his mind the prisoners would be locked behind bars and he'd been prepared to have to spend ages just trying to spot one. He wasn't expecting this at all.

"Why aren't they locked away? They could easily escape from that." He said as a group of prisoners appeared to wander right up to the fence.

There were a number of wooden huts that housed the prisoners and there were also several guard towers scattered around the perimeter, but the prisoners seemed to be allowed to go where they liked.

"What's got into you today Daggers, the fact that they're not locked up means we can get to speak to them." Blainsey said as he gave Ray yet another dig. "Come on lets go."

As the boys got closer, Ian who was probably the cleverest of them all noticed the prisoners weren't even German. "You were right Johnny, they're Italians."

Johnny gave his brother a kick up the bum. "See I told you; that will be two pieces of shrapnel you owe me."

As they neared the fence they could see the Italians laughing and joking, which proved to be another surprise as they'd expected them to be quite miserable given that they were prisoners and all. One of them even beckoned the boys over for a chat.

"Little men, you come here no?" he said, gesturing for them to approach the fence. They were rather reluctant even though it had been the purpose of their journey.

"Come on you ruddy wimps, what are you waiting for?!" Blainsey said as he took the bull by the horns and strode over to where the Italian stood. It was obvious he wanted to show the prisoner who was the boss so he asked quite aggressively; "What do you want?"

The Italian didn't seem to take offense and replied smiling. "You have a cigarette? I give you great gift if you have cigarette." He pulled out a wooden box, which had been hand carved by the soldier or one of his friends. It was exquisitely finished off and would make an ideal present for a mother or grandmother. The problem was none of them smoked; they were in the process of shaking their heads when Blainsey amazed them all by pulling a packet of twenty cigarettes out of his pocket and went to offer one to the Italian.

"Here you are then. I'll give you one of these fags

for the wooden box." He held the cigarette out to the soldier just out of reach.

"Ah no, I sorry but I would need more than one in exchange for such lovely box. I make it with own hands."

Blainsey proceeded to barter with the Italian, eventually agreeing on six cigarettes in exchange for the box. It turned out to be made from a crate, which had contained fruit.

"What have you done with the fruit that was in the box?" he asked cheekily.

"Ah, we still have some, see I show you." The Italian then produced an orange from his pocket. "You like?"

"I do indeed like. I'll tell you what; I'll throw in another two fags if you let us have the orange as well."

The Italian agreed and as Blainsey shared out the fruit with his mates, Ray reckoned the orange was worth the whole packet of fags. It had been over two years since he'd tasted one, and as he savoured his segment, sucking out the juice before chewing the pith, he remembered how he'd taken for granted the 'gifts' his uncle Walt had thrown from his passing train on a Saturday afternoon.

"Where did you get the fags Blainsey, I didn't know you smoked?"

"I pinched them of my dad." He said as he spat out

a pip. "I don't smoke, but you never know when they might come in handy. I've heard that fags are as good as money to some people, and it would appear to be true."

"Where did you hear that?" Mousey asked a little sceptically.

"I overheard me dad talking about it to his mate." Blainsy's dad, along with Obie's and Lionel's were all sergeants in the police so usually had all sorts of secret information their sons picked up on one way or another.

Over the next hour, each boy was given a ration of cigarettes for them to barter with the prisoners. They came away with several cap badges, a couple of buttons and best of all; another orange. Ray thought it strange and a little unfair that enemy prisoners actually seemed better off in terms of luxuries than the people they were fighting against.

Chapter 17 – Fame via a Banana

However, just a few weeks later it was Ray who was in receipt of a piece of fruit that was to be the envy of his entire school. Since the raids on Liverpool had stopped shortly after Christmas 1942, it was becoming harder and harder to find shrapnel. He'd therefore persuaded Ian and Mousey to accompany him to his old haunts around Wavertree in order to hunt down what were now becoming a rare commodity, and therefore a prized currency.

As they rounded the corner into Colinton Street, it felt strange for him to see his old school. He heard that it had recently reopened and he wondered how many of his old friends were still around. As he looked on the remains of where he once lived, a memory of a particular raid emerged and he began to feel a throb of excitement as he recalled the night the Germans had machine gunned the RAF crew and realised that he'd never got round to searching for the bullets.

"Ruddy hell, I've just remembered something. Listen; look out for any craters in the brick work at the end of the building while I go and see if there's any evidence in the concrete of the shelter in the alley at the back."

"Evidence of what Daggers; you haven't told us what we're meant to be looking for?"

"Bullets boys, we're looking for bullets! Remember

me telling you about the Nazis machine gunning us as we ran into the shelter? Well I never got the chance to search for any pieces of the bullets!"

The boys threw themselves into their task, as German bullets would indeed be prized possessions, but after an hour of false alarms and cut fingers due to them scouring every blemish to bricks and concrete, they were about to give up and go home. Suddenly Mousey pointed at the end of the house that backed on to where Ray used to live.

"Wow, would you look at that!" High up on the gable end there was a neat line of three clear holes. "They have got to be bullet holes."

As the boys stared, trying to ascertain if Mousey was right, they began to feel rather frustrated. "They're too high to be able to tell. Even if they were, how do we get up there to dig them out?" Ian said as he shared what the others were thinking.

However, as always, Mousey had a solution. "Look, you and Ray stand and put your arms against the wall and I'll climb up and stand on your shoulders. I'll easily be able to reach and the base that you two create should be secure enough as my weight will be balanced out."

Ray was always astounded by Mousey's ability to come up with practical solutions to problems. He never seemed to pay much attention in class and he was pretty sure he never read books or anything. It was therefore a mystery as to how he always came up with such amazing ideas.

Ray and Ian quickly made the base and Mousey clambered up on their shoulders. Within minutes he'd managed to dig three pieces of squashed metal out of the wall, which resembled bullets just enough to be lauded as treasure and meant the three boys journeyed home feeling most satisfied with their endeavours.

As he walked through the door, Ray had every intention of sharing his find with his family, but no sooner had he stepped foot across the threshold, he was summoned to the kitchen table.

"Raymond get in here!" His mother yelled from the kitchen. He was convinced he was in trouble for sneaking off back to Wavertree, but then realised his mother didn't know that's where he'd been. He then supposed she must have been frantically searching for him, meaning he was probably in for a good hiding, no tea and yet another grounding. However, he then thought of what reason she would have to look for him; he wasn't late; he couldn't recall doing anything wrong in the last day or so. As he made his way down the hall towards the kitchen, he was therefore filled with confusion and trepidation.

"At last, we've been waiting for you for ages!" his mother announced as he made his way to the table and sat down next to Joe and Dolly. "Your father refused to show us what he's brought until you arrived."

It was only then that he realised the atmosphere around the table was not one of tension, but one of excitement.

"What's going on dad?" he asked as his father came into the room and sat down in his place at the head of the table. He did so solemnly, with a large brown paper bag in front of him. All focus was drawn to the bag and there was silence as he opened the proceedings.

"When we were in work today, Joe and I received a request to help unload a cargo ship as there weren't enough men and there was a large convoy that had arrived." This was not a new occurrence as he'd been asked on several occasions to lend a hand when the number of ships arriving at the docks left them shorthanded.

"What's that got to do with the brown bag in front of you though?"

"In repayment for our labour, we were each given a bag of these." John then pulled out a bunch of six small yellow pieces of fruit that were slightly green at each end and had a hint of a curve to them. Ray had never seen a banana, let alone one like this.

"What is it?"

"It's a banana Raymond." His mother interjected. "You eat it."

As he stared at the fruit a multitude of questions swam through his brain. After his father passed him one, he was about to take a bite when his mother intervened.

"Not like that Raymond, you have to peel the skin off like an orange." She showed him how to do it, leaving him drooling in anticipation of his first taste. The reality lived up to his expectations and he relished the slight crunch followed by the softness of the texture. The taste was slightly alien but it wasn't unpleasant and he decided he could quite easily grow to love this foreign fruit.

"Can I take one into school to show Miss McEvoy? He asked, hoping to perhaps make up for all the times he'd made her cry. "I think she'll be well impressed." He didn't expect his mother to agree as the fruit was such a precious commodity.

"If I let you take one in, you'd better look after it; I mean it Raymond, if you damage that banana your life won't be worth living!" She then wrapped it carefully in newspaper. "Not even one blemish to the skin!"

As he left the house; banana in hand, he felt such a huge weight of responsibility that he kept looking over his shoulder in case there was hidden assailants ready to steal his cargo. He was still amazed his mother had agreed, and now part of him wished she hadn't. He deduced she must have been pleased he was showing an interest in school for a change, but he felt sick with nervous tension that he'd somehow damage it. When Ian jumped out from behind the hedge in his front garden, he jumped a foot in the air.

"What the ruddy hell are you playing at you blithering idiot; I nearly had a heart attack then!"

"Ian was rather taken aback by his friend's aggressiveness. "You obviously got out of bed on the wrong side; what's up?"

"I'm taking this in to show Miss McEvoy, but me Ma said if I damage it in any way I'm as good as dead."

Ian looked at the parcel clutched possessively to Ray's chest. "What is it?"

"I'm not going to tell you because you'll want to look at it and there's no way I'm taking it out until I'm safely in class. You know what the big kids are like round here; if they see it they'll rob it!"

Ian was confused and intrigued at the same time. The two of them shared everything, including secrets and the contents of mysterious packages. "Oh come on Daggers; just tell me what it is then."

"No!"

Ian looked hurt and on the verge of tears by his mate's attitude, causing Ray to capitulate. "Bleeding hell, if I tell you, you have to swear not to breathe a word to anyone else until we're in class."

"Bloody, shit, crap!" Ian said immediately. Ray had shared the secret about the railway signals with Ian shortly after they became friends and he'd found it hilarious when he heard of how Ray had used the swear words to seal the bargain; they had used the same declaration ever since when they wanted each other to keep something confidential.

"It's a banana!"

"You're kidding?"

"No of course I'm not!" he was still rather tetchy, but told of how his father came into possession of the fruit.

By the time he got to school he was still a nervous wreck. He wouldn't play football, and when Blainsey tried to take his bag to use as a goalpost, he turned on him.

"Get away from my bag! You come any nearer and I'll...."

"You'll what Daggers?" Blainsey said as he inched closer.

"I'll ruddy well run away!" He was as good as his word and headed towards the toilets where he hid until it was time to go to class.

As he stepped foot through the threshold it was like the weight of the world had been lifted from his shoulders and he started to relax. He waited until everyone was seated before putting his hand up.

"What is it Raymond. Do you want the toilet? You really should have gone before you came in." Miss McEvoy had obviously been taking lessons off Mr. Little on how to ask a question and then not wait for a reply before answering it herself. Ray reached the conclusion it must be part of the training you received in order to become a teacher, but he found it really quite annoying.

"No miss, I've got something to show you." A fleeting look of anguish, followed by fear, then surprise and then intrigue crossed the teacher's face. She had dealt with Ray's practical jokes for long enough to be wary of an artefact he wished to show.

"Is it another piece of shrapnel Raymond? I've seen enough shrapnel to last me a life time so you just leave it in your bag and show your friends later. Now I'd like you to ...."

He was becoming a little frustrated and the trauma of getting the fruit to school safely finally spilled over.

"No miss!" He yelled at his teacher. Even in his own ears he sounded harsh, but he wasn't prepared to be fobbed off after everything he'd gone through to bring the fruit in. "I have something far better than shrapnel!"

There was silence in the room as everybody looked at Ray. Many stared at him because he wasn't the type of person to be so insolent to a teacher and they were surprised at this show of assertiveness. The rest stared at him because, for him to say that shrapnel was less important than whatever he had in his bag was a huge deal. His mates gawped open mouthed, not quite believing what they'd just heard.

"I have this!" He pulled the banana from out of the newspaper and held it aloft as if it was the legendary sword Excalibur. There were gasps of amazement from most of the girls and even Blainsey looked suitably impressed. "This is a fruit called a banana; my dad gave it to me so I could show you."

The reaction of his classmates nearly made up for the stress and tension of his journey into school, but the reaction of his teacher more than made up for it. "Oh Raymond, that is truly wonderful! Come out to the front and show everybody properly."

He wasn't sure if it was the banana that had sent his teacher into raptures or simply the fact he was showing a positive interest in something for a change. Whatever the reason, he basked in the glory of being the centre of attention as he moved around the room showing off his fruit and snatching it away if grubby hands tried to reach out and touch it.

"I think you should go and show Mr. Little; he will be thrilled!"

Now Ray could remember all too well how thrilled Mr. Little had been when he'd been sent to show him his picture, so wasn't particularly eager at the prospect now. "Do I have to Miss? The last time you sent me to show him something, I ended up getting the slipper."

Miss McEvoy looked guilty for a moment before brightening. "Don't worry Raymond I will accompany you." With that, she took him by the arm and led him out of class and down the corridor to Mr. Little's office.

Having her with him made it a lot easier to show Mr. Little the fruit and when he laid eyes on the yellow treasure, he was equally as impressed as everybody else.

"This is splendid Dagnall, just splendid! I don't recall having tasted a banana for many a year so I look forward to savouring this kind gift."

Ray must have given him a look of such disgust and horror that even Mr. Little paid attention. "What is it Dagnall, what's wrong?"

"I didn't bring the banana in for you to eat it. I just wanted to show it to people. My Ma would kill me if I went home without it, and you've met my Ma sir, you don't want to get on the wrong side of her."

Mr. Little visibly blanched at the thought of a confrontation with an irate Olive Dagnall striding into his office and grabbing him by the lapel. Ray could see in his eyes, he was perhaps envisaging her ripping off his false leg and beating him with it remorselessly.

"Er, perhaps you're right Dagnall! Never mind, why don't you keep hold of the banana and go around each of the classes to show the children what one looks like."

So Ray spent a most enjoyable morning traipsing from class to class showing off his banana. For days after he was something of a celebrity, repeatedly being asked to show it off and even being invited for tea to complete strangers so he might show members of their family. He revelled in the attention and so was rather disappointed when interest finally waned after about a week. By this time the bright yellow of the skin had begun to blemish quite badly and the skin had become rather soft in places. He eventually decided it was time to eat it so called his gang together in order to share the delicacy with them. As they gathered round to watch, he carefully peeled back the skin as he'd seen his mother do. However, the fruit within was not the light creamy colour of the other banana. Neither was the texture smooth. This monstrosity was a gooey mess of dark browns and black, which more or less fell apart once the skin was removed.

"Are you trying to tell me that's what all the fuss has been about?" Blainsey looked at the mess with disgust. "I wouldn't eat that if you paid me!" He gave Ray a dig on the arm and stalked out of the headquarters in a sulk. One after the other the rest of the gang left, leaving Ray alone to wonder what had happened to his gorgeous fruit. He tried eating the less gooey bits but it didn't taste half as nice as the earlier one he'd had and later that night as he sat on the loo with stomach cramps, he was left ruing the fact he'd not eaten it a lot earlier.

Chapter 18 – Rebellion and Misdemeanours

Now the threat from above had receded, new routines began to emerge. The blackout was still in place and Ray's father still went on patrol most evenings to ensure people adhered to it. Rationing too, still dominated daily life and Olive, along with most other women, spent hours each day standing in queues. Even though the Dagnalls had extra people staying with them and therefore additional rations, food was not always available in the shops, which proved very frustrating.

Another thing that was beginning to grate with Olive was the bad habits her lodgers had developed in the many months they'd now been staying with them. At first, they had been polite and helpful, mindful of causing offense and very aware they were living in someone else's house. Nearly two years later though, they treated Clavelle Road as their own. Gone was the courtesy given around the use of the bathroom and they had the most annoying habit of eating their evening meal and then falling asleep whilst sat in the comfy chairs with the radio on and the lights blazing away. They would then wake up in the early hours of the morning disturbing everyone else as they then got ready for bed and finally switched off the lights. They only paid three bob a week and were using more than this in electricity alone. Olive would have dearly liked to be rid of them but a combination of guilt at putting them out with nowhere else to go, and Johns insistence he wouldn't treat his friend so badly, meant she had to grit her teeth and put up with them. It meant however, she spent more and more time at Sydnah's with Enid, particularly when John was on duty. This left Ray free to run wild with his mates.

They would usually end up in the deserted mansion in the park, which they now made into a home away from home. They had candles for light in the winter, comfy chairs to sit on and they even had an indoor loo they could use, which they flushed by means of a mechanism Mousey had created for transporting the water from the tap to the cistern. From this base they roamed the rest of the park and demanded payment from any other kids they found. Ray believed they were like Robin Hood and his merry men; robbing from the rich to give to the poor. The fact they never passed on their ill gotten gains or the fact that the children who they took from were no better off than the boys themselves, seemed to have escaped him. He could not deny however, they definitely diverged from the path of Robin Hood when a rival gang decided to set up a base without paying their taxes. When this occurred, Blainsey would lead his gang and mount a raid to pull their opponents den apart, giving any members who were unlucky enough to be present, a roughing up to teach them a lesson. By adopting these strong arm tactics, their gang had become the dominant force in the area, enabling them to swagger around without fear of being picked on.

Some gangs did try it on of course, but other than Ray and Mousey, the rest of the gang were very big for their age and Blainsey was such a psychopath that when it came to a fight, they'd destroy their opposition. Their reputation was enhanced even further when, during a particularly nasty confrontation, Blainsey bit off the ear of the lad he was fighting and then chased after him trying to return the chunk of lobe he had removed with his teeth yelling;

"Don't run; come back and I'll give you your ear back. They might be able to sew it back on!" Blainsey was thoughtful in his own way!

They had several punishments, which they reserved for boys who were particularly annoying. One favourite was to pile on top of him and strip him down to his underwear before tying him to a tree; with a slight variation being to hang the lad by his arms with his feet barely touching the floor. The downside for Ray however, was that he always felt guilty, which meant he'd sneak back after all the others had left and release the victim; telling them that if they told anyone he'd released them he'd "get them".

Their wanton recklessness was curbed somewhat

after being caught by the park police and cautioned. The boys had been playing 'tag' near their base when a group of girls had started taunting them.

"Look at the big hard Blains gang playing 'tick'; how very grown up!" The other girls had fallen over themselves laughing at their leader's jest, which goaded her to go further. "Do you play with dolls and have imaginary tea parties as well?!" Again her friends burst out laughing, which was too much for Blainsey to take.

"Let's get them!" He yelled and charged towards where the girls stood. They screamed and ran off giggling in mock horror as the boys chased after them through the trees. The girls didn't stand much of a chance as the boys were used to this type of hunt. They split off into smaller groups and began herding the girls towards the public toilets at the far side of the park. Each time the girls tried to change direction, they'd find boys ready to grab them. By the time they reached the toilets their screams were therefore quite real.

They ran headlong into the sanctuary of the ladies toilets believing that no boy would dare to cross the threshold; but they hadn't counted on Blainsey who had no qualms whatsoever.

"You're not laughing now are you girls?" He said as he moved into the area by the sinks followed by the rest of his gang. "What have you got to say for yourselves now?"

The girls appeared to be genuinely terrified and several of them had started to cry so Ray, ever the romantic hero, stepped forward to try and stop his mate from taking it too far.

Look Blainsey, I reckon they've learned their lesson. Why don't we just let them go now?" There were nods of agreement from a couple of the others, but Blainsey hadn't finished having his fun.

"So have you learned your lesson girls?" He said as he turned on the taps and began washing his hands. The leader of the girls nodded furiously, too afraid her voice would crack if she tried to speak.

"I can't hear you ladies."

"Yes, yes we have and we're really sorry, we didn't mean to upset you, we won't say anything ever again." She then went to move towards the door, but as she neared Blainsey, he scooped a handful of water from the sink and soaked her.

"I'm afraid that's not good enough; soak them boys!" Reluctantly the rest of the gang splashed the girls until they were dripping from head to toe before leaving them alone and heading out of the toilets. Unfortunately for them, there were two park wardens passing as they emerged, who grabbed Blainsey before he had a chance to run.

"What the hell do you think you're doing in the

ladies toilets you young hooligans?!"

Before anybody had a chance to make up an answer the girls came out soaked and bedraggled and none too happy with Blainsey and his mates.

"Officer these horrid boys chased us across the park and then followed us into the ladies toilets!" The leader of the girls sobbed as she looked at her ruined dress. "They did it for no reason at all and then soaked us with water. My mum is going to kill me; I've only just got this dress." She wailed as the policeman scowled at Blainsey and his gang.

"Right you lot, you're in big trouble! You think you can do as you please and there will be no consequences. Well you're wrong; I'm telling you now, when you're sixteen you'll all be going to prison!"

This bit of news terrified the boys and they acted on instinct and ran. Ray's logic in running was that if he didn't get caught now, they couldn't possibly be sent to prison when they were sixteen as they didn't know who they were. However, his hopes were dashed when he heard the warden yelling after them. "I know who you all are and where you live; and I know your parents as well!"

For days afterwards, he dreaded every knock at the door expecting there to be police and the paddywagon; come to take him away. They'd broken the law and ran away from the policeman; two things you just didn't do. As days became weeks and the police still hadn't arrived on his doorstep, he began to relax a little, but the words kept coming back to haunt him when he least expected it.

"When you're sixteen you'll be going to prison." It got to the point where he vowed he would leave the country before he was sixteen, and so the next time the gang met he spoke up regarding his fears.

"Look lads, I reckon we need to calm down a bit; you know, the way we treat people in the park. If we're not careful we could end up getting into serious trouble."

Blainsey just laughed at him but there were a number of nods from the rest of the gang.

"Daggers is right Blainsey, we need to keep our heads down a bit and keep ourselves to ourselves. Those parkies meant business the other week; we can't afford to be causing any more trouble."

For once the gang stood up to him and Blainsey backed down, agreeing to leave the other kids alone. However, the other kids had different ideas a couple of days later when the gang were wandering in the park. They had come across a full blown military exercise involving the Home Guard. What looked like a whole battalion had split into opposing sides, identified by the red or blue armbands they wore. It became clear the red side had to try and attack the blue side's headquarters and capture their flag. The park was alive with the shouted commands of sergeants and officers and the percussion of the rifles and machine guns as they fired blanks at each other. The first 'bodies' Ray came across were a group from the blue team who were lounging around having a quiet fag and chat. The only indication they were actually casualties were the cardboard labels hung around their necks with 'Dead' written on them.

"Alright lads, have you seen any officers wearing blue armbands anywhere near here?" A particularly healthy looking corpse asked as he looked around furtively.

"Not really, there was a bloke over that way who was yelling at everyone, but he headed off in the opposite direction." Ray was pointing over towards a clump of trees on the far side of the clearing from where they were currently gathered.

"Oh that'll be Jonsey. If he's gone off that way, we may as well see if we can't sneak back to base. We may even be able to get a pint in before he realises we're gone. What do you say boys?"

The other corpses seemed to be in agreement and where about to leave when they were suddenly assaulted by a hail of pine cones, acorns and several stones. The next moment there came blood curdling screams from the tree line and a mass of small bodies hurtled towards them. In the seconds that Ray and the others stood frozen with shock, it became apparent it was not the soldiers who were the target for this attack, but Ray and his mates. As the gap between them closed rapidly, he recognised a number of faces and with a sense of dread realised that the gangs they'd terrorised over the past year must have joined together to make a super gang in order to take on Blainsey and co.

They were vastly outnumbered, and just before the two sides clashed, Ray noticed that the Home guard, who might have protected them, had beat a hasty retreat and were nowhere in sight. It occurred to him that if these grown men were prepared to run away from a bunch of kids, it didn't bode well if the Nazis ever did invade.

The gang put up a valiant defence with Blainsey going into berserker mode; throwing kids through the air and punching, kicking, biting and head butting anybody who came within his reach. The Featherston twins worked in tandem, fighting back to back; laying low a number of the opposition before they were overrun. Lionel, Ian, Obie, Mousey and Ray had formed a defensive circle and were just about managing to keep the enemy at bay, but they realised they wouldn't be able to last much longer. They didn't realise they'd made quite so many kids disgruntled. As one wave was beaten back, there was another to take their place. Ray estimated there must have been at least fifty in the field, with many more watching from a distance. The Featherston twins had already taken a good kicking before they managed to crawl and limp into the relative safety of the circle. It was Mousey who eventually came up with an escape plan.

"Look we're going to get battered if we stay here. We need to try and get back to base. After three, all scream as loud as you can and run at them; remember stick together."

He then counted to three and the gang screamed as one and for all they were worth before charging at the point where the enemy appeared smallest. They burst through having taken the boys opposite by surprise, and proceeded to run as fast as they could towards the mansion. Once safely inside they barricaded the entrance and then the Featherstons and Blainsey took to the upper floors to bombard their foe with pieces of masonry and slate from above. The rest of the gang guarded the entrance and threw whatever debris they could find from any broken windows on the ground floor. It wasn't long before the opposing gangs retreated beyond the range of the missiles and an uneasy standoff settled over the battlefield.

An hour later they were still surrounded and it didn't look as though many had gone home for tea.

Lionel on the other hand was becoming rather agitated. "Look I can't stay any longer I need to get home. My mum will kill me if I'm not in by eight o'clock."

Ray was in the same boat but he was at a loss as to what they could do to escape. Surprisingly it was Blainsey who came up with the solution. "We'll just have to sign a truce. It's clear we're not going to get away with demanding taxes or wrecking their dens any longer, so we'll just have to come up with an agreement whereby they recognise us as being the best gang and in return we'll let them build their dens and play in the park as long as they keep away from our base."

With that he picked up a piece of white material and waved it out of the window. The countries who were at war across the world should have taken note from what followed. The opposing gangs sat around the main room of the mansion and hammered out a peace that enabled both sides to save face and ensured the park would be an area free of conflict.

By the time Ray got home his mother was waiting for him and delivered the obligatory clip around the ear. However, she was more disgruntled by her lodgers who had once again fallen asleep with the lights on, so he escaped with a telling off and a warning that if he was late again, he wouldn't be allowed out until he was eighteen. The threat held no real venom and was clearly made as it was part of their routine. He therefore retired to bed feeling exhausted, but somewhat satisfied their war had been resolved so amicably.

Chapter 19 – That Sinking Feeling!

In the months following the peace treaty, life in the park developed into a series of inter-gang sporting events, competitions and games. It was during this time that Ray grew into something of an athlete. He knew he had some skill as a cricketer and was a fairly decent footballer, but due to the variety of activities that were presented, he realised he was also a strong tennis player, a good middle distance runner and a crack shot with both catapult and air pistol.

As 1943 became 1944 he craved any opportunity to participate in sport. In the school sports day, he volunteered to run every single race, take part in every throwing event and even wanted to do the high jump and long jump. It wasn't that he had to win, he just loved taking part and trying his best at physical activities.

There was one sport however, that utterly defeated him no matter how hard he tried; swimming. Perhaps it was the fact that his first encounter involved his mother throwing him into the deep end of the pool at New Brighton baths. The icy cold had taken his breath away and he promptly sank to the bottom, only being saved by his father when he pulled him out by his hair. From then on he was petrified of water; he even got butterflies in his stomach when he had to have a bath on a Saturday.

After the failure of the 'sink or swim' strategy of his mother, Ray's father decided to adopt a more supportive approach and enrolled him in lessons at the police training centre at Mather Avenue. Every Wednesday evening, John would accompany his son to the pool where there would be an expert trainer ready to attempt the impossible. He showed Ray how to kick his legs, the technique involved in the breaststroke, the crawl and the backstroke. However, it didn't matter what the instructor tried, the result would always be the same. Ray would begin by thrashing about whilst moving nowhere, followed by him sinking like a stone to the bottom. Even the instructor realised he'd been beaten when he presented him with a large float in order to keep him buoyant, but he sank once again having only covered two yards. There was only one conclusion that could be reached; Ray didn't like water and water didn't like him. The swimming lessons were abandoned, so he concentrated on those sports that kept him firmly on dry land.

He was coming to the end of his elementary education and was ready to move up to the big school. He was now a biggish fish in a too small pool and chafed to be rid of the childish routines that left him feeling suffocated and trapped. He was not alone in feeling this way; nearly every conversation that took place amongst his friends revolved around where they would go and what subjects they thought they'd be good at. Ian, Lionel, Obie and Mousey were all intending to go to The Bluecoat School if they passed the examination and interview.

"Why don't you try out as well Daggers?" Ian asked as they strolled home one evening.

"Don't they have to wear weird clothes?" He'd seen boys in long blue coats and wearing what looked like yellow stockings walking around the Allerton area and he didn't particularly like the look.

"Yeah, but we'd look stupid together!"

This was a truth Ray had to consider. Ian, Mousey, Lionel and Obie were probably his best friends in the gang and he didn't relish going somewhere on his own. "I suppose it can't do any harm to give it a go?"

When he informed his mother of his choice she was overjoyed that he finally seemed to be taking his education seriously, so she spent most evenings coaching him on what to say in the interview, ensuring he made the most of his sporting prowess. Unfortunately, she didn't spend as much time coaching him on how to pass the exam, so when it came to the test he spent most of the time drawing cartoons in the margin of his paper. He did attempt to answer one question, which he was sure he remembered Miss McEvoy telling them when they were learning about creatures that lived in the sea.

The question asked: "How would an octopus defend itself if it were threatened?"

Ray's answer was written with confidence and only three blots of ink. "If an octopus felt threatened, it would wrap its testicles around its head and try and escape."

When the results of the examination were published, he had unsurprisingly failed. The other four boys however, had all passed with flying colours and so looked forward to an interview with the headmaster in the near future. When Olive heard this, she was adamant Ray had as much to offer, if not more. She stormed up and down the front room ranting.

"Just because you didn't score particularly well doesn't mean you are thick Raymond!"

Ray hadn't actually thought he was thick until his mother suggested it and so he began to fret that there might be something wrong with him. However, he was soon distracted when his mother slammed the door in frustration, nearly decapitating Dolly as she popped her head round the corner. Luckily she dodged back and decided now wasn't the best time to make a cup of tea as Olive continued her tirade.

"You are a brilliant sportsman and a fantastic artist; why aren't they recognising those talents?!"

"But Ma, I only got one mark out of a hundred and that must have been for writing my name. I'm pretty sure I should have got two marks, but I think I missed the second "L" off Dagnall."

His mother had embraced her fury too tightly to be persuaded by the truth in Ray's statement. "Nonsense Raymond, there must have been a mistake with the marking. I think they are just punishing you for writing the obscene answer about the octopus."

He'd been bemused when his mother received a letter informing her of her son's rudeness as he didn't even know what testicles were. "But ma, I'm sure I wrote tentacles." He paused and scratched his head as he tried to remember. "I definitely meant to write tentacles. What are testicles anyway and why are they rude?"

Olive was finding it hard to suppress a smile, but felt that now wasn't the best time to have 'the talk' about things pertaining to biology. She therefore decided to change the subject. "Raymond, an octopus squirts ink when it feels threatened."

"Squirts ink, how ridiculous is that?!" He was more than a little disappointed by the correct answer as he felt his one made so much more sense than the truth; and he was sure Miss McEvoy had said as much.

"Never mind ma, I only wanted to go there because Ian, Mousey, Obie and Lionel are going. I didn't fancy wearing the weird clothes anyway." As he said it, he realised he'd now be able to skit his mates something rotten about having to wear stockings, so felt a lot better. He expected his mother to capitulate and agree with him; however, she was far too worked up.

"If you want to go to that school Raymond, I will pay for you to go. Let's see if a bit of cash will gain you an interview at least."

A week later he found himself sat with his mother in the headmaster's office of the grammar school, sipping tea as quietly as possible and failing, whilst yearning to dip his biscuit. Each time he directed his digestive towards the cup, he'd receive a glare from his mother daring him to even try.

The headmaster was a kindly looking man who smiled after every sentence he said; a million miles away from what Mr. Little was like. "Now Raymond, what type of things do you do in your spare time?"

His mother had primed him for just such a question and so there was hardly a pause before he responded. "Well sir, I like most sport; in particular cricket, football and running. I also enjoy the high jump and the long jump but I'm not quite as good at those."

The headmaster smiled and nodded and when Ray looked at his mother, her eyes glistened with tears of pride. It appeared that her argument was paying off regarding him being prone to nerves in exams and that on the day of the exam he'd been coming down with a bad cold.

"And do you participate in any community activities?"

He was unsure what 'participate' meant, but as he glanced at his mother she mouthed "choir", which triggered his memory of his rehearsed answers.

"I've been in the church choir up until recently sir." At this point he felt things were going so well he could afford to embellish on the answers he'd rehearsed with his mother. "I'm now hoping to join Boys Brigade as I would like to learn to play the drums or the bugle."

The headmaster beamed with delight and looked at Olive who couldn't contain her pride as tears trickled down her cheeks. "Very good Raymond and most articulate. It appears you have many attributes that would make you fit in well here at The Bluecoat." Ray just nodded and smiled, not really sure what the headmaster was saying.

"What academic interests do you have? What is your favourite subject?" Ray was slightly thrown by this as he didn't really have any favourite subjects. However, he thought he best stick to the truth.

"I enjoy drawing sir." Once again this was met with a nod and a smile from the headmaster and a look of relief from his mother as if she'd just dodged a bullet.

And what type of things do you like to draw, still life; portraits?"

"Cartoons sir; i like to draw cartoons." As Ray

answered, he realised much of his good work was beginning to unwind as the headmaster's smile became a little strained and a twitch appeared in the corner of his eye. When he looked at his mother, her lips had pursed and her brows had knitted together leaving Ray feeling like he was on a precipice of disaster. He therefore added quickly. "Obviously, I only draw cartoons in my spare time; I also like to paint trees and plants."

There was an audible sigh of relief from his mother and the headmaster's twitch miraculously seemed to vanish. Ray started to relax and look forward to the next question.

"Okay Raymond, we pride ourselves at The Bluecoat School on our students' ability to undertake independent learning and research. What types of material do you like to read?"

He sighed with relief; he'd been out of his depth on the last couple of questions and felt he'd only just managed to scrape together the answer the headmaster wanted to hear. However, this was an answer he was sure would impress. Everybody he knew admired his literary taste and so it was with enthusiasm that he replied. "The material I like best sir is obviously the Beano, but I will read the Dandy as well as I like Desperate Dan."

The headmaster looked like he'd been slapped

across the face and the twitch had returned with a vengeance. As he glanced at his mother confused, the tears were once again flowing down her cheeks, but they didn't look like tears of joy anymore. The headmaster must have thought Ray was joking as he gave a little laugh. "That is very droll young man." Ray looked at him utterly baffled. "Now tell me seriously, what type of books do you read?"

"I don't read books sir, they're really boring. I tried to read Tom Sawyer once but fell asleep after the first three pages..."

Ray got a place at Heath Road Secondary School for Boys a week later, but his stinging ears lasted much longer after the repeated clips they'd received from his mother on his way home after the interview.

Chapter 20 - Fags and Apples

On the 6th June 1944 the Dagnall family heard the news the entire nation had been waiting for. Since America had joined the war at the end of 1941, Britain had become a huge storage depot of men and equipment. In the months leading up to June, rumour had been rife that the allies would finally invade the continent and take the first step towards pushing the Germans back beyond their own borders. There had been fighting in Italy of course since the autumn of 1943, and Rome had finally been captured two days earlier, but it was the invasion of their nearest neighbours in France that people had been anticipating for so long. They heard that four beachheads had been established in Normandy and by the evening, a firm foothold had been established.

Upon hearing the news a festive mood fell upon Clavelle Road and the nation in general. There was a belief that finally the end was in sight and many bandied around the well worn phrase that war would be over by Christmas.

As the allies pushed further inland in the days that followed, Olive decided they should hold a special celebration. She held a meeting, in which she managed to persuade their neighbours that a street party would be appropriate acknowledgment of the achievements of our forces in France and Italy, so in the weeks that followed, rations were saved up and clubbed together in order to mount a feast the likes of which, nobody had experienced since before the war. Every child in the road was recruited to create decorations made out of scraps of paper, which would hang from house to house and even across the street.

"I'm not making decorations!" Ray objected when his mother told him what his job was. "It's girlie! The lads would skit me rotten!"

"You will do as you're told young man or I'll make sure you miss out on the whole thing!"

He knew it was pointless to argue, but he was starting to learn the art of negotiation. "What if I add some pictures to the decorations to brighten them up?"

His mother had obviously been affected by the positive news from the war. "Now that's more like it; using your talents properly!"

On each pennant he therefore added different cartoons, generally depicting Hitler having his bum kicked in different scenarios. He interspersed these images with copies of the British flag. When he presented these for inspection, they passed muster with his mother and she beamed once more; something she'd rarely done since the fiasco of his grammar school interview. Even now her smile was tinged with sadness as she dwelt on her son's missed opportunities to develop his art work fully.

"If only you'd got into grammar school." She whispered to herself.

Unfortunately, it was said loudly enough for Ray to hear, which didn't fill him with much hope of receiving a decent education at Heath Road.

The day of the party dawned to blue skies and bright, warm sunshine. Shortly after midday the proceedings got under way with Olive, who'd organised the whole event, making a speech thanking everyone for making such an effort and saying a prayer for those friends and family who were away fighting. When she'd finally finished there was a spattering of applause and then a much larger one when it was announced the food was served. There were so many delicacies it was easy to remember what life had been like before the war. There were cakes made with real eggs, sandwiches of corned beef and even some ham, a range of pies and somebody had managed to bring several crates of beer and a number of bottles of sherry, which the adults were thoroughly enjoying.

Ray was being kept busy replenishing the tables, which ran down the middle of the road. He managed to get plenty to eat as he moved back and forth, but he wanted to spend some time with his mates. His opportunity arose when one of the neighbours decided they needed some music, so a group dragged a piano onto the pavement. Olive must have been at the sherry as she volunteered immediately to play and began giving renditions of popular songs such as 'We'll Meet Again' to which most of the adults joined in lustily. When everybody was distracted by the singing, Ray and his gang sneaked off to their headquarters with two hidden bottles of beer, courtesy of one Tony Blains.

"Here we are boys; a little something to wet the whistle as my dad puts it."

They felt incredibly grown up and rebellious as they sat around daring each other to be the first to take a swig.

"Oh for goodness sake, give it here!" Mousey said as he grabbed the bottle off Blainsey and took a large swig. He coughed a little, but seemed to like it. "That's not bad, I quite like it."

The Featherston twins quickly stepped forward. "Alright I'll go next." Johnny said.

"No you won't, I will" replied his brother. The two of them bickered for several minutes until Ray grabbed the bottle off them.

"Give it here; if you two can't make up your minds I'll take the next swig." He took a deep breath and a long draw on the bottle. The taste exploded in his mouth and was not a pleasant experience. He spat out the remaining fluid coughing furiously as he did so. "Urgh, that's ruddy horrible; why do people drink that stuff?!"

The other boys laughed at him, but as the bottle was passed round Ray was missed out as they weren't about to waste any of the precious brew on somebody who didn't like it. He was a little embarrassed by this, so sat sullenly as the others laughed and joked and got louder as the beer started to take effect. When they were suitably tipsy, Blainsey revealed another item of stolen goods pinched from his father. He presented them with such a flourish Ray thought at first it was a pack of playing cards; it was only when Blainsey opened the box he realised they were cigarettes.

"Who wants a fag?" Blainsey offered as he passed the box around, almost daring his friends to refuse. Obligingly they took one until the box came to Ray.

"I'm not sure; what if I don't like it? You don't want me wasting one do you?"

The look on Blainsey's face was full of contempt as he mimicked Ray's voice. "You don't want me to waste one do you?! You're a big girl Daggers! If you can't keep up with us maybe you should go back to the party and play with your sister and her friends." The other boys joined in with sarcastic comments, comparing Ray to a variety of things none of which were particularly masculine. In the end he felt as though he had little choice but to smoke the cigarette. It was either that or he leave, which would probably mean him never being allowed to return.

"Alright I'll try one, but if I throw up, I'm going to do it all over you Blainsey!" As always, his quick witted thrusts found their mark and the whole gang, including Blainsey, burst out laughing and clapped him on the back; fondly telling him what an idiot he was.

When he took his first drag, he did indeed nearly throw up. The smoke felt as if someone was sanding the back of his throat with a file and then he became incredibly light headed and dizzy. As he looked around at the others they seemed to be experiencing similar reactions, which made him feel slightly better. He decided to persevere with his endeavours and took several more puffs on the cigarette, each one becoming easier until the choking sensation was replaced by a rather pleasant one as the smoke was drawn down into the lungs.

He was gratified when he realised he was coping better than most of his friends. The twins were once again in competition with each other, daring the other to be the first to quit, whilst neither of them looked as though they were enjoying it very much. Ian looked like he was just holding his cigarette, willing it to burn down quickly so he didn't have to take another drag. Mousey and Blainsey were passing the beer to each other; taking a drag on the cigarette and then quickly taking a swig from the bottle to rid themselves of the taste. Lionel and Obie were sat in a corner looking decidedly green around the gills with their cigarettes lying on the ground between them. However, they didn't stay lit as both of them leaned over and threw up, extinguishing the glowing end in a tidal wave of vomit. The remaining boys laughed, but in the ensuing chaos as they made Lionel and Obie clean up their mess, Ray noticed that none of them finished their smoke.

When they emerged into the late afternoon sunlight an hour later, they realised the distinctive smell of tobacco hung over them. Whilst smoking was generally accepted in society and many actually believed it was beneficial to health, the boys believed that if their parents found out what they'd been up to, there would be hell to pay and the weather was far too good to have to give up their freedom for a week or two.

"We need to get rid of the smell boys, we stink of smoke." Ray said as he sniffed his shirt and then his fingers.

"How do we do that; my dad's clothes always stink until they've been washed."

This comment from Lionel seemed to plant a seed in all their minds telepathically and within minutes they were engaged in a full on water fight using the nearby pond for ammunition, which resulted in them becoming thoroughly soaked, but free from smoky odour.

"That's sorted out the clothes." Mousey said as they walked towards the exit, dripping water as he went. "But what do we do about our fingers; mine still stink?"

"I know, why don't we rub dandelion leaves on them? They work with nettle stings so they might get rid of the smell." Ray was quite pleased with his idea even though he received some skits, and was the first to try it out. "Yeah that works; I can hardly smell anything now."

"The smell might have gone, but look at the state of your fingers!"

As he looked down he realised his fingers had taken on a strange shade of green. "Yeah but it's better than smelling of tobacco."

Luckily when he returned home, the party was still in full swing and it appeared most of the adults were a little the worse for wear. It was therefore easy to sneak passed his mother and thoroughly scrub his fingers until there was no trace of green or smell of tobacco, even if it meant they were red raw and sore.

By the time August came around Ray was hooked on cigarettes. To begin with it seemed simple to pinch the fags from parents, but it became more dangerous after Mousey's dad noticed he had a lot less cigarettes than he should and became suspicious. He interrogated his children using police tactics, and Mousey only escaped because it turned out his elder brother was also pinching them and cracked first.

"I'm not robbing fags from the house anymore." Mousey said "That was far too close for comfort. Dad went crazy and John's been grounded until the end of the holidays."

They all felt this was pretty severe but acknowledged at the same time that they needed to change tactics for how they would get cigarettes. Daily routines therefore revolved around seeking ways in which they could make enough money in order to buy individual fags from Haswells, which was the local shop. In a normal week they'd usually be able to save up and buy two, which they'd cut up into three equal segments and retreat to their headquarters where they would share them out and smoke one each. Lionel and Obie were left out as they couldn't face smoking again after being sick the first time.

Afterwards, they'd come up with a different strategy for ridding themselves of the smell to their fingers. Instead of using dandelions they used to rub their fingers along a wall as they walked along. On several occasions Ray had rubbed too hard and was amazed his mother hadn't noticed the scrapes and blood when he returned home. He surmised she was too busy with other things, but deep down he suspected she was just turning a blind eye.

Eventually, a third of a cigarette once a week was not enough, so the gang decided they needed to raise more money to be in a position to purchase a whole packet. Blainsey called a meeting to discuss ways in which they might make the funds needed.

"We could offer a gardening service cutting grass and weeding." Ray offered enthusiastically. Since he'd moved into Clavelle Road, having a garden had been one of his highlights and he enjoyed helping his father maintain it. However, the others felt it would be too much like hard work and voted him down. Ian suggested cleaning windows, but this idea was also deemed to be too much hard work during their holidays.

"We could make perfume." There was a stunned silence as everybody turned towards Lionel who felt he then needed to justify himself. "I've seen some kids make it out of rose petals and then sell it on the street." Unfortunately for Lionel, the rest of the gang didn't think much of his idea and he received several digs and catcalls for his endeavours.

"I know how we can make loads of money; enough to buy a couple of packets of fags." Blainsey said and then sat looking smug but failing to share what his idea was.

"Well tell us then!" It was always Mousey who speak out against Blainsey, but when he saw the scowl come over his face he backed down quickly.

"Alright, I'll tell you. The apples from the nun's orchard will make us a packet of money." There was once again a stunned silence from the gang. The orchard sat not far from where they lived, but is was surrounded by an eight foot high wall and protected by nuns who could be ferocious when provoked. They had all heard stories of other reckless idiots who'd attempted to break in and steal their fruit; and of the fate that had befallen them. Many had returned battered and bruised caused by the swipe of a broom handle and one young lad had ended up in hospital after being bashed with a frying pan.

"You are kidding aren't you Blainsey? My brother tried to pinch some once and got soundly battered. He got battered again by me dad when he got home because the nuns had told him what had happened." Mousey was now genuinely worried and his concern spread through the rest of them like the flames did when Blainsey set the scrub fire.

"Ah, that's because he got caught and I have no intention of being caught. That's why we are going to plan our assault properly."

Over the following days they spent hours planning a strategy. They even attempted an assault, which nearly resulted in disaster. Eagle eyed sentries had spotted them as soon as they'd scaled the walls and chased them, screaming like banshees and armed with broom handles. As they chased the boys through the trees, one of them picked up a piece of rotten fruit and hurled it at them, scoring a direct hit on the back of Obie's head and sending him sprawling. If it hadn't been for Ray dragging him to his feet he would surely have fallen into the clutches of the nuns; a fate none of them would have wished on their worst enemy let alone good friend.

As they sat round contemplating their next assault, conversation drifted to the war. Things were still going well for the allies, if a little slower than was first expected. However, information and rumour was beginning to emerge regarding what took place on the 6th June when the allies had landed in France. It turned out the landings hadn't just taken place on one beach. In fact the attack had included dropping troops behind enemy lines via parachute and then landing vast numbers of men and machinery on four different beaches over an area that spread many miles.

Whilst the boys swapped stories they'd heard, it dawned on Ray that the solution to their problem was actually being passed back and forth as they bickered over facts and figures. He jumped up from his seat and quickly began to map out the borders of the orchard, the trees and the convent using any debris at hand. As the image became clearer, the banter from the rest of the boys died away until they were transfixed by what he was doing.

"That's the orchard isn't it Daggers? What are you thinking?"

The ideas were tumbling through Ray's head so quickly he had to take a deep breath before answering. "Yeah Johnny it is. While we were talking about the invasion it occurred to me that we could use similar tactics to get at those apples. So far we've only thought about going over the wall in the same place, which means that if we're seen, we all get chased off. But what if we were to assault it from different directions?" He indicated what he meant by pointing at different parts of the wall and explained how they might be successful. "From our own experience and everything we've heard there are normally only one or two nuns on the prowl, so if we were to go in from seven or eight different locations, they couldn't chase all of us."

Ray sat back slightly exhausted from the exertion of giving instruction as the rest of the group sat in awed silence. He was a valued member of the group but his value normally lay in his ability to make the others laugh. It was Mousey or Blainsey who came up with the master plans for their mischief. Blainsey must have realised this before anybody else as he was the first to try and pick holes in it.

"Yeah, that's not bad Daggers, but it won't work because we'd all have to go over at the same time and we haven't all got watches." He looked smug as he leaned back in his chair, which annoyed Ray a little. He considered the problem and was once again inspired by the strategy employed by the allies in France.

"We don't necessarily need to go over at the same time. When we landed in France, we first of all dropped men by parachute behind enemy lines before landing on the beaches."

Blainsey was beginning to feel rather intimidated by this new strategic Dagnall so became sarcastic in his reply. "Oh I see, so you mean to drop the twins into the middle of the convent do you? How are you going to do that Mr. Brain Box?"

Blainsey looked around the gang smirking as he looked for support for his viewpoint. However, the twins were looking at each other bemused, which caused several of the others to giggle. He took this as confirmation that he was still top dog so once again sat back smugly in his chair. Ray would normally back down at this point, but he was sure his idea was the solution they needed.

"No Blainsey you misunderstand; the troops who landed behind enemy lines not only secured vital bridges and towns, they also acted as a distraction drawing enemy troops away from the beaches and leaving them less well defended. If we go over the wall at slightly different times there's a good chance the nuns won't even see some of us as they'll be chasing the first ones they see."

There were nods of approval and looks of astonished admiration from the rest of the gang. Eventually even Blainsey nodded and threw his arm around Ray's shoulder.

"Daggers that is one good plan you have there, one good plan!" Blainsey had a habit of repeating sentences, which amused Ray no end.

They decided to implement the plan the following evening. They positioned themselves at intervals around the perimeter of the orchard wall at gaps of about a hundred yards according to the order of battle they had agreed the previous day. The Featherston twins would be first over followed by Blainsey, Obie, and Mousey. Finally, Ian, Lionel and Ray would enter the orchard on the far side from where the Featherston twins would attack, which meant the chances were that one group would be able to bag themselves a decent number of apples completely undetected by the nuns.

To protect their identity, each one of them wore a scarf around their mouths, except for Lionel who had a full faced balaclava, which his mother made him wear during the winter. The boys thought the plan was genius so launched the assault with gusto.

It was obvious when the twins had gone over as there was the screech of a female voice. "What are you doing; leave those apples alone!"

This was followed shortly after by the equally high pitched squeal of the twins as they diverted the attention of the nuns away from the true assault by running around making as much noise as possible. One by one the boys silently scaled the wall and made their way into the orchard. When Ray, Ian and Lionel went over they dropped down into the grass and crawled to the nearest tree where they hid, listening to gauge if they'd been detected.

Ray was not used to giving orders and taking the lead and he found the role quite daunting, but embraced it nevertheless. "Let's get the bags out and fill them as quickly as possible." He whispered, even though there was no sign of any nuns. The other two followed his orders and they were quickly moving from tree to tree pulling down the delicious golden treasure from the branches within reach. The chaos over the other side of the orchard appeared to show no signs of abating so they felt secure enough to climb up into the lower branches of a tree that appeared particularly burdened with fruit. Within minutes their bags were full and they were about to make their descent and jubilant return to headquarters when they realised an eerie silence had had fallen over the orchard.

"Don't move!" Ray whispered urgently as he saw Ian about to jump down. "Its gone quiet, which means the others have either been captured or they've broken off and retreated back to the park." Even in this moment of tension, he relished the opportunity to take on the role of 'hero' as if he were in one of the films he used to love.

"What do we do Daggers?!" This new found respect amazed him. The other two were deferring to him as if he had all the answers. It wasn't a welcome sensation, but he felt he owed it to them to make sure they escaped unscathed.

"Right, the nuns are bound to be on their guard so I

reckon we climb higher into the tree and wait until they've calmed down and gone back inside; then we can head for the wall." His advice proved to be sound as only moments later two nuns came striding into view, both holding planks of wood, which would cause a fair amount of damage if they came into contact with young boys backsides. The three boys sat frozen on the branches in the top of the tree afraid to even breathe and praying the women would not look up. Ray was pretty doubtful God would listen to the prayers from a group of petty thieves; particularly given they had broken into a convent to steal from the Brides of Christ. Nevertheless he prayed for all he was worth.

It came as a surprise therefore when the nuns stood for a while directly below the tree where the boys hid, but did not look up, and shortly after headed back towards the convent mumbling about heathen boys. To be on the safe side the boys decided to remain where they were in case it was a trap. By the time they climbed down and sneaked towards the wall, they were cold and aching, but they managed to climb over and beat a hasty retreat back to the mansion in the park. When they arrived the base was empty so the boys decided to eat an apple each from their stash and wait for their comrades. However, it soon became clear their mates must have got fed up waiting and gone home. Ray therefore gave his final orders of the day;

"Right lets hide the remaining apples until tomorrow and then we'll share them out and organise how we're going to sell them." They then headed home feeling pretty chuffed with their success.

The next day dawned bright and warm so Ray was up and out straight after breakfast. He called for Ian and they headed towards their headquarters expecting to find Blainsey and the others. To their surprise the base was once again deserted and when, after an hour of waiting only Lionel had shown up, they began to worry that something had gone wrong the previous day.

"What do you think has happened to them?" Ian asked as he took a bite from a juicy apple. "They're missing out on the 'fruits' of our work. Do you get it 'fruits'– apples?" Ian chuckled to himself but the other two were too worried to join in.

"What if they were captured? What if the nuns kept them all night and tortured them into telling who was with them? You saw the wood they were carrying?!" Ray was beside himself with worry. "It's all my fault; it was my plan after all!" He was now pacing up and down frantically looking out of the window each time he passed in the hope somebody might appear.

"Daggers, it wasn't your fault. If they got caught,

which I doubt, it will be because they were too slow." Ian tried consoling his friend. "I don't think nuns go in for torture either; at least not for a whole night."

This didn't make him feel any better. "They wouldn't have been there at all if I hadn't come up with the plan."

Ian was becoming a little exasperated. "Daggers, we agreed as a whole group to mount the raid so stop being stupid; it's not your fault."

After several minutes more of pacing Ray couldn't take it anymore. "We have to do something; I can't sit around here any longer."

"Let's go round to Blainsey's and see if he's there. At least that way we'll know one way or another." Lionel suggested, and so ten minutes later they were stood on Blainsey's front step knocking politely on his door. When his mother answered, it was Ray who stepped forward.

"Excuse me Mrs Blains, is Tony coming out to play?" Ray thought he'd presented himself as a polite young man, but Blainsey's mother's reply made him think he'd got it wrong.

"How dare you come knocking on my door? Anthony most certainly is not coming out to play, and will not be playing out for the rest of the holidays!"

Ray was sure this meant the others had all been captured and this was their punishment, but he had to be certain. He also realised they had to appear innocent. The fact his own mother hadn't battered him meant the gang had stood up to whatever torture was inflicted on them without divulging their names. "What's he done Mrs Blains?"

"Are you telling me you weren't with him when he tried to steal from the nuns?"

Ray paled even though her statement only confirmed his own suspicions. However, he still felt responsible and needed to protect his friends who hadn't been caught. "Er, I'm not sure I know what you're talking about Mrs Blains. Me, Ian and Lionel were playing football yesterday. I haven't seen Tony since the day before." The lie made him feel like St Peter when he denied he knew his leader when asked if he was a follower of Jesus. However, in this case Ray knew it was for the greater good of protecting Lionel and Ian. When he saw them nodding in agreement, he felt a little bit better.

"Well it's a good job you weren't. I don't know how I'm going to live this down; the shame!" With that she slammed the door, leaving them stunned and rather guilt ridden.

"Well at least we know. I still think it was a good plan Daggers, even if it did back fire!" Ian said as they walked away. "But it does mean we'll get a bigger share of the apples!" As they headed off towards the park, Ray vowed never to take the lead ever again.

Chapter 21 – Big School and a New Friend

The move to big school was pretty tough for Ray as all of his friends were going to different places, leaving him feeling isolated and alone as he stepped through the gates of Heath Road School in September 1944. What made it worse was the fact that everyone appeared to be so much bigger than him and confident in their awareness of themselves and their surroundings.

Within minutes he'd been knocked and barged out of the way repeatedly by giants as they strode passed him, oblivious to his existence or with grim threats thrown away over their shoulders such as "Get out of the way pipsqueak" or "Watch where you're going small fry if you don't want to get battered!" He eventually managed to find a corner of the yard that appeared to be deserted and sat sullenly watching as friends greeted each other as if they'd spent years, rather than weeks apart. There were kids he recognised from Springy, but he'd barely spoken to them before and reckoned if he hadn't made friends with them then, it was unlikely they'd suddenly have lots in common now. He therefore decided on a plan to keep his eyes out for people who appeared to be as lost as him. He quickly spotted several potential candidates and discarded them just as quickly as not being suitable.

His rationale for such hasty decisions; they were all flawed, which probably accounted for why they had no mates. There was a boy with thick glasses taped in the middle in order to keep them together, who twitched every couple of seconds and then proceeded to adjust his glasses after every twitch. Ray found the continuous motion of the repeated movements quite hypnotic and whilst he found it amusing to begin with, he reckoned he'd soon become tired of it with it becoming rather annoying in the end. In fact, he started to become annoyed even as he stood watching, so decided to search on.

There was another boy he spotted who appeared quite normal and at first, Ray couldn't fathom why he appeared to have no mates. It could be that he was in a similar situation as he was with his mates going to other schools. However, as he went over to talk to him, the lad let out a weird noise for no apparent reason, which actually made Ray jump. It sounded like a mixture between a car engine revving and the whistle of a falling bomb. The boy turned towards him when he was only a couple of yards away and his face lit up, obviously thinking he was about to make a friend. "Nnnnneouweeeee; Hi my names Nnnnneouweeeee; Peter what's......"

Before he could continue, Ray waved at an

imaginary friend behind the lads shoulder and ran off in a different direction. He headed off back to his corner of the yard, navigating his course so Peter couldn't see him and feeling pretty disconsolate.

It was at this point that a boy came up to him. He looked normal, there was no sign of twitches and he didn't appear to randomly make strange noises. "Alright; you look like all your mates went to other schools meaning you've got no one to hang round with; am I right?"

Ray was impressed; this lad had worked out his situation with only a look. "Yeah, I wanted to go to The Bluecoat but they wouldn't let me in. What about you?"

"I failed the exam because I wasn't well, but they wouldn't listen when me ma told them, so she said they didn't deserve me. I didn't fancy wearing those stupid yellow stockings anyway. My names Martin Mays, but my mates call me Mega; what's yours?"

Ray thought a good nickname said a lot about a person so warmed to Mega immediately. "My names Ray Dagnall, but my gang call me Daggers." He could see straight away that Mega was impressed also.

"Wow, brilliant nickname, and you're in a gang, that's impressive. I hope we're in the same class."

As luck would have it they were, and so in the weeks that followed a new friendship blossomed as they settled into the new routines of big school. They eventually got used to having different teachers for different subjects and learned how to avoid the big kids as they barged down corridors and dominated the yard at break. However, some routines hadn't really changed between Springy and here. Ray remained bored by most of his lessons, although he realised he was quite good at Maths and really enjoyed Woodwork even though the teacher said he was rubbish. This irritated him considerably as he felt that when he was working with wood he could give his creative side free reign and produce outcomes, which were imaginative and unique, even if it wasn't necessarily what he'd been asked to do.

"Dagnall you are not leaving this room until you have cut a straight line in that wood!"

Mr Entwhistle was the woodwork teacher who appeared to be in his late fifties although he could have been much younger. He wore the same clothes week in and week out, which were always caked in sawdust and he looked like he rarely washed, having greasy hair and stubble no matter what time of the day he saw him. He'd taken an instant dislike to Ray for some reason and seemed to enjoy whacking him about the head with a piece of 3x2, which he did now.

"I have never had the misfortune to teach such an untalented wretch such as you!"

As he rubbed his head, Ray wanted to say he didn't want to cut the wood in a straight line, he wanted to create curves. When they'd been introduced to the task Entwhistle wanted them to undertake, Ray was immediately reminded of the pieces he'd seen when they visited the prisoner of war camp and so decided to create a box with rounded edges, which he intended giving to his mother for her to keep her knitting in. His designs were ornate and he was proud of the sketches he'd produced, convinced he'd be able to make them a reality if he was only allowed the freedom to do so. He was therefore frustrated by being thwarted at every turn. First the designs were 'rubbish' in Entwhistle's words and now he wanted him to cut straight lines in a block of wood, which, if the truth be told, was very boring.

"Look sir, I don't want to cut straight lines; if you take a proper look at my design you'll see...."

Entwhistle didn't allow him to get any further with his speech. "How dare you speak to me like that? He screamed "I don't want; I don't want!" You will do exactly as you are told lad and god help you if you don't! Get out of my lesson!"

As he left the room and wondered where he should go, Ray reflected on the contradictory nature of teachers. One minute he was being told he wasn't leaving the room until he'd cut a straight line; the next he'd been kicked out without bringing a blade anywhere near wood. He was about to wander off when Entwhistle joined him in the corridor.

"I've had a bad feeling about you Dagnall since I met you. Are you going to be trouble? Well let me tell you now, I've eaten kids like you for breakfast! Do you think you're better than me? Well let me tell you you're not. You're a snotty nosed kid who would be wise to keep his mouth shut and his head down!" He then stormed off back into his room leaving Ray none the wiser regarding what he'd done wrong and frustrated at yet another teacher who asked a question and then answered it themselves. Why did they do that?!

He was also rather alarmed at hearing his teacher had cannibalistic tendencies and was surprised that such a person was allowed to teach, regardless of the shortage caused by so many teachers going off to fight. As for the rest of the diatribe, it just didn't make sense. He certainly didn't think he was better than his teacher at woodwork, not yet anyway, but he may have been better at other things such as cricket or running. Given the size of him, Ray reckoned it was a good bet he was better. He'd also called him a "snotty nosed kid", which he took exception to. He didn't have a cold and his mother checked his nose each morning to make sure he was 'crow' free before leaving for school.

There was also no way he was walking round with his head down and mouth shut; it took all of his agility as it was to avoid lumbering big kids. It would end up with him being shoved all over the place if he kept his head down. However, he'd learned whilst at Springy that when a teacher went off on one as Entwhistle had done, there was no point in responding or even asking for clarification. He therefore knocked politely on the door and apologised profusely before being allowed back into class.

In the days that followed it became clear that Entwhistle had been bad mouthing Ray in the staffroom to his colleagues. In almost every lesson he visited the teacher would pounce on him as soon as he'd stepped into the room.

"I've heard about you Dagnall; I don't want any of your funny business in my lesson, understood?" Or "One step out of line Dagnall and you'll be straight to the he headmasters office, understood?!" Or even

"Don't look at me like that Dagnall; you know what I'm talking about!"

But the truth was that he didn't. The fact was he'd been trying his best not to play the clown and had kept his funny business under wraps since he'd joined big school. He was also totally flummoxed about "not stepping out of line" as he wasn't aware he had to walk in lines. When he tried it for a day he kept getting told off for being stupid when he'd end every movement with a right angled turn before setting off on his next straight line. The most hurtful thing that had been said to him though, was not to look the way he did. He knew he wasn't the best looking of lads; his nose was too big to make him 'handsome', but he thought it very unfair to make an issue of it as it was impossible to change the way he looked without wearing a mask or something, which he saw as being too extreme.

These contradictions and quandaries left him dazed and hating school more than ever. He began trying to persuade his mother he was not fit on a daily basis, without much success. He tried sitting in front of the fire as close as he could and then complained of a temperature and headaches; he attempted rubbing his arms up and down on the wall of the loo in the hopes of creating a rash. He even tried chewing some soap as he'd heard this was a good way of making you vomit, which it was. However, when he crawled to his mother using his best acting skills, the answer was always the same.

"You'll feel better once you're in school; moping around the house will just make you feel worse."

She wouldn't even let him stay off when he really was ill, sending him in with nose running and eyes watering. The annoying thing was he never did feel better when he arrived in school; in fact he only ever felt better when he walked through the gates at the end of the day.

The only saving grace was that he got on so well with Mega. They discovered in each other kindred spirits who shared the same sense of humour and who came to the same conclusion that the only way to survive their education was to take the Michael out of it. Having kept his humour in check since the start of term, Ray now unleashed his inner clown with a vengeance. Each lesson became a competition to see who could make the most people laugh or who would be the first to make the teacher cry, which they achieved with some regularity. Anything was allowed, whether it be silly noises and then looking innocently around to see where they were coming from or making stupid comments in answer to questions from the teacher; that is whenever they were actually allowed to answer for themselves. Pulling faces behind the teacher's back was another favourite as was leaving pins on their chairs in the hope they wouldn't notice and sit down. Before long they'd established a reputation for themselves of which Ray was quite proud; teachers thought they were wastrels and trouble and the kids thought they were hilarious and brilliant.

There was one subject however, where they didn't mess around at all. Ray had been made up when he realised that Mega was also a sportsman and enjoyed most of the same sports as him. During their Physical Education lessons or PE for short, they therefore applied themselves thoroughly in their drive to achieve, which made them the teacher's favourites.

Miss Jones was a big woman who was as loud as she was broad. She would always choose Mega and Ray to do jobs for her and was always quick in her praise of their prowess. She was also somebody who couldn't just teach from the sidelines. She joined in every game whether it was football, rugby or running and did so with such enthusiasm and competitiveness; she could have been competing on a world stage rather than in a PE lesson. The boys suspected she just liked showing off as her celebrations if she scored or won were something to behold. To say she was a selfish player would be an understatement as Mega found out to his detriment during one game.

"Good Lord Mays, would you just pass me the ball; we're not going to win if you keep it to yourself!"

Mega ignored her and kept moving down the wing with the ball at his feet.

"Mays, I told you to pass me the ball; are you deliberately ignoring me?!" She then blew on her whistle and actually sent him off for 'insolence.'

When she got the ball she bustled down the pitch, barging kids out of the way, before blasting the ball as hard as she could at the terrified child in the opposing goal. If anyone managed to tackle her, she blew her whistle for a foul and she sulked when the goalkeeper happened to save one of her shots.

On one memorable occasion the class had been looking at passing techniques in football, which most of the boys found rather patronising as they spent a lot of their free time kicking a ball around the yard or the street or the park, so felt there was little a grown up woman could teach skilled sportsmen such as them about how to pass a ball. They'd spent twenty minutes half heartedly going through the motions of participating in the drills before she finally gave up and split them into four teams for a match. Normally when she did this, she'd place herself on the best side and operated a system of 'winner stays on'. In reality this meant that one team would dominate the competition and Miss Jones would dominate that team.

On this particular day, she must have been retaliating against Mega's insolence because when she chose the teams she decided to go on a weaker side than normal and decided her team would play Ray and Mega's team first. On paper they would normally thrash their opponents, but there was no accounting for what might happen with Miss playing on the other side.

"Right we'll have the kick off." She announced as she always did and then went bounding down the field towards Mega who was in defence. Ray was convinced she was going to mow him down ruthlessly, but as he moved out to meet her, she attempted to take the ball to the right and manoeuvre around him. However, he was too quick and deftly took the ball from her feet with a quick flick of his foot. As he went to clear the ball downfield, he felt his feet taken from under him and was left sprawling on the floor.

"Ouch! That's a foul Miss; you kicked my feet from under me!"

"Nonsense Mays, you tripped over after I'd tackled you." She then ran off after the ball barging one of her own team mates out of the way in the process, before heading towards goal and belting the ball at the quivering child who was keeping net.

"She's gone mad! She's actually gone stark raving mad!" was all Ray could say as they watched her run a lap of honour in acknowledgement of her scoring a goal; punching the air and screaming hysterically. "What a goal!"

"She wasn't like that when she played on our side was she?"

Mega was still rubbing his shin from where she'd kicked him. "No this is far worse; we have to stop her."

When the game restarted they could only look on as their teacher literally grabbed the shirt of the boy who'd taken the restart for their team and hurl him out of the way before once again heading towards their goal. By this stage no one would go anywhere near her so she had a free shot on goal. Even the despondent keeper ran away as she blasted the ball into the back of the net once more. Her celebrations were, if anything, even more exuberant, with her doing front rolls as she ran around the pitch.

"This is ridiculous, we can't just let her batter us like this, its ruddy embarrassing!" There were nods of agreement, but no one seemed to have a solution. It was therefore left up to Mega to outline a strategy during the short interval between halves.

"We need to give her a taste of her own medicine. Whenever she has the ball we need to have at least two people go in for the tackle, and they need to go in hard. If you miss the ball and kick her instead; all the better!" There were grunts of acknowledgement and as the second half started, the boys set about their task with a grim determination.

It became a painful experience for Miss Jones. Every time she took possession of the ball a crowd of boys would descend on her like a pack of wild dogs growling, kicking out and even giving a sly dig with elbow or fist. To begin with she blew the whistle for a foul, but then someone pinched it during one of the many melees and they then just ignored her cries of "Foul!" and continued down the pitch.

After ten minutes she was looking pretty disconsolate as she limped down the field, but their assault never ceased even after she'd sent Mega off for a particularly vicious kick up her backside. By the end of the match, Ray's side had been reduced to five players and lost by three goals, but as they headed back into school they were pretty upbeat as they watched Miss Jones rubbing her bruised shins and heard her vow never to play against the pupils in future.

Chapter 22 – Charging Buffalos, Bluffs and Diamonds

After the invasion of France, the situation in England had improved somewhat. There were still attacks in the South from a new type of flying bomb, which had been named a 'Doodlebug' and in the Atlantic, there were still ships that were being sunk by U boats, but these had become less, which meant that more convoys were successfully docking in Liverpool from the far flung reaches of the world. Shops were beginning to have more stock, although rationing was still in place and there was now a certainty that the allies would win the war and Hitler would be defeated. This new confidence was also drawing people back home who had spent the war years to date, living on other continents. One such person arrived in Clavelle Road in the autumn of 1944.

Ray arrived home from school one evening to find his mother's eldest sibling, and only sister Alice, sat in the kitchen sipping a cup of tea. He'd heard many stories about his aunt, but could remember little of her as she'd been out of the country since well before the war had begun. What he did know of her however, was exciting and intriguing. He knew her to have 'flamboyant' characteristics as his mother put it, and that she had been married no less than seven times. He was therefore made up to meet her and eager to hear what she'd been up to.

"Ah, this must be Raymond? My how you've grown! The last time I saw you, you were just starting to walk and you used to all me Yaya. Now look at you; a most dashing young fellow. I think we will be great friends!"

Ray had never been called 'dashing' before and so warmed to her immediately. He also noted that she sounded nothing like his mother. She had quite a posh voice with a hint of an American accent and was immaculately dressed in an elegant gown, a fur stole across her shoulders and smart black shoes. She also seemed to be wearing proper silk stockings; something he knew was much sought after by women. When she stood up to hug him he realised she was also really quite tiny. He was not the tallest of boys, but Yaya was even smaller than him and at first glance, appeared to have a fragile air about her. However, when she hugged him he felt the strength of her embrace and decided that looks could be deceiving.

She must have been in her late sixties as there were twenty one brothers between her and his mother. Even given that there were a couple of sets of twins, she had to be at least twenty five years older. However, she seemed much younger with a clear complexion. It was only as he hugged her that he saw fine wrinkles around her eyes and mouth. As she started to recount what she'd been up to, her energy filled the room to the extent that she dominated everything around her.

"Why did I call you Yaya, Aunt Alice?" Ray racked his brains but couldn't recall seeing this woman before let alone what he'd called her."

"I believe it was after I told a story of when I met a rather flirtatious German gentleman when I was on a cruise on the Nile in Egypt. If I remember correctly he used to answer every question I asked with Ya, Ya! You were only a tiny tot, but you must have been listening in and somehow the name stuck with you."

Ray loved the story and was further intrigued as she continued with her tale. Even his mother was enthralled as she told of how she'd spent the last two years in South Africa and how she had met her latest companion, Mr Benson who was an artist by trade, but had moved out there to try his hand at diamond mining and had ultimately made a fortune. They'd now returned home and he'd bought some land and a 'small' property out near Tarbuck. When Olive asked if they were married, she laughed loudly.

"Good lord no my dear, I'm far too old for that sort of thing and I think an eighth marriage would be a little greedy even for me! Reginald is a bit older than me so I will move in with him to look after his needs."

Olive looked horrified and huffed and puffed without being able to articulate her outrage, but Ray thought it was a lovely thing to do, particularly as she was getting on in age herself.

"Raymond, you must come out and visit us very soon. You'll love the house and Reginald has a passion for hunting so you could go out with him for a shoot; that way you'll also get to have a look at the land we have."

Olive looked horrified for a second time in as many minutes, which was a clear indication she was not in favour of shooting things. On the other hand Ray was overjoyed. "That would be brill Aunt Alice, can I come this weekend?"

"Most certainly you can my dear boy, and I would love it if you called me Yaya like you used to; I have a soft spot for the name. Reginald and I will pick you up in the car at say, ten o'clock? Olive, why don't you and John join us with Enid? The boys can go off and shoot bunnies or whatever while we girls have a proper catch up." Before Olive had a chance to answer, Alice had already concluded the arrangements. "That's settled then; ten o'clock on Saturday morning."

He was amazed such a short woman could dominate a room, particularly one in which his mother was present, but Yaya did this with ease. Whilst it was clear by the look on his mother's face she didn't approve of traipsing out to Tarbuck, she sat and meekly agreed, even smiling politely into the bargain; although grimace was probably a more accurate description than smile.

Ray couldn't wait until Saturday to arrive. He pictured himself creeping through jungle like vegetation, shotgun in hand as he searched for wild beasts to blast. He then envisaged himself sitting down to feast on the results, as his mother looked proudly on and his father offered him the knife as a sign of honour so that he could carve the huge joint of meat displayed on the long dining table. As he made the first cut, he imagined the guests giving him a round of applause as his mouth watered ready to devour the food.

The reality, as usual, turned out to be less flamboyant than he had imagined, but on this occasion it turned out to be a no less intriguing experience. Things started out as he expected when Alice and Reginald pulled up in a very sleek car to transport them to their new estate. Reginald seemed like an amiable old gentleman of about seventy years. However, he was trim for his age and seemed quite sprightly for one so old. He jumped out of the car and was round the other side, standing with the passenger door open a lot quicker than Ray would have thought possible. Other old people he knew, like his father's parents and his Nana were generally frail and slow moving, but this man was fluid in his walk, athletic in his build and had a healthy glow brought on by spending years in the sun. As he enthused about how much fun they were going to have hunting, Ray began to feel the tingle of excited anticipation down his spine.

When he arrived at the house he discovered a large cottage type building resting in acres and acres of fields and woodland, with orchards of both pear and apple trees. Parts of the land were well cared for and he wondered once again of how a man of this age had the energy to look after the huge lawns, flower beds and neatly organised rows of vegetables. There were also large expanses of wilderness where the grass had been allowed to grow over head height, and wooded areas, which brought back images of jungle scenarios and wild beasts.

Ray spent an agonising hour sat fidgeting, eager to pursue more manly activities, whilst the grownups had afternoon tea. Finally Reginald announced it was time for them to depart.

"I think it's time we men folk left you ladies alone

so you can gossip. Come along gentlemen, I have something to show you." He took them into a room, which had oak panelled walls and was possibly the poshest room Ray had ever seen. There were cases full of books and astonishing paintings on the walls, which depicted the beasts of his dreams captured in all their glory in acts of charging, fighting or just laying in the sun. They were so lifelike and the colours so vibrant that he was transported to the African Veldt and stood captivated as he studied them.

"Do you like them Raymond? I painted those just before I met your Aunt. I spent three months on Safari" he said as he looked into the middle distance and recalled the experience. "They were possibly the most contented times I've ever had."

"Oh yes Mr Benson, I love them, they're so real." To realise Mr Benson had created these masterpieces himself, put Ray in awe of him.

He then went on to describe the adrenaline rush of hunting big game. Ray was transfixed as he listened to the stories and looked at the pictures; he felt as though he could almost feel the heat of the sun beating down on him. "I hope our hunting today will be as exciting!"

"I'm not sure it will be as adventurous as stalking an elephant, but we'll see what we can do." He then paused as something occurred to him. "I have to say though; hunting for treasure is equally as exciting as hunting animals." He went over to a draw in his desk and pulled out a small black bag and emptied the contents onto the desktop. "These little beauties are worth a small fortune; the rush you get when you find one is second to none!"

Both Ray and his father stared in astonished silence at the small pile of glittering gems before them. Neither of them had seen real diamonds before and when Mr Benson let them hold one, their hands actually shook with excitement. Unfortunately, the old man retrieved the jewels and returned them to the bag, but as he went to lock them back in the draw, Ray decided he would become an explorer when he was grown up and travel the world looking for treasure.

"I think it's time we started with the hunt." He said as he went over to a locked cupboard, unlocked it and pulled out two shotguns and bandoliers of cartridges.

Ray was a little confused at first. "Aren't you going to shoot dad?" he asked as Mr Benson made sure the guns were empty. It was only as his father was handed one of the guns that he began to suspect he was the one who wouldn't be shooting.

"I'm afraid you're too young Raymond. These guns

give quite a kick when you fire them and I don't think your mother would be too pleased if we brought you back with a broken shoulder."

Mr Benson then chimed in. "But you will still be integral to the proceedings as you will carry the ammunition and anything we bag."

He therefore spent several hours tripping over his own feet and getting tangled in brambles and tree roots as he followed the grownups over hill and dale, burdened down with the ammunition and the carcasses of several wood pigeons and a couple of rabbits, which dripped blood down his shirt from the wounds in their sides. He'd always had a soft spot for bunny rabbits, so any idea he'd had of enjoying eating their prey was ruined. When they sat down to feast on a meat stew later that evening, he politely refused, which made him pretty fed up and hungry. What started out as a really exciting experience had developed into a fairly gruesome trek and left him with cuts and scratches on his arms and feeling rather grumpy.

However, things took a turn for the better when Alice began to regale them with stories of her travels as they relaxed around the fire after tea. Ray could tell a good story, but his paled into insignificance when compared to those of his aunt. They were so outrageous that at first, he couldn't believe they were true, but then Mr Benson would agree or even embellish a certain point or Alice would produce some sort of evidence that backed up what she was saying.

"There were several times I thought my time was up." She said nonchalantly as if death was nothing at all. "We were out in the bush trekking after a herd of elephant when suddenly this crazed buffalo came crashing through the undergrowth in a full out charge. I'm sure you've never been in that sort of situation, but you don't get much time to think."

Ray thought about the nights of air raids he'd experienced; of the destruction of his house and the sound of machine gun bullets hitting his shelter, but he supposed it wasn't quite the same as standing down a charging buffalo even though he was sure the fear must have been similar.

"As it ran towards me I suppose I just reacted. I could have run, but it would have caught me for sure so I raised my gun and shot the brute between the eyes!"

Mr Benson chipped in at that point. "I can honestly say I have never seen anything as courageous as this tiny woman calmly standing where she was as the beast came crashing to earth; landing only inches from her, and do you know what she did?"

Ray and his family really had no idea of what

Alice might have done next so meekly shook their heads.

"As cool as you like, she just placed her foot on its head and posed for a photograph!"

In that instance, Ray began to hero worship his aunt, which was more than could be said for the effect her stories had on his mother. When Alice went on to tell a rather lurid tale of a drinking competition between herself and two of the managers from Mr Benson's mine, Olive sat stony faced with her arms crossed in silent condemnation of her sister's behaviour. The fact that the managers ended up lying unconscious on the floor, and Alice pocketed a sizable pot of winnings that included several diamonds, didn't seem to matter a jot; it was the fact she had engaged with the demon drink that angered his mother so much.

"I am rather perturbed that you find pleasure in drinking to excess." His mother said as she sat stiffly and sipped at her tea.

"Don't be such a prude Olive my dear; it was just a bit of fun."

Olive began to bristle so John felt the need to intervene and change the subject."How did you two meet?" He asked as he took a puff from a rather expensive cigar, which he'd been offered by Mr

Benson. He didn't smoke normally, but felt it rude to refuse such an exuberant gift.

"Ah now there is another tale to tell! It was during a game of poker."

Olive once again looked horrified at the thought of her sister gambling, but Alice seemed oblivious as she recounted their meeting. "Fortunes can be won and lost playing this game as I know only too well having done so several times."

Ray had seen Hop Along Cassidy playing poker in one of his many films, but his own experience was limited to snap so he wasn't too sure how this could be the case until Mr Benson told of how he'd had a very strong hand of three Kings and a pair of twos, which was apparently called a 'full house' and difficult to beat.

"I was so sure I would win, I bet a ridiculous amount of money and before long the pot in the middle of the table was close to five hundred pounds." Mr Benson didn't seem to flinch at that amount of money, but Ray could see that both his parents were astounded that somebody could afford to lose that much.

"Everybody had dropped out except for Alice who sat cool and collected and matched whatever I bid. So confident was her bidding, that I started to worry she might have four of kind or a royal flush and I have to admit, I panicked a little. The pot was now nearing one thousand pounds, which was a huge sum even for me. When Alice placed a diamond on top of the pile, which amounted to a raise of several hundred pounds, I was convinced she had a winning hand and folded."

Alice had been sitting quietly listening to Mr Benson's account of their meeting, but she felt it only fair to divulge a little secret. "I've never told Reginald this, but I'm sure he won't mind. I was bluffing all along! I only had a pair of fives!"

Mr Benson guffawed with laughter. "You crafty blighter, and all this time I was sure I'd done the right thing!"

As they parted company after being dropped off back at Clavelle Road, Ray pleaded with Alice to visit them again soon to which she readily agreed. So began a new routine in which Alice would visit for an afternoon or she would pick them up and take them to the estate where Ray would join Mr Benson and act as his gun bearer, which he actually started to enjoy. However, what he truly relished were his aunt's stories, which became a highlight of every visit.

Chapter 23 – Al Capone, Mrs Louis and the Chinese Triads

On one of her first visits to the Dagnall household, Ray learned of her first marriage to a sea captain that ended so tragically. "I was only just seventeen when I met Paul; he came walking down the gangplank of his ship in full uniform and I have to admit, I fell head over heels in love with him at first sight. He was the captain of a cruise liner and was so tall and handsome with thick, dark wavy hair. We hit it off straight away and were married within the year before I was eighteen."

From the way she spoke it was clear to Ray he had been the one true love of her life. "How long were you married?"

"We were blissfully happy for sixteen years. You know, in all that time I don't think we ever had a crossed word."

"Is that because he was always at sea?" Ray asked innocently and was surprised when they all laughed. His parents didn't argue much, but they still bickered from time to time.

"No my dear, you see I used to go with him most of the time. I came to love the sea and would often accompany him on his voyages around the world."

"Wow, did you go all the way round the entire world?!" he asked incredulously as he thought of how big the world was.

"I'm sure we missed some countries out, but we pretty much visited most places." She paused as she took a sip of wine, which she'd brought with her; much to Olive's annoyance. "Things changed though in 1914 with the outbreak of the Great War. Paul decided to join the Royal Navy and for the next four years I barely saw him. "

"What did you do? Where did you live?"

"We'd bought a beautiful house directly overlooking the sea not far from Southport, so I would sit and watch the ships passing the Mersey Bar and head up the river towards Liverpool dreaming that my Captain Harrison was on board."

"You sat for four years looking at the sea?! Four whole years just sitting in a chair?!" He once again caused the others to burst out laughing, but couldn't get the image out of his head of his aunt sat in a chair with cobwebs and creepy crawlies all over her. He imagined she must have smelled pretty awful as well.

"No Raymond, I did other things as well, but I have to admit there were many days I would sit for hours at a time just looking through a telescope out to sea. Eventually in November 1918 the war came to an end and I received a telegram shortly after informing me that my sea captain would be returning for good within the next few days."

Alice suddenly stopped her story and started to cry. "What's wrong Yaya?"

"Nothing for you to worry about Raymond; it's just an old woman being silly and getting upset by a memory. I ordered my servants to lay the table with the best silver cutlery and china, ready for a sumptuous banquet for when he finally returned."

"You had servants?!"

"I did indeed; I had a cook, a maid and a driver who also acted as a sort of butler."

Ray was astounded that a relative of his had actually had servants.

"Anyway, I don't think I did move from the chair in the days I spent waiting for a glimpse of his ship as it neared home."

She paused once again as she neared the climax of the story and took large gulps from her glass of wine.

"I finally picked out his ship as it neared the coast. The thrill of seeing him come over the horizon was wonderful; but only moments later I spotted an object bobbing in the water and could see the ship heading directly for it. Everything went into slow motion as I yelled hopelessly at him to change direction."

"What was it Yaya?"

"It was a mine my dear, and I was helpless; I could do nothing to stop the collision and had to bear witness to the huge explosion as his ship hit it. It sank incredibly quickly, and with it the love of my life."

Everyone in the room had tears freely flowing down their cheeks and there was a subdued silence for several minutes before Alice continued.

"I left that house the very same day and I've never returned; I even left the dining room still laid out in anticipation of a homecoming that was never to be."

As Ray lay in bed later that night reflecting on what he'd heard, he reckoned that Yaya's recklessness was born out of the loss of her first husband. In the years following her tragic loss she'd married repeatedly but none of the marriages lasted for more than a few years. Each husband had an association with the sea, which to Ray was another indication she was trying to recapture the man she had lost, and when she grew to realise they were not him, she would end the relationship or become so outrageous in her behaviour her husband would end it for her.

In the weeks following the revelation regarding her first husband, Alice became a firm favourite at Clavelle Road and before long had an avid following who wanted to hear her stories. Ray would be hounded by his mates on a daily basis asking if Yaya was visiting today. They had all taken up the pet name and even Olive found herself using it before she quickly changed it to the more formal 'Alice'. When she did visit, any plans the boys had would be dropped in favour of sitting in Ray's kitchen and listening to her tell her stories as she sipped a cup of tea.

During one such visit she told of when she was in America in the late 1920's in a city called Chicago, and of how she'd met the notorious gangster Al Capone.

"I believe I was onto husband number three by this time; he was also involved with the sea as a high ranking officer with Cunard liners. To be honest my dears, I was more interested in the man's lifestyle than the man himself because I got to accompany him when he captained a ship on a round the world cruise; quite a perk really!"

The boys laughed even though Ray thought they

must be slightly shocked by his aunt's scandalous attitude towards marriage.

"While he was dealing with business in New York, I decided to do some travelling and experience something of what America had to offer. At this time the government had decided to ban the sale of alcohol and so an inevitable trade had grown up focusing on the making and distribution of illegal beverages. Now as you know, I like to partake of a drink from time to time so soon found myself in an illegal pub called a "speak easy" engrossed in a game of poker and on a winning streak."

Ironically it had been her first husband who'd taught her the game, but she now readily admitted to being hooked and played it whenever and wherever she could. The boys were totally enthralled in what she was telling them so when she banged on the table, they nearly jumped out of their skin.

"You should see the look on your faces boys!" She laughed. "Actually, they are not dissimilar to how many of the people in the bar looked when that knock on the door came!"

"I nearly jumped out of my skin then Yaya!" Blainsey said before he realised that made him look slightly wimpy and quickly gave one of the Featherston twins a dig on the arm for smirking.

"Anyway, the bar became silent until the large man who guarded the door flipped back a viewing panel and received the correct password, indicated everything was alright and then opened the door. You see everyone feared the knock might be the prelude to a raid by the police."

"Is that why they were called a 'speak easy' Yaya?" Mousey asked to the confusion of the other boys.

"My word young Mousey; you're bright as a button! It was indeed why. Apparently the ritual of having to give a password to gain entry and the inevitable relaxation of the customers in the bar is where the name came from. The atmosphere in the bar where I was certainly relaxed as the people around me sighed with relief. It was then that Al Capone walked in surrounded by his body guard."

"How did you know it was Al Capone Yaya?

"Oh it was simple really; his name washed around the room on a wave of whispers so I knew immediately who it was. I can tell you it felt pretty strange the way people treated him. It was if he were a hero, rather than a notorious gangster who was undoubtedly responsible for the murder of a number of his competitors and made millions of dollars each year from illicit and illegal businesses."

"What was he like Yaya?" Obie asked as he sat, like all of them, completely enraptured by her saga.

"Actually, I thought him surprisingly small for a gangster and quite tubby. He wasn't much bigger than I am and I'm no giant! The only thing that distinguished him as having a murky side was three scars on his left cheek, which had led to a nickname of "Scarface" although nobody dared call him that to his face while I was with him."

Obie couldn't contain his excitement. "You were with him?! You mean you actually spoke to him?!"

"I did indeed and he was extraordinarily polite when he asked if he could join our game; he even offered me a cigarette before he lit one himself."

"You played poker with him; Ruddy hell!"

Olive pounced on Mega as soon as he let the profanity slip. "I will not have that sort of language in my house young man, do you understand?! Any more of that and I will send you home."

Mega apologised profusely to both Olive and Alice, but Yaya seemed far less shocked than her sister.

"My dear boy I have heard language that is far choicer than yours I can tell you. Now where was I, ah yes, the game of poker. Even though he'd been polite I saw glimpses of how ruthless he could be. He had a strong "poker face", which meant it was difficult to tell if he had a good hand or if he was bluffing. His betting was also reckless, even worse than mine; but it was the way he intimated the other players that I found quite frightening."

Ray couldn't believe his ears; Yaya frightened? This was the woman who had stood down a charging buffalo. "I can't believe you were scared of him Yaya? You aren't scared of anything."

"That's not quite true Raymond dear. If you could have seen the way he stared at an opponent you would understand. It was so menacing they became flustered and either folded, or made a stupid bet. Even the way he lifted his glass towards his mouth before drinking could easily be perceived as an unspoken threat; it was very off-putting. Before long there were only him and I left at the table.

"Why didn't you give up as well Yaya?"

"I don't mind admitting I was actually terrified of the man, but I was also intrigued to find out more about him and what made him tick. After all, a girl doesn't get that many opportunities to play cards with one of the most infamous men of her generation. I also found I was in possession of four queens, possibly the strongest hand I'd ever had, so I was determined to win big. I knew Capone would try and bully me into submission as soon as I made my first bet. He gave me the cold stare as he raised my bet and when I met it and raised him, he brought the glass towards his mouth in such a threatening way I thought my heart would stop! However, I maintained my cool and calmly matched his wager. When he realised I wouldn't crack under those bully tactics, he started to try and use his money to do the bullying for him by raising his bet quite considerably in the hope I'd buckle under the pressure."

If the tension in the "speak easy" had been anything like it was in the front room of Clavelle Road, Ray reckoned it must have agonising. "What happened then Yaya?

"Well the rest of the bar sensed something was happening and became drawn to the table to watch our little battle of wills take place. There was soon a large crowd gathered who stood in silence except for collective sighs when a new bet was made. I continued to play in what appeared to everyone else, to be a cool and collected manner matching what Capone did and even raising the stakes from time to time.

"You are one cool cookie lady, I'll give you that!" Capone said as he considered his next move after I had raised him fifty dollars. "It's not often guys have the balls to stand up to me, let alone dolls."

Alice's American accent had them all in stitches as she mimicked the gangster's voice.

"Even though he said this quite affably and caused a ripple of polite laughter from the gathered crowd, I sensed the threat lying just beneath the words. I wasn't sure he'd use violence towards a woman, but I was quite sure I didn't want to find out. My emotions were in turmoil; I'd rarely had such a strong hand and the pot in the middle of the table was huge, but at the same time could I afford to make an enemy of Al Capone?

"What did you do?"

"I decided enough was enough and said to him; "Well Mr Capone, it has been an honour and a pleasure to share this game with you, but I really must be going; I'm therefore going to raise you two thousand dollars so you will either have to put up or shut up!"

"You never did?!"

"I did indeed. There was a gasped intake of breath from every single person in the room. The cigarette that had been dangling from Capone's mouth dropped to the floor as he opened it in shock and a murderous look came into his eyes."

Even though Ray knew she must have survived due to the fact she was sitting in front of them, he imagined the fear she must have felt at angering such a notorious gangster, and this made him afraid too. "Please tell me you ran Yaya."

"Actually I did not as I don't think my legs could have carried me. In that moment I realised I'd just taken the greatest gamble of my life and was glad nobody could see my legs shaking under the table. The silence in the room was unbearable, but I couldn't believe my own ears when I heard myself say.

"Well Mr Capone, what is it to be?" There was a second mass intake of breath from the crowd as a small nerve at the corner of Capone's mouth began to twitch. In that moment I honestly thought I'd made a fatal mistake and one that could possibly result in my death, but then the twitch became bigger and turned into a grin and then a bellow of laughter from Capone.

"You are one balsey doll lady, one balsey doll! I fold!"

The boys applauded the result of her gamble.

"The crowd in the bar went wild as they released the tension that had built up. People were laughing and clapping each other on the back as Capone sat back in his chair shaking his head and repeating his statement that I was 'One balsey doll' over and over again."

"That is amazing Yaya, did he let you leave with your winnings?"

"Not quite my dear. He invited me for a drink at the bar and then made me pay for them out of my winnings! He then invited me to join him for a meal and so I spent several hours being wined and dined in an exclusive club whilst he flirted with me outrageously!"

Alice received a warning glance from Olive but continued regardless.

"At the end of the evening, which was in the early hours of the morning, he had the audacity to invite me up to his hotel room! It's a good job I had the measure of him by then so I admonished him for being crass.

You see, more than anything else I believe he desired to be perceived as being a sophisticated man so I said to him.

"Mr Capone I am a married woman!" and I

presented him with my hand on which I wore my wedding ring. "A gentleman as sophisticated as you would not dream of trying to seduce such a woman I'm sure. I think we shall say good night right here, but thank you for a wonderful evening."

Capone for the umpteenth time that evening said "You are one balsey doll, lady, one balsey doll!" And then he raised my hand to his lips and gallantly kissed my fingers before escorting me to a cab, which took me back to my hotel."

When she finally finished her story, Alice received a standing ovation from the boys who stamped their feet and whooped in delight. "That was better than going to the cinema Yaya" Ian said as they were leaving. "Can we come and listen to you again tomorrow?"

As news spread of the old woman who told amazing stories of intrigue and adventure round at the Dagnall's house, so too did requests to be in attendance whenever she was holding court. Blainsey immediately spotted a business opportunity and wanted to charge people to listen to the stories.

"Look, if we charged a penny we could make a fortune. I reckon you could easily fit fifteen to twenty people in your front room at a squeeze. Think of the fags we could buy with that type of money?"

Ray was tempted, but he loved his aunt's stories because they were told for his benefit. "I'm not charging people to listen to Yaya's stories. She tells them because she loves sharing her adventures; she's not some sort of circus freak who people pay money to watch."

Blainsey wasn't prepared to give up that easily. "So who is going to keep the crowds away? There must have been at least twenty kids in your front garden the other day when she was here. I'll tell you what; I'll shoo the majority of the kids away if you let me charge a small fee to allow a handful in to listen?"

Ray wasn't too pleased, but they did need to keep the gangs of kids in check and it would mean he could afford some extra cigarettes. "I guess you can look after the door, but no more than six kids on top of the gang."

Therefore, whenever Alice's car was spotted in Clavelle road a hoard of the local children would descend on the house and it would be left up to Blainsey to clear the way and select who would be lucky enough to gain entry.

On one of her visits she'd been reading a newspaper while she waited for her audience to settle.

"Well I never!" she exclaimed as she scanned a headline. "I shall have to go down to Anfield and pay my respects to Joe. I wonder if he will remember me."

"Who are you talking about Yaya?"

"Well it says here that Joe Louis, the heavyweight champion of the world has enlisted to play football for Liverpool while he is stationed with the army nearby. I can't believe Joe would want to play football, but I would love to meet him again."

The boys looked at her askance. "You mean you met Joe Louis!?"

"I certainly did and he even signed a napkin for me, which I have somewhere. The next time I visit I'll be sure to bring it with me."

Alice then proceeded to recount a tale of a return trip to America in 1938. "By this time I was onto husband number seven; yet another sea captain who'd taken his ship across the Atlantic to New York. From the moment we docked, we'd been caught up in the hiatus regarding the forthcoming fight between Louis and the German Max Schilling. This was to be a rematch between the two men, with the earlier bout being won by Schilling and so excitement was high as thousands upon thousands of spectators headed towards the Yankee Stadium to watch the fight. Harold; that was my husband's name, had attempted to purchase tickets and was even prepared to pay well above the original price, but they were so precious he couldn't find a single one."

"Why was it so special?" Ray recalled hearing the fight on the radio, but couldn't remember much about it.

"It felt like so much more than just a boxing match between two men. The Nazis had been using Schilling as a propaganda puppet and had painted Joe as a beast of the field who never had the brains to take on one of the 'Master Race'. This competition had become a test of the two countries as well as their ideologies and politics. The entire city came to a standstill and I wouldn't be surprised if the entire country stopped to listen. We found some seats in a bar and listened to the fight over the radio whilst we enjoyed some drinks."

Alice, much to Olive's disgust included her drinking vast quantities of champagne or Gin and

Tonic in most of the stories she told. Ray suspected she included mentioning the alcohol just to see the reaction it might provoke from her sister as there was always a mischievous glint in her eye when she did so.

"It was clear from the way Joe began the fight that he meant business. I'd only taken a couple of sips from my gin and tonic when he knocked Schilling down for the first time and I hadn't even finished my first drink before the whole fight had finished and the German's trainer had thrown in the towel. The entire fight only lasted about two and half minutes; I was quite glad we hadn't wasted lots of money on tickets I can tell you!"

Ray and his mates cheered the defeat of the German even though Louis' win had already become legend. "What was it like though to actually be in New York when it happened?" Ray asked.

"When the announcer said that Joe had won, pandemonium broke out. People were yelling and cheering and even crying. Complete strangers came up and hugged us, and I received many a kiss on the cheek, which did not impress my husband one little bit! When we left to find a restaurant, the streets were packed with people cheering and honking the horns of their cars. It took us an absolute age to finally reach a decent restaurant. Anyway, we eventually did and I remember having a succulent steak."

She then went on to describe in great detail, the wonderful food she'd devoured, leaving her audience drooling and lustful to taste the delicacies that were beyond their current reality.

"Anyway, we had just ordered dessert when in walked none other than Joe Louis himself accompanied by at least fifteen others. He was seated at the table directly next to ours and ordered champagne and a steak, which when it came, turned out to be absolutely gigantic."

She once again described food in such glowing terms that the boys groaned in misery.

"Upon hearing our English accents he invited us to join him, and so we spent several hours in his presence swapping stories and generally having a good time. We went through a number of bottles of champagne until we were all really rather tipsy, including the mighty Joe Louis. He'd just asked me to dance when his mother arrived on the scene and things escalated out of hand quite quickly."

The group of boys asked in unison "What happened?"

"Well in turned out that Joe had signed a contract in which he promised to live a cleaner than clean life, which meant no drinking in public and he was also not allowed to be photographed with a white woman; so when his mother found him out after curfew drinking and about to start dancing with me, she was none too pleased."

Ray could well imagine how Joe's mother might react, as even though he hadn't signed a contract as such, he knew how his own mother would react if she caught him drinking or talking to any girl, regardless of her colour! "What did she do Yaya?"

"Well she grabbed him by the scruff of his shirt and yelled "what you doin' carousing with white folk and drinking hard spirits; what if someone was to take your picture?!""

"But Ma, they is from England and I'm just having a few drinks to celebrate my win that is all."

Ray laughed at Yaya's American accent and was rather impressed with her impersonation of Joe and his mother. "What did she say to that Yaya?"

"Well as you can imagine she was not impressed. "Don't you give me no sass boy! You should be in bed!"

"The argument had drawn the attention of the other diners in the restaurant, which was an obvious embarrassment to Joe. He therefore whispered to her through clenched teeth; "I'm a grown man ma, so either leaves me to celebrate in peace or else sit your butt down and have something to eat!"

The boys giggled at each other imagining what

would happen if they were to speak to their mothers like that. Ray could almost feel the sting of her smack as she would undoubtedly clip him around the ear. However, this was the heavyweight champion of the world we were talking about.

"What did his ma do, did she sit down?"

"Well to be honest I thought she would with it being Joe Louis and all. However, I think his mother was equally as formidable as her son because she belted him around the head with her handbag, knocking him off his chair and onto the floor. She then waded in hitting him repeatedly as she screamed; "Don't you ever speak to your mother like that boy! I was the one that raised you proper and if I say you is doing wrong, you is doing wrong!" She then grabbed him off the floor by his ear and pulled him to his feet."

By this stage the boys were in hysterics as they thought of Joe Louis being dragged around by his ear.

"All idea of Joe being a champion boxer went out the window as he cried "Ouch, get off me ma, you're hurtin' me!" As she dragged him towards the exit, the last thing I heard was Joe whining an apology and promising never to backchat her again!"

When Alice finished she received yet another standing ovation as her audience cheered and stamped their feet. Even Olive looked amused and obviously condoned the actions of Joe's mother.

"Well it serves him right! You boys should learn a lesson from that story." She warned as she folded clothes in the corner. "A boy should always listen to his mother and do as he's told because your mother knows best!"

Alice then took them all by surprise by agreeing with her sister. If ever there was a person who rebelled against authority, Ray would have paid good money that it was Yaya, and yet she said. "Olive is quite right; you should always do as your mother tells you because she knows best."

Olive smiled smugly and nodded her head, before once again looking disgusted as Alice went on to say. "If I'd have listened to my mother, I would never have gone to sea and seen the world or met the many fabulous characters that I have." She then winked at Ray before heading into her next story.

"Now have I told you about what happened when I was in China?"

The boys shook their heads in eager anticipation that they were about to find out and amazed that this old woman had travelled that far.

"Well it must have been in the late 1920's and I was on yet another cruise to the Far East."

"Which husband were you onto by then Yaya?"

Mousey asked before he realised it was a rather rude question.

However, Alice was undaunted and rather shocked them when she replied "I do believe darling that I was between husbands at that point. I was enjoying the fruits of my labour, settled on my by the divorce court."

There were looks between the boys that suggested they weren't sure what this meant. Ray actually imagined Alice hauling around a cart of fruit, selling it to the other passengers on the ship and to the Chinese once they'd reached port. However, he didn't like to interrupt so remained in rapt silence as Alice continued.

"I went ashore and travelled around seeing the sights. We had a stopover of several days and I had a small fortune burning a hole in my pocket; I therefore went looking for a high stakes game of cards."

Olive was so disgusted at hearing this she left the room.

"You have to understand my dears; China was renowned at this time for opportunities to engage in illicit gambling so I couldn't miss out on a chance to partake of such opportunities. I found a game without too much trouble and settled down to win some money.

The arena where we engaged in our battle of wills was a seedy little room at the back of a hotel. To be honest, I find the seedier the room, the more I can concentrate as there are less distractions; so after proving that I had enough money to join in, I was allowed to take a seat."

"How much money did you have to have in order to play?"

"Not enough to break the bank, but quite a sizable pot of about a thousand pounds."

The boys were shocked that anyone could have that amount of money and be prepared to lose it all in a game. Mousey couldn't keep from blurting out. "Why would you gamble with so much money? It would take my dad years to make that much."

"My dear, I had plenty more back on the ship and you have to realise I'm a really good poker player so stood to win considerably more. Anyway, by the look of the men sat around the table, they'd already been playing for many hours, which meant their concentration would not be at its peak. They were dishevelled, smelled of sweat, alcohol and tobacco and were in need of a shave. Exactly the type of men I love to play against!"

"Were they Chinese Yaya?"

"Actually there was an American gentleman, one Frenchman and several Chinese. I have to say I have played cards all over the world but I've never played against such diverse nationalities, not to mention the way they played the game. The American was loud and garrulous, which made him quite easy to read. If he had a good hand he'd become quieter and bet small to begin with, before putting a large amount of money into the pot in one fell swoop. He'd obviously had some success earlier judging by the pile of money in front of him.

The Frenchman was very quiet and sweated a lot.

He looked like his life depended on him being able to walk away with more money than he arrived with. This made him intense but unsure of what to do. If he had a good hand, he'd ponder over it, repeatedly looking at his cards before betting anything. He would rarely attempt a bluff, which made him easy to read."

The boys had heard so many stories about poker, they all knew what the terminology meant and could each hold their own when they played each other for matchsticks back at headquarters.

"The Chinese however, were much harder to make out. They were dressed identically in western suits with their jackets over the backs of the chairs and their sleeves rolled up. Their arms were covered in tattoos and they chirruped away to each other in Mandarin, which made it difficult to pick up on any "tells". The most frustrating thing was the way they seemed to play in tandem. They would follow the bet of their colleague, raise when one of them did or fold at the same time. It made me feel as though I was playing against one person rather than three."

Her audience were by now eager to discover how much she'd won on this occasion. The idea that she could lose was unthinkable as she'd become almost like a superhero; a female Flash Gordon who overcame any obstacle. "How much did you win Yaya? Did you take them to the cleaners?"

"Well boys, there is a tale to tell before I can tell you that. To begin with I made small bets so never lost or won a great deal. You see I was trying to develop a strategy to overcome my opponents. After about an hour I felt I had the measure of them so began to play with more fluidity. I quickly amassed a small fortune, mainly at the expense of the American and the Frenchman." Her eyes glistened as she recalled the thrill of winning. "There is no greater sense of satisfaction than winning a hand of poker and gathering the winnings to you."

Ray found this hard to believe as he gained huge satisfaction from plenty of things. He was sure it was probably great to win lots of money in that way, but he was certain bowling someone out in a cricket match or winning a running race in which you had to give your all were equally satisfying.

"At that point I felt invincible, which is a distinct shortcoming when you are on a winning streak. I became rather reckless with my bets even bluffing my way to winning a pot worth over eight hundred pounds in English money; when I only had a pair of twos. It was at that point however, the game shifted away from me. I'm convinced the Chinese started to cheat in some way, but I've never been able to fathom out how. All they did was give each other a look, which at the time and in my arrogance I took to be a look of admiration at my awesome skill, but soon realised must have been some sort of signal. I started to lose; small hands at first but then larger and larger pots went to the Chinese on hands that I was convinced I should have won.

I still had a considerable pile of winnings but it was dwindling rapidly so I decided it was time to leave politely saying I had to catch up on my beauty sleep. However, I was told in no uncertain terms I had to stay.

"You no leave until game is complete. You win all money or you lose all money!"

Once again the boys were thrilled by Alice's impersonation of her opponent and bellowed with laughter.

"In all seriousness, I'd never played a game like this and even though I was always prepared to lose my stake, one thousand pounds was rather a little too much even for me. I therefore decided to play cautiously until I figured out how they were cheating or I came up with a way of getting out of there with some of my money still in tack. Neither seemed very likely and I was stuck at the table for hours. Food was brought and we were only allowed short bathroom breaks. I considered using one of these to sneak off but one of the Chinamen always stayed at the table to watch the money. I was stuck; my only advantage was being slightly fresher than the others due to joining the game many hours in. I thought if I was exhausted, lord knew how the others must have felt."

Alice had once again managed to create the tension of the seedy room at the back of a hotel. The boys could almost smell the stale tobacco and sweat; although Ray suspected this might have been the Featherstone twins who only washed if their mother was standing over them.

"The Frenchman was the first to crack, recklessly going 'all in' on a hand that was clearly mediocre based upon his attitude and body language. The Chinese swooped and took his remaining money, leaving him to slope away utterly dejected. When the American went in a similar fashion not long after, it left me as the only opposition. I was still doing quite well having stemmed the flow of losses and won some small to middling pots, but I have to say I didn't hold out much hope of leaving with any money in my purse.

However, an opportunity presented itself as dawn was breaking. It felt as though we had been playing for days and it was clear the Chinamen were struggling as their stamina waned. They called for a break and for the first time, all three of them left the table leaving me alone with only the dealer in the room. The dealer moved away from the table to smoke a cigarette so I grabbed my opportunity and quickly swiped the bulk of my winnings into my bag. I then made excuses that I needed the bathroom and left the room, sneaking out the back of the hotel and down a dark alley. I'd just managed to hail a rickshaw and was heading towards the docks and the safety of my ship, when the hue and cry went up behind me. I ducked down and pleaded with the driver to go faster. I also gave him an incentive of a huge tip if he did so. Luckily the noise faded as we headed down small alleyways, using little trod shortcuts. As I started to relax I realised I was giggling hysterically. Honestly I must have looked like a mad woman with my hair in disarray, my makeup smudged and cackling like a demented witch!"

The boys applauded once again as they heard their hero succeed against all the odds.

"Ah, but I haven't finished my tale." Alice proclaimed. "When I finally reached the docks I discovered to my horror that the ship had sailed without me. I had been so caught up in the game that I'd spent a whole day longer than I'd thought. Honestly, I'd totally lost track of time.

I was at a loss as to what to do so I made my way to the British Embassy, but I received little in the way of advice other than to inform me it would be several months before another ship would allow me to continue with my journey. They also told me that the Chinamen I'd played against were undoubtedly members of a notorious Triad gang and that by crossing them I'd put my life at risk. They advised me to get out of the city and to lie low somewhere until a ship could take me away."

Alice paused to take a sip of her tea as the boys sat with bated breaths waiting for her to continue. After several minutes of silence, Ian couldn't take it anymore. "Well come on Yaya, what happened!"

"All in good time Ian, all in good time." The boys gave Ian a dig, partly for being rude to their hero and partly because they just enjoyed giving each other digs.

"The next day I disguised myself as a peasant woman travelling on the back of a cart and managed to escape into the countryside. I then spent several idyllic months living on a farm leading the simple life of a farm hand. I'd rise very early and tend to the animals, help with the cooking and cleaning and then retire happily exhausted to bed when it went dark. I learned to speak Mandarin quite fluently and even adopted an orphan dog, which I managed to smuggle on board the ship when I finally escaped the country. You know, those months taught me an awful lot about how simple things like hard work, good food and decent company can make you possibly happier than having lots of money and adventures."

Some of his mates obviously weren't as sure about that as they loved having adventures more than anything else. However, they all gave Yaya a rapturous applause before being shooed out by Olive. As they sat around their headquarters later that day, they swapped anecdotes from what they'd heard and shared their favourite bits.

"You know what; I want to be just like her when I grow up." Mousey said as he looked into the middle distance picturing the adventures he would have.

"What you mean you want to be a woman?! I suppose you're half way there already, and you've already achieved the same height!"

Everybody laughed; including Mousey, but then he felt he had to justify himself further. "What I mean is I want to travel; I want to be as fearless as Ray's aunt. I want to have adventures and make fortunes and see what the world has to offer. This war isn't going to last much longer and I reckon once it's over there are going to be some pretty amazing opportunities for people who've got ideas and the courage to try them out."

This was pretty profound stuff, but most of the boys nodded in agreement. Ray though, wasn't quite so sure.

He'd quickly come to adore in aunt like the rest of them, but he believed her recklessness was born out of the loss of her first husband and even though she always appeared upbeat and positive, he sensed a loneliness and a deep rooted sadness, which possibly accounted for why she drank so much. He also believed her attitude to life had put her in real danger on numerous occasions and whilst she dealt with the danger in an admirable and often heroic fashion, he wondered if she'd have reacted in the same way had she had a husband whom she truly loved or children she truly cared for. He realised he was also being pretty profound and given himself a headache in the process. He therefore decided to stop thinking and just go with the flow, nodding along with everyone else as Mousey described some of the adventures he was going to have.

Chapter 24 – Extraordinary Skill

1944 came to an end with scary news on the war front. Since the invasion of France, confidence had grown, even after the failure to cross the Rhine at the end of September; but then on the 16th December the Germans had mounted a massive offensive in an area between Belgium and Luxembourg known as the Ardennes, pushing the allies back. Fierce fighting was taking place and each evening they listened intently to the news on the radio to find out if there was to be another twist in the story of the conflict.

Ray's father was still confident though. "Once the weather improves the Germans won't know what hit them when the air force takes to the skies. They'll soon put a stop to the assault."

Ray had great faith in father's judgement, which proved to be accurate once again. By the end of January the Germans had been beaten back and it just seemed like a matter of time before they were completely defeated. The allies were advancing from the West and the Russians from the East. At home, things hadn't changed much. Rationing was still in place; although more goods were making their way onto the shelves and since September 1944, blackout had been relaxed a little allowing homes to produce the same amount of spilled light as the moon. This had become known as 'dim out' and although John still did his rounds of an evening, even he was more relaxed with people who breached the rules.

People were optimistic about the future and none more so than Ray. It had become clear that he had perhaps become the surrogate child that his aunt Alice had craved all her life. She showered him with gifts at the merest hint that he was interested in something. He only had to mention a new comic, or sport and the next thing he knew, she had bought him the very best or newest item. He found himself never without the newest Beano; the best tennis racquet or the most expensive football. Therefore, when he mentioned he'd gained a place in the school cricket team, he received a complete set of cricket whites, cricket boots and a brand new bat. He was the envy of the team when he turned up to training fully kitted out whilst most of them had to play in their normal school wear and pumps.

However, the first opportunity he had to wear this attire in a match, came in May 1945 shortly after the war against Germany, which had dominated their lives for the last five and half years finally came to end. Hitler had reportedly been found dead in the grounds of his bunker where he'd been sheltering from the approaching Russians, and Germany made an unconditional surrender a couple of days later. Hitler had apparently taken his own life rather than be captured, shooting himself in the head.

"What a cowardly way out!" Olive ranted upon hearing the news. "I suppose it's typical of the man to escape justice by putting a bullet through his brain!"

Ray considered his mothers opinion, but wasn't completely convinced. After the vile acts carried out on his orders and the death and destructions wrought on the world due to his warped ideology, he suspected suicide was in fact a wiser option than falling into the hands of the Russians as it was unlikely he would have received any mercy. When he intimated as much to his mother she actually got quite angry.

"Don't you dare suggest that vile little man was wise to take his own life; he should have paid for what he's done. He won't have to face up to it now though will he?!"

Ray agreed with everything his mother said, he was just trying to express logic for why Hitler killed himself. However, he wasn't prepared to argue. News was beginning to emerge of the camps the Nazis had operated and the horrors that had taken place in them. He found it hard to believe that a human being could treat another person the way the Nazis had treated the Jews and anybody else they took a disliking to. He therefore quickly apologised and agreed she was right.

A few days after the surrender of Germany and the sore heads caused by the celebration had eased; the headmaster of Ray's school decided to suspend lessons for a day and hold a day of sporting competitions instead. He enlisted the cooperation of the neighbouring girls' school, and so on a lovely sunny day the two schools descended onto the playing fields to enjoy a day of fun and frivolity. Most students had volunteered to compete as each event was to take place against the teachers. There was a football match, running races, field events, rugby match, netball and Ray's event; a cricket match.

As he walked out onto the field he felt absolutely fabulous dressed immaculately in his new cricket whites. This view was also shared by several girls who giggled as he walked passed.

"He looks rather dashing in his whites doesn't he?" They then giggled again as Ray tried to ignore them and kept his eyes facing forward. The debonair vibe was lost somewhat when he tripped over his own feet and went sprawling to the floor causing the girls to burst into fits of laughter. He'd never really been interested in girls, finding them quite boring and well;

girl like. However, hearing these compliments felt quite different. As he picked himself up and brushed down his trousers, he made a little gag of deliberately tripping over his feet and then winked at the girls who fell about in giggling excitement.

"You are one lucky blighter!" Mega said as he caught up with him. "They fancy you rotten; I wish I had a complete set of whites."

As he headed out towards the square his stride was a fraction longer, he stood a fraction taller and he felt energised by the fact that he was representing the school at cricket; and girls found him attractive.

The teachers were to bat first so Ray took up his position as first slip, with Mega taking the position of wicket keeper. They were the only first years in the entire team, so these positions of responsibility reflected the esteem in which they were held by the rest of the players, as they were both specialist positions. It may also have had to do with the fact that the ball came pretty fast to where the boys stood, which put a lot of the others off; it didn't half hurt when you got hit by a corgi ball.

To begin with the boys tried their faster bowlers against the two opening batsmen, but with little impact. The teachers had obviously played a lot and casually knocked the ball all round the field, leaving the fielders on the boundary exhausted and the team disheartened. Within ten overs the teachers had amassed over eighty runs and looked like they were going to continue to batter their students mercilessly. The closest they'd come was when they'd switched to a slower bowler and Ray had moved to silly mid off, which was a position mid way down the wicket but quite close to the batsman. On the third ball of the over the teacher miss cued a shot and knocked the ball gently into the air. Ray dived to his left, the ball almost in his grasp. As his fingers encircled the leather though, the teacher called out.

"Is that nicotine stains on your fingers Dagnall? I hope you don't smoke?!"

Ray's brain reacted quite strangely as it tried to do too many things at once. Part of it tried to complete the catch and entwine the fingers around the ball. However, there was another part, which reacted in primeval survival mode and wanted to hide the same fingers from view so his smoking wouldn't be found out. The result was several moments of confusion in which the ball was fumbled and dropped harmlessly to the floor. There was a groan from the spectators and his teammates, and a smug smirk from the teacher.

"Oh bad luck Dagnall, you nearly had me there!" He then proceeded to hit a four and a six off the last two balls.

"Don't worry Daggers it was actually a hard catch; you had a way to dive to get anywhere near it." Mega said as he tried to make him feel better as they changed ends, but Ray wanted revenge rather than platitude. He therefore approached the captain.

"Please let me have a bowl, I reckon I can get these two out. You've just seen what happened when they faced a slower ball, and they haven't seen my spin."

"You're too young Daggers; they'd knock you out of the park."

Ray liked the captain, but he wasn't prepared to give ground so easily. "They're already knocking us out of the park as it is. Give me one over and if I haven't got a wicket then take me off."

The captain was clearly at a loss as to what to do to cope with the staff so relented. "You get one over to prove yourself, but if they knock you all round the place, I'll put you at long stop out of the way." Long stop basically stood on the boundary directly behind the batsman and didn't do anything. Something that a boy who was out to impress some girls didn't want to happen; plus he also wanted his revenge.

He spent a little time loosening his shoulders and

his neck before taking his short run up to bowl. He still had no idea how he made the ball swerve through the air and then change direction so dramatically once it hit the floor, but he did know he could make it happen practically every time he bowled. His pace was ridiculously slow and should have meant the batsman had plenty of time in which to set themselves up for the shot. However, due to the unpredictability of the spin, it made them cautious. Mr Cooper, who'd made the comments about Ray's fingers, barely managed to block the ball and scored no runs off the first four balls.

"That's the ticket Daggers!" the captain said as he brought the ball back to Ray whilst polishing it on his trousers. "I think we'll keep you on after all."

Ray felt vindicated for his earlier dropped catch and put a bit of extra zip into the final two balls of the over. He didn't manage to claim a wicket but Mr Copper failed to score making it a maiden over. As he took up his position back at slip, he noticed the girls clapping him, which made him puff up with pride and gave him the incentive to try that little bit harder.

When he came to bowl again he decided to flight the ball a little further than normal, which caused Mr Copper to believe it was a full toss so he came down the ground to whack it over the boundary. However, at the last moment the ball swerved and dropped suddenly, making Cooper miss the ball completely. It then spun and went on to hit the wicket. The teacher looked unbelievably at the stumps before glaring at Ray.

"Oh bad luck sir, you nearly hit that one!"

Cooper stood for a moment, impotent to Ray's sarcasm, before walking dejectedly from the field. Ray's teammates gathered around him and patted him on the back.

"Well done Daggers, I think we've found ourselves a new star bowler." The captain said as he tossed Ray the ball. However, Ray was far more interested at the sight of the girls jumping up and down on the boundary, giggling and waving at him.

The third batsmen in turned out to be Mr Entwhistle, his woodwork teacher. Whilst he got settled at the crease Ray focused on the many negative comments this teacher had made about him and about his work. He loved working with wood but this man ruined his enjoyment on a weekly basis. He therefore decided to pour every ounce of animosity into his first ball. It zipped through the air faster than he'd ever bowled before and the swerve was more pronounced. Entwhistle lent into a forward stroke intending to block the ball, but the spin was vicious and instead of blocking it he nicked it with his bat.

"Howzat!" The cry went up from Mega as he raised his gloves in the air holding the ball. The rest of the team joined in as Ray turned towards the umpire. Entwhistle was refusing to walk, which really was bad form. He'd clearly nicked it, and in cricket you were expected to do the gentlemanly thing and acknowledge mistakes by reacting before the umpire had to make a decision. On this occasion Entwhistle was refusing to budge so it was even sweeter when the umpire raised his finger slowly indicating he was out.

"How can you give me out, we are meant to be colleagues?!"

Ray was astounded at the man's cheek; just because the umpire was a member of staff didn't mean he could blatantly cheat so the teachers won. He was therefore rather pleased at the umpire's reaction.

"Colin, you are out because you hit the ball and Mays caught it. Now be a good fellow and leave the field."

As Entwhistle slumped off towards the dressing rooms the noise was deafening. As Ray looked around the ground, the crowd were jumping up and down, arms in the air and screaming with glee. From their reaction it was clear that Entwhistle was not the most popular teacher and he felt a real sense of achievement at being able to hand out a bit of retribution on behalf of his classmates. However, he quickly had to refocus as he was now on a hat trick. To get three batsmen out with consecutive balls was something seldom achieved. The team captain gave his encouragement.

"You can do this Daggers; just take some deep breaths and relax."

"You know what skipper; I've never felt more relaxed in my life." And it was true, he was enjoying every moment of this game and confident in his own abilities, quite a rare sensation if he was honest with himself. As he took his few steps up to bowl, he therefore decided to try something different. He adjusted where he placed his fingers on the ball so that when he released it; instead of spinning, the ball went straight on. The batsman had played to block a spinning ball so missed and the ball went on to hit him on the pads plum in front of the wicket.

"Howzaaaaat!!!" the cry went up immediately, almost hysterical in its pitch. When the umpire's finger went aloft once again the crowd went absolutely wild and Ray was swamped as both teammates and invading spectators piled on top of him.

"You're a ruddy hero, that's what you are Daggers." The captain said as he dragged him back to his feet.

"Thanks skipper, but we haven't won yet and they are only three down." Inside, Ray was bursting with pride. It had only ever been in his dreams that he'd been the hero and yet here he was in reality, finally being lauded for his achievements.

By the time the teacher's innings was over he had bowled sixty balls and claimed eight wickets. Staggeringly, the teachers had not scored a single run off Ray, which meant they were all out for only 109. Upon claiming the final wicket; a stumping by Mega after the teacher had come down the ground to try and whack the ball, only to be beaten once again by the spin, Ray was lifted onto the shoulders of his teammates and ceremoniously carried back to the dressing rooms. His triumph was made complete when he spotted Aunt Alice, Reginald and his parents in the crowd. He hadn't realised they'd come to watch him play and the look of pride on their faces was something that would stay with him forever. He'd imagined it so many times before as he planned an escapade or undertook some silly endeavour, but something had always gone amiss or ended unexpectedly. This time however, the tears running down the cheeks of his mother and aunt were real and the proud grin that spread across his father's face melted his heart.

He was able to sit and watch the rest of the game in the glow of admiration and the comfort of team chairs that had been set up in front of the dressing rooms. The girls who had found him 'Dashing' before, devised a series of ploys to be near him and he heard words like 'Gorgeous, Handsome and Dreamy' being bandied around as they looked in his direction giggling. What had started out as furtive glances in his direction, were now unabashed stares, which quite frankly made him blush profusely; even more so when one of them broke away from her friends and walked over.

"You are a super cricket player." She said as she fluttered her eyelashes at him. "My friends and I think you were the best player on the pitch."

Ray didn't really know what to say as he wasn't used to this level of praise. "Er, thank you very much, but I doubt you'd say that if you saw me bat, I can hardly lay bat to ball." He realised this was probably not the best way to impress a girl, when the edge vanished from her adoration.

"Oh I see, but you bowled very well and my friend over there." She indicated a pretty blonde girl who waved and giggled before turning back towards her friends. "She was wondering if you would go out with her."

Ray found himself stumped for anything to say. He'd never had to make a decision like this and even worse, didn't have a clue what it meant to 'go out with someone.' He therefore decided to play for time so he could run the idea passed his mates.

"Come back and ask me again if we win the match."

As he said it, he had no idea what the girls reaction would be. He wouldn't have been surprised if she'd said something rude and stormed off, but instead she looked at him doe eyed. "You are so cool and dreamy" she said and ran back to her friend with his answer.

Luckily, Mega was an excellent batsman and ensured Ray the chance of a date by scoring sixty runs before being caught trying to hit a ball down to third man. However, this made it easy for the other batsmen at the top of the order to knock off the remaining runs, which marked an historic win for the students.

"Well played Dagnall well played Mays" the headmaster said as he presented them with joint man of the match awards in front of the whole school. "I must say I was rather impressed by your skills. However, I think it only fair that in the future we give other boys the chance to play against the staff so from now on you can act as coaches rather than taking part."

There was a ripple of quiet boos around the ground, accompanied by several "Shames" but the boys were unperturbed as they knew they both had dates the following week with a couple of rather attractive girls. As soon as the match was won, the girl had presented herself in front of Ray for his answer, but had first asked if he would get Mega to go on a date with her, so impressed had she been with his batting.

Chapter 25 – Peace on Earth and Wearing Long Pants

The cricket match had been something of a rite of passage for Ray. He'd gained the adoration of his peers, he'd achieved something considerable and he had a date with a girl! He realised he was growing up and this made him frustrated at being treated like a child; particularly by his mother. It wasn't just him of course, his mates chafed at the constraints of being treated as if they were unable to think for themselves or make their own decisions. Sharing tales of not being allowed to do this or wear that became an almost daily routine. One particular bone of contention was short pants. Since starting at Heath Road, Ray had been aware that the bigger boys wore long trousers, but when he asked if he could have a pair the answer was a resounding 'no'.

"You are far too young to be going round in long trousers Raymond, and besides I'm not made of money. Do you know how much trousers cost?!"

Even when he'd asked in front of Aunt Alice the answer was the same. At first he hadn't minded too much as all his mates were in the same boat, but recently Blainsey had strolled into their headquarters bedecked in a brand new pair of fashionable long slacks, which sparked renewed antagonism towards his mother.

"Ma please, I'm twelve years of age. I need a pair of long pants. I'd wear them to church on a Sunday." He was convinced playing the church card would have melted her resolve, but he was mistaken.

"God doesn't care what you wear when you worship him, he only cares that you do worship."

Ray was rather annoyed at his mother's contradiction. If God didn't care what he wore, why did he always have to dress in his best clothes and have a bath the day before? However, if he started to argue that point; he'd never get her to change her mind. He decided to change tack instead.

"Blainsey's already got a pair and Mousey and Obie have been promised a pair in a couple of weeks. I'll be the only one who still looks like a kid in short, worn out pants!"

His mother though, was having none of it.

"Raymond, I don't care what any of your friends are doing. They are not my son. You don't need long trousers yet; there are plenty of boys who are quite happy to wear short pants. I was only talking to

Martin's mother yesterday, and she's in total agreement with me."

"Yeah and he's miserable as well! It's so unfair!" With that he stormed out of the room and slammed the door hard before stomping up to his room. This didn't do much good as his mother followed him and gave him a good hiding for being insolent and moody. What was worse however, was the two week grounding he received, which meant he'd miss his date. He could have resorted to his tried and trusty method of sneaking out of the bathroom window, but he decided if he didn't have long trousers to wear it was probably better that he didn't show up.

When he told Mega what had happened he wasn't best pleased. "I'm not going on me own. What would I say?"

"You'd tell them the truth; say I'd been grounded and I'll see her in a couple of weeks."

"I don't mean that; what will I say to them in general? I'm useless with girls; I can't even talk to my sister. If you're not going then neither am I." This left two girls stood waiting outside the cinema in Woolton for goodness knew how long, waiting for two boys who didn't turn up because they didn't have long pants.

Hostilities were exacerbated in August when news came that finally the war had ended. The war in Europe had finished in May but fighting had continued against Japan until now. It had taken two atomic bombs to bring the Japanese to their knees, but after six long heartbreaking years there was peace; although if you lived in the Dagnall household you might have been forgiven for considering the conflict was still very much alive.

Ray still begrudged his mother for not allowing him to have long pants. When he'd seen the girl he was meant to date a few weeks later, she'd given him such a look of disdain he hadn't dared try and explain why he hadn't turned up for their date. Instead, he avoided her, which only made his anger towards his mother grow. She'd now decided to organise another street party and had once again persuaded neighbours to pitch in to celebrate the peace, but she was still adamant that Ray could make do with his short pants.

"Raymond, will you stop going on about me buying you long trousers! I will decide when you get a pair and I will not put up with you whining and moping about the house! Now go out and play and I don't want to hear another word about it."

"You are so mean! You love ruining my life don't you?!" Ray stormed from the house as quickly as he could before his mother could catch him, and went to find Ian. The two of them were the last of their gang without long trousers; Mega's mother having capitulated at the same time as the Japanese. This caused the two of them to gravitate towards each other in their misery.

"I'll tell you something, I'm not going to her stupid party in short pants. I'd rather stay in me room than look like a kid."

"I know; why can't they just get us some long trousers? It's not as if we don't need them. I've had the seam on me bum sewed three times on these pants. If I fart, they're likely to split in two!" Ian illustrated his point by breaking wind as forcefully as he could and bending over to show the ongoing repairs of his worn shorts.

Ray was laughing as he said "You're gross! And they haven't split so you're going to have to make do with them like me."

The day of the party dawned in glorious sunshine once again and a truly festive spirit descended over the neighbourhood. Everywhere one looked people were smiling and laughing, singing songs and shaking hands and hugging. Everywhere that is except Ray's bedroom where he and Ian moped miserably.

"It's just so unfair! Do they want to keep us children forever?! I mean what chance have we got with the Matthews sisters if we're wearing short pants; ruddy none that's what!"

The Matthews sisters were twins who lived round the corner and who flirted with Ian and Ray whenever they passed the house; giggling and making suggestions regarding what they were going to do with their time just loud enough so the two boys could hear and possibly turn up at the same location.

"Why can't they just go out and buy us a pair of long pants?! I'll tell you why; because they're control freaks that's why! They refuse to do anything unless they decide it for themselves. They won't buy us any because we asked!"

Ray realised Ian must have been spending far too much time in school, as the teacher's habit of asking a question and then answering it themselves seemed to be rubbing off. He laughed mirthlessly.

"What's so funny? I don't think it's funny; it's not a laughing matter! We need to ruddy well come up with a solution because I'm not spending the whole day up here with you!"

Ray thought his friend must be badly infected as he seemed to be getting worse, which caused him to laugh harder, annoying Ian even more. He picked up Ray's cricket shoe and threw it at him.

"Ouch, you ruddy idiot, that hurt!" Ray launched himself at Ian and they proceeded to roll around on the floor, wrestling to get the upper hand and knocking Ray's cricket whites from their hanger in the process. As the two boys entangled themselves in the clothes, an idea sprang into Ray's mind.

"I've got it; I know what we can do!" He jumped up grabbing his long white trousers and began searching through his cupboard for a suitable shirt. When he found one, he stood in front of a mirror with the clothes held up to him. "What do you think?"

Ian began to smile broadly. "Very ruddy dashing if I may say so! That is genius Daggers. I'm going to leg it home and get mine. I think I'll try and get one of my dad's jackets as well!" He then bounded from the room leaving Ray to quickly undress and don his new outfit. By the time Ian returned, he was decked out in white cricket boots, white trousers, a blue shirt and one of his dad's black jackets, which was about three sizes too big. Ian was dressed in a similar fashion, and together they admired themselves in the mirror.

"We look pretty impressive I reckon, but do you think we look a bit young?"

"I know, why don't we get some boot polish and dab it around our chins to make it look as though we shave?" Ray didn't give Ian any time to consider before he'd sneaked downstairs and returned with the tin. "We don't need to put loads on, just a smudge here and there."

Five minutes later they once again admired themselves in the mirror and were satisfied with the results. "I reckon we look eighteen easily." Ian said as he adjusted a smudge of black on his jaw." You know what; we could even get served in the pub if we wanted to."

"Too right", Ray replied as he tried dangling a fag from his mouth without using his hands. "But I haven't got any money and besides, I don't really like beer." He still hadn't acquired a taste for alcohol since the street party over a year before, even though Blainsey had been bringing an increasing amount of bottles of beer and cider to their headquarters. He didn't mind cider but still wasn't a massive fan.

"Why would we want to go to the pub when there's a party right outside; there'll be food and dancing and the Matthew sisters! I was just saying we could if we wanted." Ian was looking out the window at the gathering crowds. "We need to focus on how we're going to sneak passed your mother without her spotting us. She's bound to make you get changed and there's no doubt she'd snitch on me to my mum."

Ray didn't even need to think of a solution. "No problem at all. We'll escape the way I always do when I'm grounded; by climbing out the bathroom window and down the drainpipe. We just need to make sure to avoid them for the rest of the day."

Ten minutes later the two boys were running down the street to rendezvous with the rest of the gang before heading to the party. When Blainsey saw them, he fell about laughing.

"What the ruddy hell have you two come as; do you realise what you look like?!" You look ruddy stupid I'll tell you that much!" The tears were rolling down his cheeks by the time he'd finished.

"We do not; I reckon we look dead grown up!" Ray was rather pleased when the Featherston twins nodded in unison and felt vindicated for dressing up.

"The boot polish makes you look like you've been down the mines!" He continued to bellow with laughter, which wound Ray up somewhat.

"You're just jealous you didn't think of it!" he said as he reached up to smooth the polish out, only succeeding in smudging it further.

"I don't need boot polish to make me look like I've got stubble; I've already started shaving you idiots! Blainsey headed off towards the party shaking his head and still in the throes of much hilarity.

"Well I don't care what he says, I think we look great!" Ray said as he traipsed after Blainsey with the others so they could celebrate peace on earth and the fact they were in long pants.

The party proved to be a huge success once again, with festivities going on until the early hours of the next morning. The Matthews sisters turned out to be rather impressed with Ray and Ian's attire and flirted with them both, further vindicating their choice. After plenty of food and drink had been consumed, dancing started up and down the street. People could choose different styles of music, from the live piano playing of Olive, to the livelier big band and jazz played on a record player at the other end of the street. Naturally, Ray chose to stay as far away from his mother as possible.

"So would you like to dance with me Ray?" Elizabeth Matthews asked as she grabbed him by the hand and dragged him to where other couples were dancing.

"Er I suppose so, but I've not done much dancing

before so don't know many moves." His heart was pounding in his chest as, probably for the first time, the last thing he wanted was to look like a fool.

"Don't worry." She giggled "You just have to hold onto me and we can move around in circles together." She grabbed his arms and put them around her waist, sending a shiver down his spine.

As they moved around more or less in time with the music, Elizabeth chattered away about everything and anything, from the weather to school and the future. Ray could honestly say he didn't hear a word she said so nervous was he about stepping on her feet, and also slightly amazed that he had a girl in his arms and they were dancing!

The next record was a slower, more romantic tune and Elizabeth snuggled into his shoulder and actually stopped talking. Ray felt this was possibly one of the best moments of his life so far as he started to focus on how he could go about trying to steal a kiss. As the tune ended however, he realised he didn't have to try as Elizabeth looked up into his eyes and moved her head forward on a slight angle. He was amazed; she was going to kiss him! Without much hesitation he moved his own head forward and their lips met. The kiss didn't last that long as her sister came storming over and pulled her off.

"Have you seen what that idiot has done?" she said as she indicated a rather large black stain on her face and another on the collar of her dress, before noticing similar smudges on her sister. "He's got it on you as well! They've only gone and put boot polish on to try and look older! Arrgh, this is my best dress!!"

All plans of further smooching went out of the window as the sisters stormed off to try and get the stains out of their dresses and clean their faces. Ian then strolled over looking rather bemused.

"So did you get to snog Elizabeth at all?"

"Yeah, sort of."

"Cool wasn't it?

"It sure ruddy was!" and with that the two boys headed off to get some more food, giggling and clapping each other on the back.

Over the rest of the summer, a new routine emerged, which involved Ray climbing out of his bathroom window on a nightly basis bedecked in his dad's jacket and his cricket white long trousers so he could meet up with Ian and hang round the streets feeling rather cool. The fact that it was the cricket season and their trousers often had grass stains on them didn't seem to deter them at all.

Chapter 26 – Unfairly Treated as a Savage

In the final week of the summer holidays Olive finally took her son into the city centre to order him a pair of long trousers in preparation for his return to school. As he entered the city on the tram, he was astonished by the change that had been wrought. There was still a lot of bomb damage, but there was a bustle and vibrancy, which took the breath away. Work seemed to be taking place everywhere rebuilding what the Nazis had destroyed, and Ray noticed more men than he'd seen in a long while as he noted the fact that more and more troops had returned home to civilian occupations once more.

Although he wasn't a massive fan of shopping, he relished this opportunity to try on long trousers until his mother finally decided on a pair of black ones, which were cut fashionably with turned up bottoms. For the first time ever he actually looked forward to returning to school. However, the feeling didn't last long once he'd been in class for a couple of weeks.

Mega was off school with chicken pocks, which meant Ray was left feeling rather lonely. He'd never developed the same wide circle of friends as he had at Springy, probably because he had so many friends outside of school. Thus whilst Mega was off, he was bored and fed up. His lessons still didn't motivate him much, although he continued to be quite good at Maths and his woodwork had improved once Entwhistle realised if he left him to his own devices he could actually produce good quality work. However, he missed having a laugh with Mega and taking the mickey out of his teachers. He therefore gravitated towards Peter Dooley who was equally disaffected with his education and enjoyed undermining his teachers; although Dooley's idea of having a laugh was to deliberately initiate a conflict with his teacher and start arguing, finally laughing in the their face before storming out. This was not Ray's style at all but Dooley tended to find his jokes hilarious, which gave him someone to bounce off in lessons.

To say they became friends would be putting it too strongly, but he did start sitting by him during lessons and they hung out in the same vicinity on the yard. Dooley was also a useful ally as he was the hardest kid in their year and feared by most of the other boys in the entire school. On Dooley's part, he tolerated Ray as he made him laugh, but no more than that.

One evening Ray was walking out of the gates as normal at the end of the day along with the rest of the school. Since Mega had been off he tended to walk home on his own, but on this occasion he'd been sharing a funny story with Dooley so was stood next to him just beyond the gates.

"...And then she clipped me round the ear and sent me to bed without any tea!"

Dooley laughed at the antics he'd just heard before spotting a lad from the year above heading in their direction.

"That was really funny Daggers, but you'll have to excuse me as I have to have a word with that lad over there."

Ray was taken by surprise by Dooley's impeccable manners as he'd normally just grunt and walk off. He was also surprised when Dooley launched himself at the bigger boy and waded into him before the lad knew what hit him.

"That'll teach you to say things about me!" he yelled as he repeatedly punched him in the face. "You're not so hard now are you!?"

The other boy fell to the floor, but Dooley continued to punch and kick him. Ray was shocked and sickened by what he was seeing, but was frozen to the spot unable to intervene. The gang had been in plenty of scraps, but they always fought fairly, yet here was Dooley attacking a lad unprovoked and battering him mercilessly even when it was clear he was beaten. When a couple of teachers ran up and pulled Dooley off, Ray actually felt relieved and determined to cut all ties with the hooligan. He also reckoned Dooley should get into real trouble for the attack. However, he didn't believe he should be punished as well and was therefore flabbergasted when he was dragged to the headmaster's office alongside the said hooligan.

"You two are an utter disgrace; I will not have this type of behaviour in my school, do you understand?!"

Unfortunately Ray didn't understand one bit, but was in a state of shock and so stood numb as the headmaster continued his tirade. "You are a pair of thugs; do you hear me a pair of savages!"

Ray could hear the headmaster very well as he was stood right in front of him as he yelled, spittle flying from his mouth and landing on Ray's cheek.

"The first thing I'm going to do to you reprobates is dole out six of the best to both of you!"

Ray just dumbly raised his hand as the headmaster brought out the cane and struck him three times on each hand. He didn't even feel the sting he was so shocked and confused.

"I will be writing to both your parents, which will

probably come as no surprise to you Dooley as I normally have to do so on a weekly basis already!"

Dooley actually smirked at that and said "Yes sir" as if he didn't have a care in the world.

"However, you Dagnall are a different kettle of fish. I thought you had something to offer after that cricket match, but I was obviously wrong. I wonder how your mother will react when she hears she has bred a hooligan for a son?!"

Even after hearing this, he seemed unable to focus on the dire consequences that would befall him when his mother read the school's account of his apparent savagery. His mind seemed befuddled, and so he walked home in a daze ignoring the platitudes from Dooley who said he was a 'goodun' for not speaking out against him. It was only as he lay in bed later that evening, his hands finally stinging from the blows of the cane that the events came crashing together as one memory after the other spilled into his brain until he thought he might not be able to cope. He realised how unfairly he'd been treated and jumped up from the bed and paced back and forth, tears of frustration rolling down his cheeks until he made the decision to tell his parents his version of events.

When he walked into the living room he almost

collapsed with relief to find his father alone. "Where's me Ma dad?"

"She's at Sydnah's as usual."

"Dad I need to tell you something that happened today, but I need you to listen to it all before you say anything." He then proceeded to give his father a full account of what had occurred. When he'd finished, he waited for his father to say something, but he just sat shaking his head.

"Well aren't you going to say something dad? Do you think it's fair? I didn't do anything and I got punished. When me Ma finds out, she'll batter me and I just don't think it's fair!"

He was hoping for some sort form of agreement from his father; some statement that justified his feelings of injustice and maybe a promise that his father would sort it out with the school and his mother. Instead, his father started asking him questions.

"What are you most upset about?"

"What? All of it of course!"

"Yes I know that but what upset you the most? Was it getting the cane? Or the headmaster sending a letter home; or that your mother will probably give you a good hiding?

Ray started to think about it a bit more objectively. "The cane didn't really upset me as I've received it plenty of times before, and so I suppose getting a good hiding of me Ma wasn't that upsetting as it will hardly be the first time I've had one! I suppose the thing that really niggles is the fact I'm being blamed for something I didn't do and being called a savage and a hooligan, which I just don't believe I am."

His father actually looked quite impressed. "You know what Ray; you're growing up so quickly. I know the type of lad you are, but unfortunately life isn't always fair. Sometimes you just have to accept that you get blamed for things you didn't do." He then patted his son on the head and went back to reading the paper.

His humiliation was made even worse the next day when he and Dooley were hauled up onto the stage during assembly to be castigated in front of the entire school by the headmaster.

"Do you see these two savages standing before you?" He said scornfully as he gestured towards Ray and Dooley as if they were dog muck on the bottom of his shoes. "They are not to be trusted; mark my words nothing good will ever come from them so I advise you all to keep your distance; stay well clear of them for they are bad news; very, very bad news! They will never amount to anything so make sure you are not dragged down with them."

Ray couldn't believe his ears. He was being made out to sound as bad as the worst of the Nazis and his reputation was being torn to shreds in front of eyes. There was no way he could allow this to continue so he stepped forward and declared in a voice that sounded far calmer than he felt.

"Excuse me sir but I didn't actually do anything. I just happened to be walking out of school with Dooley."

The headmaster looked as though somebody had just told him there was an unexploded bomb in his office. He went white, started to shake and actually looked a little afraid that a pupil would speak up for themselves. "You dare to speak to me Dagnall after what you have done!?" He boomed at the top of his voice. "How dare you Dagnall; how dare you!"

"But sir, that's what I'm trying to tell you, I didn't do anything."

To give Dooley his due, he also spoke up. "He's telling the truth sir, he just happened to be there; and besides I didn't need any help in battering Smith, he's a big wimp!"

The headmaster literally looked as if he was having a seizure as his body seemed to spasm uncontrollably as he looked from one boy to the other. This was open rebellion, which wasn't helped by the few sniggers coming from the hall when Dooley called Smith a wimp. He blustered for several moments before falling back on tried and tested teacher inanity. "Yes, but you were with him, which makes you equally as guilty."

"But sir"

"Do not "but sir" me Dagnall. You were with him and that makes you guilty by association; I'll not hear another word about it!" He then stormed from the stage and out of the hall.

Ray wasn't sure what "guilty by association" meant and it appeared most of the other pupils didn't either as they didn't avoid him as they had been told. In fact he became something of a minor celebrity over the following days for standing up to the headmaster and attempting to right a certain wrong. He also reckoned his words must have had an effect on the headmaster, as even though he waited with dread, no letter arrived for his mother to read. He trusted his father when he'd told him that innocent people sometimes get blamed for things they hadn't done, but he was rather pleased with himself that on this occasion, he hadn't just accepted it and had stood up for himself instead.

Chapter 27– Waking the Neighbours and Camp

Although his reputation seemed to have escaped the accusations of the headmaster, Ray still felt he needed to improve his profile in a constructive way. He'd wanted to join the Boys Brigade for ages and now finally got his opportunity when he learned that several of the older boys had left. A few days before he went to his first session, he happened to mention it in front of Aunt Alice.

"Oh my dear boy that's wonderful; do you have the correct uniform and equipment?"

"Well not yet, but I'm sure some of the boys who are leaving will have old pieces they don't need anymore." He had an idea of where this conversation was going and whilst he loved receiving gifts off his Aunt, he did feel a bit uncomfortable about the amount she bought him compared to his sister and cousins.

"Nonsense my boy I'll not hear of it. You need a nice new drum and a brand new uniform.

"Honestly Yaya you don't need to; you do more than enough for me already." He wasn't just saying that to make her feel good about herself; it was true. She'd spent an absolute fortune on him since she'd returned to England and he sometimes worried that her money would run out. However, he didn't hold out much hope of her listening to him when all she said was. "We'll see".

Unsurprisingly, the day before he started she turned up at Clavelle Road with several packages. Inside one was a brand new uniform and in the other was a drum. Ray was overwhelmed.

"Yaya this is too much. You shouldn't have; it must have cost you a fortune for all this?!" He was delighted of course, but also felt a little awkward as he was unsure how he could ever repay her.

"Nonsense Raymond my dear; you're my favourite nephew so if I can't spoil you, who can I spoil? She then beckoned him closer and looked around in a conspiratorial fashion before whispering in his ear. "Shall I let you in on a little secret?"

Ray wasn't too sure he wanted to hear his Aunt's secret as normally when someone told you a secret they expected you to swear not to tell anyone and he didn't think his aunt would appreciate his way of swearing oaths. "Go on then Yaya, if you must."

Alice giggled at his response before continuing. "If Reginald dies before I do, he intends to leave everything he has to me in his will, and he is worth millions darling so a few pounds here and there on small presents for my favourite nephew isn't going to break the bank is it my dear?!"

Ray was astonished. He had a fair idea Alice was wealthy, but never believed she could possibly become a millionaire in the near future. Reginald was quite a bit older than her after all and had become rather frail in recent months; he'd caught the flu and had yet to recover properly meaning they'd even had to cancel their hunting trips as he didn't have the energy.

As it dawned on him that he was related to a potential millionaire, he stopped feeling awkward that she'd spent so much money and began to enjoy his new attire and drum, strutting up and down in front of her and making her howl with laughter at his antics with the drum.

As she was leaving later that evening he thanked her once again. "Yaya thank you ever so much, they're absolutely brill. You're my favourite Aunt and always will be."He then gave her a huge hug.

"Oh Raymond, you do know how to make an old woman feel young. I'm going to let you in on another little secret. Once Reginald has left me his estate, I'm going to make a will in which I name you as my sole beneficiary. That means darling that it will all be yours when I die!" She then left him standing on the doorstep open mouthed and frozen to the spot.

He couldn't believe what she'd told him. Basically, he would one day become a millionaire and own all the land as well as the house in Tarbuck. He spent the rest of the evening lying on his bed contemplating what he'd do with so much money. He'd obviously give some to his family and friends, buy a house and a car and several pairs of long trousers, but after that he was flummoxed in trying to come up with what he might do with the rest.

It was at that point he realised that for him to possess the money, his favourite Aunt would have to die and so he reached the conclusion he didn't relish the prospect at all and hoped that Alice lived for many more years so he could put off having to make decisions as well as grieving her death.

Boys Brigade turned out to be everything he'd hoped it would be. He learned to march and play the drum and the bugle, in addition to being able to enjoy the sessions with some of his best mates as Mega, Ian and the Featherston twins had joined at the same time.

He loved the way the public gazed at them when they processed on a Sunday morning, decked out in all their finery and had to admit they made a pretty impressive sight; particularly to the teenage girls of the area who would giggle and bat their lashes as the boys marched past. Even the Matthews sister's frosty attitude towards them seemed to melt and there were several occasions he caught Elizabeth staring at him during a service before she turned away and blushed when he winked at her.

Another aspect of the procession, which gave him great delight, was when Mega pointed out that lots of people tended to stay in bed on a Sunday morning; something Ray had never been able to do.

"You know, I don't think it's fair they get to stay in bed and we have to be up at the crack of dawn in order to get ready for church." Mega announced as he harnessed on his drum.

"I quite agree Mr Mears so I believe we should share God's music with them so they can enjoy his love and join in with worshipping him!"

They then made sure they put extra effort into banging their drums and sneaked waves at those irate neighbours who deigned to look out of their windows to see what the racket was that was disturbing their well earned lie in.

There were other benefits of course to being a member of the 'BB'. They learned how to make a camp fire, tie knots in rope and cook sausages over an open fire. This was a rare treat as rationing was still prevalent so allowing boys to experiment with such commodities was a rare honour indeed. Ray actually proved himself to be quite good at producing food, which on the whole was edible. This was more than could be said for Ian who incinerated everything he touched.

"Urgh it tastes like charcoal!" He said after biting into a blackened stump, which bore no resemblance to a sausage whatsoever.

"How do you know what charcoal tastes like? Mine is quite delicious. Ray made exaggerated noises of savouring his fair as Ian looked on covetously and tried another bite of his own endeavours.

"I know what charcoal tastes like because this is charcoal; I can't eat any more." He then went to throw what was left into the nearest bush.

"What do you think you're doing Davies?! Do you know what it cost to get hold of those sausages? I don't care how burnt it looks, just eat the thing!" The Lieutenant then stood over Ian and made sure he ate every single morsel, making him feel quite ill.

In order to avoid trying to find food they had to buy, they were also taught how to bait a line and cast so they could catch their own food from the sea. This took place on a Saturday afternoon in New Brighton. The whole troop journeyed across and set up along the promenade with one pole between two. To begin with Ray was quite excited, casting with enthusiasm and then reeling in the line quickly to see if his tea had miraculously appeared on the end.

"Daggers you're doing it too quickly; there's no way a fish would have time to bite anything the way you keep hauling the line in as soon as you've cast it."

"Shut up Ian! This is how we were shown; I just need to cast it further out."

Ian was not so sure but kept quiet for the next ten minutes as Ray continued to cast and haul the line in at a feverish pace. His patience finally ran out though. "Look Daggers, I think it's my turn now and maybe you could watch how I do it?"

"No way, I've hardly had a go and besides, none of the other lads have swapped yet." He continued to cast and retrieve.

"Daggers it's my turn!" Ian grabbed for the pole and the two boys began struggling for possession and ended up rolling round on the floor.

"What the ruddy hell do you two think you're

playing at?" The lieutenant said as he dragged them to their feet.

"He started it!" Ian said "He wouldn't let me have my go on the pole and he's making a mess of it anyway!"

"I am not! I've only had a go for about fifteen minutes; none of the other lads have swapped yet."

The lieutenant wasn't in the mood to negotiate. "Hand over the fishing pole to Davies." He ordered Ray." He can have a go for the next fifteen minutes and then you can swap again and if I see or hear you arguing again, you'll both come and sit next to me without a pole at all!"

They therefore spent several hours basically sitting around utterly bored as they refused to speak to each other and sullenly passed the rod over when their time was up. By the time they headed back to Liverpool, the only thing the pair of them had caught was an old tin can and possibly a cold. As they walked home from the church, Ray came up with a plan.

"I can't just arrive home with nothing; why don't we stop off at the chippy and buy some cod and chips. We could say we caught it and cooked it?"

Ian wasn't convinced, but wanted to make amends

for their earlier falling out so readily agreed. However, when Ray presented his 'catch' to his mother, he received a clip round the ear for lying and sent to bed without even getting to savour his food.

In addition to 'hunting' for food and cooking over a campfire, the boys also had the opportunity to go on a weeklong camp in Wales. When he found out, Ray signed up without even telling his mother, which turned out to be a mistake, as when she learned what he'd done, she refused to let him go unless she accompanied him.

"If I can't trust you to tell me things, how can I trust you to behave yourself and stay safe while you are away?"

"But Ma I'll be the laughing stock; I'll never live it down. Please, you can't come with me, it'll ruin my life!" He was appalled at the idea of his mother watching over him for a whole week, but she was adamant.

"Raymond, I just can't trust you to look after yourself for a whole week, you're too young. What would happen if you were constipated? You know how you hate to go on other peoples toilets."

This was in fact true, but he thought it a lame excuse to justify ruining his life. "Ma I'll be fine, I'll make sure I eat plenty of stuff that makes me go regular. I'll be nearly thirteen and I can look after myself."

"No you can't Raymond and let that be an end to it. I accompany you, or you don't go; you choose."

He seriously contemplated staying at home but when he heard about some of the activities they were going to be doing, he acquiesced. He couldn't miss out on caving, climbing mountains and the idea of sleeping under canvas for a whole week.

Olive found it quite easy to persuade the company captain to allow her to join the trip. She'd become influential in the church and helped organise most events. However, she must have been mindful of the impact her presence would have on her son, as when the captain announced that she was to go with them; he did it in a diplomatic way.

"Having seen the results of your cooking I have decided to ask Mrs Dagnall to accompany us on our camp as our resident cook for the week because I truly believe we would all starve if our meals were left up to you lot."

He obviously received some ribbing, but the boys saw the truth in what the captain had said and no one really fancied cooking for themselves.

In the lead up to the camp the excitement became almost unbearable. Ray's experience of the world extended as far as the Wirral, so the idea of travelling into Wales; a whole different country, was thrilling. He'd seen the mountains in the distance when he'd visited West Kirby, but he never dreamed he'd get the opportunity to go there. For nights before they went he lay in bed dreaming of trekking through the wilderness with his mates, fending off wild bears and wolves with spears made from sticks with their penknives bound to the end. In his own mind he cut a heroic figure clad in his 'BB' uniform with a bloody bandage around his head as he strode into camp with a slain wild boar slung over his shoulder. He revelled in the idea of slinging the beast to the floor in front of his mother.

"Cook it woman and be quick about it; all that hunting has given me quite an appetite!" he imagined; and then his mother would spring into action and meekly do as she was told to the cheers of his mates as they sat around the campfire waiting to be fed.

After a particularly long session of day dreaming in which he'd slain a lion and freed a very pretty girl from a tribe of savages, he realised it had been ages since he'd let his imagination run wild like this, and came to the conclusion that he missed the fantastic adventures he used to have within the realms of his own mind. He pondered on whether it was just part of growing up as the way he saw it, the older you got, the less time you had to dream.

On the morning of the departure he was up, washed and ready by six thirty even though the coach didn't leave until nine o'clock. He checked, rechecked and checked again that he had his knife fork and spoon, soap, towel and other necessities such as string, catapult and matches. He ensured he had enough pairs of underpants and socks to last him, and all were packed correctly. He then paced up and down, thoroughly annoying his mother as she tried to make breakfast for everyone and ensure that John knew what to do in case of an emergency whilst she was gone. Enid was to be looked after by Joe's wife and she had done the washing the day before so all his clothes were clean. When Ray knocked the pile of ironing she'd just finished onto the floor, it proved to be the final straw.

"Raymond for goodness sake, go into the garden out of my site before I do something that will see me end up in court!"

He wasn't sure what she meant but he knew when he was about to get a good hiding, so quickly retreated to the garden where he found a piece of wood to whittle with his knife. So absorbed was he with carving the lion from his day dream that it came as a surprise when his mother told him it was time to go. As he jumped up he dropped the wood to the floor and his mother bent down to retrieve it.

"You know what Raymond, you're really quite good with wood; this is super!" She then put it in her bag and they headed off to church where a coach was waiting to take them to Wales.

He'd never been on a coach before, but some instinct made him head straight towards the back seat, partly to be as far away from his mother as possible as she'd said she would be sitting at the front with the leaders, but it was also because there was more room at the back he could share with his mates. Luckily they were amongst the first to board and claimed their territory before the others got on. However, they had to spend several minutes defending their domain from older, more seasoned travellers.

"Get out of our seats; we always sit at the back!"

"Not likely, we got here first so you'll just have to find somewhere else to sit.

There followed much name calling and pushing and shoving until Olive stomped down the aisle and dragged one of the older boys away by the ear.

"They were here first and claimed those seats fair

and square so find a new one or I will put you off this coach this instance and you'll have to find your own way to Wales."

The boys moved off sullenly and found seats, but not before throwing hateful glances towards Ray and his mates who laughed and made rude gestures back in return.

"You know what Daggers, I'm glad your mum's with us; that could have got nasty then!" Johnny Featherston said as he ran his tongue over his fat lip, caused by a stray bag as it was swung around as a weapon.

"You might be but I'm not; she'll be spying on me all week!" However, deep down he supposed he was quite pleased she was there, particularly when she past him his sandwiches, which he'd forgotten.

As soon as he took charge of the package he realised he was ravenously hungry. They'd all been asked to bring a packed lunch as the journey was to take several hours so Ray had brought his favourite; connyonny butties wrapped in greaseproof paper, an apple and a flask of tea.

"I'm going to have to eat me lunch, I'm starving."

Ian looked at him in amazement. "But we're not

even out of Liverpool yet."

"Yeah, it must be the adrenalin from defending our seats or maybe the excitement of the trip, but I need to eat."

He'd therefore devoured his entire lunch before they'd travelled four streets, which gave him plenty of time to wave to passing motorists or just stare at the landscape. He was used to greenery as there were plenty of parks where he lived, but Liverpool was a fairly flat city so as they crossed the border into Wales; without even having to show any passports or papers, he looked in wonder at the mountains that seemed to reach into the sky.

"I reckon if you climbed to the top of some of these mountains you'd need oxygen to breathe they're that high." Jimmy Featherston proclaimed as he stared at a particularly high range of peaks that still had snow at the top. "I also reckon you could see into space from up there."

Ian wasn't convinced although he too was impressed. "No, I reckon you'd have to be a lot higher to see into space, but what do you reckon is up there at the top."

Ray decided to share some of his ideas from his daydreams. "There must be wild animals up there;

bears and wolves definitely. Hey, maybe we could sneak off and hunt them!" He realised he'd shared a little too much of his imaginings when the rest of his mates burst out laughing.

"Daggers you're a scream, you really are; bears and wolves became extinct in Britain centuries ago. The only place you're likely to find them these days is in a zoo, and I don't think we'll find one of those at the top of a mountain!"

Ian was his best mate, but he could really be a know it all sometimes, particularly as he'd started reading proper books since he started at the grammar school. Some of the things he came out with made Ray almost wish he was interested in reading. He kept promising himself he'd sit down and read one, but every time he tried he just couldn't get beyond the first dozen pages without becoming bored or falling asleep. He often thought it strange as he loved stories, but just couldn't seem to get stimulated by the written word.

When they arrived at the campsite just outside Conway, the first thing they had to do was erect their tents, which should have been easy as they'd practiced it in the church grounds on numerous occasions in the lead up to the trip. Given also that Ray was sharing with his mates, it should have been straightforward as they knew each other well and spent so much time together; but it wasn't. Everybody decided they knew the quickest way to get the thing erected and so spent ages arguing over how to go about it.

"You have to start with the groundsheet."

"Don't be stupid, you get the frame up first."

"You've got to knock the pegs in first you morons!"

In the end it was Ian who prevailed by grabbing a tent peg and threatening them. "If you don't all shut up and listen to me, I'm going to stick this peg where the sun don't shine is that understood?!"

The others realised he meant business, and they were also fed up with not achieving anything, so the bickering stopped and they followed Ian's instructions resulting in the tent being up within fifteen minutes.

"Now we need to stow our gear away." Mega said as he eyed the pile of instruments and bags of clothes. I reckon we ...." he quickly shut up as Ian grabbed a spare tent peg and raised it threateningly.

"What do you reckon Mega?"

"I reckon we listen to you again Ian as that way we'll sort it a lot quicker than bickering." Which is what they did, and although there wasn't much room left after everything was packed away, they managed to sort out places for each of them to sleep.

Ray loved the smell of the canvas mixed with the plastic of the groundsheet and spent a few minutes on his own, breathing in the smell before joining his mates in the canteen for tea.

After having a singsong round the campfire and drinking warm milk, the boys retired to their tent where they were told they had half an hour before they needed to go to sleep. They washed, cleaned their teeth and went to the loo in the toilet block next to the tents, which reminded Ray a little bit of what it was like when he had to go to the loo in the back yard. They then got ready for bed and settled down before the officers did their rounds to ensure everyone was tucked up tight.

However, Ray was nowhere near ready to go to sleep. He supposed it must have been the mixture of the canvas and the plastic having an effect on his brain because he felt giddy with excitement and proceeded to make stupid noises, which made the rest of the tent giggle.

There was a sudden banging on the tent flap that made them all jump and laugh even louder. "If you lot don't shut up and go to sleep I'll have you running round the field in the dark for the next hour!"

As the lieutenant walked away Ray did an uncanny impersonation "If you lot don't shout up and make lots of noise, I'll have you sitting around the canteen with some connyonny butties!" The others rolled around laughing before there was a second thumping of the tent flap.

"I said sleep! And I know that was you Dagnall; you better be careful!"

The second warning seemed to do the trick for the rest

of the group and before long there was just the sound of deep breathing and the odd snore, which made Ray giggle to himself. "Is anyone awake?" Ray whispered as he stared into the darkness.

A voice came from the other side of the tent. "I am"

"Who is I am; I don't recall any of my mates called I am; there's an Ian, but definitely no I am." Although people said you shouldn't laugh at your own jokes, he found this particular one hilarious and sniggered to himself.

"It's Mega you dick!"

"You think I've got a Mega dick, that's very nice of you but a bit saucy!" The pair of them thought this hilarious and had to sneak out of the tent to avoid waking the others with their laughter.

The next day they would be unable to explain what came over them, but as they stood in the darkness just beyond their tent, Ray came up with an idea, which they thought would be yet another hilarious joke.

"I reckon we get our drums and sneak up to where the officers are camped. We then drum like hell and leg it back to our tent and pretend to be asleep. It'll be brilliant!"

"What if we get caught?"

"We won't get caught it's too dark to see who we are and we'll be back in our tent and tucked up asleep before they can search everywhere."

The two of them therefore crept back into their tent and retrieved their drums before crawling up the field like commando veterans. When they finally located the officers' tent, they found it hard to contain their giggles.

"Shush! Right after 3: - 1 - 2 - 3!" They bashed away at their drums for about five seconds before running down the field laughing hysterically and whooping with joy. However, things started to go wrong almost immediately as Mega tripped over a guide rope and went flying headfirst into the side of the next tent in the row, bringing the whole thing toppling down onto the occupants inside. Then when Ray went to help him, he got tangled in the mess and kept slipping to the floor as he tried to drag his friend free whilst giggling uncontrollably.

The next morning they were paraded in front of the rest of the company in disgrace. Ray had to admit he was a little taken aback by the scowls coming from most of the other boys. He'd expected them to find the whole thing really funny, but in retrospect he reckoned that a night of disturbed sleep hadn't gone down that well after all. After taking a walk of shame up and down the rows of tents, they had to report to the captain in his tent.

"What have you two got to say for yourselves?" The captain had recently returned from the army and had instilled the same ethos in his company of BB. "Stand to attention when you are in my company unless I say otherwise!" He bellowed, causing Ray and Mega to jump at the sudden change in tone and volume before they quickly stood as straight as they could.

"We don't know what came over us sir." Mega offered timidly; but by the look on the captain's face it didn't appear this was enough so Ray also made a contribution.

"Perhaps the mixture of canvas and plastic got to us sir and sent us a little bit loopy. I know I felt a bit weird all evening." Mega turned to look at his friend in astonishment, not quite believing what he'd just heard.

"What are you talking about Dagnall; I've never heard such rubbish in all my life; I've a good mind to send the both of you home!"

The boys looked at each other in horror as they'd been looking forward to the trip for ages and now they'd put the whole experience in jeopardy before they'd even begun.

"Sir, please don't! We're truly sorry and we promise we'll be as good as gold for the rest of the week. We'll do anything sir, but please don't send us home!"

To give him his due, the captain seemed to accept their apology as the tension went out of his shoulders and his face lost some of the redness and anger, making the boys believe they might just have got away with it. However, just as they started to relax the Captain dropped his bombshell.

"Very well I'll not send you home, but you will be

punished. The pair of you will spend today pealing spuds and cleaning out the toilets. After tea this evening you will then do the washing up for the entire camp; and you will hand over your drums for the rest of the week."

The boys thought the punishment a bit harsh, particularly the last part as the grand finale of the week was to be a large procession around the streets of a nearby village, which they would now miss out on. However, it was better than being sent home and so accepted with alacrity. "Yes sir!" they responded before saluting and leaving the tent.

Ray's mother however, was not as compromising. Upon hearing of her son's escapades she gave him a good hiding in front of his mates and threatened all kinds of retribution if he should step out of line for the remainder of the week. When she learned of their punishment though, she was less than impressed.

"He can't take your drum off you, it's your drum!" she ranted as she paced up and down. "Peeling spuds, washing up and cleaning the toilet block is punishment enough. I'm not having you missing out on the procession through the village." She then stormed off in the direction of the captain's tent before banging on the flap rather aggressively. As the captain stepped out to see who was disturbing his peace, Ray and Mega stood horrified, with any thoughts of a reprieve vanishing into the mountain air as Olive launched her tirade

"How dare you take Raymond's drum off him; I know he was naughty and deserved a punishment but the spuds, the toilets and the washing up was enough. He's said he's sorry so I want you to give him his drum back!"

His mother in full flow was a wondrous, if not scary thing to behold as the captain found out. He'd just spent five years fighting the Germans and seen action in Italy, France and Germany itself, but he'd never faced opposition like he did now. His first tactic was an attempt to defend his position.

"Look I'm sorry Mrs Dagnall but your son broke lots of rules by sneaking out of his tent, using his drum in an inappropriate fashion and then causing damage to a tent and bringing mayhem into camp. He's lucky I didn't send him home. In my judgement the punishment was fair and appropriate so I don't feel any need to rescind any part of it and I hope you will support my decision."

It was clear the captain was rather satisfied with his initial rebuttal of her assault, and by the look on Olive's face it was also clear that such a rigorous defence had left her attack in disarray. She wasn't used to people standing up to her and was also taken aback by the reasoned argument he presented to justify his position. However, like all good battle commanders, she was not prepared to be beaten at the first assault and so adapted her strategy.

"That drum does not belong to you captain. Raymond's aunty bought it for him especially so he could join the BB. You therefore have no right to take it off him."

The captain, believing he'd already won this battle, became reckless in his counteroffensive. "I'm sorry if you feel that way Mrs Dagnall, but my decision is final."

Unfortunately he had underestimated the strength of Olive's arsenal of weapons, which she now turned on him to dominate and batter him into submission. Her face became like stone and she fixed him with her most steely glare; her body language spoke of a dangerous wild animal that was about to pounce on its prey and her gesture as she slowly raised a pointed finger at him felt as deadly as any gun. As she took a threatening step towards him, he actually flinched and took a step back. She spotted the chink in his defences, and as quick as a flash, pressed home her advantage by bringing out her most lethal weapon. She switched from loud aggression to quiet, sinister threat.

"If you do not hand Raymond's drum back to him, I will refuse to cook another thing for the rest of the week. Will *you* be able to cope with cooking for so many boys?!"

The captain knew he was beaten. There was no way he could sort out feeding the boys at such short notice, and the idea of allowing the boys to cook for themselves sent shivers down his spine. However, he couldn't just surrender unconditionally so opted for a strategic withdrawal. "Look, I'll tell you what. I will keep the boys drums for the rest of today, and if they behave themselves I will return them tomorrow."

Olive was magnanimous in her victory and so agreed to these terms without hesitation. The boys received their drums back the next day and behaved like angels for the rest of the week.

Chapter 28 – All Change

When Ray and Olive returned from camp, there were a number of surprises in store for them. The first one was rather sad as they found out that his father's mother had died. She had apparently gone into hospital for a routine operation and had then fallen out of bed in the middle of the night and burst her stitches, which caused an infection resulting in her death. His father was quite stoic about the situation and seemed to make more of a fuss than normal about finding out what his son had got up to while he was away.

Ray had never really known his granny other than when he'd stayed with them after being bombed out. They'd rarely visited, and his father shared few stories about her. All he knew was that she had lots of tattoos, smoked a pipe and could swear like a trooper. He also thought she was full of life and energy and was therefore sad she had died, shedding a few tears upon hearing the news.

The second surprise was also a little sad for Ray, although his mother was overjoyed. Joe and Dolly and her mum and sister were finally moving out after having lived with them for nearly five years following them being bombed out in the May blitz of 1941. Even though their habits aggravated his mother, he'd come to look on them as part of the family and he was actually sadder they were moving, than the death of his grandparent. He even called Dolly's mother grandma, so after she'd made him his final chip butty, he hugged her and cried.

"I'm going to really miss you grandma."

"I'm going to miss you too Ray, but the corporation has finally found us a house so we have to move. After all, we can't stay here forever; imagine what your mother's reaction would be if we did." She then winked at him and started clearing away the dishes.

She was right of course; Olive was over the moon to be finally getting her house back and went about her daily business with a grin like a Cheshire cat on her face. "They said they were only going to be with us for a couple of days! Can you imagine how much money we'll save on hot water and electricity alone!?"

This was true of course, but the house felt empty once they'd gone. Ray realised that for as long as he could remember, except for a few months after they'd first moved into Clavelle Road, there had always been additional people living with them. At first there'd been Nana, then the Irish navvies and finally Joe and his family. After all this time, he wasn't sure how he'd cope with the extra space, let alone the additional quiet of having four less people in the house. He supposed that now Enid was getting older she'd probably start taking up more of the space, but she was a quiet child who seemed happy to just sit and play with whatever toy was at hand. She certainly didn't run about the house like he used to. That might change now she'd started school as she'd probably bring friends back with her, but so far that hadn't happened, which meant he would have to get used to the new space and the quiet.

However, he didn't have to get used to it for long as only six weeks after Joe had moved out, there was a knock on the door one evening. Being the only person at home, it was left to him to get up and answer it. When he opened the door, there stood Aunt Alice.

"Hello Yaya, we weren't expecting you; I'm afraid no one else is in." He was used to Alice turning up unannounced but he certainly wasn't used to seeing her upset. He was therefore taken aback when she burst into tears. "What's wrong Yaya? Is it Mr Benson; has something happened to him?" From the way she sobbed even louder, he suspected that is was.

"Oh Raymond!" was all she could manage to say between heart wrenching sobs, which sounded like she was genuinely in pain.

"Come in and sit down and I'll make you a nice cup of tea. Me Ma's at Sydnah's but she'll be home soon." He thought being kind and considerate was the right strategy, but it just made her worse.

"Oh Raymond!" she wailed again and fell into a chair where she sobbed even louder, causing Ray to wince in pain of his own.

"Yaya, what's wrong?" He thought it was an innocent enough question to ask, but apparently it was not.

"What's wrong? What's wrong? Oh, if only you knew!" She got to her feet and started pacing up and down as she wrung her handkerchief between her hands.

He would have dearly liked to know, but she seemed determined not to tell him. "Yaya, why don't you sit down and tell me what has happened?"

"How could this have happened to me Raymond; please just tell me?!"

"I don't really know Yaya." He wanted to add 'because you won't tell me!' but thought it might aggravate her further. He therefore decided to leave her to calm down and went into the kitchen to make the tea. When he returned she seemed a little calmer, but he felt he daren't say anything for fear of setting her off once more. After several minutes of intermittent sobs, interspersed with loud sips of tea, she finally managed to say a few more words.

"What am I going to do Raymond? What am I going to do?!"

In all honesty he didn't have clue what she was going to do as he still didn't know what was wrong. One thing was certain though, he wasn't going to offer any answers after the way she'd reacted to his voice so far. He therefore just sat beside her on the sofa and patted her hand, which proved to be just as bad as being kind and considerate as she once more began to wail.

"Oh why Raymond, why?!"

'Raymond' wanted to scream "I don't know why Yaya because you won't tell me why!" However, he was pretty sure that wouldn't be the right tack to take and so merely shrugged and smiled, which also proved to be a mistake.

"Please Raymond, you have to help me; please!" She wailed once again and began to sob and hiccup at the same time she was so distraught.

All he wanted to do was escape and hide away in his room, but by the way she looked at him he knew he'd have to provide an answer. It was at that point he suddenly had an inspiration, which surprisingly he'd learned in school. He decided to adopt a strategy he'd picked up from his teachers who were masters at being able to answer a question with another question.

"Why do you think Yaya?" He wasn't really expecting any success; his main objective had been to try and calm his aunt down. He was therefore surprised when she responded.

"Oh Raymond you are wise beyond your years, you truly are. It's my fault of course, all my fault; I've ruined everything just like I've ruined things my entire life."

Ray was starting to get worried about where this conversation was heading as he didn't feel equipped to deal with an old woman's regrets. He'd just decided to try and distract her by telling a tale of his adventures on camp, when she said something that piqued his interest.

"It would have all been yours Raymond. If only I hadn't been a stupid old woman, it all would have been yours." She then took another loud sip of tea and sat silently brooding, shaking her head repeatedly.

Having calmed her down by saying as little as possible, the last thing he wanted to do was set her off again by asking her questions, but Ray was intrigued to learn more about what she'd said regarding it all '*would have*' been his.

"Look Yaya, you are obviously really upset, but I don't understand why. Are you able to tell me what happened? I may be able to help."

"Raymond that is a lovely thing to say but it's too late; he's kicked me out and never wants to see me again!" She started to sob again.

"So Mr Benson has kicked you out Yaya? Why did he do that?"

"Please don't think badly of me Raymond, I'm a weak woman and always have been." This shocked Ray as his impression of his aunt was of an invincible force of energy that couldn't be stopped. "You see, I've always had a weakness for the drink ever since my first husband died, and well I've got into the habit of joining a couple of friends I've made at the Adelphi Hotel a couple of afternoons a week."

He was impressed as the Adelphi was very posh and probably the most expensive establishment in the whole of Liverpool.

"We normally have lunch and share a glass of wine or two; have a good gossip and then head home. Raymond I don't know what happened today, honestly I don't, but the glass of wine turned into several bottles instead."

He was shocked his aunt would drink so much in the afternoon, but he was still unsure of why that would have caused Mr Benson to throw her out. In many of her tales, she had quaffed vast amounts of champagne and other forms of alcohol without it having any effect so was still unclear as to what had taken place.

"So what did you do to upset Mr Benson?"

"My dear, I can't hold my drink like I used to and so returned home rather later than I'd said, and a little the worse for wear. When I tried to get into the house I found the door locked and no matter how much I knocked, the horrid man would not answer. At first I thought he may have gone out; I even considered he may have gone looking for me, but he hasn't been well since he had the flu and rarely ventures further than his office. He's become distant with me of late, which is perhaps why I've found the need to spend so much time with other friends."

This was all getting a bit much for Ray, but he remained silent as Alice continued. "But then I heard movement from inside the house and when I looked towards the window in his office, I actually saw him peeking out from behind the curtains. I thought perhaps he didn't realise it was me so yelled through the letterbox and tried to get him to let me in."

She stopped talking and pulled out a tissue to blow her nose. After a rather loud and sustained blast she reverted to a silent brooding, interspersed with a sob and hiccup. Although Ray felt completely uncomfortable, he needed to learn what happened next.

"Did he let you in Yaya?"

"My dear that's the thing that sent me over the edge. I spent about tem minutes trying to attract his attention to get him to open the door, and he ignored me. The next thing I knew he'd opened the window a fraction and screamed that he was sick of me leaving him alone to swan off and visit friends and family, and he said I drank too much. Raymond, I tried to reason with him that I felt I had to seek company elsewhere because he had become distant, but he wouldn't listen and slammed the window on me. How dare he slam the window on me Raymond?! I mean, the absolute cheek of the man?!"

Ray sensed her sadness was turning to anger so he thought he should calm her down by agreeing with her.

"What an absolute Cad!" He'd heard the word 'Cad' in a film and loved the sound of it, although he hoped he'd used it in the right context as he wasn't totally sure what it meant.

Alice smiled before continuing. "I quite agree Raymond, an absolute Cad! Well as you can imagine, I was livid and well, I suppose I overreacted. I picked up a rock and threw it through his window before trying to climb in." She then started to giggle uncontrollably. "I think the horrid man was genuinely scared as I heard him scream and run from the room. Raymond, I beg you, please don't think badly of me, but you see I couldn't get in through the broken glass so I followed him around the house throwing stones through each of his windows. He called the police on me, and they came and took me away. They actually handcuffed me Raymond; me an old woman. I've been in the station for hours; they've only just let me go."

He was amazed at the fact he had a relative who was a criminal as he envisaged her following in the steps of her one time poker colleague Al Capone. "Are you going to prison?" He said, worried that he wouldn't get to see her any more.

"Of course not my dear; he's said he doesn't want to press charges, but he doesn't want to see me again. He told the police he'd pack all my belongings up, but he won't let me near the house. He said somebody else has to pick them up for me. What am I going to do Raymond? I've got nowhere to go and not much money left. I was banking on Reginald leaving me his fortune, but I can't see that happening now." She paused then as she contemplated the wider implications of losing the fortune. "Oh my dear boy, I was going to leave everything to you. I've ruined your future as well as my own; I'm an abominable old crone; I'm so sorry!" She began to sob again only quieter this time.

Ray was shocked on so many different levels. His aunt, who he idolised and thought of as a sophisticated lady; getting drunk and taken away by the police; the fact that Mr Benson had kicked her out so heartlessly, and she now had nowhere to go; the surprise at the news she had little of her own money left after the way she had spent money on him; and the fact that any dreams he might have had of receiving millions of pounds and acres of land had more than likely gone out the window; or more accurately gone through the window when Yaya threw the rock!

When his mother arrived home shortly afterwards with Enid in tow, she automatically took control. "You will obviously move in with us Alice; we have plenty of space since Joe and the others moved out."

"Olive I can't impose myself on you and your family it wouldn't be fair on you."

"Nonsense, you would be doing us a favour. The house has seemed empty lately and after everything you've done for our Raymond; we owe you more than a bed. Now I will not hear another word about it. Raymond, go and make up your bed so Alice can get a good night's sleep. We'll sort everything out tomorrow.

The next day Ray and his father travelled to Reginald's house to pick up Alice's things. When they arrived he was shocked by the change that had come over Mr Benson in the few months since he'd seen him last. He knew he was an old man but he'd always appeared much younger than his age. The frail, stooped figure who answered the door looked ninety at least. He was hunched forward and had to use a stick to help him walk. His hands shook and it took him several moments before he recognised Ray and his father.

"I suppose you've come for her things?" he said in a cold, hard manner. "It proved too difficult for me to pack all of her tat so you'll have to do it yourselves."

Ray was taken aback by the sternness of the man he'd spent hours hunting with. "That won't be a problem Mr Benson; are you alright, is there anything we can do for you?" He expected the old man to thaw towards him as he'd always valued courtesy highly.

"Don't be impertinent boy; of course I'm not alright! That harpy nearly scared me to death; she was so aggressive. I won't be alright until she is out of my life for good! Now be off with you and make sure you only take the things that are in her room. I don't want you touching anything else, is that understood?!" He then turned abruptly and hobbled down the hall to his office before slamming the door behind him leaving Ray and his father shocked and confused.

"I can't believe what has just happened dad. How can he speak to us like that? I've spent so much time with him; I thought he liked me, but he was acting then like he didn't even know me." He was genuinely upset at the way Mr Benson had treated him. "It wasn't us who got drunk and smashed his windows, why is he taking it out on us? I'm going to talk to him."

As he went to follow Mr Benson, his father put a restraining hand on his arm. "Ray there really isn't any point. He's far too upset and angry to listen to anything you have to say and you may just make matters worse."

"How could they possibly get worse dad? He's kicked her out and doesn't want anything more to do with her or us by the look of it."

"Be that as it may, I still don't think you should talk to him. He's old and obviously ill. I think it's best if we just get your aunt's things as quickly as possible and get out of here."

Ray still wasn't convinced, but he listened to his father's advice and they went to pack up Alice's few personal possessions. As he worked in silence he realised he wouldn't know what to say to the old man anyway. The whole situation was heartbreaking for all involved. He also thought it incredibly sad that a woman, who'd led such an extraordinary life, had so little to show for it. After only an hour they were ready to leave with everything that Alice possessed, which fitted into just three suitcases and a carrier bag. As they were about to leave they heard the front door slam and a man's voice.

"Father where are you? The front door was wide open, you shouldn't do that; not after what happened yesterday."

Ray and his father made their way into the hall to leave and were confronted by a man in his mid forties who looked remarkably like Mr Benson only slightly chubbier. Ray took an instant dislike to him as he looked them up and down with disdain.

"I suppose you are related to that woman are you? Well let me tell you, she'll not see a penny of my father's money! I always knew she was a gold digger, but I could never make him see what bad news she was. Who would have thought it would be her own stupidity that would be her undoing!"

Ray had never seen his father use violence before, but on this occasion he honestly thought he was about to hit Mr Benson's son. He saw him clench his fists and he seemed to coil his body as if he was about to strike. Ray decided one relative being arrested was enough for one week so decided to act to defuse the situation in the only way he knew how. He blew a loud raspberry, which seemed to do the trick as he saw his father take several deep breaths before responding.

"And I suppose you must be the son that Reginald never sees and who he speaks about even less." He paused for effect before continuing. "In fact the only time I can recall him mentioning you was when he said you were a waste of space and certainly not worthy of remembering in his will. I suppose in his weakened state he's succumbed to you trying to wheedle your way back into his good books."

In that moment, Ray was genuinely proud of his father. His words hit home harder than any punch and Mr Benson's son reeled as if he'd actually been hit. He looked as if the wind had been knocked out of him and seemed to find it difficult to breathe as Ray and his father walked passed him and out of the house not even glancing in his direction.

The sad irony was that just two weeks later they heard that Mr Benson had died having changed his will and leaving everything to his 'grieving' son. If Alice had behaved herself for only a couple of weeks more, she and Ray would have been millionaires. As it was, he wasn't particularly bothered about the money as he much preferred the daily company of his favourite aunt, and to him, her stories were far more valuable than any fortune.

Chapter 29 – A Peaceful Coup and Cycling

In September 1946 Ray returned to school far more excited than usual. Seeing that he would be fourteen the following May, this would be his final year and he could start to look forward to getting a job and making some money. There was a challenge however, he had to overcome before then, which was to decide what he wanted to do. Early on in the autumn term he went to visit a careers advisor for some advice.

"So Raymond, what type of things interest you?" The man appeared on the wrong side of fifty and showed little interest in what Ray had to say. He had a newspaper on his desk and was clearly trying to work out a crossword clue.

"Well I like cricket and football, working with wood, drawing pictures –" He saw no point in continuing seriously so decided to throw in a couple of exaggerations to gauge if the man was paying any attention at all. "I also like hunting wild beasts with my bear hands and I'm training to become a Lion tamer with the local circus."

"That sounds wonderful; you seem to have a lot of interests. Have you thought of a job down the mines? There are always jobs going in that sector."

Ray left the office disgusted that the man was

actually being paid to give advice! However, he had enjoyed caving when he was on camp and so didn't discard the idea out of hand. He'd found the concept of there being a whole different world under his feet to be quite thrilling and the time he'd spent underground made him feel like an explorer or even Flash Gordon on another planet. The more he thought about it, the more the idea became enticing, which led to him changing his opinion about the man; he did appear to know what he was doing after all.

When he told Mega what the advisor had said he received quite a surprise. "That's weird; I told him I was interested in Science, History and running and he told me a job down the mines would be suitable as well!"

"I reckon he's being paid by the mining company to get workers. We should report him."

However, as they talked, the idea of working together seemed like something they'd both really like to do and it turned out Mega had shared Ray's enjoyment of being below ground when they went caving. There was the slight problem of there being no mines in Liverpool, but the boys overcame that quickly.

"We'll just have to move away. We'll be fourteen

so we should be able to cope. The mining company will probably have houses and we could share one." As Ray said it, he started to get excited at the prospect of living with one of his best mates and being able to decide for himself when he got washed or whether to leave the toilet seat up or not.

"What do you reckon our mums will say?"

"I don't care; I'm going to do it regardless!"

Ray's assertiveness was put to the test as soon as he mentioned it to his mother that evening. "Raymond, don't be stupid! You can't go and work down a mine; you get scared of the dark." His mother's tone was dismissive, which riled Ray considerably.

"I do not! I haven't been scared of the dark for years; I actually loved it when we went caving on camp. Anyway, the careers advisor in school said it would be a good idea and Mega and I agree. I'll be fourteen by then so I don't see why I can't."

His mother didn't seem to know what to say to that so fell back on a stock tool of the trade of parenting.

"Because I said you can't that's why!"

He'd never really stood up to his mother before, but her dismissive tone and her refusal to discuss it properly was like lighting the touch paper of a firework as far as he was concerned. He'd talked this through fully with Mega and he'd made up his mind. However, his manners were ingrained so he tried to make his rebuke as polite as possible.

"I'm afraid you won't get much of a say in it Ma. Once I leave school, I'll have to leave home as well in order to find a job at a mine, which means I'll have to make decisions for myself." He thought he'd articulated his argument rather well; he'd made it clear he was prepared to take responsibility for his future and been assertive to the fact he'd make decisions for himself rather than his mother making them for him. He'd also committed himself to mining as a profession, and whilst his mother may not like it, she should surely be proud of the mature approach he was adopting towards his future. He was therefore not amused in the least when she slapped him repeatedly before taking a heavy wooden spoon and beating him. Each hit was interspersed with a word.

"You (hit) will (hit) do (hit) as (hit) I (hit) say (hit)"

It was a sustained attack lasting several minutes as she apparently had quite a lot she wanted to say regarding him still being a child and about the fact that he was not leaving home until she said, so he could put any such ideas out of his head. By the time she was finished he was covered in red welts and bruised up and down his arms where he'd tried to defend himself; his head also throbbed from the blows that had got through his defence. He retreated to his room defeated and frustrated, unsure of how he was going to break the news to Mega who seemed as set on the idea as he'd been.

However, Mega merely shrugged his shoulders when he'd broached the subject with him. "I don't think I'm going to be able to be a miner." He said, and waited for Mega to explode in frustration. When he didn't say anything, Ray felt he had to continue. "Me Ma went mad and battered me round the house with a wooden spoon; look at the lump on my head." He indicated quite a large lump to the left of his forehead. "I'm really sorry."

"We'll just have to come up with something else then."

"What did your Ma say?"

"She didn't think it was a good idea and when we discussed it, she pointed out a lot of things we hadn't thought of. Do you realise we would have had to buy our own food and cook it?! Not to mention having to wash our own clothes, do the ironing and pay bills! I'm actually glad your ma said you couldn't go because I don't thing I wanted to do it anyway."

"But she didn't batter you? Ray was incredulous that Mega had been able to discuss the issue with his mother.

"Batter me? Of course not; I've got to do something really bad to receive a good hiding."

"Oh, I suppose we need to start thinking of another career."

They therefore spent most lessons passing messages to each other with suggestions of what job they might do. It never occurred to them to seek separate jobs. It had become a given they'd work together and if need be, move away together if they could find a job that included somebody else doing their shopping, cooking and cleaning.

Ray was still good mates with Ian and the rest of the gang but they had started to see less of each other now they were in their final year of school. They were all starting to look towards their futures and it was clear their dreams and desires were becoming quite different.

Lionel and Obie wanted to follow in their father's footsteps and join the police. Whilst Ray thought there was nothing wrong with this; indeed a career in the police sounded exciting, he didn't see how it could come to pass as they all knew they were going to prison when they were sixteen, something he expressed to Lionel.

"How will you be able to join the police when you have a criminal record?"

Lionel looked at Ray baffled. "What?"

"When the park police caught us coming out of the girl's toilets, he told us we were all going to prison when we were sixteen. You must remember; it wasn't that long ago."

"Lionel looked at him utterly baffled and repeated "What?"

"He said he knew our names and where we lived, so he must have put it on our records. I intend to do a runner just before I'm sixteen and I don't care what me Ma says!"

Lionel looked at him open mouthed before falling about laughing until the tears streamed down his cheeks. "You're not serious are you Daggers?! God you really do know how to make me laugh!"

Ray joined in with the laughter but he wasn't sure why. It was clear he was sceptical about the policeman's threat, but how could he know for sure? Ray had had nightmares about being carted away, and whilst he'd convinced himself he was worrying over nothing most of the time, there was still the small niggle at the back of his mind that his nightmares would come true.

"So you don't reckon he was serious?"

"Of course not you ruddy idiot, he was just trying to scare us!"

"Well he succeeded then!" Ray said as they headed off to meet up with the rest of the gang.

Another of his friends who had clear leanings towards a career was Mousey. He'd always been brilliant at working out solutions and making things out of rubbish; the device he created for carrying water from the kitchen to the toilet in their headquarters was genius and allowed them to flush properly without lugging buckets of water around. Therefore, when he announced he was interested in doing some type of engineering it came as no surprise.

Ian, like his father had developed a penchant for numbers and appeared to be heading towards a job in a bank or office, which dealt with money. However, after listening to Alice's stories and adventures around the world, he declared that deep down he'd really like a job that involved travelling, perhaps at sea but not necessarily as a sailor.

The Featherstons were quite keen to work at the docks with their dad and Blainsey was convinced he was going to become a professional footballer, which to Ray's mind was a little delusional as he was probably the worst player out of them all. In an attempt to moderate his ambition, Ray sought to find out if there was anything else he'd like to do.

"What will you do if football doesn't work out or you get injured or something?

"I reckon I'll become a bank robber. With me dad being a copper I know all about what they do to catch criminals, which means I know how to avoid capture. I reckon I'd be really good at it!" He then burst out laughing, but the scary thing, was that Ray reckoned part of him was being serious and he began to have doubts as to whether hanging round with Blainsey was in his best interests. He came to the conclusion he needed to start distancing himself as he was certain he didn't want to end up in prison at sixteen or at any other age.

It wasn't just Blainsey's declaration of wanting to become a bank robber that made Ray uneasy; in recent months some of his exploits were becoming seriously reckless and dangerous. Only a few weeks earlier he'd turned up at their headquarters with a motorbike.

"Who wants a go?" he asked expecting everyone to be eager to try it out. When nobody seemed inclined to volunteer he became more assertive. "Come on you wimps, you can all have a go; Daggers you go first."

"Where did you get it from Blainsey?" He was pretty sure no one in his family owned a bike.

"I borrowed it off my next door neighbour; come on I'll show you what to do."

"Does your neighbour know you've borrowed it?" Ray asked, suspecting they probably didn't.

"Will you stop going on Daggers, you sound like an old woman. Get on the bike; now!" Ray didn't appreciate being ordered around quite so aggressively, but at the same time didn't fancy getting into a confrontation with Blainsey at this point. After being given some rudimentary instruction he set off round the paths in the park going at what felt like a fast speed but was probably little more than ten miles an hour. It did feel exhilarating riding the machine without a helmet, but he was quite glad when he'd completed his circuit and was more or less hauled off the bike by Blainsey.

"God that was rubbish Daggers, I could have run

faster than you were going! Right Ian, you're next and this time, open the throttle up and get some speed going."

Ian certainly seemed to go faster than Ray, but it still wasn't enough for Blainsey who decided he'd show them what he meant by speed. He went hurtling off around the paths with no thought towards anybody who might be walking in the park. They could hear the scream of the engine as it roared in the distance and then appeared again, but as he came into view, he took the final bend too fast, skidded and went flying through the air; the bike somersaulting over him and smashing into a tree. As they ran over, Blainsey got groggily to his feet.

"That was ruddy brilliant, did you see how fast I was going?!"

"Are you alright? Look at your trousers."

As Blainsey looked down he realised he had a huge rip in his trousers and blood was pouring freely down his leg, and as he tried to walk he stumbled. "Ruddy hell, I think I've done my ankle in!"

"Never mind your ankle." Mousey said "Look at the state of the bike" As the boys looked over they saw the machine crumpled against the tree, smoke coming from the engine and clearly beyond repair. "Your neighbour is going to hit the roof when he sees it. There's no way he's going to be able to repair it, it's wrecked."

Blainsey took one look at the mess he'd made and took off as fast as his injured foot would carry him.

"Where the hell do you think you're going?!" Mousey yelled after him. "You can't just leave us with your mess!"

"It's not my mess boys." He called over his shoulder as he limped into the trees. "My neighbour doesn't know I took it, I nicked it while he was out!"

The boys had to push the wreck to the nearest police station and say they'd found the bike lying in the park. They got away with it, but after it was over, it wasn't just Ray who was beginning to have doubts about their friend; the rest of the gang were fed up and becoming tired of such stupid antics as well.

"What are we going to do about it though?" Obie asked as they sat around the now deserted pill box holding a secret meeting to discuss their psycho friend. "There's no way he'd take the hint and just stop hanging round with us and I don't fancy getting my head kicked in for telling him to do one."

He was right of course; Blainsey had been their leader for over five years and they each felt guilty that it had come to this. Nevertheless, they were in agreement that he was becoming dangerous and to date, any actions they'd taken to try and moderate his behaviour had been ignored or met with abuse and even violence. When Mousey had tried to persuade him that siphoning petrol from cars to sell on the black market was neither wise, nor safe; Blainsey had taken the can he'd just filled and poured the contents over Mousey's head. He'd then lit a match and threatened to set him alight. They were pretty sure he didn't intend to follow through with the threat as he walked off laughing, but their real fear was that none of them could say for certain as he'd become so unpredictable.

They debated for hours how they might rid themselves of his influence, but to no avail. Eventually, Ray decided he needed to get some fresh air as he felt stifled in the pillbox and by the atmosphere caused by the lack of a solution.

"Lads, I'm going for a bike ride I need to clear my head." Aunt Alice had bought him an amazing gift for his thirteenth birthday shortly before she'd been kicked out by Mr Benson. He'd come down on the morning of 31st May to find a bicycle, wrapped in brown paper in the front room with Alice standing over it beaming.

"This is for my favourite nephew's birthday; happy birthday Raymond!"

When he'd unwrapped the parcel he realised it wasn't just any bike; this was a top of the range racing bicycle with extra thin tyres, chrome covered plating and a brand new type of brake. It also had a set of ten gears, which was unheard of at the time, thus allowing him to conquer the steepest of hills without having to get off to push. He'd quickly become the envy of his friends as they had to jog along beside him whenever they were out and about, and before long most of them had followed suit by pleading with parents and relatives to buy them their own bikes.

It was as Ray was walking out of the pillbox it occurred to him that here lay the possible solution to their problem. "Blainsey is going to be held up for a while with that sprained ankle isn't he?"

"Yeah I reckon it could be three to four weeks before he's fully fit, which means that's all the time we've got to come up with something."

"He hasn't got a bike has he?"

"No, he said he couldn't get used to the seat and it hurt his bum, but I reckon it's because his parents won't buy him one after they found out he'd been nicking sweets from the shop."

Blainsey had received a full months grounding after Mr Holborn had dragged him round to his parent's house after catching him stuffing sweets down the front of his trousers.

"You know what, I reckon I realised I didn't miss his company during that month he was grounded." Mousey said and received nods of agreement from the others. It had been during this time they'd started going on bike rides; racing each other down the country lanes around Halewood. However, any hope that Blainsey might have learned from his incarceration and engaged with them in their new pursuit went out of the window after only a couple of days.

"This cycling lark is ruddy boring and it chafes me bum. We're going to have to do something else." This resulted in them returning to inane activities, which just weren't fun anymore.

"So he's not going to be around much for the next three to four weeks, he can't stand cycling and he doesn't have a bike. If we join a cycling club or just go on bike rides, it's highly unlikely he'd want to join in."

The penny dropped with the rest of the group and there were vigorous nods of agreement around the circle. "We need to make sure we invite him to join us." Obie chipped in. "So he doesn't think he's being left out and end up battering us."

"Yeah but we have to stick to our guns." Mousey

advised. "We can't give in when he says we have to do something else like we did last time." Mousey was forceful in his argument for the need of solidarity. "I reckon he'll soon get tired of not being involved so will either join in, which will be fine as there's not much mischief he can cause from the back of a bike, or he'll start hanging round with other kids; either way I think we're on to a winner. What's more I love cycling!"

Over the following weeks the boys embraced their new hobby with a fervour that saw them explore further and further afield and become much fitter in the process. When Blainsey recovered from his injury and they invited him to join them on an excursion to Southport, his reply was succinct.

"I'd rather stay in bed than getting me bum rubbed raw by them bleedin' seats!"

The boys therefore headed off, minus Blainsey, on a ride that took them all day. They'd packed butties and enjoyed eating them in a bus shelter near Formby. They got to go on the beach and even though it rained, it didn't dampen their spirits; all agreeing it had been a brill day. By the time he got home Ray did indeed have a sore bum, but unlike Blainsey he thought it was well worth it. He was also rather chuffed with himself that each time they'd raced each other, he'd won by a huge margin. He put it down to having a superior bike when he was conversing with Yaya after he'd had a bath.

"It must have been the extra gears that allowed me to beat them every time we raced."

"Nonsense Raymond, you must have a talent as well. A machine is only as good as the person operating it."

He reflected on her words in the weeks that followed as his hobby grew into a passion. Each weekend he'd arrange some sort of challenge, whether it be a leisurely bike ride into the countryside or a full blown race further afield. He loved the feel of the wind on his face as he raced down a deserted road; and for him, there was nothing better than experiencing the burn in his muscles as he pushed himself to go faster and faster. As they became fitter, they spent whole days in the saddle, marvelling at new sights and realising the world wasn't as big as they'd once thought as Wales became just a half days cycle away. These experiences opened his eyes to the possibilities the world might have to offer now the war was over, and he started to think seriously about what he might do at the end of the year.

Mousey's prophesy regarding Blainsey came true as he quickly tired of not being able to persuade them to give up on their cycling and started to hang round with none other than Peter Dooley, who'd got Ray into trouble the year before. He wasn't sure how they'd teamed up, but they now terrorised the neighbourhood and had already had several close shaves with the police.

The group fragmented further as Mega, Ian and Lionel became more focused on schoolwork. They still saw themselves as a gang, but the dynamic had shifted with the core cycling crew being made up of Ray, Mousey, Obie and the Featherston twins. For this group, cycling became something of an obsession as they planned bigger expeditions and longer treks on a weekly basis. Even Ray's mother approved of his new hobby and actually encouraged them to join a proper club, which they did. Each month there would be a hundred mile race, which took them as far as Blackpool and back or into the mountains of north Wales. Ray found he preferred the steep routes through the mountains as he strangely enjoyed the pain of exertion and proved to have stronger stamina than most other members of the club. Mr Jenkins, the club leader even suggested he consider taking up competitive cycling full time, but when he mentioned this to his mother she was rather dismissive.

"Raymond, how would you make any money?

You'd probably only get paid if you won a race and that would be a pittance. Keep it up as a hobby, but think about a proper job you might do."

"I suppose you're right; I'm just struggling to come up with something I'd really like."

"Don't you worry son, something will turn up."

He didn't really mind his mother's negativity towards him becoming a professional cyclist as he hadn't expected anything less. His reason for bringing it up at all was to use it as a ploy to distract her from the true purpose of the conversation. His strategy was to be as accommodating as possible so he might make her more amenable to his real request.

"Yes I know ma, but its Easter soon so I really need to get a move on."

"That's very sensible Raymond; I do believe you've started to grow up now that you're not going round with Tony Blains."

Ray sensed now was the time to get her permission. "Actually Ma, I was thinking that during the Easter holidays I might try and get away for a few days on my bike with the other lads; you know, to clear my head and really focus on identifying what I want to do."

His mother was silent, which made Ray think she was going to shoot him down in flames, so he was slightly taken aback when she asked; "And where is it you intend to go?"

They had been planning for weeks, and had come up with the idea of cycling to Anglesey and camping there while they toured around the island. "We were just thinking of going to Anglesey, and actually it would help me with school work because we've been learning about the Romans and they went to Anglesey and we could go round all the ancient sites as there are apparently lots of them on the island. We could camp out because Obie said we could use his tent and that sleeps six..." He thought he best pause at that point so he could gauge his mother's reaction

"Oh, you seem to have already planned it all out?"

He realised this was the delicate part of the negotiation. Any wrong move at this point could well ruin the whole thing. "Well we didn't think it would be fair to just say we wanted to go to Anglesey. We thought we needed to show that we'd thought things through. I've even saved up some money so it won't cost you or dad anything."

"You have, have you, how very thoughtful."

Now was the time to play his trump card. "I would

really love to go, but if you don't want me to, I'll try and understand."

The look on his mother's face told him she was positively surprised, but that didn't mean she was going to say yes; when she started to make a humming sound in the back of her throat, he went all in with the last card up his sleeve.

"Mousey, Obie and the Featherston twin's parents have already given their permission, and even Ian and Mega have said they're going to come along as their mothers thought it would do them good to have a break. I was just waiting for the best time to ask you."

He'd played every card at his disposal, and so it was with bated breath that he waited for his mother's response.

"I suppose if the other parents have agreed I'd look a little mean if I didn't let you go too, but you had better promise me you will be sensible and don't do anything stupid; and I want you back here in time for Easter Sunday."

He felt exhilaration like never before and bounded out of the house to tell his mates and put the final touches to their planning now he knew for certain he'd be able to join them.

When they met up to leave, each boy wore a backpack with spare clothes and food and they also had a second pack tied to their bike in some fashion, which contained other elements for their survival such as the tent. Ray's held a bag of tent pegs and some spare food, which he'd managed to fix behind him making him look like he had saddlebags. As they set off it was clear they weren't going to be able to go at any great speed, but that wasn't the point of the journey. They all knew this was possibly the last opportunity they'd have to spend quality time together before they all left school and started in a job or an apprenticeship. They'd made a pact in which they vowed to remain close friends, but deep down they understood how hard that would be having experienced the fragmentation of the original gang over the last six months. They therefore rode at a leisurely pace, talking and laughing and stopping off if they happened to see something of interest.

By early evening they had only just passed the border into Wales and therefore decided to stop for the night. They'd been travelling on a road that ran through several miles of woodland and had just emerged onto a lane that was surrounded by fields and farmland.

"Do you think we need to get permission or something from the farmer?" Ray asked as they began to unpack the tent.

"Nah, I'm sure he wouldn't mind; besides how the heck would we find him, it's already starting to go dark and I can't see any buildings. Let's pitch the tent at the edge of the wood and that way it's unlikely anybody will see us."

As always Mousey had a sensible solution so before long the tent was up and a campfire lit. After a tea of baked beans and corned beef, which they all agreed was possibly the best meal they'd ever had due to the fact they'd made it with their own hands over an open fire, the boys settled down to contemplate the heavens and share simple camaraderie. It was a warm night for April, and the skies were clear leaving them with an unobstructed view of the cosmos. They sat in silence and stared at the vastness above them. Ray was swallowed up by his thoughts as he contemplated how insignificant their planet must appear when compared with the billions of others out in space. As an avid fan of Flash Gordon, he was a firm believer in aliens and so concentrated hard to see if he could catch site of a spaceship in the void above. When he saw a shooting star he nearly jumped out of his skin.

"Ruddy hell it's a spaceship, we're being invaded!"

"You're the alien Daggers; that was a shooting

star!" Mousey said as he pointed towards the point where the light had vanished. "Do you realise that was a planet burning up and it probably happened hundreds of years ago; it's just taken that long for the light to reach us."

Ray was often amazed at how much Mousey knew and his brain ached as he tried to make sense of what he'd been told. It also reinforced his earlier thoughts about how insignificant they were when compared to the whole universe. In an attempt to explore the possibility there was more to their existence than birth, life and death he decided to make a proposal.

"Seeing that we have the campfire and we are on the edge of a dark and rather spooky wood, how about sharing some ghost stories?"

The idea went down well with the rest of the group although Obie was a little reticent. "I'm adding more wood to the fire though, I can't stand the dark!"

They therefore gathered round, eerily illuminated by the glow of the leaping flames and began sharing their tales. After several classics, which the boys had all heard before, Mousey leaned forward.

"Right, the story I'm going to tell you now is, as far as I know, a true one because it happened to my cousin Matt and it only happened last year. He and his mum had gone down to London to visit his elder sister and her husband for a few days. When they arrived she showed them the room where they'd be sleeping. It was the spare room at the back of the house and it had twin beds in it. Matt said the room felt strange as soon as he saw it; he said it felt colder than normal, but when he mentioned this to his sister, she just said it was because it needed airing."

"That's really scary!" Johnny said sarcastically. "A cold room; I've heard nursery rhymes that are scarier than that!"

"I haven't even started yet." Mousey replied. "In the middle of the night on the first day of his visit, Matt woke up to find his blankets were on the floor. He leaned over, picked them up and went back to sleep."

"I don't know how I'm going to sleep tonight!" Jimmy interjected equally as sarcastic as his brother.

"Will you two shut up and let me tell the whole story – Exactly the same thing happened on the second night, but this time when he woke, he found his blankets were on the other side of the room forcing him to get out of bed to fetch them." He stopped and referred to the Featherston twins. "Yeah, I know, not particularly scary, but on the third night when he awoke again to find his covers on the floor and leaned out to pick them up, his mother asked him what he was doing. Matt was half asleep so he replied grumpily that he was picking up his blankets and then rolled over and went back to sleep.

The next morning as they were getting dressed his mother turned to him. "Matthew, what were you doing last night?" At first Matt couldn't recall what had happened, but then he said. "Oh, I keep waking up to find my blankets on the floor. I was just picking them up."

His mother looked at him strangely. "No Matthew, why were you standing at the bottom of my bed?"

Matt was utterly confused. "Mother I don't know what you're talking about. I didn't even get out of bed. I woke up for the third night in a row to find my covers on the floor; I leaned over to pick them up at which point you asked what was I was doing, and I told you I was picking up my blankets."

His mother's face had gone white and her hands had begun to tremble. "Matthew, I swear the reason I asked you what you were doing was because I heard a noise, and when I opened my eyes you were standing at the foot of my bed staring at me. You then said something about picking up your blankets then you walked round the bed and stroked my hand!"

"Mother I didn't get out of bed, it wasn't me!"

"Matthew I believe you" she responded. "But there was someone standing and staring at me and then they stroked my hand."

By now the rest of the group were in rapt silence, leaning in to hear the rest of the story, and to gain courage by the proximity of their friends.

There was suddenly a loud crack as a log spluttered in the fire and the boys screamed in unison, even Mousey who was telling the story.

"Ruddy hell, I nearly pooed me pants then!" Ray said giggling as he tried to calm his racing heart. After a bout of nervous laughter, Johnny asked. "Well what happened?"

"They went downstairs for breakfast and Matt decided to confide in his brother in law what had taken place. When he heard what had happened he sat in silence for several minutes before enlightening Matt as to what he thought.

"I'm really sorry" he said "but I'm pretty sure it's a ghost that's been disturbing your sleep. A couple of years ago my uncle had been staying with us when he died in that bedroom, and since then numerous people have said they've experienced similar things like covers being pulled onto the floor and sensations of being watched. This is the first time though that anybody has actually seen him." Matt and his mother got the train home later that day!"

When Mousey finished the rest of the boys actually applauded him. "There's no way I'm going to be able to sleep tonight after hearing that, but I think I'd like to get into the tent now." Ray said as he scoured the shadows within the gloom of the encroaching forest. There was no argument from the others so they quickly climbed in and made sure the ties were securely fastened. Even though he'd said he wouldn't be able to sleep, after only a few minutes of banter, the day's exertions started to take their toll and the boys began to drift off to sleep.

"Get out here now!"

There was a loud crash on the tent flap and the whole tent shook as if it were being attacked by a wild beast. The boys were already in a heightened state of hysteria due to the stories they'd heard; even Mousey was scared, and Ray was convinced they were being attacked by a crazed monster that was half human and half bear.

"We're all going to die!"

"I said get out here before I call the police!"

Ray was pretty sure a crazed half bear, half human monster wouldn't feel the need to call the police to sort them out, so calmed down a little. "I think we should do as he says." He then went and untied the tent flaps and crawled out, which he immediately wished he hadn't as he was met by a huge man holding a shotgun. He threw his arms in the air.

"We surrender mister, please don't shoot us!"

This caused pandemonium as the boys who were still inside the tent screamed even louder.

"Will you all just CALM DOWN and SHUT UP" The man bellowed loudly, which broke through the hysteria and forced the boys into an uneasy silence. "Now will someone kindly tell me what the bloody hell you are doing camping in my field and leaving a fire unattended? Do you know how dangerous that can be? One spark could catch alight and before you know it, we've got a forest fire."

The relief was palpable as the boys realised it was only the local farmer rather than a monster, and Ray noted he must have trained to be a teacher due to his questioning skills. He was going to mention this, but thought better of it when he saw the look of anger on the farmer's face as he doused their fire.

"We are so sorry mister; we're on our way to

Anglesey and it became too dark to cycle any further after I got a flat tyre. It took ages to fix and by the time we did, we couldn't see a building where we could ask for permission to sleep here." Nobody had actually had a puncture, but Mousey was very convincing and they saw the farmer relax a little.

"Alright you can stay here tonight, but I want you gone by first light and don't light any more bloody fires." He then stalked off into the darkness leaving the boys wondering why he'd been out so late armed with a shotgun in the first place. It was fair to say, none of them slept well that night.

When they finally arrived on Anglesey the next morning, the first thing they did was find a legitimate campsite and set up their tent before going off to explore. Ray felt as if the past was reaching out to him, as wherever they went the landscape seemed steeped in history. They visited an ancient burial mound that dated back several thousand years, and discovered what looked like the remains of an ancient settlement as they made their way through some woodland.

"There's history all around us" Ian noted as he came across a medieval church just a few hundred yards from the settlement. "People must have been living here for thousands of years. Just imagine they probably stood exactly where we are now seeing the same view; it's amazing really."

Ray had never been interested in history, but even he was enthralled by their surroundings. "Is it true the Romans killed loads of Druids when they invaded?" It was about the only thing he remembered learning about Anglesey and was proud to contribute something to the conversation.

"That's right" Ian said; "but that was on the other side of the island. Anglesey was the religious heart of what they called Britain, so most of the local population had retreated onto the island for safety. When the Romans came across they slaughtered everybody including women and children."

As they made their way back to the bikes it struck

Ray that even though they currently enjoyed peace, it was clear that war and violence were part of human nature. "Do you reckon there'll be another war in our lifetime?"

Most of their life to date had been spent experiencing the horror that was war and yet their answer was almost immediate. "Without doubt" Ian said "It's inevitable really; look at the amount of wars there's already been, and nothing seems to have changed. They said after the Great war it was the war to end all wars, but we were at it again only twenty odd years later."

Being young and immature, he was quite excited by the prospect as he imagined himself looking pretty cool in a uniform and cutting a dashing figure as he protected his loved ones from, at that point, an unknown enemy.

"Do you reckon the men who did the slaughtering were put on trial after the Romans had taken over the country?"

The truth about the death camps Hitler had set up was now known and the trials of those accused of crimes against the human race were taking place in Germany.

"I doubt it Daggers because the Romans won. They ended up being here for nearly four hundred years. In the end, most people adopted their way of life."

Over the next two days they cycled the whole way around the island and explored many historical sites. Ray considered it to be a fitting way to close this chapter of their childhood because they repeatedly had to combine their knowledge in order to deduce conclusions about the landscape, and in that way it felt as though this was their final examination, which in Ray's mind, they passed with flying colours.

Chapter 30 – Not quite the end after all

Ray returned to school refreshed and ready to tackle the last term of his schooling before being unleashed onto an unsuspecting world. His trip to Anglesey had focused him on the urgency and need to identify a job he'd like to do, and energised him into wanting to do well in his upcoming tests. However, all his enthusiasm and motivation were blown to smithereens when his whole year was called into assembly on the first day back. Normally there'd only be an assembly for a year group if someone had done something particularly bad and the teachers wanted to know who'd done it. He suspected it was unlikely someone could have done something so early in the term; even Dooley, so he was perplexed as to the reason. Looking round the hall he could see most of the familiar faces so thought it also unlikely that something had happened to one of their peers. The headmaster entered, strode up onto the stage and put them out of their misery immediately.

"Right you lot, I have received a letter from the government over the holidays. It has been decided to up the leaving age to fifteen."

There were looks of incomprehension up and down the rows as the boys tried to make sense of what they'd just heard. Ray had heard 'government letter' and 'leaving age to fifteen', but it still hadn't registered what it meant.

"Obviously many of you are still confused so I will make it as simple as possible. The government have decided to change the rules regarding when a child leaves school. This means that you will no longer be leaving in the summer and will have to stay on for an extra year."

Pandemonium broke out in the hall with boys yelling objections and turning round aghast to complain to anybody who would listen. As the news sunk in, Ray too felt furious at being denied the right to leave in a few weeks time, particularly as it was so close to his fourteenth birthday. He was ready now; had spent the whole year preparing psychologically to make the transition. His trip to Anglesey had confirmed his preparations were complete, and yet now he was being told he'd have to wait another twelve months; it just wasn't fair!

"Silence!" the headmaster yelled with little effect as some of the boys started to get up from their chairs. Ray noticed Dooley savagely kick his chair to where a teacher stood. "I said silence or by God I will thrash every single one of you!" With the support of the rest of the staff, some sort of order was restored and the year was left mumbling obscenities under their breath.

As Ray looked around he realised the news had taken his teachers by surprise as well. By the look on their faces it was clear they knew nothing about the change, and to be fair to them, looked as outraged as their pupils.

Over the next few days it became apparent that the change meant teachers had to plan a whole years worth of new curriculum in a matter of weeks and there appeared to be little by way of guidance from the government. The current curriculum ended at fourteen so they would have to start from scratch whilst still teaching the old one.

Whilst he didn't envy the task facing his teachers, he thought it a little unfair for them to take the whole fiasco out on their pupils. In every lesson, teachers were bad tempered and would overreact at the slightest provocation. He spent weeks being punished for anything and everything;

"Get out of my class Dagnall!"

"Why sir, I've only just walked through the door."

"I don't like the way you walked through the door, now get out."

Or if he was lucky he might just get a whack across the head. "Ouch, what was that for miss?"

"You looked at me the wrong way; now get on with your work!"

In woodwork, which was still one of his favourite lessons despite the teacher, he became astute at dodging pieces of wood as Entwhistle took to prowling the classroom and throwing blocks of wood indiscriminately at anybody who caught his eye. However, this enthusiasm was finally curbed by the headmaster after Entwhistle had hit one child on the head and knocked him cold. Evidently the child's parents complained and threatened to sue, which forced a reaction from the school and resulted in Entwhistle remaining behind his desk for most of each lesson; well away from any bits of wood.

The pupils for their part reacted with sabotage and subtle rebellion. In History, learning was undermined by mysterious coughs that moved from one angelic looking boy to the next, utterly destroying the teacher's ability to sustain a thread of discourse. In English, every single child seemed to need the toilet one after the other and the teacher became so overwhelmed, she eventually burst into floods of tears and sat with her head in her hands. In one Science lesson, Ray's class decided to remain silent for the entire time refusing to answer questions; in another nobody seemed to be able to find their pencils, rulers or even books.

An uneasy truce descended whilst they took their tests but hostilities resumed shortly afterwards. Ray lost count of the times he received the cane, but he knew it was enough to make him immune to the sting. In fact it became a badge of honour and the boys competed to see who could receive the most strokes in a day or a week.

There seemed little the staff could do to bring the rebellion to an end. Corporal punishment had always been the mainstay of keeping unruly boys in check, but if that didn't work there was little else to act as a deterrent. They could exclude a pupil of course, but that would only give the child what they wanted; namely to leave school, so it acted as an incentive to some.

The first to go was Dooley who was caught making stupid noises in a lesson.

"Dooley, leave the room please."

"No"

Ray suspected the teacher genuinely couldn't believe he was being refused so probably thought he'd misheard. "I beg your pardon?"

"You heard, I said no! What are you going to do about it?"

To give the teacher credit, he tried to remain calm. "Listen Dooley, I'm not having you ruining my lesson and effecting the learning of the other kids in the room. Get out and go and stand outside the headmaster's office."

Dooley just sniggered in the teacher's face. "I've already told you; no I don't feel like leaving."

"I am going to give you three seconds to get out of my sight or I'm going to drag you out, and God help you if I have to do that."

Dooley's response was succinct "Get stuffed!"

As the teacher grabbed Dooley's arm to drag him from the room he stood up quickly and shoved the teacher with both hands, sending him flying across a desk and tumbling to the floor.

Dooley burst into laughter. "What are you going to do you dickhead!?" He then called him several more unsavoury names before picking up his chair and throwing it across the room, smashing a window in the process.

Ray was shocked by this incident. His school was quite tough, but there had always been strict discipline and he found this type of behaviour extreme to say the least. However, in the weeks that followed, several more pupils reacted in a similar way, fronting up to members of staff, resulting in them getting kicked out.

The war was finally brought to end when the headmaster called another assembly. "I want you to listen very carefully to what I am about to say because I am fed up with your rebellious attitude and stupid behaviour. I am going to be inviting every one of your parents in for a meeting with myself to share with them, the fact that it is the government who have made these changes, not me or my staff. I will also be asking for their support in ensuring that you boys toe the line."

When Olive returned from her meeting at the school, Ray received a good hiding even though he hadn't been in trouble that week.

"Ouch, what's that for?!" he whined as he cowered in a corner trying to cover his head with his arms as his mother beat him once again with the wooden spoon. She seemed to have developed a fondness for the utensil and it was now her weapon of choice when it came to punishing her son.

"The headmaster said that no one was blameless and knowing you Raymond, you will have been at the centre of any mischief."

He thought this was a little harsh as he'd only instigated about a third of the japes and those he had developed were amusing and witty rather than downright rebellious. However, he sensed his mother was only half hearted with her retribution as her whacks lacked the normal fervour she put into her strokes and she soon tired of even that.

"Just behave yourself for the next year Raymond." She then left the kitchen to go and see to Enid saying "This change affects all of us you know."

Ray wanted to ask her what she meant. How could having to stay in school for an extra year affect her? He racked his brain but couldn't fathom what she meant. When his father returned from work he asked him for his thoughts on the matter. After contemplating the question as he always did, his father shared his wisdom.

"How much do you reckon you eat each week Raymond?"

He didn't have a clue. "I suppose I eat the same amount as you, but I don't see what that's got to do with what I'm asking you?"

His father merely looked at him and said "Think; how much does it cost to buy you clothes?"

He thought hard but still couldn't see the connection with him having to stay in school for an extra year.

"I'm sorry dad you're going to have to spell it out for me."

"Raymond, if you'd been leaving school now, you would have started a job next week and therefore begun to pay your way. The fact you've got to stay in school means you won't be contributing financially."

The penny dropped and it suddenly made perfect sense, but it didn't make him feel any better. In fact he now felt guilty as he realised he'd be a burden on his family for another twelve months. As he left school on the last day of term, he fumed at the politicians, blaming them for ruining his life; why did they have to meddle?

Chapter 31 – The Wrath of Ma

Ray could honestly say his home was a happy one. His parents rarely argued and Alice had been a nice addition, bringing with her many stories of her journeys and a genial personality that made her a good listener and wise in her advice. Enid was now nearly seven and had remained a quiet child, which meant she didn't annoy Ray like some of his friend's sisters.

However, when his parents did argue, his mother could hold a grudge that lasted weeks, which happened just after the summer holidays had started. His father had always excelled at a number of sports from snooker, darts and football to crown green bowls. He played this latter sport for a local team and was considered the star player. One evening after a particularly successful match, he returned home bursting with excitement.

"There was a representative from the English Bowling Association at the match today, and he thought I showed lots of potential."

Olive was in the process of serving up tea so wasn't really paying attention. "That's nice dear." She said, placing his plate in front of him.

"He said he thought I was good enough to represent the North West of England."

"Did he now? That's wonderful news isn't it?"

Ray was sat watching and knew his father was leading up to something as he was normally far more straightforward when talking to his mother.

"I thought so; he wants me to play in a huge competition."

"That's nice, when is it?" His mother was still only half listening.

"Next week on the Isle of Man; I'll only be away for a week."

"Well that's – What did you say, the Isle of Man?!"

There followed a rather intense battle of wills in which John tried to persuade Olive that it was a huge honour. "Olive, do you know how many bowls clubs there are in the North West? This man had the pick of literally thousands of people and he chose me."

"I don't care if you were chosen from millions, you can't just swan off for a week and leave me here on my own; it is the school holidays you know."

"Darling you won't be on your own, you have Alice here as well and you're always round at Sydnah's anyway."

The amount of time his mother spent at her friends became a bone of contention sometimes.

"Don't you bring that up again, Sydnah has been very good to us and she's my best friend."

"I'm not bringing Sydnah up, I'm just trying to point out that you are often out in the evening so won't miss me that much."

"I won't miss you at all, you inconsiderate oaf!"

Both Ray and his father knew that when Olive resorted to name calling, she felt she was losing the battle and would start to play dirty. Therefore John tried to push his advantage home.

"I will be representing the whole of this region. The man said there was a good possibility of the Echo wanting to talk to me."

"The echo may want to talk to you but I certainly don't!"

Ray wasn't sure how a newspaper could possibly talk to anybody and had a fleeting image of a giant paper flapping its pages in an attempt at communication. The image made him giggle.

"What are you laughing at Raymond; do you think it's funny?!"

He received a weighty clout round the ear as his mother rampaged around the room until she got to the point whereby she was obviously going to cause some sort of damage. She therefore decided to storm from the room, when a thought suddenly occurred to her and she launched a counter offensive.

"I take it your travel and accommodation will be paid for by the 'Association'?" She asked cynically.

John was taken by surprise and felt ambushed; he therefore retreated into mumbling.

Olive pressed her attack. "I can't hear you John; are they paying for your travel and board?"

"Actually no, I have to pay for it myself."

Olive exploded into fury, but Ray also thought she looked like the proverbial cat that'd got the cream. "I have never heard anything so ridiculous in all my life. If it's such an honour then why do you have to pay for yourself?! I'm sorry, but you'll just have to turn him down."

She folded her arms in a clear sign that for her, the battle was over and she had won. However, whilst the money aspect had put his father on the back foot, he certainly didn't feel defeated. In fact by the look on his face, Ray thought he looked truly angry, which in itself was a scary thing to behold as he never got angry. He'd gone a dark shade of red and was inhaling deeply trying to control his temper. He placed his knife and fork down quietly and then ran his hands over his face before clenching and unclenching his fists.

"And I'm sorry as I have already agreed to go and there is no way I'm letting him down." He then quietly rose to his feet and as he left the room said. "I seem to have lost my appetite."

For several moments Olive stood with her mouth open looking rather stunned. Her husband had never truly stood up to her before, let alone walked off. "You come back here this instance John Dagnall!" She yelled at empty space, but all she heard was the click of the front door as John left to go for a walk.

The next morning hostilities were still very much in evidence with Ray feeling like he was the now defunct League of Nations trying to keep the peace and failing miserably. As they sat around the table having breakfast, Olive turned to her son.

"Tell him to pass me the teapot please Raymond."

Ray looked from his mother to his father in bewilderment. They were sat no more than five feet from each other; why she couldn't ask him herself beggared belief. However, he felt it better to comply so turned to his father.

"Dad, me Ma said can you pass her the teapot."

John passed the tea with good grace. "Raymond, can you tell your mother that I'm going to the bowls club straight from work as I need to practise for the competition so I will be late home."

Olive took a sharp intake of breath through her lips, which sounded as though she was slurping tea loudly. She visibly tensed, squeezing the spoon tightly as she stirred her tea. She took a second intake of breath and became almost rigid when Ray repeated the message.

"Me dad said he'll be late home from work because he's going to practise his bowls.

"Tell him he can make his own tea in that case."

"Dad, you can make your own tea in that case."

It was now his father's turn to take a sharp intake of breath. "Raymond, please tell your mother that's fine I'll stop off at the chippy on my way home."

Alice had been sat looking rather awkward and decided to try and smooth things over. "I know why don't we all have fish and chips for tea? It can be my treat."

If she thought this would bring peace to the table, she was sadly mistaken as Olive shrieked. "We most certainly will not be having fish and chips! I stood for hours to get some meat to make a stew and we are not going to see it go to waste!"

Ray wanted to ask why, if his mother had gone to so much trouble to get some meat; she would not save some for when his father came home from work. However, he didn't get the chance as his father had more to say; via his son of course.

"Raymond can you please tell your mother it doesn't matter how petty she becomes, I'm still going to represent our region at the competition on the Isle of Man."

"Ma, me dad said it doesn't matter how petty.... sorry dad, what else did you say?" His father didn't need to repeat the rest of the message as Olive had a message of her own.

"Raymond, you tell him if he thinks this is petty, he is in for a big surprise as I haven't even begun to be 'petty' yet!" She then stormed from the room and slammed the door with such force, the plates shook on the table.

"Dad, Ma said..."

"It's alright Ray, I think I got the message!"

In the days that followed the weather may have been warm and sunny, but the climate inside Clavelle Road was frosty to say the least. Ray was sick and tired of playing the intermediary, but it appeared to have become a routine whereby he had to be present if his parents wanted to communicate in any way, shape or form. One evening when they were both out, he sought advice from Yaya.

"Oh my dear, don't worry yourself about it; you should have seen how I fought with my third husband, or was it my fourth, I can't remember? Anyway, we used to go at it hammer and tongs; I actually put him in hospital once after I threw a perfume bottle at him and it hit him in the head, knocking him cold! He needed seven stitches in that cut!" She chortled to herself as she pictured the scene. "It was my fifth husband; that's right silly me!"

Ray loved his aunt dearly, and she'd always been a font of knowledge and wisdom when asked for advice. However, recently she'd developed the tendency to meander through memories of her life and ended up telling stories rather than offering the advice he needed.

"But Yaya, how does that help me in this situation?"

"My dear, I'm telling you that all couples fight and bicker, but it doesn't mean they don't love each other. I'm sure things will sort themselves out before too long."

He wasn't convinced by this advice. Firstly, he was a little sceptical that putting your partner in hospital was a true indication of love and secondly, in his aunt's case, things didn't sort themselves out on seven separate occasions if you included her relationship with Mr Benson. In fact, as he came to this conclusion, he realised that Alice was probably the last person he should be seeking advice from regarding marital relationships!

Things came to a head the day John left for the bowls competition. Olive was still refusing to speak to him and this was putting a strain on the whole family. Even Enid had been playing up; taking a tantrum because she couldn't find a favourite doll; something that was truly out of character. As his father entered the kitchen on the morning of his departure armed with a small suitcase, Ray prayed his mother would finally relent.

"Well I'll be off then. Come and say goodbye to your dad." Ray and Enid ran to him and squeezed him tightly. In many ways Ray felt this whole situation was ridiculous as he was only going away for a few days. It wasn't as if he was going off to war, which would have taken him away for years, if not permanently. However, if his parents parted with this rift still between them, he feared the departure could well turn out to be permanent.

"Aren't you going to say goodbye to me dad?" he said to his mother as he pulled away from his father's hug. Olive just stood stonily silent with her back to her husband, refusing to speak.

"Don't worry Ray; I'll see you in a few days; hopefully with a trophy!"

As his father turned to leave, Ray grabbed him by the sleeve. "No, wait you can't leave like this! Ma, me dad's going on a journey across the Irish Sea. How would you feel if his boat sank and he drowned?!

"Thank you for the positive images Raymond, I won't be scared at all now!" his father said in an attempt at light heartedness.

Ray knew he was being desperate, but he didn't realise he was being insensitive until Alice sobbed and quickly left the room having been reminded of what happened to her first and only true love.

"Tell him to look after himself."

Ray was furious at his mother's stubbornness. "Tell him yourself!" He too then stormed from the room but not before he heard his mother speak to her husband for the first time in over a week; even if it did sound rather sullen.

"Take care of yourself."

While his father was away, his mother rampaged about the house like a bear with a sore head, although Ray found it hard to imagine what a bear with a sore head would look like. He'd heard Alice use the term and felt it summed up his mother's mood as she was like a wild beast who growled if anybody encroached into her vicinity. She slammed draws, snapped out orders when she wanted something done and clipped her son round the ear purely because he was in reach. Even Alice wasn't immune from her fury and kept her distance by staying out as much as possible.

Ray was therefore overjoyed when his father returned home at the end of the week, accompanied by a rather impressive trophy.

"Wow did you win that?!" he asked as he admired the silver cup, which had his father's name engraved on a plaque at the base.

"Well they didn't just give it me for turning up!" His father was obviously very proud of his accomplishment. "I won every one of my matches and received this cup as player of the tournament. There was even talk of me representing the National team."

Ray was hugely impressed, which was more than could be said for his mother. "Well I hope you told them it wouldn't be possible?! There is no way on earth I am putting up with you swanning off all over the place to play a stupid game!" She then flounced out of the room leaving Ray and his father in stunned silence.

Later that evening he overheard his father trying to reason with his wife, but to no avail. The daily routine was therefore quickly re-established by which Ray acted as the go between whenever the two of them wanted to speak to each other. He found excuses to stay away from home as much as possible and spent many hours honing his speed and stamina by going on rides on his bike.

A week later, John came home early from work in what appeared to be an exuberant mood. Just from the way he walked through door made Ray believe he was excited about something.

"You look pleased with yourself dad?"

"Do I, where's your mother?"

"She's upstairs; you're not going to start arguing again are you? He was reaching the end of his tether with the pair of them and felt that if they didn't sort things out between them, he would end up doing something drastic. He had no idea what that would be, but he was sure it would be drastic.

"Come with me Ray, I want you to tell her something."

He'd never answered his father back before, but something inside him snapped and he supposed the 'something drastic' was his response. "I'm sick of this; you're both acting like a pair of kids! You're pathetic, the pair of you! If you want to speak to your wife, do it yourself!"

He was convinced his father would explode at that point or maybe even kick him out of the house. He braced himself for the consequences, but was surprised and confused when his father agreed.

"I couldn't agree more Raymond." He said, still wearing a big grin on his face. "But I think we should be able to put things right any minute now. Please come with me."

Ray still didn't have a clue what was going on but he got up and accompanied his father upstairs. When they entered his parent's bedroom, Olive was sat at the mirror brushing her hair.

"What does he want?" She said with such hostility that Ray reckoned his father would need a miracle to make her attitude thaw.

"Can you please tell your mum that she is the love of my life?" Ray felt a little sick having to repeat such soppy endearments, but did as he was told; only seeing a minor thaw in his mother's body language.

"Can you also ask her if she remembers the fact that I buy a ticket for the Irish sweepstakes?"

Ray looked at his father in confusion. He was convinced this 'conversation' was going to take the form of a grovelling apology after his father's initial foray. He was therefore unprepared for it to go off at such a strange tangent. Evidently, so was his mother who'd stopped brushing her hair and turned towards her husband.

"Please pass the message on Ray." Ray did as he was told and was rewarded with his mother actually speaking. "Well?" However, her attitude had thawed considerably and her tone was genuinely interested. In addition, she'd directed the question at her husband rather than her son.

"Well I won!"

John then brought his hands from behind his back and threw two huge wads of money into the air. His mother screamed with delight, jumped up and began to hug her husband as the banknotes floated down to cover every surface. Ray had never seen so much money in all his life. There must have been several hundred pounds at least.

"We're rich!" he yelled as he scooped up five pound notes and threw them in the air again.

"Not quite rich but five hundred and fifty pounds should go quite a long way!"

His mother was ecstatic and the three of them proceeded to dance around the room. All thoughts of hostilities; completely forgotten.

Chapter 32 – Blackpool or Bust

Now that peace had been restored in Clavelle Road, the family had to decide how they would spend their winnings. At least that's what Ray thought they should do; his mother, always frugal at the best of times, had other ideas

"We should put most of it away in the bank or something. You never know when we might need it."

"But surely we could spend a little bit of it on having some fun?" It was quite amusing to watch his parents now they had made up. They smiled at each other more than normal and acquiesced to the smallest of requests from the other.

"I suppose we could spend a bit of it; how about a nice holiday for a few days. I think that would do us all good?"

Even Alice thought that was a good idea. "That sounds like a perfect way to enjoy the summer. Where do you think you'll go?

"Wherever we go Yaya, you'll be coming with us; your part of the family now." Ray said immediately.

Alice had to dab at the sudden tears that came unbidden to her eyes after hearing his proclamation.

"Raymond that is so sweet of you, it really is."

After only a little debate, the family decided on Blackpool; so a few days later the Dagnall family headed towards Liverpool Lime Street in order to catch the train. Ray was so excited he hadn't slept the previous evening. It wasn't just the idea of Blackpool that was appealing, although it was even more popular that Southport and New Brighton put together; he'd never been on a train before and couldn't wait to experience this form of travel.

When they arrived at the station he was in awe of the high vaulted ceilings made of carved iron and glass, and the smell of coal and steam. It hung in the air like fog and created a magical atmosphere. What struck him most was the underlying excitement of people as they waited to embark on their journeys or merely waited to greet somebody they knew. He realised he'd experienced something like it before when he was waiting for the ferry to cross the Mersey and supposed it was the anticipation of the journey itself, combined with whatever was to take place at the destination, which caused the excitement. For him on this occasion, it was also the additional excitement of the unknown.

There were a number of families who were obviously off on their holidays complete with suitcases and giddy children, which meant that when they were called for boarding, there was a mad scramble as everyone tried to get on at the same time. After a small amount of chaos they found their seats and Ray claimed the one next to the window and spent a most enjoyable couple of hours staring at the countryside through the smoke from the engine as it wrapped itself around the cabin having been blown back on the wind. He could honestly say the journey lived up to his expectations as he fell in love with the speed and the comfort.

When they arrived in Blackpool he was almost sorry the journey had ended, but quickly overcame any shortcomings when he first caught sight of the promenade and the tower. He'd never seen so much ornate architecture in his life. Extravagant oriental domes vied with Italianate arches, with vivid enamelled signage that created a visual feast of colour and style. He was used to seeing rows of houses and drab shops, and so the bombardment of so many colours, sounds and smells made him feel as if his senses would overload. As they headed towards their bed and breakfast, they came across men whose job was to wander around and entice the holiday maker to enter their arcade and play the slot machines and other game, which was almost too much for Alice. It took all of Olive's formidable powers of persuasion to stop her entering one of the establishments there and then.

"For goodness sake Alice, you can surely wait until we have booked into the guest house before you start feeding your addiction!"

"My dear, I'm not addicted to gambling, I just love it!" Ray had to admit, his aunt was as giddy as the children he'd seen at the station earlier, at the mere prospect of gambling. He concluded that perhaps his mother was right regarding her being addicted.

His suspicions were reinforced when Alice grabbed him by the hand as soon as he'd put his case down in the room he was sharing with her.

"Lets you and I head out and have some fun Raymond?!" She then whisked him out of the guesthouse and into the nearest arcade. As they entered through an open fronted area, he was once again mesmerised by the brilliance of the colours and the myriad of sound. As he gazed at the rows of machines, he had to admit to himself that they were things of beauty. It wasn't just the colour and sound; he was enthralled by the engineering and the mechanics of how they worked.

"Yaya, this is amazing!"

"You wait until you win some money my dear." She said with a hungry look in her eyes. "Then it will feel truly amazing!"

While he was slightly concerned by the feverish way in which his aunt attacked the machines, he had to admit she was right about the feelings of exultation when you won. On only his third go, he pulled the lever to make the dials turn around and they landed in a combination, which triggered multiple coins to drop. The sound of the coins as they were deposited in the tray at the bottom of the machine gave him such a buzz of satisfaction that he was soon lost in a world of pulling the lever and watching the dials go round.

It was some time therefore, before he realised he was alone; his aunt nowhere to be seen. He'd also lost all the money he'd won and a little more besides. Having made sure Yaya was definitely gone; he decided to head back to the guesthouse. As he exited the arcade he was slightly shocked to discover it was already going dark and realised he'd been gambling away for several hours, which scared him somewhat. He was also more than slightly scared of what his mother would say when he returned. He could hear the raised voices as soon as he stepped out onto their floor.

"How could you just up and leave without telling us where you were going; and then come back having lost my son?!" Olive was pacing up and down the room as she ranted and Alice attempted to defend her actions.

"I haven't 'lost' him as you put it, I've just

misplaced him. I went to several arcades and just can't remember which one it was where I left Raymond."

Ray thought this might be an opportune moment to make his entrance and hoped his mother's anxiety over her missing son would generate hugs at his return, rather than a clip round the ear.

"Ma, I'm here."

Olive strode across the room and hugged her son to her, causing Ray to overestimate her feelings of affection towards him.

"I was fine Ma, I just lost track of time."

Olive clipped him round the ear. "Don't you ever go off and not tell me where you're going, do you understand?!"

"But Ma I was with Yaya." He thought this was a reasonable enough response, but the way his mother looked at her sister made him think perhaps it was not.

"I don't care who you are with, you still tell me; now let's go down and have dinner."

Ray thought his mother was so upset she'd forgotten what time of day it was. "Ma we have dinner at dinner time; in the middle of the day like at school.

Its tea time now, surely you mean we'll go down to have tea?"

Olive smiled indulgently. "We may call it tea while we're at home, but seeing we are on holiday we will refer to our meals in a more sophisticated way. That means we will have breakfast, 'lunch' in the middle of the day and dinner in the evenings."

Ray rolled his eyes at his aunt as he followed his mother down to 'dinner', but didn't bother to suggest this was rather snobby as he knew his breath would be wasted because his mother was something of a snob.

After their meal, they went for a walk along the promenade and out along the pier.

"Just think" his father said as he looked along the sea front at the mass of illumination that made the promenade look like daytime. "Not so long ago you wouldn't have been able to see a single light back there."

"And if there was one, we would have heard you yelling for it to be turned off!"

They laughed as they headed further out over the sea. It felt strange to Ray to be so far out and yet still on dry land. Nevertheless he was rather nervous as he still hadn't come to terms with water; in fact if anything his fear had become greater as he'd grown older.

"Can we head back now?" he whined petulantly. Even to his own ears he sounded like a spoiled brat, but he couldn't help how he felt. He was unsurprised when his mother refused.

"Raymond, when was the last time you got the opportunity to walk so far out to sea? I want to head to the end and see what's there."

He therefore spent the next hour staying as far away from the barrier as possible and yearning for the solid ground of the promenade. As they made their way back to where they were staying he vowed never to step foot on another pier or boat as long as he lived; he even promised himself he'd not go on the ferry anymore.

The only thing that got him through the ordeal was the promise of a visit to the Tower Ballroom to be part of the audience while Reg Dixon recorded a broadcast for the radio. He was a firm favourite with the Dagnall family who had a ritual of gathering around the wireless several times a week to hear him play a range of tunes on his Wurlitzer organ. They loved the way his music had such a strong base line whilst having fabulous accompaniment and melody.

His regular broadcasts had stopped during the war when he joined the RAF, and so they'd only been able to listen to him on rare occasions. Now the war was over, he was back to his regular performances, and had become more popular than ever.

John must have used some of his winnings, as they had the best seats in the house; although they spent much of the show on the dance floor. Ray had never seen his parents dance together before and was amazed at how good they were. They twirled around the room using such intricate steps he wondered if they didn't practice in secret when he was asleep; or maybe his father would sneak home during the day whilst he was at school. However they managed it, he was impressed and applauded energetically when they finished.

He'd been dancing with Yaya and although she could dance, he didn't feel as though her heart was in it. She basically moved around in circles with no energy or enthusiasm.

"Are you alright Yaya, I'm not stepping on your toes too much am I?"

"You're doing fine my dear; it's just that I'm getting a bit too old for this type of thing." He'd noticed her slowing down somewhat in recent weeks and worried that she'd lost some of the verve and energy she'd had when she first returned to England.

"Nonsense Yaya, you've got more energy than the rest of us put together."

"Be that as it may, I have a nice gin and tonic waiting for me back at our table so why don't you dance with your sister to the next tune while I rest my aching feet?"

As he twirled his sibling round and experimented with a couple of steps he'd seen his parents using, he looked down at her and realised she appeared to be entranced by the music.

"Are you having a good time?" he asked.

"Oh yes, this is wonderful; it's like being in a fairytale!"

Being seven years older than his sister had meant he didn't really have much to do with her; they shared meals together with their parents, went to church together and generally inhabited the same house. Other than that, he realised he couldn't remember a time when he'd actually had a proper conversation that lasted more than a couple of sentences. He therefore decided to try and instigate one now.

"What type of fairytales do you like?"

Well it was like a set of floodgates had suddenly been breached as Enid's eyes lit up. "I love all types of stories, even the ones where there are wicked witches who want to eat you, like Hansel and Gretel; but I think my favourite is Cinderella..." She twittered away gleefully as they moved around the floor and as she did so, it occurred to Ray his sister wasn't just the additional body who lived in his house. She was a girl with a personality of her own, who had likes and dislikes and dreams and ambitions just like him. As he reflected on this he realised also that he must be growing up himself. Even twelve months ago he would never have considered analysing the type of person his sister was, and this scared him.

For the rest of the week he reflected on this new found self awareness as the family enjoyed numerous highlights he would remember for years to come. The weather was glorious so they were able to spend lots of time on the beach, but Ray held back on truly enjoying himself as he felt he had to start behaving in a more mature manner. Therefore when Enid pleaded to ride on a Donkey and his father offered him a go as well, he refused.

"I'm a bit too old for that type of thing now dad." But inside he yearned to have a go, and when he saw how much fun his sister was having he capitulated. "Oh alright then, I'll just have one go."

As he plodded along the sand, memories came flooding back of the times he'd ridden Uncle Walt's dog to the shops, and it was with a sense of nostalgia that he imagined himself for one last time as Hop Along Cassidy saying 'Howdy' to the people as he passed, doffing an imaginary hat.

Chapter 33 – Tennis

When they arrived home from their holiday, the first thing Ray did was go to find his mates. He called for Ian first.

"You look really tanned you lucky beggar!" his friend commented as they headed towards their headquarters. "It's been pretty boring here; I've hardly been out."

As they approached the big old house in the park they were surprised to see lots of activity with Lorries parked outside and men swarming all over the building.

"What the ruddy hell are they doing to our base?!" Even though they didn't frequent it as much as they used to, they still felt an ownership over the premises.

"Hey mister, what are you doing?" It was pretty obvious what they were doing, but Ray felt he had to ask.

"We're renovating the house before the new owners move in. I'll tell you what, you won't recognise it once we've finished."

As the boys cycled away, they admitted to being shocked. "I was convinced that building would eventually fall down, and until then we'd have the run of it." Ian said as he scratched his head.

"You know what, it feels like every day something else changes and I'm not sure I like it. That building was part of our childhood, and well, I suppose it feels as if it's yet another chapter that's coming to an end."

Ian braked hard, nearly causing Ray to come off his bike. "Ruddy Hell Daggers, what happened to you on that holiday? Did you read a book or something!?"

Ray gave him a dig on the arm. "Don't be stupid, I'm not that much of a swot." He paused as they cycled in silence. "Where are we going to go to hang out now?" he asked miserably as they cycled through the park in search of the Featherstons, Mega, Mousey, Obie and Lionel.

"I'm not sure really, we could try out the new youth club down at the church?"

They had been a couple of times after boys brigade, and it had been quite fun. They had all sorts of clubs and games like table tennis and badminton.

"I suppose we could, but it's not open during the day and we've got another four weeks off until we have to go back to school."

They pondered how they were going to fill their days whilst they rode around the area trying to find their friends. They planned several bike rides but were still floundering for things to do as they entered Calderstones Park, which was yet another lovely green space in Allerton, Liverpool. It was here that they found the rest of the gang playing tennis on the courts, which were laid out over quite a spacious area in one corner.

Ray hadn't played tennis for ages, but soon got the hang of it once he'd had a chance to play a few games. After several hours, he realised that here lay the solution to filling their time.

"Why don't we start a tennis league? Each match could be a set long and you get two points if you win your match. At the end of the holidays, whoever has the most points wins the league and gets a prize. We could all club together to create a prize fund; what do you think?"

His idea was met with a good deal of enthusiasm and so on the way home they hammered out the finer details of how the league would work. When he told Yaya, her reaction was unsurprising.

"Here you are my dear; you go out and buy

yourself a new racket." She said as she pulled money out of her purse.

"Yaya, you don't have to do that anymore. You've already bought me too much and you no longer have Mr Benson's money to fall back on. You need to look after your money."

"Raymond, it's very kind of you to think of me, but I want to buy you this racket and I want to come and watch you play with it in this league of yours. I will not hear another word about it. Take the money or I will be most upset."

He reluctantly took the money and so turned up for his first match equipped with the very latest wooden racket that the man in the shop said was used by professional players.

Tennis became something of an obsession in the weeks that followed. They played every day and were soon hitting the ball so cleanly, that it fizzed across the court with speed and venom. News of the boy's competition spread quickly; Mousey told his brother, Obie mentioned it to his sisters, Mega told his cousin and the Featherston twins told anyone who'd listen. Before long there were kids from all over the area congregating around the courts asking if they could join the league.

"We could use their interest to increase the prize pot." Mousey said as he mopped his brow with a towel having just been beaten by Ray.

"What do you mean?"

"We could charge each person a small fee for joining the league and put the money into the pot for the winner."

Ray was currently sitting third in the league, but hadn't played as many games as Mega or Obie so reckoned he was in with a chance of winning the whole thing. "Seems like a ruddy good idea to me!"

Therefore, by the end of the first week there were twenty players involved and matches went on all day and into the evenings until there wasn't enough light to see the ball properly. There were several girls who'd joined, but each match followed the same rules regardless of the genders involved.

At the beginning of the second week Ray saw his opportunity to close the gap on Mega and Obie as they had to play each other, whilst he had a match against a girl. It wasn't that he had anything against a girl's ability to play a good game; indeed one of his hardest fought matches to date had been against a girl; it was just that this particular girl didn't seem to know one end of the racket from the other and was scared of the ball. He wondered why she'd wanted to join the league in the first place. Her name was Joyce, and she was a couple of years older than Ray.

When he turned up at the courts on the day of their match he found her already warming up against her friend Nora. To say 'warming up' was perhaps a slight exaggeration. Nora was hitting the ball over the net and Joyce was swinging her racket wildly about.

"Joyce for goodness sake, aim the racket at the ball!" her friend pleaded as Joyce nearly decapitated herself with a positively vicious swing. "You're playing tennis, not fighting a battle."

"I'm trying!" Joyce responded panting. "And I'd do a lot better if you didn't criticise me so much!"

Ray stood watching for five minutes to gauge any strength, but sadly could not gleam any insight as Joyce didn't manage to hit a single shot. He surmised this was because she shut her eyes tightly and moved away from the ball as she swung her racket.

"Are you ready to play?" He asked whilst trying not to laugh after Joyce fell over following a move in which she'd made it look as if her racket was actually attacking her.

"I suppose so, but I'm telling you now, if you hit the

ball hard I'm not going to play!"

He couldn't quite believe what he was hearing. "But the whole idea of the game is to hit the ball as hard as you can and try and stop your opponent from returning it."

"I don't care; I've given you fair warning!"

Ray smothered a laugh and headed down to his end of the court. To be fair, he did feel a little guilty as Joyce looked thoroughly exhausted already. She was panting for breath and beads of sweat were already running down her face.

"I'm going to serve now." He said as he bounced the ball on the service line. "Just try your best to get it back over." He tried to take pity on her and served a soft shot, but placed it well into the corner; Joyce ran in the opposite direction and therefore came nowhere near hitting it.

"I told you not to hit it hard, that's not fair!" She yelled before she threw her racket to the floor and crumpled into a sulk at the side of the court."

The last thing he'd intended was to make the girl cry so he tried to make amends.

"Look I'm sorry, it was an accident; come back

onto the court and I promise I won't hit it hard."

"Alright, but this is your last chance!"

For his second serve, Ray decided to serve a nice, simple underarm serve and gently sent the ball sailing in Joyce's direction. He saw her bite her lip as she hurtled towards the ball, but unfortunately tripped over her own feet and went sprawling to the ground. Ray ran round the net.

"Are you okay?" he said as he leaned down to help her to her feet. He considered he was being gallant and gentlemanly so was unprepared when she took a vicious swing at his legs with her racket.

"You promised you weren't going to hit the ball hard and then did exactly that. You are a horrid, horrid boy!" she sobbed as she connected with his shin before regaining her feet and flouncing from the court.

"Does this mean you're forfeiting the game?" he casually asked as he rubbed his leg, which was already starting to bruise.

"Well I'm not playing with someone like you who uses bully boy tactics to try and win, so if that means I have to forfeit, so be it!" She then stormed off leaving Ray a little bewildered as to what had just happened.

With daily tennis matches and the occasional bike ride, the remaining weeks of the summer holidays flew by and before they knew it, it was almost time to return to school. Ray had maintained his good form on the tennis court and it came down to a match between him and Ian to decide who won the league and the cash prize of £3 7s 6d; a huge sum for any teenager.

Quite a crowd gathered to watch the final, and even Aunt Alice kept her promise and was in attendance to cheer her nephew on over the three sets of the match. As Ray walked out onto the court he was amazed to see so many people. What had started out as a way of passing the time until they had to return to school had blossomed into an event such as this, with people lining every side of the court. There was already talk of repeating the league the following year, but by then of course, Ray and his mates would be in some sort of employment and far too grown up to take part.

It turned out to be a hard fought and extremely close match. Both he and Ian had honed their skills in recent weeks, so every point lasted for many strokes as the boys returned shots with skill and agility. Ray preferred playing from the baseline whereas Ian took any opportunity to come into the net. The contrast in styles made for many thrilling rallies and so by the end of the first set, which Ian won narrowly, the crowd were animated in their support; cheering winning shots and gasping in admiration when either player managed to return a seemingly impossible ball. The support was generally impartial with the audience merely appreciative of good tennis; however, there were exceptions. Alice was obviously biased towards Ray, and was therefore vocal in her advice of how to beat Ian, even if she did have a soft spot for him.

"Lob him Raymond" or "Put some backspin on the ball."

Unfortunately, Ray found this more unnerving than supportive, and so during a break between games he went to ask her to be a little quieter.

"Yaya thanks ever so much for coming to support me."

"Raymond it's my pleasure and you're playing very well."

He wasn't sure quite how to broach the subject so decided to give a holistic view of the support. "Thanks, but I'm finding the noise of the crowd a little off putting."

"Oh my dear, you just need to block out the noise; pretend there's no one here except for you and Ian."

He thought this was good advice, but still felt the need to ask his aunt to be a little less vocal. "Yaya that's great advice; I'll try it in the next game. However, could you possibly keep your advice until between games as I'm finding hard to concentrate."

As always she took no offence and merely responded positively. "Oh my dear, of course I can!"

Therefore when he started the next game, Ray focused on there being just him and Ian there, which seemed to work for a while. However, his aunt wasn't the only partisan individual in the crowd only this one was very much in favour of his opponent. She had even made a banner with 'IAN TO WIN!' written in large black letters, and every time Ian won a point, she'd yell and jump up and down holding the banner aloft. Ray reckoned Joyce's support for his friend was as off putting for Ian as Yaya's had been for him, but Ian was far too polite to ask her to stop. By the way he kept glancing over at her, Ray also suspected his friend was rather pleased to be receiving such adoration and smiled back at her; even waving once or twice. The distraction played to Ray's advantage and he won the second set by breaking Ian's serve in the tenth game, thus winning 6-4.

They'd been playing now for over two hours and the sweat was pouring off them both. Some of the more fickle supporters had gone home, but there were still plenty of people watching as the cheers had attracted new people who'd been relaxing in the park or were just passing by. With a shock, Ray realised his parents had joined Yaya and were looking rather proud as they stood amongst the spectators. However, their presence somehow seemed to unnerve Ray and he made several avoidable mistakes. It wasn't that he was embarrassed by them watching; in fact he was pleased they were there; it was the fact that they'd seen him play so rarely, he wanted to do his best, which put him off a bit. The last time they'd seen him was when he'd beaten the teachers at cricket, and that was such a special occasion, he feared he would not be able to replicate his success.

The third set was as hard fought as the previous two. Both the boys hit the ball with power and skill, taking many games to 'Deuce' on numerous occasions. By the time it was five games all, they were both exhausted, but the rules they'd created said the win had to be by two clear games.

"Can't we just call it a draw?" Ray asked Ian as he tried to catch his breath between games. "I'm absolutely shattered! We could share the prize money?"

Ian looked as tired as Ray. "That sounds like a good

idea to me. The way this is going we could be here for another couple of hours."

As they headed over to Mega who was the umpire, to tell of their decision, they were stopped in their tracks by a female voice yelling for the sidelines.

"Ian Davies, don't you dare give up now! I want you to thrash that ghastly boy!"

As they turned to the voice, they saw Joyce with a face like thunder and hands on her hips. To be fair, she did look formidable and Ray was reminded of his mother when she was in one of her determined to get her own way moods. However, he was still a little hurt when Ian said.

"I think I'd better do as the lady asks because I certainly don't want to get on her wrong side like you've obviously done."

The final two games were a bit of an anticlimax compared to the rest of the match. Ray felt somewhat betrayed by his best mate and Ian was obviously buoyed up by the flirtatious smiles and giggles coming from a certain female in the crowd. When Ian hit a perfect backhand down the line to seal his victory, Ray sportingly waited as Ian jumped the net and they shook hands.

"That was some game Daggers"

"It certainly was mate, well played.

As Ian went over to receive the adulation of his new found admirer, Ray felt rather deflated. He assumed it was mainly because he'd lost, but he suspected that deep down he felt rather empty now the tournament was over. The summer was gone and he only had a year of school to look forward to. As he watched Ian and Joyce flirt around each other he also suspected more changes were afoot as his mates paired up with girls, thus potentially driving a wedge between them.

"You played brilliantly, hard luck"

He turned to see his parents and Yaya beaming at him. "But I lost." He said as he shrugged his shoulders and gathered his belongings together.

"When has winning or losing ever mattered to you? His father said. "You get your satisfaction from trying your best and by just playing the game. You played a wonderful game and should be proud."

His father's insights never ceased to amaze Ray. He'd never articulated his personal philosophy regarding sport, so was therefore once again in awe of his father's ability to see through to the core of who his son truly was.

"In celebration, I reckon you deserve a bag of fish and chips for tea!"

"You know what dad, I think you're right!" As they walked off towards Menlove Avenue, he whispered to himself so nobody else could hear. "You're right about so many things."

Chapter 34 – Projects and Plans

Ray returned to school in the September of 1947 for the second time in his final year. He wasn't looking forward to it one bit, but the reality turned out to be not half as bad as his imagination had built it up to be. The teachers basically didn't know what to do with them as the curriculum they'd taught for years ended aged fourteen. It was therefore decided to give the boys a series of 'projects' to undertake in preparation for a life in work and which actually turned out to be more useful to Ray than the rest of his education put together.

His first project was focused on painting the entire school, so after some initial instruction from Entwhistle, he was provided with a set of overalls, brushes and paint and left to his own devices. The thing that surprised everybody the most was that they didn't mess around and actually got on with the job at hand. Ray took great pride in his work for a change, which earned him the gratitude and respect from the Headteacher.

"Dagnall, if you'd only applied yourself with such diligence to your proper school work you could have gone far!"

Ray reflected that if he'd applied himself properly,

he probably would have known what 'diligence' meant, but he didn't dwell on it as he became absorbed in his painting. Within six weeks the whole school looked like new and the head had written to every parent expressing how pleased he was with their efforts. Ray suspected it was more to do with the Headteacher avoiding criticism from parents for not teaching their children anything academic. However, he kept quiet as he was enjoying the sense of achievement that doing 'proper work' brought him.

The next project they were given was landscaping the school grounds, which were basically in a state of overgrown abandonment. His whole class spent some time designing how they wanted it to look before putting a spade in the ground.

"We should allocate space to grow some food; we could plant potatoes, cabbages, lettuce and even try some tomatoes." Mega suggested as they were trying to decide a use for a quite sizeable plot in the corner of the playing fields. "We could then sell the produce to the school kitchen or even open a stall on the market to make some money."

The idea of making money was most appealing to the rest of the boys and so after completing the rest of their plans, they devoted themselves over a number of weeks to clearing the brambles and nettles, before preparing the ground and planting their crops. They even drew up a rota for who would tend it on a weekly basis. This entire endeavour proved to be most successful, and they looked forward to reaping the fruits of their labour the following spring and summer.

Before they knew it, Christmas was upon them and thoughts turned once again to what they were going to do when they finally left school the following July.

"I never really fancied going down the mines." Mega announced one Saturday afternoon as they sat down by the Pier Head watching the ships travel up and down the Mersey. "The idea of being in the dark all day really wasn't appealing. How do you fancy joining the navy?"

This took Ray by surprise as Mega had never so much as mentioned going to sea before. "What made you think of the Navy all of a sudden?" It wasn't that he was against the idea as such, it was just the idea seemed to have come from nowhere.

"I suppose it's sitting here watching the ships and wondering where they're headed. I've always fancied seeing the world and joining the navy would be a good way of doing it."

Considering a life at sea should have been a fairly obvious choice for Ray seeing that so many of his uncles and relatives had been sailors going back generations. However, he concluded the reason he hadn't done so was the fact that he was afraid of water.

"I've not told many people this, but I'm scared of water and even though I've had loads of lessons, I just seem to sink when I'm trying to swim."

Mega looked at him thoughtfully. "But you're not 'in' the water you're 'on' it Daggers, that's a big difference, and imagine all the amazing places we'd be able to visit and the things we'd see. I want to see dolphins, whales, turtles and flying fish." He seemed to have vanished into a world of his own. "I want to see the pyramids and the Great Wall of China."

If Ray were honest, he couldn't get past the idea that it was all very well that the ship was 'on' the water, but what would he do if the ship sank? A number of his uncles had been torpedoed during the war and spent hours 'in' the sea. This thought blocked any desire for him to see any of the things Mega was talking about. If anything, he'd prefer to explore his own country rather than travel to the far flung corners of the world. He'd been to Wales and holidayed in Blackpool, but other than that he'd only been on the ferry over to New Brighton and he reckoned Britain had quite a lot more to offer. In addition, he rather liked his home city and didn't feel the need to up and leave, not at that point anyway.

"I don't think the navy is for me Mega, I'm looking for something nearer home."

In the silence that followed, Ray believed he'd put the idea well and truly to bed, but then Mega changed tack.

"But what if neither of us can think of what we want to do? All's I'm saying is the navy pay is brill and you get all your meals cooked for you and you don't even have to do your own washing."

Ray hadn't considered this and the idea suddenly became a little more attractive.

Mega pushed his advantage some more. "I'll tell you what, if we haven't come up with another idea by, let's say, your birthday; we go down to the recruiting office and get the papers to join the navy."

Ray contemplated this idea seriously. Everything

Mega said was true; they didn't have a clue what they wanted to do even though their parents had supplied them with various options.

"Raymond you are going to have to make up your mind sooner rather than later you know. You only have a few months left!" had become his mother's daily mantra.

This idea of Mega's therefore provided an easy solution to the problem. The idea of making good money was also very appealing as he was sick of having no money of his own and having to ask parents or Yaya if he wanted anything. This proved difficult when the something he wanted was a packet of fags, which he still kept secret for fear of reprisals from his mother. He therefore thought over his friend's proposal and came to a conclusion.

"Alright, if we haven't come up with another idea by the end of May, we'll join the navy." They then spat on the palms of their hands before shaking them, thus sealing the deal.

As they headed home that evening, Ray suggested they go to the club, which had become a focal point for most of the youths in the Allerton and Garston areas of Liverpool, and was deemed a pretty cool place to hang out; mainly because it was the only place to hang out. It had become so popular in fact that it now opened each evening except Sunday and the types of activities on offer had grown even though the space was quite basic. The hall was a basic oblong shape, but it had a protrusion off one end where there was a kitchen area and some offices. It had a boarded floor and at the other end was a raised stage. Activities ranged from table tennis and badminton to drama productions and a weekly dance.

Ray generally opted for the more sporty activities, but would still turn up when Ian dragged him to attend on the evenings when the more artistic events were taking place. He was never sure why Ian wanted to go on these evenings as he'd never shown any leanings towards the theatrical or the artistic, and all he ever did was sit around watching rehearsals while Ray made fun of the 'arty' people as they endeavoured to be creative. This behaviour brought him into conflict once again with the girl who was proving to be his arch nemesis; Joyce, who happened to be passionate about her amateur dramatics.

"Raymond Dagnall, why do you have to be such an ignorant pig?" She spat at him after a particularly witty foray from Ray in which he mimicked her voice as she rehearsed her lines.

"And you Ian Davies, I expected more from you!" I don't know why you find him so funny!?"

"Maybe it's because I am?" Ray responded in a slightly petulant tone. He was a bit irked by her calling him a pig; he wasn't too sure what ignorant meant but he knew 'pig' was a bit strong. "Why do you have to get your knickers in a twist so easily?"

Ian giggled at that but stopped abruptly when he saw the look on Joyce's face.

"You are such a horrid boy; I'm telling the vicar!" With that she ran from the hall in tears.

"Why do you have to always wind her up Daggers? I thought I might be in with chance with her."

"Ray was slightly incredulous with Ian's attitude. "I don't!" he cried "I only need to look in her direction and she flies off the handle; I don't know what's wrong with her."

"Well you certainly seem to upset her enough. That must be at least the third time you've made her cry."

Ray experienced a feeling of guilt as he never intended to upset her; there was just something about her that pushed his buttons, and it seemed obvious the feeling was mutual. He thought he might be feeling a touch of jealousy as it was clear Ian fancied her and she could therefore come between them, but he suspected it was more than that. They just seemed to rub each other up the wrong way whenever they met, and he couldn't put his finger on the reason why.

His guilt evaporated however, when he was called before the vicar.

"Raymond, why have you been bullying Joyce here?"

Ray didn't know what to say. "Vicar, I haven't been bullying anyone; she just has no sense of humour whatsoever. Is it my fault if she can't take a joke?" He was trying to put a reasoned case forward, but his first attempt obviously didn't go down too well with both his accuser and his judge.

"You see vicar; you see what he's like? He's utterly horrid and beastly!"

The vicar played it a little more conciliatory. "Raymond, you may have thought you were merely joking and having a laugh, but does it look like Joyce is laughing?"

Ray actually thought she looked like she was smirking behind her handkerchief. "No vicar" was all he managed to say.

"No, that is correct, which means that your words and actions have led to Joyce feeling sad and upset, which in my book means you have been bullying her. What have you got to say for yourself?"

Ray could think of plenty of things he'd like to say about the way she flew off the handle at the slightest thing he said or did, but he knew it was pointless. "I'm sorry Vicar."

"It's not me you need to apologise to, it's poor Joyce here; and make sure you mean it."

He therefore had to turn to the girl who seemed to find fault with everything he did and apologise. "I am truly sorry if my messing about has upset you. I never meant for that to happen and I promise I won't do it again."

It nearly choked him to say the words, but he managed to do it without making eye contact so he didn't have to see the gloating look of triumph in her eyes.

"I do hope you meant every word you've just said Raymond because if I find out you've been causing mischief again, I will have no alternative but to ban you from the youth club.

As they walked out of his office he caught Joyce smirking at him out the corner of his eye before she threw her head in the opposite direction and flounced off.

"What did the vicar have to say?" Ian asked as Ray

joined him at the tuck shop.

"I had to apologise for upsetting her, and he told me I'd be banned from youth club if it happens again."

Ian shook his head. "You may as well start looking for somewhere else to hang out because you're bound to wind her up somehow!"

"What is it with her anyway? Why does she fly off the handle at the slightest thing?"

Ian didn't seem to have an answer other than. "Keep out of her way." He then did the exact opposite and went over to talk to her, leaving Ray to twiddle his thumbs on his own in the corner. It appeared his premonitions were coming true when Ian came back over to him.

"You know what, she's not that bad when you get to know her; you just need to give her a chance."

"Not that bad?" he said bitterly. "She's just nearly had me kicked out of the youth club! Just because you fancy her, you don't need to take her side over me!"

Ian blushed profusely, which was something he rarely did. "What if I do fancy her; it wouldn't do me much good anyway after your antics. She associates me with you, which makes me only a little bit better than dog muck! It'll take a miracle, or you being nice to her forever for her to be interested in me, and I can't see either happening any time soon!"

Ray was rather hurt by being referred to as dog muck so his reply lacked the sincerity his friend would have liked. "Oh ruddy hell; alright I promise to try and be nice to her if it will help you out."

"Thanks Daggers, thanks a lot."

However, he realised it was not going to be easy when he attempted his best smile at her as they left, only to be met with a scary scowl before she stuck her tongue out at him.

Over the weeks that followed, Ray came to realise it wasn't just Ian who'd been wounded by the arrow of love and was saddened to observe the effect the poison from the barb had on his mates. One after the other, they seemed to fall victim to the disease and began mooning over some girl or other. He was used to having a laugh, with few things being taken seriously, but now he felt he had to walk on eggshells as their sense of humour vanished overnight and they became sensitive to how their behaviour might appear to any girls who were nearby. This resulted in them being serious about everything for fear of offending with their laughter, and it made Ray frustrated and mad.

It wasn't that he didn't find the opposite sex attractive, he did; he just didn't understand them and therefore didn't see the point in starting a relationship at that point. Luckily Mega seemed as immune to the disease as Ray, and so they stuck together and basically took the Michael out of their mates for their foolishness.

In school too attitudes had changed. Conversation, which had always revolved around masculine things such as football, survival crafts and film genres such as westerns and Flash Gordon, now tended to revert to how pretty a certain girl was or how another had winked at someone, which was a sure sign she was interested. Ray wanted to yell in exasperation "Interested in what?!" They certainly weren't interested in football, he rarely saw any play table tennis down at the club and they just rolled their eyes when he talked about any of his heroes such as Flash Gordon and Hop Along. The bottom line was that they were a mystery to him, and a mystery he wasn't interested in solving any time soon.

Sadly for Ray, the mystery of the female gender only deepened after a trip with his father to watch Liverpool play. John had begun taking his son to Anfield in the latter days of the war. The football league had been suspended in 1939 shortly after

Germany invaded Poland; at first due to fear of the impact a bomb could have on crowded places, but later due to the fact that most of the players had been called up or volunteered to serve. However, the government recognised the positive effect football could have on morale and so relented to allowing matches to continue. To begin with, crowds were limited to eight thousand, but by 1943 after the blitz, they raised the number so that fifteen thousand could attend. The league was still suspended due to lack of players, but regional divisions were set up and teams were allowed to use 'guest players', thus tapping into the resource of any professional footballer who happened to be stationed nearby.

It had therefore become a Saturday afternoon ritual when Liverpool played at home, for Ray and his father to make the journey to the hallowed turf and watch their heroes. The team had played fairly well during the war years, given that the only regular players were all past their best; and in the first proper season after the war they had actually won the championship. However, this season had turned out to be mediocre at best, which left them feeling morose after a humiliating 3-0 defeat to Portsmouth. John felt the need to steer the conversation away from the match and he'd also received orders from his wife that it was time he had 'the talk' with his son.

"You'll be fifteen this year won't you Ray?"

Seeing that the man asking the question was his father, Ray felt the question to be rather stupid. "Er yes obviously, and my name is Raymond and I live with you in 59 Clavelle Road and I'll be leaving school in July."

He'd expected some sort of retort from his father for using sarcasm, but he merely nodded and continued walking in silence, which was a clear sign he wanted to discuss something of importance.

"Are we going to talk about what job I'm going to do because I've already told you, if I haven't come up with something by the end of May, Mega and I are going to join the navy." He'd had numerous arguments with his mother about joining the navy, but as yet, he was determined he was going to stick to his guns.

"No, no you need to make your own mind up about what you're going to do. There's nothing worse than ending up in a job you can't stand; it makes you miserable."

Ray was surprised by his father's statement as he'd always thought he'd been happy in his work. "Don't you like your job dad? What did you want to do?"

"I do like my job most of the time but I suppose deep down, I would have loved to play football. I was a pretty good player you know; I was even offered a trial for Liverpool, but my dad said I needed a proper job. I suppose I've always wondered what would have happened if I'd done the trial."

Ray was amazed his father could have played for Liverpool and pondered how little he knew about him as they once again walked along in silence.

"Anyway it wasn't jobs I wanted to talk to you about. Your mother thinks it's about time you learned about the facts of life; the birds and the bees." John looked hopefully at his son. "You know what I mean don't you?"

Ray had heard talk of birds and bees linked to talk about facts of life in school, but if he were honest, he didn't have a clue what it was all about. In one Science lesson the teacher had stood at the front looking rather nervous.

"Now listen up, when a bee lands on a flower, he takes nectar from it in order to make honey." At that point Ray had switched off and started doodling on his paper. The next thing he caught was. "And then the female bird lays eggs, which she incubates by sitting on them until they hatch."

That was as far as his knowledge about the facts of life went. To date, none of his mates seemed any more clued in than he was, but the pleading look on his father's face made him feel he had to offer something.

"I've heard about them in school."

His father took a huge sigh of relief and actually whispered "Thank God!" to himself. "So you know where babies come from?

"No not really."

His father's face dropped and he began to stammer. "W-well, oh dear lord; well they c-come from the mum!"

Ray looked at his father incredulously; he wasn't that stupid. "I know that, I'm not stupid. I know me Ma gave birth to Enid. I remember she went off for a few days and then came back with the baby." If he was honest, he wasn't too sure exactly how she'd given birth, but he hoped it wasn't anything like the way a dog did, as he'd observed Obie's pet Labrador give birth to pups and that looked pretty messy to say the least.

"You see, the erm, a baby grows from, erm a seed that is planted in the mother's stomach." John looked pleased with himself at the description he'd given. "So now do you see?"

Ray was a little clearer, but still failed to see the connection between birds and bees and facts of life, and he had another question. "How does the seed get into the mother's tummy?"

John paled once again and remained silent for several streets as they walked into town to catch the tram home. Finally he brightened. "Her husband plants the seed."

He looked at his father in utter confusion. "What?!" He envisaged a farmer with his father's face and armed with a rake, hacking at his mother's stomach and trying to shove some seeds in. "That's impossible! How can you possibly plant a seed inside her stomach without taking her to hospital for an operation? You'd end up killing her!" Ray was disgusted and quickened his pace so he didn't have to walk along side his father, leaving him well and truly flustered.

"Well we do" he called after his son as he tried to catch up. "And that is how babies are made; and we don't have to go to hospital to make one. If you want to know more, you'll have to ask your mother." It was then his father who increased his pace, almost running away from his son and leaving him more confused than ever.

When he shared his confusion with his mates as they headed towards the youth club that evening, he heard varying suggestions about the mysteries surrounding reproduction. Obie had been told that the woman produces an egg and the male fertilised it. Ian had been told the man and woman slept together in order to create babies; the Featherston twins hadn't been told anything and Mega had been told to watch dogs mating, as it wasn't that different for how humans created babies. As they entered the club for the weekly dance, a montage of images swirled around Ray's head, but he started to look at girls in a new light and spent the whole night standing in a corner avoiding any glances made by members of the opposite sex.

Chapter 35 – Finally!

As the weeks ticked by Ray still couldn't decide what he wanted to do, and he became resigned to the prospect of joining the navy despite his fear of water. On a daily basis he racked his brains for things he'd like to do. He knew he liked making things with his hands and he was quite creative. He therefore considered some form of engineering, but knew he wouldn't have the right qualifications by the time he left school and didn't believe he was clever enough to go on and do further study. He mentioned this to Mega.

"If you tell the recruiters you are interested in engineering, they are bound to be able to help set you up as part of your training on board ship."

Ray was impressed. "That's another good reason for joining I suppose."

However, everything changed just before the Easter holidays when Mega had an accident. He had a part time job helping to deliver coal, which involved him sitting on the back of the wagon and helping the coalman by opening gates and doors to allow him easy access with the sacks. He'd then help deposit the coal in the coal shed or bunker before going round and helping collect in the money. On this particular occasion they were coming to the end of the round when Mega jumped back up onto the wagon after collecting some money just as it pulled away from the kerb, causing him to lose his balance and plunge headfirst to the ground. He smacked his head hard on the concrete floor and knocked himself out. Luckily the driver saw what happened and braked.

"Are you alright son?" He said anxiously as he leaned over him. When Mega didn't reply the coalman panicked and started to slap him across the face. "Come on boy, wake up!"

Mega came round to a rather heavy slap across his face. "Will you get off me you ruddy idiot that hurts?!"

"You were out cold lad; I needed to bring you back round; you look a bit peaky now as well."

"So would you if you'd just fallen on your head!" This wasn't like Mega who was normally quite a placid individual.

"I'm going to take you to hospital to get you checked out and I don't want any arguing about it." Mega spent a night in hospital while they observed him to make sure he wasn't concussed and he was released the next day.

When Ray first heard about the accident he assumed Mega was fine as they would have kept him in hospital if he wasn't, but in the days that followed he noticed subtle changes come over his friend. The Mega he knew was enthusiastic and full of energy; he was adventurous, mild mannered and witty, but following the accident all these qualities seemed to vanish. He lost interest in all the things he'd loved and started to make excuses to avoid taking part.

"We're going on a bike ride this weekend; are you coming with us?" Ray asked him.

"I can't I've pulled a muscle in my calf

A few weeks later he asked him if he wanted to play football.

"I can't I have to go and visit my Nan."

When the cricket season started, he even came up with an excuse not to play for the school team even though it would be his last season and he was the best batsman and wicket keeper the school had ever seen. When hearing his friend had dropped out of the cricket team, Ray finally confronted him about his lethargy.

"What is wrong with you Mega? You don't seem to be interested in doing anything lately and to be honest, I'm worried."

He was astounded when Mega couldn't even

summon up the enthusiasm to argue. "I just can't be bothered" was all he said.

"But you don't seem bothered about anything these days. Come on, talk to me."

Mega just shrugged his shoulders. "I dunno I just find things boring."

"We're meant to be joining the navy next week and then we've only got a couple of months before we leave school. We should be trying to cram in as much as we can before we go away."

He was convinced his rationale was sound and believed he'd be able to persuade his friend to buck up, but he merely shrugged his shoulders once again.

"I don't think I want to join the navy anymore."

Ray was shocked "What? But it was your idea! You've been going on about it for over a year; why have you suddenly changed your mind?"

Mega shrugged yet again. "I don't know I just don't fancy it anymore; I suppose I've lost interest, but you can still join if you want to."

Ray had never been a violent sort of person, and he always managed to keep his temper in check, but

Mega's attitude made him furious and it took all of his will power not to give his friend a good hiding.

"I could have been thinking about other careers seriously if you'd told me you'd lost interest!"

He had to walk away when Mega responded with yet another shrug of his shoulders. Ray knew it was pointless in arguing further if all he got in return was a sea of apathy. He therefore returned home to ponder his future. He toyed with the idea of still joining the navy as he'd come to look forward to doing so, but when he analysed his reasons for this, he realised they mainly centred around the adventures he'd have with his mate and didn't look forward to having to do it on his own. He therefore dismissed the navy as an option and began to re-evaluate what he was going to do.

However, after several hours of racking his brains he was no nearer to coming up with a solution and he began to panic. He'd spent over two years trying to decide on a pathway to follow and he now had less than two months. He decided to do what he always did when faced with a dilemma; he went to Yaya to ask her advice.

"What is it you like to do Raymond?" she asked as she sipped noisily from a cup of tea. "I suggest you start there. Make a list of all your interests and then try and match them to a job."

This sounded like decent advice but he'd already done this in the past. "But Yaya, I like cricket and football and cycling and drawing, but I don't think there's a job that will enable me to combine those types of things."

His aunt tapped the side of her cup as she thought. "Alright, you mentioned you like drawing; what other subjects do you like in school?"

He'd been over this with his teachers, his parents and even his friends. He'd tell them what he liked and they would suggest possible careers, but none of them ever sounded appealing so he didn't really see the point of doing it again. However, he didn't want to offend his favourite aunt so complied with her wishes.

"I like Maths and I like making things with wood, although the teacher says I'm rubbish."

"And do you think your work is rubbish?"

Nobody had ever actually asked him what he thought of his own work, so he reflected for several moments before replying. "No I don't; I honestly don't. I think I can create good quality things with wood. I made you that ashtray last year, which you seemed to like."

"You are absolutely right my dear, I thought you did a wonderful job, and I agree with you, you are extremely good with wood. So do you think there are careers that might allow you to work with wood?"

"Yes there are lots." The realisation dawned on him he maybe on the brink of finally identifying a chosen career, and he became excited. "There are furniture makers, joinery jobs, cabinet makers; I love it!"

"And how would you go about acquiring a job in this field?"

"I suppose I'd have to serve time as an apprentice; we've been given talks about what happens and how long it takes and that sort of thing."

"So do you think that would suit you?"

And that was all it took. All those months of searching for an idea of what to do; all the sleepless nights discarding one job after another had been sorted in a five minute conversation with his aunt in which she didn't tell him anything or even make suggestions. All she'd done was ask the right questions, which allowed him to come to his own conclusions.

"You are an absolute genius Yaya!" he said as he hugged her and kissed her on the cheek.

"Oh I wouldn't go that far, but I do try." She said with a wink.

In the days that followed it felt as though the pieces of the jigsaw that made up Ray's life started to fall into place. He began to scour the newspaper for any jobs in the field of woodwork and was rewarded after only a few days by finding an advert looking for school leavers to undertake an apprenticeship in cabinet making with a renowned company called Hampsons. He wrote a letter and was successful in being invited to interview.

"Raymond, this is only the second interview you've ever had and we all remember what happened in the first. Whatever you do, do not mention the Beano, or the Dandy or drawing cartoons!" His mother appeared far more nervous than Ray was himself. She flustered round him, spitting on a handkerchief and wiping an imaginary stain from his face.

"Mother I'll be fine, please stop fussing; I still need to get some examples of what I've made together." The invite to attend an interview didn't say he had to take anything with him, but he thought it would be a good idea. As he rooted around looking for the carved lion he'd made before camp and the ashtray he'd made for Yaya, it struck him that it was indeed him who had decided to take the items; nobody had made the suggestion for him and he was proud at his emerging ability to think for himself. The second thing that struck him was the fact he'd just called Olive 'mother' for possibly the first time in his life; she had always been 'Ma', and he took this slip of the tongue as yet another indication that he was becoming a man.

The interview itself was a total contrast to his interview for grammar school. He felt he was able to be himself and shared witty anecdotes with Mr Hampson, which had the man holding his sides with the pain of laughter; and he appeared genuinely impressed with the fact Ray had brought examples of work and the quality of what he'd produced.

"Ray lad, I think you'll fit in just fine with us. I'll send you details of what you need to get in terms of clothes and equipment, and we'll see you the first Monday after you've finished school."

It was that easy. When he returned home and told his family, his mother actually shed a tear before grabbing him in a bear hug that was so tight he thought his ribs might crack. His father shook him by the hand, which felt just as extraordinary as the bear hug because his normal show of affection was a ruffle of the hair;

and Aunt Alice sat and beamed with delight not saying anything, which was also extraordinary.

"Raymond, we are so proud of you." His mother stated as she cuffed away a tear and returned to the stove to hide her emotion.

"Thanks Ma, can I have a connyonny butty, all this work stuff doesn't half build up your appetite!"

The final days of his schooling flew by in a whirl of having a laugh and working hard harvesting the produce from the allotment and trying to sell the goods to the school kitchen, which didn't work out so well as the headmaster made them 'donate' the vegetables for free.

On his final day when he awoke, he could have sworn he felt different. It was as if he'd gone to sleep the evening before as a boy and awoke that morning as a man. When he went to get washed, he searched as he always did, for any bristles on his chin, which would allow him to start shaving; and low and behold there were three definite bits of fluff protruding from his face. Even his mother noticed the change.

"You look different this morning Raymond; have you done something with your hair?"

When he got to school, his teacher commented also.

"You look taller somehow Dagnall; have you grown over night boy?"

Even Mega noted the change, which was somewhat of a miracle as he didn't seem to notice anything anymore. "I see you've finally got some bum fluff Daggers; you'll be shaving soon!"

But as he headed towards the gate as the final bell tolled, Ray new the change wasn't an external one; he felt different inside. He felt a sense of freedom and of hope for the future; a future that for the first time he knew he could make successful, as he was about to embark on a job he knew he'd love and one in which he was confident he had the right skills. He paused as he reached the gate and turned to look back on the school building as kids swarmed around him.

In that moment he couldn't see what lay in store for him; could not imagine he would journey to a far flung corner of the world and fight in a forgotten war. He was totally unaware he'd already met the love of his life and the fact he would be go on to raise children of his own; or just how successful he would become in his career of choice. All he knew in that moment was a significant chapter of his life was coming to an end. He took one final glance at the school before bringing his hand to his head in an informal salute.

"See yer!" He said before turning and running through the gates as fast as he could.

Historical Note

The vast majority of the events within this book did take place and were imparted to me by Ray himself over several months. Any inaccuracies are my own or gaps in Ray's memory. There was a Nazi zeppelin over Liverpool at some point prior to the outbreak of war, however none of the eye witness accounts seem to be able to recount exactly when. Ray believes it was some time in 1938, but many others put it at any point between 1934 and 1937.

Although New Brighton has had a certain revival in recent years, it has for a long time been quite forgotten as a place for relaxation and enjoyment. However, in 1938 it was indeed one of the most popular holiday and weekend destinations around. There are film clips on line that show the crowds crammed onto the ferry, and the packed beaches. The City Mission did use to hold their summer services on the beach and Ray did indeed deliver regular 'sermons'.

All of the events surrounding Uncle Walt, his dog and the other daily routines are as they were imparted to me. The air raid shelter that was built in the alley is also accurate although I was unable to find examples elsewhere. The incident which led to the death of the soldier when he got caught in the ropes of the barrage balloon did happen, as did the slicing off of the Sergeants fingers as he was having a smoke.

I have not been able to ratify Ray's claim that railway signals were ever used to signify a coming raid. However, he was adamant that this was the case, and claims to have been saved by the foreknowledge on several occasions.

Searching for shrapnel was prevalent with most young boys at the time and I'm fairly certain Ray will not have been the only one who inadvertently picked up an unexploded incendiary bomb as they were usually dropped in vast quantities and often failed to explode.

The incident with the unexploded lamppost did take place, and although the exact date of when Colinton Street was hit has been forgotten, I have determined it was on either 28th, 29th or 30th of November 1940 as Wavertree in Liverpool was targeted repeatedly on those dates with over one square mile being destroyed.

There was a lone German Ju88 shot down by 3 Hurricanes from no 312 squadron based at Speke Airport at around 4:15 pm in October of 1940. Ray is certain he saw this, but believes he was in Clavelle Road at the time, which is why I have brought the incident forward to 1941.

The mansion used as the gang's headquarters has

since become known as 'The Pub in the Park' and frequented by many a family to this day. The pill box is still in the park and Ray assures me his name is written on its walls, although I have failed to find it.

The May Blitz of 1941 saw Liverpool targeted each night for the first week of that month and intermittently over the following weeks. The devastation was wide spread and thousands of people lost their homes. Joe and his family did indeed end up living with the Dagnalls for nearly five years before being given a house of their own.

The Battle of the Atlantic was waged for most of the war with Liverpool being pivotal in the survival of the country as it acted as the gateway to America and the rest of the world. Red Cross parcels were literally life savers for many, and Ray truly did love the red clogs! The banana tale is also true, but apparently they were a super small variety, which is why they were seen as so special.

In my research, I could not find any official evidence of a Prisoner of War Camp based near Speke Airport, but there are numerous eye witness accounts of it in various forums on line. The prisoners were exclusively Italian, and by all accounts were better off than some of the local residents.

Aunt Alice was every bit as flamboyant as I have tried to portray her on these pages. She is someone I would dearly have liked to meet. The seven marriages, fortunes won and lost and the events of her downfall all took place. If you ever drive down the M62 motorway you will pass Tarbuck Island. The land where the motorway now sits, and the fields surrounding it all used to belong to Mr Benson (Although I have changed his name).

The stories she told were legendary and her accounts of meeting Al Capone, Joe Louis and the Chinese Triad are all recorded here with little embellishment. There is even a report in an archived Liverpool Echo that Joe Louis did indeed sign for Liverpool when he was stationed nearby. However, I have no corroborating evidence that he actually played.

The change in the leaving age, increasing it to 15, came into force in April 1947 thus leaving teachers with little time to plan a whole new curriculum for their frustrated students. Ray remembers feeling rather miffed, but the level of rebelliousness is perhaps a reflection of my own experience of education rather than his! There are several amusing Pathe News exerts of the time, showing the education secretary patronising rather glum looking children.

Liverpool FC did win the championship in the first proper season after the war, but then their fortunes took a downward turn for several years, resulting in them actually being relegated. This obviously before the great Bill Shankly turned things around.

And so Ray left school at 15, ready to embark on his new career. He will make new friends, travel the world and fight in a major conflict as the ordinary boy becomes an ordinary man.

5371047R00279

Printed in Great Britain
by Amazon.co.uk, Ltd.,
Marston Gate.